THE
SECRET FORMULA

THE
SECRET FORMULA

a novel

JAMES GABLER

BACCHUS PRESS LTD
PALM BEACH

Book design by Maureen Cutajar
www.gopublished.com

First Edition: 2013
Crime Fiction

ISBN: 978-0-9613525-9-2

Published by:
Bacchus Press Ltd
146 Sunset Ave, #3
Palm Beach, FL 33480
bacchuspr@aol.com

CHAPTER 1

Atlanta, June 1999

Boris Forsenko, a Russian Mafia boss has hired an assassin from Russia to kill you. This man arrived in the United States today . . . The words cut through Alex Ivanovich like a knife.

Alex stares at the answering machine. It's after midnight. It's been a long day and he's very tired. He hesitates, then hits the rewind button and replays the message. The voice he hears is deep and resonant, and the words are in Russian. *Alex, my name is Demitri Sadkov. You may remember meeting me through the KGB. I am also a member of HAC. Boris Forsenko, a Russian Mafia boss who operates from the Brighton Beach Moscow Social Club in Brooklyn, New York, has hired an assassin from Russia to kill you. This man arrived in the United States today with a forged banking visa, but he is not here as a banker. His only purpose is to kill you and immediately return to Russia. I do not know his name or what he looks like, but I have learned that he will arrive in Atlanta tomorrow morning at nine-thirty aboard Delta Air Lines flight 695 from New York. You will now erase this message and never reveal that I called you.*

Alex stands motionless. *Who is Forsenko? Why does he want to kill me?* He's sure the message isn't a hoax. He met Sadkov several times when they served in the KGB together, and they are both members of HAC, a group of ex-KGB officers scattered around the world that have sworn to help one another. Alex presses the erase button.

Alex arises in the morning at seven. It was a restless night with Demitri's message playing over and over in his head. He showers, shaves, dresses in casual clothes, and makes a pot of coffee. Sitting with his coffee he searches his mind for why he has been marked for execution. At eight o'clock he dons a raincoat, slides his taut six foot-two frame behind the wheel of his Lincoln Town Car, and heads to Atlanta's Hartsfield International Airport. He doesn't want to be late for the assassin's arrival.

Striding down the corridor leading to the Delta terminal, Alex could be just another man on his way to catch a flight or meet a friend, but his calm exterior does not reveal the internal turmoil he is feeling. He is in his late thirties, 195 pounds, with rugged good-looks accentuated by high cheekbones, dark blue eyes, an angular nose and black curly hair. His former KGB colleagues admired him for his physical strength, his ability to speak six languages fluently, and a memory bordering on total recall.

Leaning against a wall, Alex scrutinizes the passengers of flight 695 as they walk down the Jetway and enter Concourse B. He knows that his ability to identify the Russian assassin is a matter of life or death.

As the passengers come into view, he makes quick mental impressions of them. He figures that the man sent to kill him traveled first class and will be one of the first off the plane. He is confident that he can quickly pick him out, but the plane continues to empty and his confidence ebbs; he feels a flash of panic. *Have I missed him? Is he coming on another flight? Was Demitri's call a hoax?* Then he sees him! He is dressed like a thousand other thugs Alex met before he left Russia eight years ago.

Wearing a rumpled, ill-fitting black double-breasted suit, the man is about six feet tall and over two hundred pounds. He looks to be about forty. A few paces beyond the Jetway he stops, looks around, lights a cigarette, takes a deep drag, throws it on the floor and crushes it with his right foot. Alex gets a good look at his round mottled face. His nose looks like it has been broken more than once, but his gray-green recessed wolfish eyes are what set him apart. They are the eyes of a man who would slit your throat and laugh. There is no mistaking him. His business is murder.

The assassin hesitates, then turns right and walks rapidly down a long corridor that leads to the terminal train. After he enters the train, Alex gets aboard the car in the rear. The assassin leaves the train at Terminal A. At the top of the escalator he walks directly to the Hertz counter. Knowing he will have to take the shuttle bus to the car rental area, Alex drives directly there and parks below the Hertz exit gate. Within minutes the shuttle bus arrives. The assassin steps off, speaks briefly with an attendant and walks to a red Chevrolet Lumina. Alex notes the license number as the car exits the parking compound and heads north on Route 85 toward Atlanta. Alex follows.

The Chevrolet leaves the expressway at the 10th Street exit ramp. Alex assumes the assassin will turn on Peachtree Street to reach his hotel, but he doesn't turn on Peachtree, he continues east. *That's strange,* Alex thinks, *that's not the way to the Downtown and Midtown hotels.* When the car turns right on Myrtle Street, it strikes Alex that the assassin is heading in the direction of his apartment. Alex turns off at Juniper, a parallel street, and speeds ahead. He turns left on 3rd Street, and parks a block from his apartment. He runs toward Myrtle, crosses to the south side of the street and ducks into a doorway that gives him a view of the wood-framed house that stands in front of his cottage-apartment located in the rear. Within seconds the Chevrolet comes into view moving slowly along Myrtle. As the car creeps along the assassin's head moves from side to side. The car stops in front of the house that hides Alex's apartment from view and then moves slowly forward, turning left at 3rd Street. It stops at the alley. The driver gets out and walks into the alley.

Alex's pulse quickens. *He knows exactly where I live!* Minutes later the man returns. Standing beside his car he gives the neighborhood a once-over. Alex slides out of the doorway, walks back to his car and waits until the assassin drives off. By maintaining a discreet distance behind, Alex keeps the Chevrolet in view and follows it until it pulls into the driveway of a small hotel on 14th Street.

The Russian speaks with an attendant and goes inside. Alex glances at his watch. It is 10:50 a.m. Twelve minutes later, the assassin returns, enters his car and drives east on Ponce de Leon Street. At Highland Avenue he turns right. Several blocks later he parks in front of a women's apparel shop and enters.

Alex waits a few minutes and drives by the store, but he can't see inside because of sunlight reflecting off the storefront window. He continues on for a block, makes a U-turn and parks on the other-side of the street facing the shop. He reaches in the glove compartment, removes a set of binoculars and focuses them on the storefront. He watches the Russian exit the shop carrying a package about the size of a shoebox.

The man enters his car, glances around, and begins opening the box. Suddenly, his hands and the box fall from view, but Alex can tell from the movement of his arms that he is removing something from the box. The man raises his right hand and places something in his jacket pocket. He moves his left hand across his chest and slips an object into what appears to be a shoulder holster. *A gun,* Alex thinks, *and surely it has a silencer.*

Alex follows the assassin back to the hotel. It is 11:40 a.m. He decides he must start his own plan.

Chapter 2

Alex drives to a Home Depot and places an order with the lumber department for delivery later that day. He buys a circular saw, an extension cord, a ball of twine, a large plastic bag, six sheets of one inch thick Styrofoam and a roll of bubble wrap. He puts the purchases in the car trunk and drives to an icehouse on Marcus Street. Here he purchases four slabs of dry ice and returns home.

Alex's apartment is a two-room cottage located behind a Victorian-like house on Myrtle Street in Midtown. He moved there eight years ago when he arrived in Atlanta. It is a neighborhood of individual houses, many of which have been converted into apartments with well-tended lawns on wide, tree lined streets.

Alex parks his town car in one of the two spaces adjacent to his cottage. He enters the apartment through a gate that opens onto a small porch. The front door opens into a room that serves as kitchen, dining nook and living room. The kitchen utilities are strung along the far wall with a table and two chairs next to a window looking out to the porch. A sofa rests against the wall to the left of the entrance door.

Alex reverses the positions of the sofa and the table and chairs. He pushes the sofa beneath the window and places the table and two chairs in the area where the sofa was. From the bedroom he carries a television and night table into the living room and sets them next to the sofa. He positions the television facing the table and chairs. This arrangement requires anyone watching television to sit with their back to the archway that connects the living room and the bedroom. He turns on the television and adjusts the sound slightly higher than normal.

He returns to the bedroom and unlatches the lock on the bedroom window. He lifts the window to determine the ease with which it moves, and if it makes noise when raised. The window moves easily. He decides that with the television playing its movement will not be heard. He closes the window but leaves it unlocked.

He walks to the closet, reaches overhead and searches along a ledge until his hand feels a hard object wrapped in a soft cloth. Bringing it down, he uncovers a Smith & Wesson automatic and a clip holding twelve rounds. He inserts the clip into the handle, chambers a round, checks to be sure that the safety is locked, and slips it under a pillow.

AT THREE-THIRTY a Home Depot truck pulls into the alley. At Alex's direction the driver and helper discharge a pile of lumber in the area of the vacant parking space. With a circular saw, hammer and nails, Alex sets about building the assassin's coffin, a 4' x 4' x 2' slatted wooden crate lined with the Styrofoam sheets. He finishes two hours later and moves it on to the porch.

Alex showers and at six o'clock he phones David and Richard, neighbors who live in the first-floor apartment in the main house. David answers.

"David, will you do me a favor?"

"Certainly, Alex, what is it?"

"When you walk Max tonight, will you let me know if you see a red Chevrolet parked in the vicinity of my cottage?" Hesitating, he adds, "And if there's someone in or near it, let me know what he looks like."

Although Alex speaks in a measured tone, David detects a tinge of emotion at the edge of each word. "I normally take Max out at about six-thirty, but I'll leave a little early tonight so that I can cover more ground. I'll call you as soon as I get back."

Thirty minutes later Alex's telephone rings.

"Alex, he's there!"

"Where, David?"

"Alex, are you in trouble? Do you want me to call the police?"

"No, David." Alex thought David might be suspicious and he has an explanation ready. "He's a private investigator who has been hired by the husband of a woman I'm seeing. She overheard her husband speak to him on the phone, and she warned me that I might be followed tonight."

"Okay, but he's a large, sinister looking man."

Alex laughs. "David, trust me, I'm not going to be seeing her tonight so there's nothing for me to worry about."

"Okay, Alex. His car is parked about five car lengths below the alley and facing Myrtle. He was slumped down in the driver's seat when I passed it."

"Do you think he was suspicious of you?"

"No, no. It was perfect. Max decided to take a leak on the tree just in front of his car. That gave me the chance to casually look around."

Alex feels a flash of relief. *If he's positioned himself so he can see me when I leave the apartment, he won't try to kill me then. That will attract attention. He's going to break-in after I leave and kill me when I return.*

"Alex?"

"Sorry, David, I was checking something. Thanks. I owe you one."

"You don't owe Richard or me anything, Alex. You've been our friend, and I'm glad to help."

CHAPTER 3

ALEX WAITS UNTIL dark before leaving his apartment. He removes the gun from under the pillow, releases the safety, and slips it in his belt. Behind the wheel he places the gun on the seat beside him, starts the engine and drives down the alley, stopping before entering 3rd Street. He looks to his left and sees the red Chevrolet. He turns right on 3rd, and then left on Myrtle, and heads south toward downtown, all the while glancing in the rear view mirror to see if he is being followed. He drives around the downtown area until he is satisfied that he has not been followed.

At Churchill's, a pub featuring live jazz, Alex takes a seat at the far end of the bar where he can see everyone who enters. Churchill's is his favorite nightspot, a place where he usually drinks beer, but not tonight. During the next two hours he drinks water, keeps his eyes on the doorway, and his ears on the music. At about ten, he heads home.

He parks a block away. He places the automatic in his pocket, locks the car and jogs toward Myrtle Street. There is no one in sight. A shoulder-high hedge and a stone pathway run from the front of the wood-framed apartment house to his cottage in the rear. Except for a small hall light, the lights are out in the main house. Alex creeps around the side of the house. The sole illumination in the backyard comes from his porch light and a light further down the alley. He moves quickly and silently to a position under his bedroom window, pauses, takes a deep breath and listens. Any anxiety he feels is completely masked by the adrenaline surging through him.

He does not hesitate. He carefully raises the bedroom window and crawls in. He had turned the television on when he left and it is still playing. Hugging the wall, he edges forward until he is able to see through the archway into the living room. The flickering television light silhouettes the assassin. He is seated in the chair closest to the archway with his back to the bedroom, watching and waiting for Alex. The rearrangement of the furniture has positioned the assassin exactly where he wants him. With cat-like quickness, Alex lunges forward and thrusts his right arm around the assassin's neck, yanking him backward. The man screams, but somehow gets to his feet. With incredible strength, he jerks forward carrying Alex on to his shoulders. They crash to the floor. On hands and knees the gunman scurries toward the television where his gun fell. Alex leaps on the man's back, throws his left leg around his waist, locks the foot of that leg inside his other leg and pushes his assailant's arms out from under him.

With the assassin sprawled on the floor face down, Alex slides his hands and arms under the assassin's arms and applies a full nelson by gripping the back of his neck with both of his hands. Exerting pressure on his neck and head, Alex bends the man's head down and, at the same time, applies pressure with his legs to his victim's midsection. He hears what sounds like fire crackers exploding as the assassin's ribs crack. The assassin gasps. Alex increases the pressure on the assassin's head and neck until he hears a loud snap. The assassin's body falls limp. Keeping his left hand over the man's neck in the half nelson hold, Alex feels his pulse. There is none. His neck is broken. He's dead.

Alex remains on top of the dead body until he catches his breath. He turns the body over. In the flicker of the television light he examines the corpse: the head flopped sideways, the tongue clenched between rotten teeth, the nose bloody, the eyes open but nearly popped out of the sockets. He feels a cold shiver.

Alex leaves his apartment and returns with his car. As he gets out, David and his roommate, Richard, approach.

"Is everything all right?" David asks.

"Thanks for your concern, David, but everything is just fine."

"Richard and I are really glad to hear that. Frankly, we were worried about you. That's why we came home early." David stares hard at Alex. "Do you know your nose is bleeding?"

Alex hesitates but rubs the back of his left hand under his nose and looks at it. "Yes, that happens sometimes, high blood pressure." David continues staring at him and Alex stares back. Finally, Alex says, "Good night, David. Good night, Richard," and turns toward his apartment.

After David and Richard return to their apartment, Alex removes the dry ice, the roll of bubble wrap, and a small cylinder from his car trunk and carries them inside. Next, he pushes the crate into the living room and lays it on its side. He closes the kitchen blinds and turns on the overhead light. He rolls the body over and places it against the sofa for support. He pulls the limp legs and knees up to the chest and wraps heavy twine around them. He continues stringing the twine around the chest and arms, pinning the arms to the sides. He positions the head in the up position and ties it back. He places the plastic bag on the floor and slides the body into it. He raises the corpse and pushes it feet first into the crate. He lifts the crate to the upright position and stuffs it with the bubble wrap.

With the corpse positioned face up, he drops in the dry ice, scrunches the top of the bag together creating a small opening, inserts two plastic tubes into the opening, tapes it closed, and attaches the outlet of the cylinder to one of the tubes. The cylinder contains Argon, an inert gas heavier than air that does not burn or support combustion.

Next, he opens the cylinder valve and pushes the air out of

the bag by allowing in the flow of the Argon gas. After purging the air in this manner for several minutes, he lights a match and holds it to the opening of the second tube. The flame immediately goes out indicating that the plastic bag is completely purged of air. He removes the tubes and tapes the opening closed. He decides not to nail the top on until after David and Richard leave for work in the morning.

From the moment he heard Demitri's message he realized that he would have to dispose of the assassin's body when he killed him. By shipping it back to Forsenko two purposes are served: the body disappears, and it sends Forsenko a message. Demitri mentioned that Forsenko operates out of the Brighton Beach Moscow Social Club in Brooklyn, New York, and Alex secured the address earlier by calling information.

Alex reaches in his wallet, removes the paper on which he has written the address, prints the address on the plywood panel with a black felt pen and places clear tape over the panel to protect the address in case of rain. On the loose top panel he slaps on a "This Side Up" label.

Ever the optimist, Alex made arrangements for the pickup of the crate in the morning with delivery to Brooklyn two days later. He knows, however, that if the temperature of the corpse is not kept cool, it will start decomposing and give off foul-smelling odors. If that happens, the body will be traced back to him. He is counting on the dry ice and the Argon gas preserving the body until it arrives at the Brighton Beach Moscow Social Club.

ALEX'S ENTIRE BODY aches from the fight with the assassin and preparing the body for shipment. He climbs wearily into bed, and with the events of the day tumbling through his mind, another thought intrudes. What has happened in his life that he was left with only two choices—kill or be killed?

CHAPTER 4

EVENTS LEADING TO the attempted murder of Alex Ivanovich started three weeks earlier at Atlanta's Hartsfield International Airport.

After dropping off a CNN executive at the Delta Air Lines terminal and helping with her bags, Alex gets into his Lincoln Town Car and prepares to maneuver through the maze of traffic that has his car pinned against the curb. Seeing a break in the traffic, he eases down on the accelerator. Suddenly, the right rear car door flies open. He stops, turns, and sees a woman starting to climb inside. Their eyes lock.

"Please, it's my mother's sixtieth birthday, and I'm late for her party." Alex stares at the woman and shakes his head.

"Please!"

"Lady, I'm not allowed to pick up passengers in the airport. The airport has its own service, and it's just behind you."

The woman is half in the backseat leaning forward, her eyes fixed on Alex. "I know. I stood in line for over a half-hour, and it's still a mile long. I'll never make it to my mother's party if you don't help me."

Alex looks back to the taxi area and sees a long line. "Where's your baggage?"

"On the sidewalk, only two bags."

"Get in," Alex says, as he hits the trunk release button and gets out. The woman watches as Alex walks toward the baggage. He is dressed in black trousers and a white short-sleeved shirt open at the neck. His muscular arms sweep up the bags and he throws them into the trunk.

"Thanks," the woman says, as he slides behind the wheel.

Alex looks in the rearview mirror. "I just hope it doesn't cost me my airport privileges."

He starts forward and out of nowhere a man steps in front of his car. He slams on the brakes and stops. The man looks like a scarecrow, head cocked, legs spread and bowed, arms flapping, and a twisted grin on his face. He is carrying a leather travel bag in his right hand and a small black case in his other hand. The man lurches forward and falls onto the hood.

A drunk. Alex puts the car in park and jumps out. The man rolls off the hood, staggers to the passenger side, opens the front door and falls in. Alex's first reaction is to pull him out but realizes that it might create an incident, just what he doesn't want. He glances around. No one seems aware of his situation. He gets in, slams the door, edges the car forward, and enters the flow of traffic.

The man stares at Alex, and after a moment, says, "That was very kind of you to stop for me." Sensing movement in the backseat, the man turns and sees the woman. "Oh, I didn't know you were there. Please, let me introduce myself. I'm Harold Vanderbork."

"I'm Kia Williams," the woman says, extending her hand. She looks past Vanderbork to Alex. "I wanted to introduce myself sooner. I'm Kia Williams. I've been in Bermuda with some friends from work. Our plane was due in at three but it was delayed over two hours."

Alex smiles. He's no longer angry. "I'm pleased to meet you, Ms. Williams, and you too, Mr. Vanderbork. My name is Alex." Directing his remarks to Kia, he adds, "Where can I take you?"

"My father is giving a surprise sixtieth birthday dinner for my mother at the Azio restaurant. I think it's on . . ."

"International Boulevard just off Peachtree," Alex says.

"If you would drop me off there, that would be perfect," Kia says, glancing at her watch.

After several minutes of silence, Vanderbork says, "Doesn't anyone want to know where I'm going?"

Alex looks over at Vanderbork. "After I drop off Ms. Williams, where can I take you?"

"The Ritz Carlton in Buckhead, and speaking of being sixty," Vanderbork says, twisting around so that he can see in the backseat, "that's why I've been celebrating. I'm going to be sixty in three months. Unfortunately, they're putting me out to pasture." He bangs his right fist on his travel bag. "It doesn't make any difference who you are, that's what happens at Coca-Cola. You're out at sixty." Vanderbork's head slumps. "I've given Coca-Cola thirty-eight years. And now, like trash, I'm thrown out."

Leaning forward Kia places a hand on his shoulder. "I know who you are. You're the company's chief chemist. I've made travel arrangements for you."

"How do you know . . .?"

"I work for Coca-Cola. I'm in the travel department."

Vanderbork nods. "Coca-Cola is the only company I've ever worked for. It's my life."

"After thirty-eight years, I'm sure you have a nice pension coming to you."

Vanderbork's face flushes. "It's not a question of money. I love what I do, and I don't want to give it up. I'm still a young man. There's no one in the company that knows more about how Coca-Cola is made than I do. As of yesterday, Coca-Cola had a market value of one hundred and forty-six billion dollars and most of that value comes from one thing—the formula. I'm one of only three people in the world that know the formula's contents. Think about it, I'm a guardian of a secret worth billions of dollars and the company is going to dump me." Vanderbork turns and lifts over his head the black case he is cradling in his lap.

Vanderbork leans his head against the headrest and closes his eyes. "Perhaps retirement won't be so bad after all," he mumbles. "I'll buy a house in Chincoteague, Virginia. I love Chincoteague oysters. I'll sit on the beach . . ." He falls silent.

Alex looks over. Vanderbork's head is slumped on his chest; he's asleep.

Alex leaves the expressway at exit 96 and heads up International Boulevard. Three blocks later he stops in front of the Azio restaurant. He lifts Kia's bags from the trunk and opens the right rear door.

As she leaves the car Kia fumbles in her purse. Without looking up she says, "How much do I owe you?"

"Please, lady, no money. I violated the rules by giving you a ride. I don't want to make it worse by taking money. It's my favor to you so that you can celebrate your mother's birthday."

Kia's head snaps up. Their eyes meet. Extending her hand she says with a smile, "Thank you, Alex. Perhaps sometime I'll be able to return the favor." She looks in the car. "I hope Mr. Vanderbork will be all right."

Alex smiles. "He'll be okay."

Alex watches as Kia walks up the steps and enters the restaurant. *Some pretty woman,* he thinks.

Vanderbork is still sleeping when Alex heads north on Peachtree in the direction of the Ritz Carlton. Stopping in the Ritz's circular driveway, Alex leans over and gently shakes his passenger. He does not respond. He shakes him harder. Vanderbork stirs, "How much? How much?"

"Nothing, Mr. Vanderbork."

By the time Alex reaches the passenger side, a hotel attendant has Vanderbork in tow and is maneuvering him toward the front door. It is six-thirty. Alex is tired. He heads home.

CHAPTER 5

ALEX PARKS IN his driveway. As he starts out of the car, he catches sight of something on the front passenger floorboard. He reaches across the seat. It's the black case containing Vanderbork's laptop computer. Standing in the humid air cradling the case, thoughts flood his mind. He remembers Vanderbork lifting the computer case over his head in a sort of triumphant gesture after saying he was the guardian of a secret worth billions of dollars. Could the Coca-Cola formula be in Vanderbork's computer? Does it contain secret ingredients?

Inside his apartment Alex places the black case on the kitchen table. It is hot and humid and sweat trickles down the back of his neck. He removes his tie and turns on a window air conditioner. He opens the refrigerator and grabs a can of beer. He removes the computer from the case, plugs it into a wall outlet and turns it on. Within seconds he is staring at a blank screen with a flashing cursor next to the words "Enter Password." Since he doesn't know the password, the only way into the computer is to find a crack.

IN 1989 ALEX spent three months in computer training at a KGB school on the outskirts of Saint Petersburg where special classes were conducted in the use of "password recovery tools," a sophisticated term for "cracking." After thinking for a moment about the best way to proceed, he reboots the laptop and discovers that the BIOS were manufactured by Award Technologies. He turns on his own computer and goes to Yahoo looking for a crack for Award's BIOS. He types in the keywords, "BIOS CRACK AWARD and hits enter. Within seconds a long list of matches flash on the screen. He selects the one that claims to have cracks for almost any BIOS.

He scrolls down the page and examines a variety of cracks: Windows screensaver cracks, Microsoft Word password breaks, zip file workarounds, and finally, what he is looking for—Award BIOS cracks.

He downloads the file and follows the directions on how to place the crack onto a diskette and boot up the laptop so that he can run the cracking program. To his dismay the program reports that the BIOS version is incompatible with the crack. He goes back online and finds other cracks, all useless until he comes across a Russian website that specifically mentions the BIOS version he is looking for. He runs the program and when the Windows banner screen appears, he knows that whatever the password was, it has been deleted.

Alex browses through each folder on the hard drive starting with the "my documents" folder. He opens each document one by one but finds nothing but corporate correspondence. He runs a search of the hard drive looking for all files ending with the extension "doc" that Windows stamps on the end of every "Word" document. He finds nothing.

He takes a break and drinks a beer. *Where is it?* Suddenly, the answer hits him. Vanderbork had entered the formula file so as to avoid a search for files with the extension ending "doc."

Alex now begins the long and tedious task of checking through every directory for a file that might be named in some way for what he is looking for. After hours of searching through hundreds of files on the hard drive, he comes across a file titled

"UNIQUE." He opens the file and a recipe for a cola drink appears on the screen. He isn't sure it's the Coca-Cola formula, but it's the only cola recipe in the computer.

He studies the cola formula, its grams, milligrams, parts per hundred, and its constituents: phosphoric acid, carbohydrates, salt, sugar, caffeine, carbonated water, caramel, and the natural flavors, the ingredients that distinguish Coca-Cola from its competitors. Compared to some chemical formulas he had to memorize in getting his chemical engineering degree, the Coca-Cola formula is relatively simple. He repeats it several times and locks the formula in his memory. For a brief moment he's excited. He is one of only four people in the world who know the Coca-Cola formula, but his excitement is ephemeral. He doesn't own the formula. It's the property of The Coca-Cola Company. He turns off the computer and puts it back in the case. He will drop the computer off at Coca-Cola headquarters in the morning. It is nearly 3 a.m. He goes to bed.

THE PHONE RINGS. Alex reaches for it and glances at the bedside clock. It is 5:42 a.m.

"Alex, this is Debbie at Peachtree. I'm sorry to call you at this ungodly hour, but we just got a call to pick up a client in Macon at eight-thirty and all of our limos are booked. Can you handle it?"

Peachtree Limousine Service is an agency that sends Alex some of its overflow business. Over the past three years, Peachtree has become his most important source of business and he accommodates their requests whenever possible. The day is open. He planned on going to the automobile auction with Avon Jones to buy a Porsche to recondition and sell but . . . "Sure Debbie, I can handle it. Where in Macon?"

"Alex, you're a sweetheart. You're to pick him up at the 1842 Inn on College Street. His name is Winfred Armstrong. He'll tell you where he wants to go, but it's an all day job because you're to deliver him to the Atlanta Airport for a four o'clock flight to Boston. We'll take care of the billing." She pauses. "If this guy gives you a big tip, will you take me to dinner?"

"Absolutely."

"Alex, you say that every time, and I'm still waiting."

DRIVING FROM THE airport Alex reflects on his day. It was busy but uneventful. Armstrong didn't talk to him except to give directions to places in and around Macon that he wanted to visit. His directions were precise and Alex had no difficulty in finding each location. At about one-thirty Armstrong instructed Alex to take him to the Atlanta airport. Alex isn't sure what Winfred Armstrong's travels were about, but he is satisfied with Armstrong's hundred dollar tip.

Alex exits the airport and speeds off in the direction of Atlanta. It is 3:30 p.m. He hasn't exercised in two days and he wants to drive to the YMCA on Edgewood Street and work out, but returning Vanderbork's computer had been on his mind all day. If he works out first, it will be too late to return it today. He heads home for the computer.

ALEX PUTS THE key in the front door lock, opens it, steps inside and reaches for the wall light switch. A sharp pain explodes in the back of his head.

CHAPTER 6

WHEN ALEX AWAKES he is engulfed in darkness and silence. He doesn't know where he is. The pain in his head is so intense he can't think. His entire body is numb. He tries to move his arms but he can't move them. *I'm paralyzed.* Panic streaks through his body with unthinkable terror. Remembering his KGB training, he reminds himself, *don't panic.* He takes deep breaths, exhales slowly, remains calm and motionless. His mind is a complete blank. He repeatedly asks himself, *Where am I?*

He lies still, and after what seems like forever, he feels the numbness recede and his memory starts to return in bits and pieces. *I stopped at my apartment to pick up Vanderbork's laptop. I'm on the floor of my apartment.* Cautiously he tries to move his arms. They move! Relief surges through him.

Raising his head slightly he sees a sliver of light, and though every muscle in his body aches, he crawls toward it. As he pushes forward on his elbows, blood oozes into his eyes, along the bridge of his nose, over his lips, and down his chin, but he keeps crawling. Finally, he reaches the bathroom. The light that guides him is from a street lamp in the alley.

Exhausted, he rests for a moment, and then pushes himself up along the doorframe. Standing braced against the doorframe, he switches on the bathroom light. In the mirror he sees he is covered with blood. He opens the shower door and turns on the cold water. Standing with his head bent and both hands pressed against the shower sides for support, he watches swirls of blood spin clockwise down the drain. When the bleeding fades, he steps out of the shower, removes his clothes, towels off, and wraps the towel around his head. The bleeding has almost stopped, but he knows he needs medical attention.

After changing into clean clothes, he goes into the living room, turns on the lights, and looks around. Blood is all over the floor, especially near the front door where he fell. It is clear that someone was inside the apartment and struck him on the head with a heavy object when he entered. *Who? Why?* His eyes sweep the room. Nothing appears disturbed. At the kitchen table, his gaze stops. Vanderbork's computer is missing. He remembers seeing it on the kitchen table when he left in the morning.

ALEX DRIVES TO the emergency room of Gary Hospital. He tells the registration nurse that he stumbled in his apartment and struck his head against the edge of a dresser. He repeats that story to the ER physician who orders his head shaved and puts fifty-two stitches in a deep laceration that runs across the top of his head. When the last stitch is laced in, he asks for a mirror.

The nurse looks up and a playful smile crosses her face. "Are you sure you're ready for this, Mr. Ivanovich?"

Alex forces a smile and extends his right hand.

The nurse hands him a mirror. "It will take about a week for the black eyes to clear up. As for the hair," she says, with a shrug, "that will take longer." Alex stares in the mirror. If he didn't know that he was looking at himself, he wouldn't know who it was in the mirror.

Alex has not eaten all day and he's hungry. Despite his appearance, he decides to stop at Manuel's, a pub in the Virginia-Highland's area. For a disguise he slips on sunglasses and a Braves baseball cap. He parks in the lot across the street from Manuel's and almost falls when he gets out. He realizes that he is still weak, and he walks cautiously, like a drunk trying to walk a straight line for the police.

Alex likes Manuel's. It has good food, reasonable prices, and verve. Almost every night, including tonight, it is crowded with college students, baby boomers, truck drivers, professors, lawyers, investment bankers, secretaries, all mingling to the blare of music, the din of voices, and the clatter of glasses.

He sits at a table against the wall. A waitress hands him a menu and takes his order, a Killian's Red and a hamburger with steak-fried potatoes. Waiting for the waitress to return with his order, he people watches. Suddenly, he hears someone say, "Alex, what happened to your head?"

He turns around and there stands Kia Williams. She is dressed in a sleeveless cotton flower-print dress cut just above the knees. Her face is long and thin with high cheekbones, smooth light-brown skin, and shoulder length, jet-black hair. She is about five-eight or nine inches tall with shapely legs and long, elegant fingers.

"How, did you know who I am? Almost no one recognizes me in my Friday night disguise."

"Well it wasn't easy. What's with the sunglasses and the head bandage?" She hesitates, "You do remember me, don't you?"

Alex, dressed in clean, well-pressed khakis and a black linen shirt open at the neck, stands. "Yes, Miss Williams, I remember you. How was your mother's surprise birthday dinner?" He is at least six inches taller than she. The baseball cap only partially hides the bandage that circles his head, and the purple discoloration around his eyes seeps out beyond the sunglasses.

"Oh, it was wonderful but . . . what happened to you?"

Alex looks around. "Are you waiting for your husband?"

"I'm not married. I'm supposed to meet a girlfriend, but she's already a half-hour late. I was standing at the entrance when you came in, but I didn't recognize you until you sat down."

"That's better than I did when I looked in the mirror at the hospital."

"Hospital? What happened?"

Alex points to a chair. "Will you join me until your friend comes?"

"Yes. Thank you."

The waitress returns and Alex says, "I ordered a Killian's and a hamburger. What will you have?"

Kia thinks for a moment, "Just a glass of water." When the waitress leaves, Kia leans forward, "Please, Alex, tell me what happened to you."

Alex takes a sip his beer. "If I tell you, will you keep it to yourself?"

"Certainly."

"After I dropped you off at the restaurant, I took Vanderbork to the Ritz-Carlton in Buckhead. When I got home I noticed that he had left his computer in my car . . ." Alex goes on and details what happened after that, including memorizing the Coca-Cola formula.

"Who do you think did this?"

"I don't know, but I suspect it was someone acting on orders from Coca-Cola."

The room is crowded and noisy and they are leaning their heads together to be heard. Kia pushes back in her chair. "You can't be serious."

Alex nods.

"Have you reported it to the police?" Alex shakes his head. "Why not?"

"Because I'm a Russian immigrant. I'm in this country on a green card. To get a one way ticket back to Russia all I have to do is say something that impugns the integrity of mother Coca-Cola and I'm on the boat."

"I know a Georgia accent when I hear one, and you were raised here in Georgia."

Her eyes flash. "Why are you saying that you're a Russian?

Why are you saying Coca-Cola is responsible for what happened to you?" The waitress places the hamburger and Kia's water on the table between them.

Alex stands, fishes in his pocket and pulls out a wad of bills. He removes a twenty dollar bill and places it on the table. "This should take care of the bill," he says, and turns to leave.

Kia jumps up and grabs his arm. "Why are you leaving?"

Alex glares at her. "You called me a liar."

"I didn't call you a . . ."

"I told you I'm Russian. You said, 'No, you're American.' That means you don't believe me. In Russia, that calls me a liar."

"I . . . I apologize and . . . mean that sincerely. It's just . . . hard to believe that you're Russian and speak fluent English." Her eyes are pleading. "You told me that you haven't eaten anything all day. Please stay and eat your hamburger." She smiles. "If it won't make you feel better, it will me."

Alex sits down. "I apologize too. I don't mean to be rude, but I'm not myself. I shouldn't have come here. I should have gone home." He takes a swig of his beer and bites into the hamburger. A smile flickers across his face. "I'm also fluent in German, Italian, French, Spanish and, of course, Russian."

Kia feels her body relax. She studies him. "What are you going to do?"

"About what?"

"What happened to you."

Alex runs his right hand across the back of his head. "I was thinking that I'll buy a wig tomorrow, a blonde wig."

"No, no. You have beautiful black hair," Kia says, and feels a flush of embarrassment. She scrunches her face into a flippant smile. "Besides, you're not the blonde type."

"Will you go with me?"

Kia is surprised by the invitation but quickly says, "I'd love to." She reaches in her purse, takes out a pen and a slip of paper and writes her address and phone number.

"Here's my address. Do you know where it is?"

"In Druid Hill?" She nods. "I'll find it."

"What time can I expect you?"

"What about eleven? We can have lunch afterward."

Kia stands and extends her hand. "And Alex, bring along some 'before' photographs of yourself."

CHAPTER 7

THE NEXT MORNING at eleven Alex turns into Kia's apartment complex. He follows the road around, and when it forks, he swings to the left and makes an immediate right into a cul-de-sac rimmed with townhouse-like apartments.

He rings the buzzer for apartment 1A. The door opens almost immediately and Kia greets him with a cheerful, "Good morning." She is dressed in jeans, a plain white cotton blouse and a navy-blue cardigan. With her hair hanging curled around her shoulders, she appears taller than she did last night.

"Are you feeling better today, Alex?"

"Much better."

She motions him in. Alex follows her through the living room into the dining room where the Yellow Pages lay open on the table. "I was just looking under 'Wigs and Hairpieces' when you knocked. Can you believe this? Two pages of places that sell nothing but wigs and hairpieces."

Alex looks down at the open pages. "Where do you suggest we go first?"

"This one," she says, stabbing her finger on the page. "They advertise that they specialize in 'solutions for hair lost medically or trauma related.'"

"That's me. Let's go."

PURCHASING THE HAIRPIECE turns out to be less of an ordeal than he expected. There is only one other customer in the store when they arrive. Alex is taken to a private sitting room. He took Kia's advice and brought along several photographs of himself, including one that shows him with a full crop of curly black hair. The saleslady uses the photographs to search through her inventory, and the choices are quickly narrowed to two. After considering the opinions of Kia and the saleslady, Alex makes his selection. Before leaving the store, he takes a final look in the mirror. It isn't a perfect match but it comes close and, except for the blackening around his eyes that can be hidden by sunglasses, he looks and feels almost normal.

Walking to the car Alex says, "You know, Kia, I was half-kidding when I said I was going to buy a wig, and I probably wouldn't have bought it, except for you. Thanks."

"Hey, you don't get off that easy. You promised me lunch, and I'm hungry."

ALEX DRIVES TO Virginia Highlands, and they go to a little Thai restaurant off Highland Street. They take a table by a front window. Kia places her elbows on the table, her chin in her hands, and grins. "From the smells alone, I know that I'm going to like lunch." They laugh. The waitress hands them menus and Alex the wine list. Alex studies it for a moment. "Would you like a glass of wine?"

"Why not? It's Saturday."

"White or red?"

"With Thai food I prefer white or rosé."

Alex orders two glasses of a California chardonnay, and he gives their orders for a double order of sliced chicken sautéed with hot chili and onions.

When the waitress leaves, Kia says, "I have the feeling that there's something mysterious about you. It's not a bad feeling . . ."

She waits before continuing. "You don't like to talk about your-self, do you?"

He shrugs. "All my life I haven't."

"Why not?"

"I suppose because of my training and my job."

"And what was that?"

Alex takes a deep breath. "I was a member of the KGB." He pauses. "Do you know what the KGB was?"

She stares at him, "The Russian secret police?"

"Yes," he says, with a nod.

"Isn't the new president of Russia an ex-KGB agent?" Again, Alex nods. "And you were a spy?"

Alex stares at her but says nothing.

Kia feels a flutter of excitement. "Was the KGB as bad as I've heard?"

"I don't know what you've heard. It was very powerful and, some say, the most ruthless intelligence organization in the world." Alex frowns and shuts his eyes. "If you decide to leave, I'll understand."

"Leave? Are you kidding? It sounds exciting." The waitress returns with the wine.

"When you said that you would understand if I left, did you say that because you are ashamed to have been a member of the KGB?"

"No. I said it because of how some people feel about the KGB. Actually, I was designated by the authorities for the KGB at an early age. In school I had aptitudes for languages, math and the sciences. The authorities recognized this and my schooling followed directions that led into specific training for the KGB. In other words, I had no choice. I was selected to be in the KGB, and that was that. You were told it was for the good of the Soviet Union, and you didn't argue with the authorities. I accepted what I was told to do."

"You speak in the past tense. What happened?"

"In August of 1991 a plot to overthrow Gorbachev failed. Vladimir Kryuchkov was the chairman of the KGB at the time, and he and several of his deputies were implicated in the attempted coup. Kryuchkov was arrested and put in prison, and a few months later the KGB was disbanded. Before anyone realized it, the Soviet Union began unraveling. I was in the foreign intelligence service, and with budget cuts and the general chaos that was sweeping the Soviet Union, we didn't know from day to day what we were supposed to be doing, or if we would be paid. There was a terrible national confusion." The waitress arrives and places the chicken course on the table. "What do you say I leave it at that for now?"

She takes a sip of wine. "What brought you from Russia to Atlanta?"

Alex fidgets with his wine glass. As they eat Kia studies Alex. *He is*, she thinks, *quite handsome.*

"My uncle sponsored me. He was working and living in Atlanta. After the collapse of the Soviet Union there were two forces tearing my life apart. I had grown to hate my job in the foreign-service, and my marriage had become a nightmare."

Kia's eyebrows arch. "Are you still married?"

"I am."

Kia holds her hand up. "Alex, I was recently involved with a married man, and it ended on a very sour note. He made a lot of promises that turned out to be nothing but lies." She bites her lower lip. "He made a fool of me, but I developed enough self-respect to end it. After it was over, I made myself a promise to never again go out with a married man. As much as I enjoy your company, I'm going to keep that promise."

She slides out of the booth. "I'd appreciate if you'd take me home."

THEY RIDE IN silence. As they approach Kia's apartment, Alex says, "Let me add something to what I was saying, and then if you don't want to see me again, I'll understand." He looks over at her. Their eyes meet. "Okay?"

"Will it be the truth?"

"Yes. The three years before I left Russia, my wife and I had not been intimate. We stayed together for the sake of our son, Grigory. Eventually, living together became unbearable and we separated. Because my job required me to travel often and unexpectedly, my wife, Tatyana, was awarded custody of Grigory. When I was advised that I had been accepted to immigrate to the United States, I asked Tatyana to allow Grigory to come with me so that he would have more opportunities than in Russia."

"How old was Grigory?"

"He was six at the time." Alex pauses, but his eyes never leave Kia's. "She refused. To this day I've continued to send monthly child support payments, and every June, I return to Moscow and spend two weeks with Grigory. We have a good time together. We go into the countryside and hike and fish. We visit museums, and we talk. He loves to hear about the United States. We're more than just father and son; we're what you call in America, buddies."

"How do Grigory and his mother get along?"

"Grigory has never said, and I've not asked him, but from personal observations, they seem to tolerate one another. You have heard the expression, 'Every person has a price.' I know my wife's price because every year when I return to Russia she tells me what it is."

Kia's hands are sweating and she rubs them on her jeans. "Her price for what?"

"To sign the necessary consent documents that would allow Grigory to come to the United States and live with me."

"What is her price?"

"Over the years she has continued to up the ante. When I was there in June, she demanded $200,000. But, of course, I don't have $200,000, so it's a moot issue. Grigory is now fourteen, and time is running out. But that's my quest, to get enough money to buy his freedom out of Russia."

Kia sits slumped in the seat facing Alex with her right fist pressed against her mouth. "Why is she asking for so much money?"

"She thinks because I live in the United States I'm rich."

"How will you get that much money?"

"I don't know, but I'm going to do it."

Kia jerks down the door handle and opens the door. "Thanks for a wonderful day." She smiles, "If you don't call me, I'll call you."

CHAPTER 8

Alex's telephone rings. He glances at the clock radio. It's 7:10 a.m. He decides not to answer, but on the fifth ring he picks up. "Hello."

"Did I awaken you?"

"Kia?"

"Yes. I'm sorry to call you so early, but have you read this morning's *Journal-Constitution*?"

"No. Why?"

"There's an article in the 'Atlanta' section about a man who claims he owns the Coca-Cola formula, and he wants to sell it."

There is silence at Alex's end. "Alex, are you there?"

"Yes. Does the article say how much he wants for it?"

"No, but you should read the article."

"Why?"

"I don't know. Since you've seen the formula, I thought that it might interest you." Alex says nothing. "Alex, is anything wrong?"

"I'm fine. I just need to take a shower and wake up. I'll read the article and give you a call."

Alex opens the front door, walks to the end of the porch and picks up the *Sunday Journal-Constitution*. The article is on the first page of the "Atlanta" section.

THE SECRET FORMULA · 33

He tosses the paper on the kitchen table and takes a shower. As the hot water pours over his body, he thinks about the Coca-Cola formula. *If I owned it, what would I do with it?*

An idea begins to form. It is a long shot, but worth exploring. He towels down, slips on sweat pants and a T-shirt, and starts a pot of coffee. While the coffee brews, he turns to the article. The caption reads: "Grandson of Thomas R. P. Calderman Offers To Sell Coca-Cola's Secret Formula." After reading the article he calls Kia.

"I've read the article, and I thought it might be fun to drive out and meet the man who claims he owns the Coca-Cola formula. Would you like to come along?"

"That might be interesting." She pauses. "I was planning on going to the ten o'clock Mass. Can we leave after church?"

"Sure. What time shall I pick you up?"

"What about eleven-thirty? Are you going to call him first to be sure he'll be there?"

"I don't think so. Why don't we just drive out, and if he's home, fine. If not, it will be a nice afternoon in the country. I know the area fairly well."

KIA IS WAITING outside when Alex arrives. He drives through the city and takes the entrance ramp onto Interstate 85 North. Kia has been thinking about Alex all through church. She wants to know more about him.

"Alex, tell me more about yourself."

He glances over at her. "Like what?"

"Like where in Russia were you born?"

"I was born and raised in the city of Vladivostok, and my mother, sister and brother still live there."

"I'm sorry, Alex, but my geography of Russia is terrible. Where is Vladivostok?"

"Well, if this is Russia," Alex draws in the air with his right index finger the configuration of Russia, "then, here," he points, "would be Vladivostok. It's located in the extreme southeastern part of Russia. Our neighbors are North Korea, China and Japan." Alex looks over at Kia. "Wait a minute. I keep telling you about me, but I know next to nothing about you. What about telling me something about you?"

"Okay, fair enough," Kia says, her face taking on a solemn look. "On my last birthday, two months ago, I turned thirty."

She falls silent for a moment and then continues, "I didn't go to college because I got pregnant during my senior high school year. I graduated but they didn't let me on the stage to receive my diploma. He was a ghetto bum, and when he learned I was pregnant, I never saw him again. And, of course, he never paid one cent towards my son's support. In fact, I later heard I was the third girl he had gotten pregnant. It is a game ghetto bums play. They brag about how many women they've made pregnant."

"Your son? Where is he?" Alex asks, his face etched with confusion.

"Tony died two years ago from spinal meningitis." Her eyes well with tears.

"What happened?" Alex pulls the car to the side of the road and stops.

"I was at work and got a call from the school nurse saying that Tony had the flu and to come take him home. When I got there, Tony complained of a headache and achy joints. I was told he had a temperature and had vomited. I took him home, called his pediatrician, described Tony's symptoms, and he agreed that it was probably the flu. He prescribed an antibiotic, called it into the druggist, and I picked it up. Later that night, I noticed that Tony had clusters of tiny pin pricks on his neck. I called his pediatrician again, but it took nearly two hours for him to get back to me. I told him about the pin pricks on Tony's neck, and he told me to take Tony to the hospital." Kia bursts into tears.

Alex hands her a handkerchief. "I'm terribly, terribly sorry. I know how much I miss my son, but it's entirely different to lose a son forever. In a very small way, Kia, I know the tremendous loss you feel every day."

They sit in silence. When Kia regains her composure, Alex says, "Shall I take you home?"

"No," she says, shaking her head. Speaking in barely a whisper, she continues, "In the morning a physician told me that Tony had died from bacterial meningitis. My father, who is ten years older than my mother, had a stroke two days later. I'm sure Tony's death caused it. My parents loved Tony. Tony and I were their only family."

"Do you still want to go on?"

Kia nods and they continue on in silence.

Suddenly, Alex pulls over and stops. He reaches in the back seat and finds the newspaper article. He studies it for a moment. "The article says he lives a mile east of here on Backlash Road." Alex looks up at the midday sun to get his bearings. "East is straight ahead. It doesn't say whether Backlash Road is on our left or right. You look on the right for Backlash and I'll look on the left."

Alex pulls back onto the roadway and drives slowly. After traveling a mile or so, Kia points ahead to the right, "There it is."

Alex slows and looks for a signpost but doesn't see one. "How do you know?"

"It's on that mailbox."

Alex sees on the side of a rusting mailbox, "257 Backlash." He turns into a narrow dirt road pitted with deep ruts, lowers his speed and creeps along with the under-carriage bumping along the twisting path. Suddenly, the undercarriage strikes something hard and the car crashes down. He stops and swears under his breath.

Kia sees his concern. "Do you want to turn back?"

"I wish I could, but I'm afraid we're at a point of no return." As he slowly maneuvers a ninety-degree turn, a shack, set on a barren dirt knoll, comes into view.

"Alex, let's get out of here."

Alex shares her tension. An old, dilapidated Ford pick-up truck sits in a rut near the shack. Alex pulls in behind the truck and starts backing up. A thin, unkempt man dashes out the front door carrying a shotgun. He runs directly toward them. Alex stops. The man halts his charge two feet from the front bumper, raises the shotgun and points it directly at the windshield. The man's eyes bulge with excitement. "What the hell are you doing here?" the man screams.

"Don't move," Alex whispers to Kia, and lowers his window. "I'm here to see Simon Calderman about the sale of the Coca-Cola formula. I'm sorry if I came to the wrong place."

The man is wearing dirty overalls and nothing else, no shoes, no shirt. His red, puffy eyes give the impression that he was sleeping and in haste threw on the first thing he could lay his hands on. Alex guesses his age at about fifty.

"You," the man says, waving the barrel of the shotgun at Alex, "git out." Alex opens the door and steps out keeping his hands in full view. He doesn't want to give this crazy an excuse to shoot him.

"I'm sorry if I disturbed you mister . . .uh . . . I'm sorry but I don't know your name. Let me introduce myself. I'm Alex and I'm from Atlanta. That's my wife in the car."

"Why'd you say you came here?" the redneck says, spitting in front of Alex.

"I came to see Simon Calderman."

"Why?"

"There's an article in today's *Journal-Constitution* about Mr. Calderman wanting to sell his Coca-Cola formula." The tension in the man's thin, drawn, boozy face seems to ease. Alex feels he's talking to Simon Calderman. "I want to talk to him about possibly buying the formula from him."

"How much?"

"Are you Simon Calderman?"

The man spits again. "Yeah, I'm Calderman. How much?"

"I don't know. I thought we could talk about that." The man shifts his weight and lowers the barrel of the shotgun. "I'm glad you're Mr. Calderman," Alex says, as a feeling of relief sweeps through him. "For a moment I thought I might be trespassing."

"You are trespassing. Ain't nobody invited you here." Calderman again spits.

"But now that I know why you're here, I ain't gonna shoot you." He keeps staring at Alex. And after a long moment says, "Why do you want to buy the Coca-Cola formula, boy?"

"I don't know. Maybe I'll give it to the world."

"What are you talking about? Give it to the world? How could you do that?"

"Put it on the Internet."

"On the what?"

"The Internet, have you heard of it?" *Nobody's that stupid,* Alex thinks.

"Yeah, I heard of it." He glances toward the car. "Ain't you gonna introduce me to your girly?"

"Sure." Alex turns. "Honey, Mr. Calderman wants to meet you." Alex moves to the passenger side, opens the door, and leans in. "You're my wife."

"I know," Kia murmurs. She slides out, walks straight up to Calderman, extends her hand, and says, "I'm Kia Williams."

Calderman looks her over greedily, his handshake moist and weak. Calderman turns to Alex, and rubs his right hand across his upper lip. Alex notices that his fingers are covered with cigarette stains, and his right index finger bent from arthritis.

Calderman smiles at Kia and spits near Alex's right shoe. "I'll sell you the formula for a hundred thousand dollars."

Alex shakes his head. "I don't have a hundred thousand dollars."

Calderman's eyes narrow. "Then git out of here, you fool."

CHAPTER 9

ALEX'S EYES SWEEP the property: the falling apart shack-of-a-house, the junk heap of a truck, the rutted, unpaved road, the desolation of the land. "I've got two thousand dollars and I'll pay you that in cash, but only if I can see the formula and confirm that it's real, and only if you can prove to me that you own it."

"Two thousand dollars," Calderman sneers. His predatory eyes again run over Kia. "How's a fruit ball like you gonna know if it's the real Coca-Cola formula?"

Alex cautions himself to stay cool. "I'm not interested in the original formula. I want the formula that Coca-Cola uses today. I understand that as the grandson of Thomas R. P. Calderman you inherited that formula and claim sole ownership of it."

Calderman takes a step forward. There is no breeze, and standing not more than three feet apart, Alex can smell his stale, boozy breath.

"Where'd you hear that?"

"I read it in today's *Journal-Constitution*."

Calderman spits and shakes his head. "The dumb bastard who wrote that was too lazy to come out here and talk with me . . . called me on the phone. And I never told him I owned the original formula. I own the formula that Coca-Cola uses today. It's the same formula that they've illegally used since my granddaddy invented it in 1921. That's the one I own, but I ain't selling it for no stinken two thousand dollars."

With a wave of his right hand, he adds, "Now git." Calderman shuffles a little closer and stops, the shotgun barrel in his left hand and resting against his thigh.

Alex stands his ground. "Tell me something, Mr. Calderman. If Coca-Cola bought the formula from your granddaddy, how can you claim to own it?"

"You ain't too smart, are you? Well, let me tell you how it happened, and then I want you to take your wife and git off my property. In 1921, the government brought a lawsuit against Coca-Cola. As a result of that litigation, Coca-Cola was required to change its soft drink formula. My granddaddy, Thomas R. P. Calderman, a chemist, owned a small pharmaceutical company located on lower Peachtree Street.

"Roscoe Hatfield, president of Coca-Cola, was my granddaddy's friend. They played golf, hunted and drank together. When the government won the case, Hatfield asked my granddaddy to formulate a new recipe for Coke. Hatfield promised that if my granddaddy's recipe was accepted and used, Coca-Cola would pay my granddaddy one percent of gross revenues from future Coca-Cola sales."

Alex's brain slips into gear. He doesn't know the sales figures for the intervening seventy-eight years, but billions of dollars flash through his mind. "Was Hatfield's promise made on the basis of a handshake or . . .?"

"Handshake my ass! I got the original letter signed by Hatfield and witnessed by Wilma Streeter, his secretary. And I also got my granddaddy's original recipe that they attached to that letter. The letter is dated August 14, 1921. My granddaddy died of a heart attack a month later, and you know what? My granddaddy's recipe became the new Coca-Cola formula, and Coca-Cola has never paid my granddaddy's estate, or my father, or his estate, or me, one thin dime."

"How do you know that your granddaddy's recipe is, in fact, today's Coca-Cola formula? Did you ever see the formula from which Coke is made?"

"The bastards won't let me see it. They wouldn't let my daddy see it either. Twice I hired a lawyer to make em let me see it, but they refused, and the judge both times sided with Coca-Cola saying that it's a trade secret that they don't have to disclose. I know that it's my granddaddy's recipe because on his deathbed he told my daddy that Hatfield told him that they was gonna use it, and dying Christian men don't lie."

Alex's instincts and training tell him that Calderman's arrogance and bravado are a façade and he will sell his claim to the formula for far less than a hundred thousand dollars. But before Alex increases his offer, he has to be sure that what Calderman claims to own actually is the Coca-Cola formula. He remembers the percentages of grams and milligrams of every component and, most importantly, every natural flavor in Vanderbork's formula. A glance at it is all he'll need. *Give it one more try,* he tells himself.

"Mr. Calderman, if you'll just let me glance at your granddaddy's formula, and if I'm convinced that it's the real formula, and you own it, I'll increase my offer and . . ."

He falls silent and waits for a response, his eyes fixed on Calderman.

"Listen pal, I own it. It came to me from my daddy who inherited it from his daddy. But here's your problem . . ." Squinting into the sun, Calderman wipes the sweat from his forehead. "I ain't gonna sell it to you for no measly two thousand dollars."

Calderman reaches in a pocket and pulls out a crumpled pack of cigarettes. He takes one out, rests the barrel of the shotgun against his crotch, and lights it. He takes a deep drag, inhales, and expels the smoke slowly. His body heaves a sigh of relief. He takes another deep drag.

"You know, your idea of giving it away, of putting it on the Internet . . ." He waves his hand, the cigarette dangling from his puffy lips, "It would serve them rotten sons-of-bitches right."

Alex knows from the newspaper article that the Coca-Cola authorities have not only refused to consider buying the formula from Calderman but have issued press releases disparaging his claim.

The sun is broiling the back of Alex's neck. "I have one request. Let me have a quick glance at your granddaddy's recipe."

The two men stare at one another. Calderman says, "What's your name?"

"Alex."

"Okay, Alex, I'm gonna let you have a glance at it, but let me warn you, don't git no ideas about running off with it, unless you think you can outrun these shotgun pellets." Calderman turns and stalks back to the shack.

Kia whispers, "Alex, let's get out of here. The man is crazy and . . . and dangerous."

"This is what I came for, Kia. Get back in the car. I want to have a look at what he has."

"No. I'll wait here with you."

Calderman emerges from the shack and strides toward them. In his left hand he carries the shotgun and in his right hand some papers. "Here, this is a copy of my granddaddy's 1921 recipe, in his handwriting. And here's a copy of Hatfield's letter setting out the agreement to pay my granddaddy one percent of all future Coca-Cola gross revenues. These are the only copies I have. The originals are in my safe deposit box in Atlanta."

Alex unfolds the wrinkled, dirty papers. His eyes scan the first few lines, and Vanderbork's formula pops into his head. He reads on. Calderman's grandfather's recipe is identical with the formula in Vanderbork's computer. He reads Hatfield's letter and it confirms Calderman's story. He refolds the papers and hands them to the sweating redneck.

"Well?"

Alex points to his car. "That car is owned by South Trust Bank. Every month I pay the bank five hundred dollars to keep it because that's how I make a living. Wealthy people hire me to drive them around." The sun's flaring rays are now at full strength. He glances at Kia. She looks withered by the heat and the emotion of the moment. It is time to make his bid and leave. "For me, two thousand dollars is a lot of money, but I'll increase it to five thousand dollars for the original of your grandfather's recipe and Hatfield's letter. You must also sign an affidavit of the source and authenticity of your ownership, and sign a contract of sale."

Alex takes out his business card and hands it to Calderman. "Here's where you can reach me if you change your mind. If you get a better offer . . . take it."

"Let's go," he says to Kia, and holds the passenger door open while she gets in. Walking around the front of the car, he gives a little salute and says, "It was nice meeting you Mr. Calderman. I hope we meet again."

Alex maneuvers his car backward and forward until he has it pointing back down the dirt road. As he starts forward, he sneaks a side glance of Simon Calderman. His appearance has changed. He no longer looks angry.

ALEX DRIVES OFF the property more confident than when he arrived. Neither Kia or Alex speak until they are on the main road and heading back to Atlanta.

"That was the scariest thing I've ever experienced," Kia says. "When he came charging out of that dirty little shack, I thought he was going to kill us." She breathes in deeply, "When he ordered you out of the car, I thought he was going to shoot you on the spot."

Alex stares ahead thinking about a plan for the use of the

formula, and the pieces begin falling into place. *Funny how things turn out, without Kia it won't work.*

"Well?" Kia says. "Is it the same?"

"Is what the same?"

"Alex, you're a million miles away. Thinking about the Coca-Cola formula, aren't you?" He nods. "Is Calderman's formula the same as Vanderbork's?" She watches him carefully. His face is expressionless.

He glances at her. "Why don't we talk about it later?"

THAT EVENING ALEX'S telephone rings. "Alex, it's Kia."

He feels a stab of disappointment. He had hoped it was Calderman. "Hi, Kia."

"I'm dying to know. I take it Calderman's formula is the same as Vanderbork's or you wouldn't have increased your offer. Am I right?"

Alex hesitates. By training and culture, he doesn't feel comfortable talking on the telephone. In the Soviet Union telephone service was limited and completely controlled by the authorities. Every phone call was monitored. *Do the thugs who burglarized my apartment have my phone number? Is my phone tapped?* "Kia, can we get together sometime later this week?"

"You are going to make me wait that long?"

"I would rather not discuss it over the phone. Can we meet at Manuel's Friday night? "

Kia mentally runs through the week's after work activities. "Yes, that works fine."

If I'm going to hear from Calderman, I'll have heard by Friday. "What time?"

"I usually stop by my parents' at about five-thirty and spend a couple of hours with them. I can meet you at eight."

"Great. We'll go to dinner."

CHAPTER 10

KIA IS WAITING inside the front door of Manuel's when Alex arrives.

"Been waiting long?" he asks.

"A few minutes."

Alex looks around. Manuel's is already crowded and noisy. "I want to talk to you about something, but it's too noisy here. Do you mind if we have dinner someplace quieter?"

"Not at all, wherever you like."

"Have you been to Lafayette's?"

"No."

"You'll like it. It has good food."

Alex's suggestion that they dine at Lafayette's surprises her. "I'm not dressed for Lafayette's. I'm told that's a fancy place."

Alex looks her up and down. "I guarantee that you'll be the most beautiful woman there."

"It's very nice of you to say that, Alex, but won't we need reservations?"

"When I thought about it, I figured this place would be too noisy, so I made reservations."

Kia stares at him and wonders what he wants to talk to her about. "I understand Lafayette's is very expensive but . . ." She shrugs, "Okay."

THEY ARE MET at the door by Harry, the maître d', and it is obvious from his greeting that he knows Alex. Harry shows them to a table in a small, cozy room in the back.

After being seated Kia says, "I don't have a lot of experience with expensive restaurants, but from looking around this room, and the other rooms we passed through, I would say that we have the choice table in the restaurant, pretty good for a limousine driver who just happened to make a last minute reservation." She gives him a searching look. "Alex, an aura of mystery surrounds you."

"I'm sorry to demystify myself but the answer is simple. I play handball with Harry at the YMCA, and when I called him, he said he would find a table for me."

The waiter approaches and hands them menus and Alex the wine list. Alex glances over the wines. "What would you like to drink?"

"Whatever you select."

Alex hands the wine list to the waiter, "The 1990 Chateau Beaucastel, please." The waiter nods and leaves.

"What did you choose?"

"It's a Chateauneuf du Pape from the southern Rhone region in France. The grapes are all organically grown. Some experts think it's the best Chateauneuf-du-Pape. I like it and I think you will too."

"The plot really thickens with the mysterious Alex Ivanovich."

Alex grins. "Speaking of the plot thickening, you don't know how prophetic those words are."

The waiter returns. They stop talking while he removes the cork and splashes some wine into Alex's glass. Alex takes a sip, nods his approval to the waiter who pours the wine.

Alex raises his glass and touches it against Kia's glass, "To good health and wealth."

"To good health," she says.

Alex swirls the wine in his glass, "Kia, if you woke up tomorrow and found that you had a million dollars in your bank account, how would it change your life?"

Kia thinks a moment. "I've never really thought about having a million dollars, but the answer is easy. I would take care of my parents financially. Their only income is my father's social security, and the money my mother makes working three days a week as a domestic. But my mother has severe arthritis, and she shouldn't be working." Kia fidgets with the stem of her wineglass and pauses. "I'd register at Emory, and if I got accepted, I'd quit my job at Coke. I'd be the oldest freshman at Emory but that wouldn't bother me." Kia stares off for a moment. "I would major in English. I've always liked to read and . . . and maybe, I would buy a small house." She shrugs.

"That's it?" She nods. Alex raises his glass. "Here's to the two of us becoming millionaires, courtesy of your employer, The Coca-Cola Company."

She takes a sip of wine, looks down and unfolds her dinner napkin. "I knew the evening was going to be more than just dinner when you said you wanted to talk. So, what do I have to do to become a millionaire? And I want to be very clear with you that if it's illegal, I don't even want to hear about it."

Before Alex can answer, the waiter reappears. "Are you ready to order or would you like more time?" he asks.

"I'm hungry," Kia says.

"Have you decided?"

"Order for me. I like most everything."

Alex scans the menu. "Do you like buffalo steak?"

"I've never had it,"

"Want to give it a try?"

"Sure."

"How do you want it done?"

"Medium."

Alex nods to the waiter. "Two buffalo steaks, one medium, and one medium rare, with rice and asparagus." The waiter leaves.

Alex takes a sip of wine. "Last night Calderman called and said he wants to sell the formula, but not for five thousand dollars. After a lot of haggling, we agreed on a price of ten thousand dollars."

Kia's jaw drops. "I suspected your get-rich-quick scheme had something to do with Calderman's formula." She leans back in her chair and studies Alex. "Alex, what in the world do you think you can do with Calderman's formula that he couldn't do with it? I've checked around and learned that he's been trying to sell that formula for years, and he's had no takers, and that includes The Coca-Cola Company."

She pauses, takes a deep breath and leans forward. "Alex, you're a nice guy. You work hard for your money. Don't throw it away."

"Are you telling me that you aren't interested in making a couple of million dollars? There are no guarantees, of course." He shrugs "We might end up with nothing."

"I would like to be a millionaire, but . . ."

Alex senses her discomfort. "I'm sorry. Let's talk about something else and enjoy the evening."

CHAPTER 11

THE WAITER BRINGS their dinners. Kia cuts into her steak, takes a bite, and rolls her eyes. "It's very good." Alex pours more wine. "And the wine's even better with the steak. Where did you learn about wine?"

"When I was on assignments in France and Switzerland, I always drank wine with dinner, and over time I acquired a taste for it. I started reading about it, visited the vineyards every chance I got, and before I knew it, it was a hobby. I started . . ."

Kia interrupts. "When you spoke about making a lot of money with the Coca-Cola formula, would it involve anything illegal?"

"Do you mean . . . could we go to jail if it doesn't work out?"

"Yes."

"I'm not an authority on American law, but I don't think so. But you would probably lose your job at Coca-Cola."

"And you?"

"I would be deported to Russia."

"And you're willing to chance that?"

"Yes. And spend the money I've saved to finance the venture."

Kia stares at her empty wine glass. "I make thirty thousand dollars a year. I've been with Coca-Cola eight years. On my next birthday I turn thirty-one. If I work there until I'm sixty . . ." She looks up. "So, unless I meet a rich prince charming, I'll never get to do what I want to do. And since I'll never meet a rich prince charming, I'm doomed to remain a travel clerk."

"That's not true. You're a beautiful woman and you can do anything you want."

Kia stops him with a wave of her hand. "Alex, don't say that because it's not true. I don't know about in Russia, but here in Atlanta white men don't want to be seen in public with black women. Wealthy black guys like a pretty black woman to show off and screw, but when it comes to taking her home to mommy, or getting married, they want a single woman who has a college education."

Her eyes flash. "But because my father was a truck driver and my mother a domestic, and neither went to college, I'm viewed by these so called princes charming as the by-product of some drunken backseat fuck." Her mouth tightens. "And, of course, because I didn't go to college, I can't be smart."

The waiter, who has been hovering near, steps forward. "Would madam care for dessert?"

Kia shakes her head, "But I'll have a coffee." She notices Alex look away. "I'm sorry if I'm boring you."

"No. On the contrary, I feel privileged that you've shared these pent up emotions with me. Look, Kia, I don't know whether you realize it but what you've just told me defines where you are with your life. You're in a sort of personal prison. What I'm offering you is a chance to get out of that prison, a chance to make choices for yourself that you'll never have if you stay where you are. What I'm proposing is a long shot with no guarantees, but it gives you an option you may never have again. You've got to decide whether you'd rather spend the rest of your life where you are, or take a chance on getting to where you'd like to be."

"You said that you've agreed to buy Calderman's formula for $10,000. What do you plan to do with it, and how would I fit in?"

Alex leans forward, "If you decide that you're not interested in what I'm about to tell you, can I have your promise that you'll keep it to yourself? The reason I ask that is because the success of my plan depends on secrecy."

Kia stares at him long and hard. "If I come in with you and we're successful, what's my split of whatever we get?"

"One-third to you, two-thirds to me, and I pay the expenses."

The generosity of his offer surprises her. "Okay, you have my promise that I'll not tell anyone. What's your plan?"

"First, I'll need an attorney to draw up a contract that transfers Calderman's ownership of his grandfather's formula and the contract with Coca-Cola to me." He pauses. "Calderman will come to Atlanta tomorrow if I can make those arrangements. Do you know an attorney who could do that?"

Kia thinks for a moment. "I know a lawyer that I see from time to time at the fitness club." She digs in her purse, roots around, and pulls out a card. "Here's his card. I don't know what kind of law he specializes in, but I'll call him tomorrow morning if you like. If he can't do it, I'm sure he'll be able to recommend someone who can. "

Alex nods. "Suppose I call you at nine tomorrow. Calderman will need about an hour to get into Atlanta. If this lawyer can see us in the morning, it might work out."

"Alex, if I decide to become your partner in whatever you are about to propose, I'd also want a contract drawn up regarding our split: one-third for me, two-thirds for you."

"Don't you trust me?" Alex says with a wry smile.

"I know almost nothing about you. You tell me you're a Russian, but for all I know, you could be a Chinaman with a facelift. I want some kind of written agreement that sets out our understanding. Agreed?"

Alex nods. "No problem, but just the terms of our agreement, not the specifics of how we're going to obtain the money."

"One-third to me, two-thirds to you, and you pay the expenses. Is that our deal?

"That's our deal." They shake hands on it. "By the way, Kia, do you keep a diary?"

"No."

"Good. Don't start one."

"Why?"

"Diaries leave trails, and we don't want to leave a trail."

"Okay, no diary." She glances around the room. "Tell me something Alex. What makes you think that you'll be more successful in selling the formula to Coca-Cola than the son and grandson of the man who is supposed to have invented it?"

"What makes you think I plan on selling it to Coca-Cola?"

"That's the only thing I can think of that you can do with the formula and make money."

CHAPTER 12

HIS EYES MIRROR the answer. "You're right. We're going to sell it to Coca-Cola, but let me give you some background. When the KGB decided to recruit a spy, from England, France, the United States, or wherever, it didn't haul off and offer just money because, by itself, money usually isn't enough. What the KGB did was find someone who was vulnerable, someone who harbored a secret that they desperately wanted to keep secret at all costs. If the secret also needed money to nurture it, then that made the situation even better."

"Give me an example," Kia says.

"A closet homosexual with an expensive gambling or drug habit."

Kia rocks back on her chair ever so slightly, never taking her eyes off Alex. "I'm not sure I get the significance of what you're saying."

"The point is that high-profile people of great wealth and power usually harbor secrets that they want no one to know about, secrets they hide at all costs. And if you don't believe me, look at your President Clinton. He lied to the entire world in an attempt to keep his affair secret."

"Okay, but how does all this help us sell Coca-Cola a formula that it claims it owns and has used for the past seventy-eight years?

"We find out the hidden secrets of Coke's top executives."

"Do you know for a fact that they have secrets?"

"No, but experience tells me they do."

"How can you be so sure?"

"Coke's executives are no different from other wealthy, powerful people. Wealth and power breed arrogance, and arrogance breeds indiscretion. And indiscretion usually leads to conduct that must be kept secret."

"Why?"

"Because arrogance feeds on itself and breeds a sense of omnipotence. Narcissistic people become their own first victims by believing in their grandiose sense of self-importance. They have no regard for the feelings of others, and they do what they want and take what they want. Yet they know that certain aspects of their behavior are beyond the bounds of propriety and, if found out, unacceptable to their spouses, their children, their business colleagues, and their own images."

"You're pretty confident about this, aren't you?"

"Yes."

"If I join you, what's my part?"

"As an employee of the Coca-Cola travel department you know where the CEO, President and CFO are going almost as soon as they know. I want you to supply me with their travel itineraries."

Kia eases back in her chair. "And what else do I have to do to earn my one-third share?"

"That's it."

"What will you do with this information?"

"Follow them, and if they have a secret, video it, photograph it, and at the appropriate time, reveal it to them."

"When you reveal it, will it be in the form of blackmail?"

"No. We will never threaten anyone with the information we obtain."

"Then how will you use the information? Assuming you obtain it."

"We will put together a portfolio of photographs, videos, au-dio-tapes and transcripts and discretely present it to them—individually, without anyone else knowing about it. In fact, when they receive the incriminating evidence, they will not know that it was me who sent it to them. That will come later when I offer to sell them the Calderman formula."

"And why will they want to buy it?"

"To avoid the bad publicity of a law suit, to get undisputed ownership of the formula, to eliminate the probability of the for-mula becoming public knowledge, and . . ." He takes a sip of wine.

"And?"

"To keep their secrets secret."

"What's your asking price?"

"More realistically you should ask me what will I accept, and I don't know the answer to that. As you Americans say, I'll have to play that by ear."

There is a sudden loud clap of thunder. They both look out the window and see lightning flash across the sky. "Think about it Kia. With a million dollars you could afford to help your parents, and get that college education you've always dreamed of."

"What I don't understand is how you can speak so confident-ly about a scheme that sounds crazy to me. What makes you so sure it will work?"

Alex takes a deep breath. "I can't guarantee that I can pull this off. There are so many unknowns. But it's a once in a lifetime op-portunity, and I'm going to give it my best effort—with you or without you." He pauses to let the words sink in. "I hope it will be with you."

"And what if it doesn't work and you get shipped back to Russia or, worse yet, you go to jail. How will you feel about that?"

"Better a fallen rocket than never a burst of light," he says with a smile.

Kia stares at him for a long moment. "Who are you quoting?"

"A man who went to jail. Oscar Wilde."

She smiles, lifts her glass and tips it against his. "Here's to the formula, partner."

"Are you in?"

"Yes," she says with quiet resolve.

Like changing masks, the tension in Alex's face breaks into a broad smile.

CHAPTER 13

The next morning Alex gets up early, drives to Piedmont Park and jogs four miles around the lake. He stops for a coffee at a nearby Starbuck's and arrives home a little after eight. He showers, put on a pair of jeans and a white T-shirt and calls Kia.

"Good morning, Alex. I called the attorney. He can see us at ten if that's convenient for you?"

"That's fine. How far from your place is his office?"

"He told me it should take about twenty minutes, but it's an area I'm not familiar with."

"What's the address?"

Kia reads the address. Alex recognizes it as being in a run-down neighborhood. "No problem," he says. "I have a map of the city, but to be sure we're there on time I should come over now. Can you be ready in about fifteen minutes?"

"I'll be waiting outside."

When Alex pulls in front of Kia's apartment, she runs out the front door and to his car.

"Good morning, Alex."

"Good morning. I see you haven't changed your mind."

"No, I've been awake all night thinking about what you said. I think it could work." She hands him a card. "Here's his business card."

Alex glances at it. "I've forgotten. How did you meet this lawyer?"

"I met him about five months ago at the City Fitness Club. I've only talked to him a few times, but he's always been friendly."

"Okay, let's meet Harvey Slinger. I think I know how to get there."

They drive along chatting about different things and Alex learns that for the past year Kia had been taking karate lessons at the Coca-Cola exercise center. Abruptly Kia says, "Are you sure we're in the right neighborhood?"

Alex looks around and sees an unbroken ugliness of deserted streets littered with debris and crumbling houses. He points to the map that is on the seat between them. "According to the map, we should be at his office in three blocks."

Alex slows the car. He glances to his left at a string of decaying buildings.

"Wasn't that 5500?" And without waiting for an answer, adds, "This must be 5502."

He turns left and pulls onto a rutted macadam parking lot that is already half-full with cars. In front of them stands a cinder block building with a neon light proclaiming, "Kitty's Topless Rampage."

Kia grimaces, "This can't be right."

They sit staring at the building. Kia looks troubled. Alex shrugs, "Let's go in and see if we can get directions to where we're supposed to be."

It is raining. Alex reaches under the front seat and pulls out an umbrella. He runs to the passenger side and holds the door for Kia. They walk quickly toward the building.

A red canopy marks the entrance. The front door has a sign listing the hours of operation: 9 a. m. to 3 a. m. Sunday through Saturday.

They are met by the bouncer, a burly man, who says, "Can I help you?"

It is dark inside. Alex squints and focuses on the object of every patron's attention, a young blonde woman prancing down a long neon lit runway clad only in a G-string and gold colored spiked shoes. True to Kitty's motto, she is topless.

"I said, buddy," the bouncer mumbles, spinning Alex around, "Can I help you?"

Kia moves between them. "We're trying to find a lawyer by the name of Harvey Slinger, but we're lost."

"You ain't that lost, sweetie. You just came in the wrong door. Our resident shyster's office is upstairs."

"How do we get there from here?"

"Go back out the front door, turn right and at the far end of the building there's a sign with Slinger's name on it. He's upstairs."

Alex takes one last glance at the stripper, takes Kia's arm, and they leave through the front door.

They climb a rickety flight of stairs and enter a room featuring a gray metal desk piled high with stacks of files. On the floor beside the desk is a man on his knees, his back to them, rummaging through an open file cabinet. The walls are paneled with cheap mahogany plywood, and two folding chairs face the desk. Alex's reaction is to leave, but before he can make a move, Kia says, "Harvey?"

The man's head snaps around. "Kia!" He bolts straight up and stumbles as he moves forward.

The man reminds Alex of a squirrel, brown thinning hair, pointed, pinned back ears, a long thin face with bulging eyes and a large sharp nose. He is short and slight of build, about five-six, with soft, fleshy arms, and a big stomach. He is dressed in jeans, a short-sleeve denim shirt, a silver bolo tie and black boots.

"Harvey, this is Alex. Alex meet Harvey." They shake hands. Harvey's handshake is wet, cold and weak. Instinctively, Alex wipes his hand on his pants.

Harvey's eyes take in Kia. "It was wonderful to hear from you this morning, Kia. I've been hoping for a long time that you would call me." Harvey motions toward the two folding chairs. "Please, have a seat." He holds the chair for Kia and then walks back behind the desk.

Speaking to Kia, he says, "I'm not sure that I understand what type of document you want me to prepare for Mister . . ."

"Ivanovich," Alex says.

Harvey's eyes narrow, "Polish?"

"No, Russian." Alex glances at Kia who seems oblivious to the tension developing between the two men.

Harvey's eyes sweep from Alex to Kia and back to Alex. "What is it you want me to do for you?"

"I'm going to buy something from someone, and I would like for you to prepare a contract that makes it legal," Alex says.

"What are you buying and for how much?"

"I can't tell you what it is, but I'm paying ten thousand dollars for it."

Harvey's eyes shift between Alex and Kia, resting on Alex. "Why won't you tell me what you're buying?"

"The seller wants to keep it a secret."

Harvey's brow furrows. "How do I account in the contract for what you are buying?"

"Leave a space and we'll fill it in."

Harvey slams his fist on the desk and papers fly. "I can't do that! I could be guilty of malpractice."

Alex's eyes move across Harvey's desk, and he wonders how much malpractice lays buried there.

"Please, Harvey," Kia says.

Harvey breathes in deeply. "Okay, for you, Kia, I'll do it, but it's going to cost your friend here one hundred dollars."

"How long will it take?" Alex asks.

"What do you mean how long will it take?" He pushes his hand through his thinning hair in a gesture of disgust. "I can have it for you in two or three days."

Alex shoots Kia a glance.

"Perhaps you've forgotten, Harvey, but when I called this morning, I said we needed it today," Kia says.

Oh, so they need it today. What are they up to? Harvey positions himself in front of a computer, clicks the mouse several times, brings a document to the screen, and says, "Give me the name, address, and the correct spelling of who you are buying it from, your full name and address and the price you're paying for this . . . Tell me as much about the transaction as you can without identifying exactly what it is."

After typing in the information, he asks. "Is it a goods or a service that you're buying?"

Alex thinks for a moment, "A goods."

Harvey types for a minute or so, hits a key, and takes a two-page document from the printer. He peruses it, staples it, and hands it to Alex. "Read it carefully and tell me what if any changes you would like." He glances at Kia. "Would you like a copy to read?" Kia shakes her head.

Alex reads the document and hands it back to Harvey. "It looks okay, but I'm not a lawyer. What I want to know is, if a dispute later develops over whether or not I own this item . . ."

"And, of course, you haven't told me what this item is, but the answer is yes. This contract will give you good title, provided . . ." Harvey stares at Alex and pauses before adding, "provided this Calderman fellow has good title in the first place. I suggest you pay Calderman by check so that if a dispute arises, the consideration for the purchase can be easily identified. Also, have your signatures witnessed by two people."

He notices Alex glance at Kia. "Yes, Kia can be one of the witnesses but the other person should be someone with whom you are not quite so friendly. In fact, it would be a good idea for you and Calderman and the witnesses to sign the contract in the presence of a notary."

Harvey stands, leans back and stretches, a motion that accentuates his stomach. He holds his right hand out, palm up.

"But in my case, no checks. Cash only."

"You just told me that it's better to pay by check," Alex says facetiously.

"Only when we wish to identify the payment, Mr. Ivanovich, but I don't wish to have your payment identified—cash."

Alex hands Harvey a $100 bill.

Kia says, "Harvey, there is something else Alex and I would like you to prepare."

Harvey gives her a quizzical look. "We're going to do a project together, and if it works out, we're going to divide the money on a one-third, two-third basis with . . ."

"With the two-third's, of course, going to him," Harvey says, nodding toward Alex and rolling his eyes.

Alex feels like punching him but counts to ten slowly.

Kia continues, "That's correct, with Alex paying all expenses."

"And, of course, I don't get to know what this project is either, I suppose."

"I'm sorry, Harvey, but Alex and I have agreed to keep it secret. Can you do that for us?"

"For you, Kia, yes, but are you sure that the split of only one-third to you is fair?"

"Yes."

Harvey extends his right hand, all the while looking at Kia. "I hope the Russian has another hundred bucks—cash."

Alex reaches in his wallet and takes out another Franklin. Harry snatches it from his hand, examines it as if trying to determining if it's counterfeit, puts it in his pocket and sits down at the computer, "Your full name and address, Kia."

After a few minutes he takes from the printer two copies of a two page document and hands Kia and Alex each a copy. "Read it carefully. I've left blank spaces for you to fully identify the project and what each of you will do to bring it to fruition. Whatever you hand write into the contract, you should both initial. Sign both copies before a notary public, and each keep a copy. Oh, and before

I forget let me print another copy of your contract with Calderman so that you can give him a copy." Harvey hands the extra copy of the contract to Alex.

"Thank you, Harvey," Kia says, extending her hand.

As he shakes her hand, Harvey says, "Kia, are you sure you don't want me to help you with your part of this project?"

Kia nods, "I'm sure, Harvey, but thanks."

As they start out the door, Harvey calls, "Kia, I'll see you at the gym. I'm going to start working out again." Kia turns and waves.

CHAPTER 14

AS SOON AS the door shuts, Harvey picks up the phone, presses the buzzer and says, "Stilton, get your ass in here."

Harvey's office door opens and Stilton Geronsky stands in the doorway. From below comes the blare of music. "Don't stand there," Harvey says, "come in and shut the door." Stilton closes the door and muffles the musical strains of *The Devil Wants To Fuck Me In The Back Seat Of My Car.* Stilton lumbers forward.

Stilton is five feet ten inches tall with broad sloping shoulders. He has a large head, a round forehead, bulging eyes, and fat, protruding lips. Although he looks a bit like a Neanderthal man, he is a proud member of the Georgia and Atlanta Bar Associations.

Harvey studies Stilton. *He's not only ugly but dumb.* Harvey tries to think back to why he hired Stilton, and the only reason he can think of is Stilton's willingness to work for three hundred dollars a week. *But he's not even worth that. He's a legal malpractice time-bomb about to go off.*

"Stilton," Harvey begins, "I've got some bad news. I've got to let you go."

Stilton scrunches his face and squints. "Go where, Mr. Slinger?"

Harvey shakes his head, "How'd you ever pass the bar exam?"

"You forget, Mr. Slinger, I failed the first three times I took it."

"Yeah, I forgot." Harvey leans forward, elbows resting on the desk. "Stilton, I don't have any work to give you. The goddamned insurance companies have ruined everything."

"How'd they do that, Mr. Slinger?"

"What do you mean, 'how'd they do that?' You know how the bastards did it. They stopped paying those fender-benders, that's how they did it."

Harvey stands, "I used to make a damn good living off of fender-benders. Shit, nowadays the bastards won't pay more than specials, and only when they know we've got liability locked up."

He doesn't like what he's about to do and that annoys him. "Stilton, what I'm saying is, you can't work here anymore." Stilton's face remains impassive. "Stilton, read my lips. You're fired!"

"You mean you don't want me no more? What'd I do wrong? I know I ain't . . ." He bursts into tears and his head flops onto the desk. He sobs uncontrollably.

Harvey moves around the desk and put his hand on Stilton's shoulder and waits until Stilton stops crying.

Stilton turns his head and looks up at Harvey. "I don't care about me. I really don't, but I don't know what I'll do about my mother. She depends on me. She's sick, Mr. Slinger, very sick. We only got each other, and except for a little money she gets from Social Security, we live on what I make."

Harvey has never asked Stilton about his personal life. Until this moment, he really hasn't cared. He has never been to Stilton's house or Stilton to his. Their relationship has been strictly business. He is feeling sorry for Stilton and feeling sorry for someone is unusual for him. He walks back to his desk and sits down. He looks at Stilton's wet, swollen face and pushes a box of tissues toward him.

Stilton wipes his face and looks up. There is an empty look in his eyes. "The answer to this whole situation is to find more business. If I can find a way to get more business, will you help me get it?"

"Sure, Mr. Slinger, I'll do anything you want."

Harvey reaches over and squeezes Stilton's hand. "Remember that, Stilton, because I'm gonna hold you to it."

CHAPTER 15

AS ALEX PULLS out of Kitty's parking lot, Kia says, "Well, what do you think about Harvey Slinger and the contracts he prepared?"

"I think Slinger's an enormous piece of crap. I don't ever remember forming a more intense dislike for a person on a first meeting. However, he seems bright enough, so hopefully the contracts are okay."

Kia smiles to herself, "Any other piquant observations?"

"Oh! You want a piquant observation. Well here's one you can bet your mother's savings on. Before long you'll hear from Slinger and before the conversation is over he'll try to find out what we're up to. And if he finds out, he'll ruin everything."

"He won't find out from me. I promise."

"Good," Alex says, and swerves the car to the curb and stops. "I forgot to call Calderman."

He reaches in the side door pocket, removes a cellular phone and calls. "Mr. Calderman, this is Alex Ivanovich. I have the contract, and if you can come to Atlanta today to . . ."

"Is the ten grand in cash?" Calderman asks.

"I won't have cash, but I'll give you a cashier's check for ten thousand dollars."

"You said cash, goddamn it!"

"I know I said cash, but a cashier's check is the same as cash. Any bank will accept it . . . ."

"I want fucken cash!"

"Simon, the reason for the cashier's check rather than cash is simple. It will serve as proof that I bought the formula from you should The Coca-Cola Company later dispute my ownership of it. We'll need to sign the contract before a notary public . . . ."

"Listen pal, there ain't gonna be no need for a notary if you don't come up with ten grand in cash."

Alex rolls his eyes. "Tell you what. It's now eleven-twenty. The bank closes at three. If you'll meet me there at two, I'll have the cashier's check. The bank has a notary, and after we sign the contract, I'll introduce you to the bank manager and you can convert the cashier's check into cash right there on the spot."

"I ain't got the letter and formula on me. I gotta go to my bank and git em from my safe deposit box," Calderman growls.

"I forgot about that. Will you have enough time to get the formula and the contract from your safe deposit box and meet me?"

"I think so, but ain't you gonna tell me the name of your bank and where it is?"

"That would help, wouldn't it. Sorry. It's the South Trust Bank on Virginia Avenue at Todd . . . ."

"I'll get there as soon as I can, and I'd better git cash or it's no deal."

"Remember, the bank closes at three."

CHAPTER 16

ALEX CALLS THE Midtown branch of the South Trust Bank and speaks with the manager, James Campbell.

"Mr. Campbell, this is Alex Ivanovich and . . ."

"Hi, Mr. Ivanovich, what can I do for you?"

"I want to withdraw $10,000 from my savings account in the form of a cashier's check payable to Simon Calderman."

"When do you want it?"

"I'm going to meet Calderman at the bank at two o'clock today. Can it be ready then?"

"Certainly."

"Calderman is then going to present the cashier's check for cash."

"No problem."

"Oh, and Mr. Campbell, I'll need a notary."

"I'm a notary."

"Good. I'll be there in about an hour."

Alex and Kia stop at a deli, share a corn beef sandwich and add to their agreement the information they didn't want Harvey Slinger to know about.

At the bank they sign their agreement in the presence of the bank manager.

Campbell witnesses and notarizes the agreement. He hands

Alex an envelope. "Here's the $10,000 cashier's check you requested payable to Simon Calderman."

"Thanks, Mr. Campbell. This check is the consideration for something I'm buying from Calderman. When he comes in, I'll need a little time alone with him to finalize our agreement, and then I'd like you and Kia to witness our signatures."

"You can use my office to meet with Mr. Calderman," the manager says. "Call me when you're ready."

Campbell and Kia leave the office. Alex starts working on the contract. A few minutes later he looks out the window and sees Calderman closing the door of his Ford pickup truck. His clothes are a bit more presentable than when Alex first met him. He is wearing sandals, jeans with a large tear along the right leg, and a soiled T-shirt.

Calderman enters the bank and Alex waves him back to the manager's office.

"Do you have the cashier's check?" Calderman says. Alex nods and holds the check up for Calderman to see. Pointing to the check, Calderman asks, "Can I get it exchanged for cash today?"

"You can, provided you have your grandfather's 1921 formula, his contract with Coca-Cola, and we get our contract signed before three o'clock."

Calderman glances at his watch. "I got em. Where do I sign?"

"First, we have to add the exact terms of our agreement to the contract,"

Calderman seems puzzled. "You mean you didn't do that when you had the contract prepared?"

"I didn't want the lawyer to know the specifics of our business."

"All right, let's do it."

Alex has written his understanding of their agreement on a separate piece of paper and he reads it aloud.

Calderman points to the contract. "That's what we agreed to. Add it."

As Alex writes, Calderman says, "Where are the ash trays? The goddamned non-smokers have taken over the world. Fuck em." He pulls out a cigarette and lights it.

Alex hands Calderman both copies of the contract. "Read both copies to be sure I've accurately stated our agreement."

Calderman scans the papers. "Yeah, that's fine."

Alex motions to Campbell. Campbell and Kia enter the office. Alex hands Campbell two copies of the contract. "Mr. Calderman and I would like Kia and you to witness our signatures and have you notarize it."

The contract is signed, witnessed, notarized, and a copy given to Alex and Calderman.

Calderman hands Alex the originals of his grandfather's recipe and the 1921 contract with Coca-Cola. Alex gives Calderman the cashier's check for $10,000.

Calderman looks at Campbell. "How do I exchange this for cash?"

Campbell points to his cashier's booth, "The lady will provide you with cash in any denominations you want."

WHEN KIA AND Alex leave the bank it is raining.

"Where to? Home?" Alex asks.

"No. I promised my parents that I would have dinner with them." She gives Alex directions to her parents' apartment. As they approach the apartment building, she says, "What executives do you want the travel itineraries of?"

"William Brannon, chief executive officer, Sharon Talbot, president and chief operating officer, and Nelson Foster, senior vice-president and chief financial officer."

"When do you want to start?"

"Monday morning."

"What information do you want from me?"

"I want to know the travel itineraries of those three executives including their means of transportation, times and places of departures, destinations, expected times of arrival, and where they stay on arrival." He pauses. "It would also be helpful to know the purpose of their trips. Is this kind of information available to you?"

Kia stares zombie-like straight ahead.

"If you want to change your mind about doing this, tell me now."

She shakes her head. "I'm just tired, and scared, and feeling guilty. But, no, I don't want to back out." She turns and faces him. "The information that you want is available to me."

"Kia, always call me from a pay phone, never from a company phone, your home phone, or cell phone. That is very important." Kia nods. "And call me on my cell phone. I may not always be able to answer immediately, so let's agree that if I don't answer, you'll leave the time of your call and the number you called from. I'll call you back at that number one hour later. Is that do-able?"

Kia thinks for a moment. "Yes, there are pay phones at work."

Alex stops in front of Kia's parents' apartment building. The intensity of the rain has increased. Alex reaches under the seat for an umbrella.

"Please, don't bother." She sits for a moment, her eyes fixed straight ahead.

"Alex, I'm scared and . . ." She opens the door. "I'll call you as soon as I know something." She jumps out of the car and runs toward her parents' apartment.

CHAPTER 17

AFTER THE MEETING with Stilton, Harvey spends the rest of the day working on a criminal brief that must to be to the printer on Monday. He calls his wife and tells her that he is going to work until he finishes the brief, and he will not be home for dinner.

He reads the brief a final time. It isn't his best work, but considering the facts he has to work with, it will do. He has a headache. It is five minutes after seven. He decides to stop on the way home for a sandwich and a drink or two, but not downstairs. Rather, he thinks, some quiet place where he can be alone with his thoughts.

While putting on his coat Harvey hears loud, shrill voices below. The commotion seems to be coming from the front of the bar near the main entrance. He decides to find out what's going on.

As he moves through the bar, a young stripper by the name of Georgia continues to bump and grind on the runway. At the entrance door Harvey sees the bouncer, Tony Angeleno, pushing a well-dressed customer up against the wall. Tony has him in a hammer lock and is screaming, "Don't you ever come back here again, you drunken son-of-a-bitch!"

The victim's appearance catches Harvey's attention. He doesn't look like a typical Kitty's Topless Rampage patron. Harvey knows Tony well. In fact, he represented him in his last divorce. He taps Tony on the shoulder. Tony turns. "What'd he do, Tony?"

"He grabbed Clarette's snatch when she came around for the money stuffing, the bastard." Clarette is Tony's current girlfriend.

"I'll take him off your hands, Tony."

Tony releases his grip on the man, and Harvey takes him by the arm and walks him out the front door. Outside, the man steadies himself by leaning against the doorframe. He isn't falling down drunk, but he's too drunk to drive.

"Is your car here on the lot?" Harvey asks.

"Yes," the man says, shaking his head.

"I don't think you should be driving. You've had too much to drink." The man nods in agreement. "What's your name?"

"Doctor Irving Smalkin."

"Doctor, I'm Harvey Slinger. I'm a lawyer and I think you should let me drive you home. You can get your car tomorrow." He pauses. "What do you say?"

"Yes. Thank you."

As Harvey maneuvers Smalkin in the direction of his car, he says, "Where do you live?"

"In Vining."

Classy neighborhood, Harvey thinks. *I can't afford to live there.*

On the way to Smalkin's house, the doctor says that he's a psychologist specializing in sexual dysfunction. He goes on to explain that he attended a party at a client's place of business and heard two guys talking about Kitty's. He felt horny and decided to check it out. He rarely drinks too much, he says, but tonight it got away from him.

Harvey sees Smalkin into his house. Smalkin thanks Harvey, and they exchange business cards.

THE NEXT MORNING the telephone awakens Irving Smalkin. On the sixth ring, he picks up. "This is Doctor Smalkin."

"Doc, this is Harvey Slinger. How are you feeling?" Silence. "Doc, don't you remember me? I'm the guy who drove you home last night."

"I have a tremendous headache, and I'm having trouble getting things in focus, but yes, Harvey, I do remember you. I appreciate what you did for me last night."

"We left your car on Kitty's parking lot. If you'd like, I'll come over in about an hour and drive you out there. Will that give you enough time?"

"Yes. I'll leave the front door unlocked. Come in."

LATER, IRVING SMALKIN and Harvey Slinger are drinking coffee in the lounge section of the Caribou Coffee House on Piedmont and Fourteenth Streets.

Harvey is bemoaning the drastic decline in his income because of the refusal of insurance companies to settle soft tissue injuries for anything more than twice special damages. "The situation is so bad that I'm going to have to let my associate go unless I can find a new source of business," he says.

"You know, the situation is almost as bad in my profession. The HMOs, Blue Cross, you name it, none of the health care institutions want to pay mental illness claims and, when they do, they limit it to two or three visits. Fortunately, insurance companies are a bit more generous in how they view the need for treatment in my specialty." He sees the look of surprise on Harvey's face. "Don't get me wrong, I get plenty denials . . ." He shakes his head and lets his gaze drift to the window and the traffic outside.

"You mentioned last night that you treat people with sexual dysfunction. I thought Viagra took care of that problem."

"No, Harvey, you're thinking about erectile dysfunction. What I treat is entirely different. Sexual dysfunction or, as it's often called, sexual addiction is one of the least talked about diseases facing society today. And it's more difficult to give up or, perhaps I should say, more difficult to conquer than alcoholism or smoking."

"Oh, come on Doc," Harvey says, pushing back in his seat and letting out a soft chuckle. "What the hell is wrong with wanting a little extra pussy? God knows I mentally crave it all the time. To tell you the truth, Doc, I want to screw every good-looking chic I see, and some that aren't so good-looking, especially when they've got big tits. Now, is that a form of sexual dysfunction?"

"Yes, but since I gather you just think about it and don't actually do it, it's a harmless addiction. If you were to convert your sexual fantasies into realities, and carry on an obsessive course of sexual promiscuity, it would eventually destroy your marriage, your career, everything that's important to you. You can't imagine how many people in this country suffer sexual addictions. And it's not just, as you put it, 'wanting a little extra pussy.' It takes many forms other than sexual intercourse."

"Like what?"

"Pornography. Do you realize that every day millions of people are compulsively engaged in surfing the Internet to view, buy, sell, distribute, and write pornography. Do you know what the business savants, who are constantly hyping e-commerce Internet sales, don't talk about?" Harvey shakes his head. "They don't talk about the Internet's biggest source of consumer business—pornography." Smalkin takes a sip of his coffee. "Want some more examples of sexoholism?"

"Is that what it's called?"

"That's a cute word for it. It's usually called an addiction or dysfunction, but regardless of what you call it, it's a disease. And like cancer it comes in different forms and spreads its venom indiscriminately throughout society, rich and poor, weak and strong, successful and unsuccessful. It's no respecter of who you are."

"What do you mean like cancer it takes different forms?"

"There are many different kinds. For example, someone who engages in anonymous phone sex . . ."

"You mean like getting a phone call from someone who says filthy things and hangs up?"

"Yes. That's a form of sexual dysfunction that's entirely different from prostitution, another form. Other sexual addictions that come to mind are compulsive masturbation, voyeurism, and exhibitionism." He pushes his empty coffee cup to the side. "There are other kinds, but those are the main ones."

"I had no idea. What the hell causes it?"

"We don't have all the answers but one consistent thread that is common to many sexual addiction patients is that they were sexually abused when youngsters."

"Christ," Harvey says, shaking his head, "they're starting to blame sexual abuse for everything. I read an article in the *New York Times* that attributes welfare free-loading to sexual abuse."

"I read the article, and do you know something? I believe it. I can't think of a greater trauma for a child to suffer than to be sexually abused."

"Is this sexual addiction stuff very prevalent?"

"No one knows exactly. I've heard the figure three percent, but because of the nature of the problem, I suspect that it's a lot higher. It's not something people talk about at cocktail parties." He pauses. "But hell, three percent represents over nine million people in this country alone."

"Yeah, that's a lot of people." Harvey leans forward. "How do you treat these people?"

"Through private counseling and group therapy."

"How much do you charge for a consultation?"

"$125 an hour"

"Christ, you mean to tell me that you only get $125 for an hour consultation?"

Smalkin nods. "Actually, consultations are fifty minutes but, yeah, that's all those stinking health care insurance companies pay."

"Tell me something, Irving. How the hell can you afford to live in that big house making only $125 an hour?"

Smalkin's eyes sweep the room. Satisfied that no one is listen-

THE SECRET FORMULA · 77

ing to them, he leans forward grinning. "It's my way of fucking those stingy, no good health care providers, but you've got to keep it to yourself." Harvey nods. "When you came in this morning did you notice the living room?"

"I sure as hell did. It's huge."

"Did you notice anything else about the room?"

"Yeah, it's almost empty, just some folding chairs and a table. You know what went through my head? It struck me that you're so mortgage poor you can't afford to buy furniture."

"Fortunately, that's not the case. Every morning on Monday, Wednesday and Friday at nine and eleven, I conduct therapy sessions in the living room for about fifteen patients. The living room serves as the stage for the various scenarios my patients act out during therapy."

"Let me see if I have this right. Twice on Monday, Wednesday and Friday mornings you hold therapy sessions in your living room for as many as fifteen patients at a time, and you bill each patient at $125 per hour. Do I have that right?"

Smalkin grins, "You got it."

"If I calculate correctly, that earns you about eleven grand a week."

"Your math is excellent, and I have my afternoons and Tuesdays and Thursdays free for research, private consultations, golf and tennis."

Harvey smacks himself on the head with the palm of his right hand. "You're a genius."

Smalkin glances at his watch. "I'm afraid I have to get going." He stands and extends his hand. "I can't thank you enough for last night."

Walking toward their cars, Smalkin stops. "I know what I wanted to ask you. What are you doing Friday evening?"

"This coming Friday?"

"Yes."

"Why?"

"The National Association of American Psychologists is holding its annual convention in Atlanta at the Anchor Hotel. I'm president of the Atlanta chapter, and we're hosting a cocktail party Friday evening before the dinner-dance. I'd be pleased if you and your wife would be my guests. It's an opportunity for you to meet a lot of local psychologists, and who knows, you might end up making some important contacts."

Slinger's mind races ahead. "How many psychologists will be there?"

"Over five hundred plus spouses and significant others."

"I'll check with my wife, but she usually doesn't like that sort of thing. But even if she won't come, I will, so count me in. Like you say, it never hurts to meet new people. Besides, I might need a shrink someday."

CHAPTER 18

MONDAY MORNING FINDS Alex driving into Atlanta from Harts-field International Airport. The two young lawyers in the back seat of his limousine are in Atlanta for a breast implant seminar, and from the gist of their conversation they are full of themselves, court victories, women conquests, drinking prowess, athletic skills.

After dropping off the attorneys at the Hyatt Hotel, Alex turns south on Spring Street and has not traveled more than a block when his cell vibrates. It's Kia.

"Yes Kia."

"William Brannon is flying to Paris tomorrow evening on the company Gulfstream from Fulton County Airport. I have his itinerary. Do you have a pen?"

He doesn't, but says, "Yes, go ahead." He will remember it.

"He leaves Atlanta at nine-thirty and arrives at Charles de Gaulle Airport at about eight the next morning. A company limousine will meet him. He'll stay at the Ritz on Place Vendome. He'll rest an hour or two before meeting for lunch with Monsieur La Foulette, Coca-Cola's Director of European Operations. They, and others, will lunch at Taillevent at one-thirty. After lunch they'll confer at company headquarters located on Champs-Elysées. Dinner reservations for the evening are at Lucas-Carton at nine o'clock. Alex, do you know where all these places are located?"

"No, but I'll find them."

"The next morning Brannon will be picked up at ten and taken to company headquarters."

"Where is Brannon having dinner?"

"Le Grand Vefour at eight-thirty. The next morning he'll leave at ten-thirty for a flight to Brussels. He'll not spend the night in Brussels but fly out after meeting with representatives of the Coca-Cola Bottling Company. His flight is scheduled to leave Brussels at about nine. He'll . . ."

Alex interrupts, "I don't need to know about Brussels. If it's going to happen, it will happen in Paris. Thanks Kia. You've done a great job. Wish me luck." Before she can reply, he hangs up.

ALEX SPENDS THE evening at the computer searching for the cheapest round-trip airfare to Paris. He finds it aboard a Delta flight leaving Atlanta at eight the next evening and arriving in Paris at 9 a.m. He e-mails his friend and ex-KGB colleague, Yuri Natskov, advising that he will arrive in Paris Wednesday morning for a two-night stay, and asks if it will be possible to stay with him. Alex and Yuri worked together in England in the late '80s and have remained friends. Yuri lives in Paris, has an apartment around the corner from Place des Vosges, and works for IBM in its encryption division.

It is eight o'clock in Atlanta, but because Paris time is six hours ahead, it is two in the morning in Paris. Within minutes, however, he receives an e-mail from Yuri. "Alex, I leave Paris in the morning for a business trip to Berlin. I'm sorry that I will not see you, but you are welcome to stay at my flat. The address is 15 Rue de Bourbon, second floor. I will leave the apartment key with the concierge, Madame Lourette. Her apartment is on the first floor. Show her your passport for identification, and she will give you my apartment key. I will also leave on the kitchen table the keys to my Fiat and Vespa. Madame Lourette will show you where I garage them. It is just a block away. You know Paris, and I won't tell you how to entertain yourself. Have fun, but try to give me more notice when you next come to Paris. Regards, Yuri."

ALEX'S PLANE TOUCHES down at Charles de Gaulle Airport on schedule. He takes the train from the airport to Paris. He meets Madame Lourette, a woman of about seventy, and she escorts him to Yuri's apartment. Pointing from an open window, she identifies the building where Yuri garages his car and Vespa. When Madame Lourette leaves it is almost noon. The keys to the Vespa and Fiat are on the kitchen table with a sealed envelope. Inside the envelope is a note and five lock-pick keys. The note reads, "These keys will open most doors in Paris. They are an extra set so you can keep them." Alex smiles and places them in his jacket pocket. There is just enough time to shower before silently greeting William Brannon outside of Taillevent.

ALEX SPENT MOST of yesterday at the main branch of the Atlanta Public Library looking at every photograph and reading every bit of information that he could find on William Brannon. He read through every "Who's Who" in which Brannon was listed. He left the library knowing Brannon's age (fifty-seven), colleges, degrees, and honors: Princeton, B.A. Economics, Magna Cum Laude, Harvard Business School, MBA, Baker Scholar, family status: married to Virginia Longsworth Brannon for thirty-two years, three adult children, Sharon, thirty-one, William, Junior, thirty, and Suzanne, twenty-seven.

A PROCESSION OF well-coifed women and impeccably attired men have entered through Taillevent's elegant brass framed doors before the arrival of Brannon and his entourage. Alex had once overheard Brannon's public image of quintessential family probity sullied in a conversation between two visiting executives while driving them from Coca-Cola headquarters to the airport. The conversation was not meant for his ears, but he remembers it, and it now flashes through his mind as he watches a black Rolls Royce stop in front of Taillevent. The chauffeur, dressed in a black uniform, holds the right rear door open and five men step out. Brannon is easily identifiable from the photographs. He is tall, trim and good-looking. Impeccably dressed in a dark blue suit, Brannon is, Alex thinks, a Hollywood casting director's ideal of what the CEO of Coca-Cola should look like.

At three o'clock Brannon and his coterie leave the restaurant and return to Coca-Cola headquarters. At six-thirty a limousine pulls in front of the headquarters entrance. A few minutes later, Brannon leaves the building, enters the limousine and returns to the Ritz.

CHAPTER 19

AT THE VERY moment Coca-Cola's chief executive steps out of his limousine in front of the Ritz, Joe Creamer is parking his car in the Kitty's Topless Rampage parking lot. Coming to Kitty's has become a daily routine for Joe Creamer, a routine he can ill afford, but he has nothing else to do with his time. He has been separated from his family for over a year and a recent on the job injury has left him unable to work. With no girlfriend, hobbies or interests, time lays heavy on him. As for television, he can watch only so much of it before he feels like jumping out of his skin. So Kitty's is his refuge.

The expense at Kitty's isn't so much in the two or three beers he usually drinks but the obligation he feels to stuff a dollar into the garter belt of every stripper who circles the bar following her act.

He enjoys watching the girls perform, but today he's having trouble concentrating on the well-proportioned redhead humping the pole in the center of the runway to the joint's favorite tune, "He Loves My Mother More Than Me." An insurance representative called earlier in the morning and advised that at the end of the month the insurance company is going to cut off his weekly worker's compensation payments.

"Shit," he says out loud, "I gotta get a lawyer."

The man seated on Joe's right turns and says, "Buddy, if you need a lawyer there ain't no better shyster alive than Harvey Slinger. He got me money when I wasn't even injured."

"Where's Slinger's office?" Joe asks.

"Right upstairs," the man says, pointing to the left.

"How do I get up there?"

"Go out the front door and turn right. Near the end of the building there's a sign with his name on it. Harvey's office is upstairs."

"Thanks," Joe says, and calls for his bill.

JOE CLIMBS THE wooden staircase and knocks on the door. A voice calls out, "Come in." Joe steps in and sees a man seated behind a cluttered metal desk. The man stands. "Don't be afraid," he says, "come in. I'm Harvey Slinger and I notice you're walking kind of funny. Back injury?"

"Yeah, how'd you know?"

"That's how I make a living, getting people money when they get injured. How'd you hurt your back?"

"At work attempting to move a lab table."

Harvey points to a metal folding chair. "Have a seat and tell me about it. But first, what's your name?"

"Joe Creamer. I live up the street in the Albion Apartments."

"Who do you work for?"

"Macrand Laboratories. I've been with them eighteen years."

"What do you do there?"

"I'm a lab technician."

"Doing what?"

"I run tests for foodborne infections, bacterial and viral."

"What are foodborne infections?"

"Infections that cause various types of food poisonings."

"Food poisoning?" An idea pops into Harvey's head. He closes his eyes and thinks of Gloria Ripdon, a woman he represented in a worker's compensation case. Gloria, a banquet waitress at the Anchor Hotel, slipped and fell on some lettuce and injured her back. Harvey remembers Gloria's story and her description a large machine resembling a top load washer that the hotel used to prepare salads for as many as a thousand guests. The machine served two functions: dry the lettuce via a spin cycle, and mix the salad's ingredients and the dressings via a tumble cycle. *It's perfect, hundreds of psychologists for clients.* "That's interesting. I want to learn more about that, but for now, tell me how the accident happened."

"Well," Joe says, shrugging, "I was trying to move a lab table so it would be closer to where I was running my tests. I needed the extra space, and all of a sudden, I felt a sharp pain in my low back and . . ."

"Were you pushing the table when you felt this pain?"

"Actually, I was pulling it."

"Is pulling or pushing a lab table unusual in your work?"

"Nah, we do it all the time."

"Did your foot slip when you were pulling the table?"

Joe thinks for a moment. "I don't remember."

Harvey leans forward, the fingers of both hands pressed together in the form of a steeple, his eyes fixed on Joe. "Let me tell you something about the Worker's Compensation laws of Georgia. If a worker is carrying out his routine work and nothing unusual occurs, but he experiences a pain in his back like you did, that is not considered an accidental injury arising out of and in the course of his employment."

His eyes narrow. "Under that scenario, do you know how much the worker gets for his injury?"

Joe shakes his head as though confused.

Harvey holds his left hand up and places the tip of his index finger against the tip of his thumb. "He gets zero, nothing, zilch." Harvey sees Joe's anger smoldering. He sits back in his chair and waits.

Joe's lips quiver. "I've got what the doctor calls a herniated disc. He told me I'm going to need an operation. I'll be off work for a long time. If I don't get paid, I can't make it. I've got a family and monthly support payments to make. That's not fair. It's not fair." His fist strikes the desktop.

"Of course, it's not fair. The insurance companies got that law passed by paying off a lot of crooked politicians. Insurance companies are predators. They just want to rake in the money. They never want to pay it out. But," Harvey says, springing to his feet and throwing a clenched fist into the air, "if your foot slipped just a little bit when you were pulling that table, then that shit-pot insurance company has got to pay all of your medical bills, has got to pay you temporary weekly payments until you return to work, and has got to pay permanent partial disability payments depending on the percentage of your disability! Now, did your foot slip when you were pulling that heavy table?"

Joe stares knowingly at Harvey, the faintest trace of a smile forming around the corners of his mouth. "Yeah, my right foot slipped out from under me, and that's what caused me to fall."

"And is that when you felt the pain? When you fell?"

"Yeah, that's when I felt this knife like pain shoot through my back."

Harvey smiles and nods, "Very good, those bastards owe you a lot of money, and I'm here to see that you get it." Harvey returns to his desk, sits at the computer and begins typing. "You'll need to file an amended claim form setting out the fact that your foot slipped. I'll do that at the time I enter my appearance on your behalf. Here," he says, handing Joe a blank claim form, "sign your full name where I've placed the X. I'll fill in all the necessary information." Joe signs the form.

Harvey explains the Worker's Compensation procedures, why the insurance company will contest the issue of accidental injury, how his fee is set by statute, and the doctors he will use to secure a permanent partial disability rating.

When he finishes, Joe says, "I'm glad I came here." They shake hands, and Joe starts for the door.

CHAPTER 20

As JOE STARTS for the door, Harvey says, "Joe, there's something else I want to talk to you about," and waves him back. When Joe is seated, Harvey says, "I take it you know a lot about what causes food poisoning?"

"Yeah, I know quite a bit about it. Why?"

"If I wanted to play a trick on someone and cause them to have a slight case of food poisoning, how would I be able to do it?"

"Who do you have in mind to play this trick on?"

"Some relatives. They're always playing tricks on me at family outings. You see, they don't like me because I'm a lawyer. They're jealous."

"When you say a slight case of food poisoning, do you mean throwing up with diarrhea and stomach pain?"

"Yeah, that's exactly what I mean, with the symptoms clearing up in two or three days. I don't want anybody to get sick and die."

"You know, that happens sometimes. Children and old people are especially vulnerable."

"No, no, I don't want anything so strong that someone could die. I've read that certain types of salmonella and E. coli cause the kind of symptoms I mentioned. Which would you recommend?"

Joe looks around the room. It is, at best, a shabby sight. He feels a tremendous urge to leave, but he's afraid to leave for fear Slinger will drop him as a client. He wants Slinger to represent him in his worker's compensation case. "There are different strains of salmonella and E-coli, but for what you have in mind, I think a virus called SRSV might be best."

"What's SRSV mean?"

"Small, round, structured viruses. They are transmitted by contaminated foods and cause the symptoms you described."

"How soon after eating a food contaminated by SRSV will the diarrhea and vomiting occur?"

"It varies, but somewhere between fifteen and seventy-two hours."

Harvey leans back in his chair, eyes staring up at the ceiling. "How long do the symptoms last?"

"It's different with different people, between a half day and three days, with some slight discomfort possible as long as two weeks."

"Okay," Harvey says, "I'll go with the SRSV."

"How will you get the culture?"

Slinger laughs. "I thought you understood. You'll get it for me." They sit facing each other in a strained silence. Slinger edges forward in his chair, his eyes appraising Joe as he speaks. "At the end of this month the insurance company is going to do what it said it will do, cut off your weekly payments. I'll immediately file with the commission a request for a hearing, but we may not get a hearing for two or three months. Unfortunately, during that time, you're going to be without money."

"Can they do that?"

"Not only can they do it, but they will do it, and there's nothing I can do to stop them. When you filed your claim, you didn't say anything about your foot slipping before you felt the back pain. The insurance company routinely started making the weekly payments to you, but when their lawyer reviewed your file, he realized that what you said about how the accident occurred doesn't amount to an accidental injury. And that's why they told you your payments will be cut off at the end of the month, which is four days from today. If you do me this favor, I'll advance you money against the recovery you get in your case."

Joe feels himself tighten. "If I get the SRSV culture for you, it'll have to be for cash and not an advance against what I get later." He pulls out a pack of cigarettes and lights one.

Harvey is about to tell him that he doesn't allow smoking in his office but has a second thought. He reaches in the bottom desk drawer and takes out a coffee mug, "Here, use this."

"I will have to sneak into the lab at night to prepare the culture, and there's a night watchman. It's against the law to do what you are asking me to do." Little beads of sweat form across Joe's forehead. He takes a deep drag on the cigarette and blows the smoke out the side of his mouth. "And if it's ever found out that I prepared the culture and gave it to you, I'll go to jail. So you see, Mr. Slinger, my getting you that culture has got to be for cash."

"Joe, how about a beer?"

Joe moves his tongue across his dry lips. "That would be good."

Harvey picks up the phone and punches some numbers. "Cindy, this is Harvey. Will you bring four cold beers up immediately?" He looks over to Joe, "Is Budweiser okay?" Joe nods. "Four Buds, Cindy, and put them on my account along with your tip." Harvey puts the receiver down and stares off in space. "Now, where were we? Yes, you said you'll need cash." Harvey's eyes narrow, "How much cash, Joe?"

Joe lights another cigarette, takes a deep drag and says, "Fifteen thousand."

"I was thinking more like two thousand."

Joe shakes his head. "That ain't enough to live on for two or three months.

"Besides I ain't risking going to jail for no measly two thous . . ."

There is a knock on the door.

"Come in," Harvey calls out.

The door opens and a big breasted young blonde sashays in, clad only in a G-string and carrying a tray containing four Budweisers. "Hi, Mr. Slinger," she says, in a throaty voice.

"Hi, Cindy," Harvey removes the beers. "Thanks, Cindy." He pats her on the butt as she turns to leave.

Harvey twists off the caps of two beers and hands one to Joe who puts it to his lips. With one swig he finishes off half the bottle.

"I don't like doing what you've asked me to do, but I need the money to hold me over until I start getting my comp payments again." He takes a final drag on the cigarette and crushes it out in the coffee mug. "I'll do it, but not for a penny less than five thousand."

"Do you think there's any chance that you'll get caught when you go back to the lab tonight to prepare the culture? If there is, I obviously don't want to be involved."

"Did you say tonight?"

"Yeah, we're having the family outing tomorrow afternoon, and that's when I want to play the trick on some of my mean relatives." Harvey eyes his client and repeats, "Is there any chance that you'll get caught preparing the solution?"

"There's a chance, but not much of one. I know the watchman's routine, when and where he goes to take his nap. I'll be in and out before he makes his second set of rounds. And if he should find me in the lab, I'll tell him I've come to get some of my personal belongings. We're pretty good friends, and I don't think he'll report me."

Harvey nods. "Okay, you've got a deal—five thousand dollars. When will you have the stuff for me tomorrow?"

"If everything goes okay, in the morning."

Harvey smiles and twists off the caps of the other two beers and hands Joe one. "Joe, I like you."

CHAPTER 21

AS JOE CREAMER leaves Harvey's law office and walks down the rickety steps leading to the parking lot, William Brannon strides out of the Ritz, climbs into his waiting limousine and says to the driver, "Lucas-Carton."

Lucas-Carton, a three star Michelin restaurant on Place de la Madeleine, is considered by many gourmets to be one of the best restaurants in Paris and where Brannon is meeting business associates for dinner. Alex follows Brannon and parks the Vespa at the top of the street where he can keep an eye on Brannon's limousine.

At eleven Brannon leaves the restaurant and is driven back to the Ritz. He dismisses his driver and enters the hotel. Alex parks the Vespa in the center of Place Vendôme, next to the Austerlitz Column. From this vantage point he can see across the square to the Ritz entrance. *This is it,* he thinks. *Either Brannon goes to bed or he comes out.*

Alex focuses the binoculars on the entrance. There is sufficient light to see the features of persons entering and leaving the Ritz. Fifteen minutes after Brannon entered the Ritz, a tall lanky man wearing sunglasses, a beret, and a cream colored windbreaker appears in the entrance doorway. He hesitates and then turns right toward Rue de Castiglione. Suspicious of someone wearing sunglasses at night and sporting a beret inside the Ritz, Alex follows him with the binoculars. He knows it's Brannon when the figure flexes his left shoulder, the same way Brannon did when he entered Taillevent.

The man strolls across the square and turns into Rue de Castiglione. At its intersection with Rue Saint Honoré, he hails a taxi and gets in. The taxi moves along fashionable Rue de Saint Honoré to Rue de Royale where it turns left and enters traffic circling Place de la Concorde. With Alex close behind, the taxi swings right onto the Champs-Elysées and races by flood lit buildings until reaching Avenue Franklin D. Roosevelt. Here, the taxi turns left and heads toward the river. Sensing the taxi will cross the Seine at Pont des Invalides, Alex accelerates and narrows the distance between the two vehicles.

To his surprise the taxi turns left before crossing the bridge. It follows a cobblestone roadway that skirts the Cours la Reine, a tree-lined terraced park running parallel to the Seine. As the taxi exits the Cours la Reine its brake lights come on, and it pulls to the right into an access driveway and stops in front of an iron gate. Alex slows the Vespa, kills the headlight, and jumps the curb onto the Cours la Reine. The scooter moves across its wide expanse and stops at a row of plane trees lining the walkway bordering the Seine.

Alex parks the scooter behind a large tree and runs to the wall separating the Cours la Reine from the river. He watches Brannon pay the driver, slip through an opening to the right of the gate, and walk down the service road toward the bank of the Seine.

Brannon walks past two bateaux and hesitates beside the third bateau before walking onto the dock. A man wearing white trousers and a navy blue jacket waves him aboard. The two men shake hands. Brannon ducks below deck. A deckhand frees the moorings, and the bateau starts up the Seine.

Alex mounts the Vespa and travels slowly along the Tuileries and Louvre quays, keeping the bateau in sight. The bateau moves to the opposite side of the river, and with the dappled lights of Paris reflecting off the water, it glides past the Tuileries Gardens, the Musée d'Orsay, the Louvre and Notre-Dame Cathedral. It is a view of Paris that Alex had seen many times, and yet, *pure poetry*, he thinks. At the tip of Île de Saint-Louis the bateau turns, crosses to the Right Bank of the river, and starts its return trip.

Anticipating the bateau's return to its docking berth, Alex returns to the Cours la Reine and takes a position at the wall that gives him an unobstructed view of the dock.

The deckhand ties the boat to the dock. As if on cue, a taxi pulls into the service drive and stops at the gate. The captain knocks on the stateroom door. Brannon emerges wearing the beret and sunglasses. The captain assists Brannon off. Brannon ambles up the service road and climbs into the waiting taxi. The taxi speeds off in the direction of Place de la Concorde.

Alex glances at his watch. It is 1 a.m. *Who's next?* He doesn't have long to wait. A chauffeur driven black Mercedes approaches the gate and the gate opens. The Mercedes drives down the service road and stops at the dock beside the bateau. The captain knocks on the stateroom door. A tall, svelte woman with long blonde hair steps up on deck. Silhouetted by the distant lights of the Invalides, a soft breeze blowing her hair around her shoulders, her face clear in the moon's light, she is as beautiful as any woman Alex has ever seen.

Standing about fifteen feet below where Alex is crouched at the wall, and not more than sixty feet distant, she begins talking to the captain. Alex reaches into the backpack strung on his back, removes and snaps on a pair of "Bionic" earphones, a listening device that allows him to hear distant conversations. "Pierre," she says in French, "I am going to want to use the bateau again tomorrow night at about the same time. My friend not only has an insatiable appetite for sex but also fine Champagne. So, be sure that we have on board two bottles of 1990 Dom Pérignon—well chilled."

"Everything will be in order as usual, Madame Secour."

She has her own private floating whorehouse, Alex muses.

As she starts to leave, the captain offers his assistance. She refuses and steps off the boat with an effortless grace. The chauffeur holds the door. She gets in, and the Mercedes roars away.

Alex fingers the handle of the black leather briefcase containing a micro-miniature wireless audio-video surveillance system that he brought from the United States. Fearful that his continued presence in the Cours will arouse the suspicion of a patrolling policeman, he is about to leave when a light colored Renault pulls up and stops at the gate. The captain and deckhand appear on deck. Alex activates the earphones. The captain says, "Madame is going to be using the bateau tomorrow at about the same time. Be sure that you refuel and have all of the necessary provisions aboard, including two iced bottles of 1990 Dom Pérignon. And, of course, Madame's stateroom must be immaculate. I have a number of personal errands to attend to tomorrow, and I probably won't be aboard much before eight."

"I have to attend a funeral in the morning. I will clean the stateroom before I leave tonight and take care of the other matters in the early afternoon," the deckhand says.

"A family member?"

"Yes. Uncle Phillipe, my favorite uncle."

"I'm sorry, André. If you would like to take the day off, I will come in and take care of matters and get someone to replace you for tomorrow night."

"No, no, captain. I will be here tomorrow afternoon in plenty of time to have everything ready. Everything will be in order when you arrive, sir."

"Do you have your alarm key?" André nods. "Good. Be sure you activate the alarm when you leave." The captain waves, walks to the waiting Renault and heads off into the night.

Alex reviews in his mind all of the significant parts of the conversations. *When the deckhand finishes cleaning the stateroom, he'll leave and not return until the afternoon. Before leaving, he'll lock the stateroom and activate the alarm system. Should I go on board after he leaves, or wait for sunrise? Both have advantages and disadvantages, but being able to work during daylight outweighs the disadvantages. Besides, I need some sleep.*

Alex climbs aboard the Vespa, rides to Yuri's apartment, and sleeps for three hours.

CHAPTER 22

IN THE GRAY of morning with the sun just beginning to reach across Paris' mansard rooftops, Alex strolls across the Pont de la Concorde. He parked the motor scooter on a side street in the Left Bank. Street traffic on both sides of the Seine is sparse, and the river is quiet and lonely. At the service gate, he studies the situation.

There are three private boats moored to the dock and no sign of activity aboard them. He walks down the service drive keeping close to the wall. When he comes parallel with Madame Secour's bateau, he stops and looks up and down the service drive. It is empty.

Dressed in a dark brown windbreaker, brown corduroy trousers, black crepe-soled shoes, and carrying a briefcase wrapped in newspaper, Alex ambles across the roadway and onto the dock. Without hesitating, he jumps down onto the deck of the Secour bateau.

The main cabin door is locked with a simple bolt lock that Alex easily picks. On entering Madame Secour's quarters he finds the alarm pad. Working quickly but carefully, he turns the alarm off on the third try.

The stateroom is large and elegantly appointed with a mix of French provincial furniture, Oriental rugs, and modern art. The centerpiece of the room is a Louis XVI canopied bed. Looking around, Alex quickly identifies a *Sortie* sign above the entrance door as the place to conceal the transmitter, the camera and the microphone. *It's perfect. It faces into the room and I can adjust the camera lens so that it takes in the entire room with special focus on the bed.*

Alex unscrews and removes the plastic *Sortie* cover from the wall. He tapes a battery pack, a .25 watt audio/video transmitter, and the antenna connector to the wall directly behind the cover. Using a hand drill with a special bit, he makes two pinholes in the plastic cover, positions the miniature color camera lens and microphone behind the holes, and repositions the *Sortie* cover on the wall. He then extends the antennas out along the sides of the cover and against the wall and screws the sign cover to the wall. The lighting in the room is furnished by four lamps and when turned on bathe the entrance wall in shadows making it impossible to see the antennas.

The entire operation takes less than half an hour. Before leaving the bateau, Alex checks the boats moored fore and aft. There is no activity aboard either boat. He looks up along the wall that skirts the Cours la Reine walkway. He sees no one. It is too early for tourists. He reactivates the alarm system, jumps onto the dock, walks up the service road, crosses the Pont de la Concorde, retrieves the Vespa, and heads back to Yuri's apartment.

ALEX SLEEPS UNTIL noon. After showering and changing into clean clothes, he lunches at a bistro near Place des Vosges. Sitting over a steaming bouillabaisse, a glass of wine, and the morning edition of *Le Monde*, he calculates that he has nine hours before he starts preparations for monitoring the activities of William Brannon and Paris' most expensive and beautiful courtesan.

It is a clear, sunny day and Alex decides to skip the museums and wander the streets of Paris absorbing the architecture, the people, and the sounds. And that is what he does. He takes the Metro to the Champs-Elysées station and people watches as he walks down the elegant boulevard. He crosses to the Left Bank and strolls east along the quays, occasionally examining the books and art displayed in the stalls lined along the banks of the Seine. He stops at an outdoor café on Île de Saint-Louis, orders an espresso and absorbs the 17th and 18th century charm of the island's houses and mansions. Leaving Île de Saint-Louis, he walks to the Luxembourg Gardens, sits on a bench, turns his face to the sun and dozes-off. From the gardens he walks to Boulevard St. Germain. It is too early for dinner so he sits at a terrace table at the famous Café des Deux-Magots, drinks an espresso, and watches the passing parade of people.

At about six o'clock, he finds a nearby outdoor restaurant on a side street off Boulevard St. Germain, orders a glass of Chateauneuf-du-Pape and thinks about the evening ahead. After dinner he will return to Yuri's apartment and double-check the receiving equipment to be sure that it is in working order. Brannon is scheduled to join business colleagues for dinner at Le Grand Véfour at eight-thirty. If he follows last night's itinerary, he will return to the Ritz, change into casual clothes, and take a taxi to Madame Secour's bateau. To be sure that he misses nothing, Alex decides to take up his position in the Cours la Reine at ten o'clock.

CHAPTER 23

WHILE ALEX SIPS espresso in Paris, Harvey Slinger sits slumped at his desk.

It is raining and the howl of the wind outside his office drowns out the music downstairs.

But his dwindling law practice, not noise, is on his mind. The tough attitude of insurance companies toward settling fender-benders is certainly a contributing cause, but that doesn't entirely explain the fact that he is seeing fewer clients come through the door.

Then his thoughts turn to Joe Creamer. *What the hell has happened to Creamer? Creamer said he would have the* SRSV *solution to me this morning. Did he get caught?*

Harvey glances at his watch. It's eleven o'clock. The psychologists' convention dinner-dance is tonight.

The phone rings. "I've got the product. Do you have the five grand?"

Is this a set-up? Harvey asks himself. *Has Joe gone to the police? Is he wired?*

"Let's meet downstairs at Kitty's in an hour."

"Kitty's? Why Kitty's?"

Because if you're wired or carrying a recording device, the music will drown out our conversation. "We should have a beer to celebrate."

"Oh, okay. I'll see you at Kitty's in an hour."

Harvey calls ahead to his bank and orders the withdrawal of five thousand dollars in hundred dollar bills from his office checking account. Many of Harvey's clients want cash at the settlement of their cases so it's not unusual for him to make large cash withdrawals.

At the bank Harvey slips the money into his briefcase, locks it, puts the briefcase in the trunk of his car and drives to Kitty's. Tony Angeleno is on the door.

"Good morning, Tony."

"Hi Mr. Slinger."

"Tony, how long have you been on the door?"

"Been here since we opened this morning, Mr. Slinger."

"Has anyone come in that you didn't know?"

Tony thinks for a moment, "Nah, all regulars."

"Do you know Joe Creamer? Little guy, walks with a slight limp . . ."

"Yeah, yeah, I know what he looks like. He ain't been in today."

"I'm going to meet him here in a few minutes. If anyone comes in that you don't know between now and when I leave, will you let me know immediately?"

"I sure will."

"Thanks, Tony." Harvey hands him a twenty. "One other thing, as soon as Joe Creamer joins me at the bar, I would like you to check the parking lot to see if there is anyone out there . . . anyone you don't know."

Tony smiles, "Like cops?"

"Yeah, Tony, like cops."

"I sure will, Mr. Slinger. And if anyone's out there that fits that description, I'll let you know right away."

"Thanks, Tony." Harvey moves to the bar.

A few minutes later, Harvey is joined by Joe. Harvey orders a beer for Joe and glances over at Tony. Tony turns and goes outside. The bartender places the beer in front of Joe who takes a swig from the bottle. He never drinks from a glass in a joint like Kitty's. Over the din of the music, Joe says, "I got the stuff."

"Any problems?"

"Nah."

"Good." Harvey glances over his shoulder toward the entrance. Tony is just entering and their eyes meet. Tony shakes his head from side to side indicating, *nobody out there.* Harvey feels his body relax. "Follow me," he says to Joe.

OUTSIDE THEY GET into Harvey's car. "Where we going?" Joe asks.

"I'll let you know in a minute." Harvey's eyes sweep across the parking lot.

Tony's assessment was correct. There is no one in the parking lot.

Harvey drives at a crawl through the parking lot and turns north, all the while glancing in his rear view mirror. After traveling several miles, he is satisfied he has not been followed. He pulls over to the curb and stops. He turns to Joe. "Joe, you'll have to forgive me, but as a lawyer I'm paranoid by profession. I'm going to ask you to empty all of your pockets or allow me to frisk you."

"What's this all about?"

"I want to be sure you're not wired or carrying a recording device."

"Are you joking?" Joe rips off his windbreaker jacket and throws it at Harvey, unbuttons his shirt and exposes his bare chest, empties his pockets and turns them inside out.

Harvey removes a small plastic bottle containing a yellow liquid from the jacket. "Is this what I think it is?"

Joe glares at Harvey but nods. "Does that satisfy you?"

Harvey slips the bottle into his jacket pocket. "I'm sorry to put you through this."

"You really are paranoid."

"Better paranoid than in jail."

"Speaking of jail, I risked going to jail to get you that stuff, so where's my money?"

Harvey gets out of the car, opens the trunk, lifts the briefcase out, unlocks it, climbs back in and tosses it to Joe. "It's in there. Five thousand dollars. Count it."

Joe lifts the briefcase. "I trust you."

Harvey drops Joe off a block from the Albion Apartments. As Joe gets out, he says, "Remember, that stuff can cause serious harm to children and old people."

"I'll keep that in mind. And Joe, drop the briefcase off at my office. If I'm not there, leave it with whoever's on the door at Kitty's."

CHAPTER 24

HARVEY RETURNS TO his office. In anticipation of Creamer providing the SRSV solution, Harvey has thought through every problem that might occur, even stopping by the Anchor Hotel, inspecting the physical layout of the banquet kitchen, and taking a photograph of the salad machine. He is satisfied that his plan will work. The only possible kink in the operation is Stilton. *He's so dumb.* Still, he has to use him.

There is no alternative. He can't do it himself. He has to be with Dr. Smalkin throughout the cocktail reception and dinner.

It is two o'clock. He calls Stilton who is in the office next door. "Stilton, I want to see you."

A few moments later there is a soft rap on Harvey's door. "Come in Stilton,"

"Mr. Slinger, I'm sorry to bother you, but you said you wanted to see me."

"That's right, Stilton, come in and have a seat. I have some important business for you to handle tonight."

"Tonight? I take my mother to bingo on Friday nights."

"I've never before asked you to work a Friday night, but when I explain what it's about, you'll understand why you have to do it tonight." Stilton takes a seat facing Harvey. "Do you remember a few days ago when I told you that business was so bad that I was going to have to fire you?"

Stilton nods.

"Well, I think I have a solution to that problem, but I'm going to need your help."

He pauses and thinks how to best put it to Stilton. "You told me that you would do anything I asked of you. Do you still feel that way?"

"Sure, Mr. Slinger, I still feel that way. What do you want me to do?"

Harvey pulls open the middle desk drawer and removes the plastic bottle containing the SRSV. He places it on the desk. Next he pulls out a bottle of water and a stainless steel whiskey flask. From another drawer he removes a white cotton jacket, the type worn by the Anchor Hotel banquet kitchen employees. He opens it and holds it up. It is extra-large. "Think this will fit you?"

"I think so. Do you want me to try it on?"

Harvey hands Stilton the jacket. "Yes, try it on."

Stilton stands and puts the jacket on. "What'd you think, Mr. Slinger?"

Harvey eyes the jacket. It is a bit snug in the shoulders, but otherwise it fits. "It passes muster, Stilton."

Harvey opens the bottle containing the water and unscrews the cap on the whiskey flask. The cap is attached to the flask by a small chain. Carefully, he pours the water into the flask. "Roll up your right sleeve, Stilton." As Stilton removes his sweater and rolls up his sleeve, Harvey continues, "Tonight I want you to wear a T-shirt under this sweater." Harvey walks around to where Stilton is seated and places the curved side of the flask against the underside of Stilton's right forearm and wraps it with masking tape. "Now, put on the sweater and the jacket." Stilton complies. "Good. The flask is not visible under the jacket. How does it feel?"

"It feels okay, but why are we doing this?"

"Ah! The million dollar question. But first, can you unscrew the cap without difficulty? Don't totally remove the cap. Just see if it turns easily."

Stilton places his left hand inside the right sleeve of the jacket and under the sweater. After a moment he says, "It turns easy. I can remove it."

"Good, now to answer your question. Tonight at ten minutes to six, wearing that white jacket and with the flask taped to your right arm, you're going to enter the banquet kitchen at the Anchor Hotel at this point here." Harvey points to a diagram that he has unfolded on his desk.

"How will I know how to find the banquet kitchen? I've never been to the Anchor Hotel."

"When we finish here we're going to stop by the Anchor, and I'll show you the kitchen, the door you enter, and everything else you'll need to know. Relax." Again pointing to the diagram, Harvey says, "As you enter the kitchen through this door, you will see in the middle of the kitchen a large stainless steel machine. Here is a photo of what it looks like."

Harvey removes a photograph from an envelope and hands it to Stilton. "The machine is used to prepare salads and when you see it, it will be filled with salad. If someone should be working at the machine, don't approach it, wait until they leave. When there's no one at the machine, remove the flask cap, walk over to the machine and, while pretending to look at the salad, pour in the contents of the flask. It will not take more than a few seconds. The whole operation must be done so as not to attract attention. Be casual. As soon as you've emptied the contents of the flask into the salad, turn and leave by the same door you entered. Stilton, it's very important that you not hurry when you leave. Walk normal. If anyone should stop you, just say, 'excuse me, but I have to go to the bathroom,' and leave. Do you understand what you're to do?"

"I think so. But why am I doing this? What will be in the flask? Poison? Will anyone get sick?"

"Calm down, Stilton. No one is going to be poisoned. Are

their stomachs going to be upset? Yes. Are they going to vomit and shit? Yes. Is anybody going to die? No. Let me tell you something, Stilton. If we don't get new business in this dump soon, your ass is going to be slinging hamburgers at McDonald's because I'm going to fire you."

Stilton's head is bobbing, his eyes fixed on the floor. "I'm sorry, Mr. Slinger. I know you wouldn't do anything to hurt someone."

Harvey lifts a large plastic bowl from the floor. He walks over and places it on a small table to the left of his desk. He moves the table to the center of the room. Motioning toward the table and the bowl, he says, "We are going to have rehearsals, Stilton. This table and bowl are going to represent the salad machine. I want you to go out the door and reenter just as you'll enter the kitchen tonight. Then I want you to approach the plastic bowl and empty the contents of the flask into it, the same way you'll do it tonight. If I'm standing by the machine when you enter, you must remain by the door until I leave. Remember, no one can be working at the machine when you empty the flask. After you empty the flask, you'll turn and leave, the same as you'll do tonight and walk normal. If I attempt to stop you, you'll use the bathroom excuse. Okay, let's go through every possible scenario until we get it right."

Harvey is delighted to discover that Stilton is more adept as an actor than as a lawyer. His performances are flawless and convince him that his plan is sound and Stilton can pull it off.

Following the rehearsal, they drive to the Anchor to view the actual physical layout. Harvey parks in the hotel garage. They walk up the stairway to the third floor, the location of the banquet kitchen. Harvey points to a telephone booth near the kitchen where Stilton will change into the white jacket and wait until he enters the kitchen. Harvey suggests that Stilton pretend to be speaking on the phone during this waiting time. He shows Stilton the swinging doors through which he will enter the kitchen. They peek through the door window and see the salad machine.

On the ride back to the office Harvey says, "I know how close you are to your mother, but it's very important that no one . . . I mean no one, finds out what we're doing. Do you understand, Stilton?" Stilton casts his eyes down, and nods his understanding. "Look at me, Stilton." Stilton looks at Harvey. "I want to hear you promise out loud that you'll not mention a word about this to your mother."

"I won't tell my mother, Mr. Slinger, I swear, but . . . but what do I tell her when I say I can't go to bingo with her tonight?"

Christ, he's worse than a baby. "Tell her," Harvey says, trying not to lose his temper, "that you have to help me with a brief that's due at the printer's tomorrow morning. Tell her it's very important . . . that it's a matter of life or death."

"Okay, Mr. Slinger, "I'll tell her," Stilton says, in a whisper.

They agree to meet at the office at five for final preparations.

HARVEY IS BACK in his office at four-thirty. He is dressed in a tuxedo. He pours the SRSV solution into the flask with the aid of a small plastic funnel. Next, he places the jacket, a blue plastic bag, and masking tape on the small table. From his wallet he removes two ten dollar bills and places them by the tape. He wants to be sure Stilton has enough money to take a cab from the Anchor Hotel back to the office where he will leave the flask, jacket, tape, and bag on his desk.

A few minutes before five, Stilton arrives wearing a white T shirt, the same brown V-necked sweater, brown trousers and rubber soled shoes. "Am I dressed okay, Mr. Slinger?"

"You look fine. How do you feel?"

"I feel good. I've never done anything like this before. I'm looking forward to it."

"Good. That's good, Stilton," Harvey says, feeling a tightness in his stomach.

"Let's get you ready."

Seated at the desk Stilton removes his sweater. Harvey positions the flask under Stilton's forearm and secures it with the tape. Stilton slips the sweater over his head, dons the white jacket and stands for inspection.

"It looks good," Harvey says. "You can't see the flask. It's completely hidden under the sleeve. Want to do another run through?"

"Sure."

HARVEY AND STILTON leave the office at five-fifteen. Traffic is light and the drive to the Anchor Hotel takes only twenty minutes. Harvey parks in the hotel basement garage. Stilton leaves first carrying the white jacket wrapped in the plastic bag. He takes the stairs. On reaching the third floor, he turns left and walks about sixty yards along a wide corridor to the public telephone booth located around the corner from the kitchen entrance. He passes only one person, a woman dressed in the uniform of the maid service. She walks past him without a glance. He scrunches into the booth, closes the door, and checks the time. It is five-forty-five. He has five minutes to kill. He removes the jacket from the bag, crumples the bag, puts it in his right pants pocket and slips on the jacket. He picks up the receiver and pretends he's having a conversation. After five minutes of self-conscious gibberish, he leaves the phone booth and walks toward the kitchen.

CHAPTER 25

ALEX IS WAITING when a taxi pulls into the service drive entrance and stops at the gate. It is eleven-thirty. Brannon exits the taxi and jogs down the service drive. With the spring of a teenager he jumps from the dock onto the deck of Madame Secour's yacht. He is greeted by the captain and disappears below deck.

Alex's backpack contains a frequency audio/video receiver, 6.5 MHz audio sub-carrier, female audio output, and 3db dipole omni-directional antenna. He plugs the power supply line into the Vespa's cigarette lighter and switches on the remote control button that activates the transmitter hidden behind the *Sortie* panel. Almost immediately he hears the sound of the cabin door shut, followed by, "You look absolutely ravishing, Michelle."

"Then I look like I feel, William darling, because tonight I'm going to ravish you."

Michelle Secour, clad in a silk-robe and slippers and seated on the sofa, motions for Brannon to join her by patting the sofa seat. Brannon sits beside her. Placing her arms around his neck, she kisses him. On the table in front of them is a silver ice bucket containing two bottles of 1990 Dom Pérignon and two champagne flutes. She pours the wine and hands Brannon a glass. "Here is to what I hope will be one of the most memorable evenings of your life."

Brannon raises his glass, "If it's like last night, I'll be more than satisfied."

They tip glasses. "You will be ecstatic, that I guarantee."

They sip the champagne in silence. Michelle Secour places her glass on the table, takes Brannon's glass from him, and places it beside hers. She leads Brannon to the bed that stands high off the floor. She places her arms around his neck and kisses him.

Brannon's arms encircle her. His right hand feels beneath her robe. There's no clothing underneath. His hand moves along soft, warm flesh. Her nakedness heightens his excitement. Secour's experienced hands seek and unfasten his belt, lower the zipper, and his pants fall to the floor. She removes his boxers and slips out of her robe. She pulls him to her with both hands clasping his buttocks. Her soft moans and labored breathing fuel his anticipation. She turns, lays her upper body on the bed, spreads her legs, and guides him into her.

Brannon wants to delay the throbbing pleasure that flows through him as long as possible, and he tries to think irrelevant thoughts but to no avail. Madame Secour's writhing motions and cries bring him a physical and emotional intensity that he has rarely felt before, ending with an explosive rush of pleasure. As his orgasm subsides, he feels her twitching beneath him. Michelle Secour, her head and upper body still lying on the bed, says between gasps for air, "Let's get in bed."

What a wonderful beginning, Brannon thinks, and more to come. And, indeed, more does come in the form of one of the best blow jobs this captain of American industry has ever had.

They spend the last thirty minutes of their outing drinking champagne and talking.

There is a rap on the door and the captain's voice booms out, "Madame, you wanted me to notify you when it was one-thirty."

"We're docking?" Brannon asks.

Secour's face bursts into a wide grin, "William, darling, we never left the dock."

"I never noticed," he says, with a sly smile. "I hope that you have no objections to my paying you in the same currency that I've used in the past?"

The beautiful prostitute smiles, "Not at all, darling. I made enough money on your last visit to buy my Mercedes."

"If I paid you in cash it might leave a trail, and I want our rendezvous to remain secret. Do you understand?"

"I understand completely, William. So, what should I buy?"

"Orangina."

"Why?"

He glances around the stateroom. "We're going to make an offer for it. A big offer and Orangina's price will shoot up. But don't hold it. The French Government with its obsession with national pride might withhold approval of the sale. So, get in and get out. And Michelle, don't breathe a word of this to another person."

"William, do you take me for a fool?" she says, kissing him lightly on the cheek.

It has been a heady evening and as he pulls her to him for a farewell kiss, he says, "This is a night I'll remember." Little does William Brannon realize the prescience of his statement.

CHAPTER 26

AT ABOUT THE time William Brannon is receiving fellatio from the practiced lips of Madame Secour, and Harvey Slinger is waiting nervously at the entrance to the Grand Ball Room for the arrival of Dr. Smalkin, Stilton Geronsky leaves the telephone booth and approaches the kitchen doors. He does not hesitate. Pushing the right door forward, he enters. Two women are working at a long table located to the right of the salad machine, but the machine is unoccupied. With his left hand inside the right sleeve of his jacket fidgeting with the flask cap, Stilton walks directly to the machine. When he is within a few feet of his goal, the cap won't come loose. *Darn it, it's stuck.* He feels a flash of panic. Suddenly, the cap comes free.

The machine is filled with the salad mixture. He glances to his right. The two women are chopping vegetables and focused on the task before them. He moves his hand within inches of the top of the salad mixture and begins pouring the SRSV solution. He keeps his head and eyes down, as though examining the contents. It seems to take forever for the flask to empty. His armpits are wet and his pulse races.

"You!" someone calls out. Stilton's body stiffens. He snaps to attention and looks in the direction of the voice. His body sags with relief when he sees a large black man dressed in white and wearing a toque berating a small Latino man who looks tired and confused. The small man starts shouting back. With everyone's attention focused on the confrontation, Stilton turns and walks out of the kitchen.

He walks down the empty corridor to the stairway. Inside the stairwell he removes the jacket, peels the tape from the flask, and places the flask, tape and jacket in the bag. He scoots down the steps, leaves the hotel from a side door that exits onto Peachtree Street, and crosses the street to the Hyatt Hotel.

AT THE MOMENT Stilton crosses Peachtree Street, Kia is on her way to a computer show at the Hyatt and turns onto Peachtree from Harris Street. At the hotel entrance, Stilton walks in front of her. Kia sees him and thinks, *What a strange looking man.*

Stilton speaks to the doorman who hails him a taxi.

"Where to?" the driver asks.

"Do you know where Kitty's Topless Rampage is?"

"Yeah, I take fares there all the time."

"That's where I want to go."

"Good choice," the cabbie says with a wink.

At Kitty's Stilton pays the taxi driver, and after the taxi drives off, he walks to the office and leaves the bag on Harvey's desk. Feeling pleased with himself, he drives home and takes his mother to bingo.

WHILE STILTON GERONSKY is poisoning the dinner salad, Harvey Slinger stands at the entrance of the Anchor Hotel's Grand Ball Room. It is cocktail time. The crowd is punctual and streams of people file in. A few minutes after six, Smalkin appears and the two new friends disappear into a clamorous crush of humanity gathered to celebrate the final hours of the thirty-fourth annual North American Convention of Psychologists.

As he pushes his way through the noisy crowd, Harvey is thinking about Stilton. Not because of compassion for his safety, but because he's afraid that if caught, Stilton will squeal on him.

The dinner is in the Grand Ballroom. Harvey is seated between Smalkin and a matronly female psychologist from Toronto who is excited about a paper she wrote about the psychological impact to children from being left by parents in daycare centers.

"It is," she tells Harvey, "tantamount to child abuse." He pretends to listen but has his mind on the salad that is being served as the master of ceremonies introduces the first speaker. He watches a waitress approach with a tray of salads. She first serves Smalkin and then places a plate of salad in front of him. *If Stilton has done his job, this salad is poisoned.* He pretends to eat it, but he doesn't take a bite. He watches the people at his table eat the salad, and it makes him nauseous. He turns to Smalkin, "Irving, I feel sick to my stomach."

"What is it?"

"I don't know but I think I'll go home."

"Are you okay to drive?"

"Thanks, Irving, but I'll be able to drive."

"I'll call you tomorrow," Smalkin says.

HARVEY DRIVES TO his office. The bag containing the jacket, flask and tape are on his desk. He takes the flask to the bathroom and flushes it out with hot water. He leaves the office and walks to the rear of Kitty's where a large trash dumpster is located. He throws the bag and its contents into the dumpster, confident the bag will be buried beneath a ton of bottles, cans, and other trash before the night is over.

THE NEXT AFTERNOON Harvey is at home watching television. The Notre Dame-Michigan game is playing, but his mind isn't on the game. He's thinking about the events of last night. He has not heard from Stilton but figures he was successful in lacing the salad with the SRSV solution. Still, he wonders if anyone noticed Stilton in the kitchen? Did Stilton run into any problems? Has anyone reported being sick? He reaches for the phone to call Stilton, and the phone rings.

"Harvey, this is Irving. How are you feeling?"

"I feel better than I did last night, but I'm still a little nauseous."

"I'm glad you're feeling better, but you are not the only one who got sick last night. I'm getting calls from colleagues complaining of diarrhea, nausea, and stomach cramps. Joe Murphy, a psychologist from St. Louis, called me sick as a dog just minutes ago from the Grady Hospital Emergency Room. He said the emergency room is filled with people who attended last night's dinner."

"What do you think caused it?"

"Food poisoning! And this is probably just the tip of the iceberg. It usually takes between fifteen and seventy-two hours for the symptoms to develop. So let's see . . . we sat down to dinner at about seven and it's now one-twenty, that's only eighteen hours. We have more than two days left before this thing runs its course."

"What can I do to help?"

"Nothing for now, but Harvey, Joe Murphy was hopping mad and talking about suing the hotel. I'm sure there will be plenty of others who will feel the same way. If some of my colleagues decide to sue the hotel, would you be interested in representing them?"

A smile crosses Harvey Slinger's face. "Well, if we're able to prove that these people were actually poisoned at the hotel dinner . . ."

"Don't be ridiculous, Harvey. Of course they were poisoned at the dinner. It is the only place where they were all together. Besides, the lab studies will prove it."

"All I'm saying, Irving, is that from a lawyer's perspective I have to be able to prove it. It can't be based on supposition. So, yes, if the lab studies prove that these people were food poisoned, and they identify the type of bacteria or virus that caused it, and if the treating doctors are able to state to a reasonable degree of medical probability that, in their opinions, the bacteria or virus causing the illnesses came from food eaten at the Anchor Hotel last night, then I'll be honored to represent your colleagues in this matter. But that's what we'll have to prove."

"I understand."

Prepared for this development, Harvey continues, "You could help tremendously by asking your colleagues to secure the names of their treating physicians, and to sign hospital authorizations releasing copies of their hospital records directly to me. That will simplify obtaining their hospital records. Didn't you tell me that psychologists attended from forty states?"

"Forty-three states!"

"Irving, when you speak with your colleagues don't assume that they want me to represent them. Explain that some of your colleagues have already retained me. If they're considering making a claim, recommend that they employ me. They respect you. Your recommendation will make the difference." As he speaks, Harvey opens his liquor cabinet, pulls out a bottle of twenty year old VSOP Cognac and pours two fingers into a brandy glass. He doesn't normally start drinking this early, but this is a special occasion. He takes a big sip and feels it burn down his esophagus.

"Explain to your colleagues that because there will be many claims, it makes sense to coordinate all of the claims through one law office. If they agree to have me represent them, get a telephone number and a convenient time when I can contact them. In fact, I would like the names, addresses, and phone numbers of everyone who reports being sick as a result of last night's dinner." Harvey pauses and breathes in deeply. "I know that's a lot to ask, but if you can do it, it will expedite processing the claims."

"It's the least I can do. I feel responsible for what's happened. I chose the Anchor Hotel as the convention site."

"Irving, you're a professional, and you know it wasn't your fault, so get rid of that silly guilt feeling. And thanks for asking me to handle this matter. I'll do a good job."

"I know you will, Harvey, and when I learn more, I'll be in touch."

"One other thing would be helpful, Irving. If you speak with a colleague at the hospital today who expresses an interest in having me represent him, suggest that he invite me to the hospital to meet him. That will give me an opportunity to meet others who are there for treatment." The prospect of getting into the hospital and signing up clients excites Harvey. "If you call later and can't reach me here, I'll be at my office. There's a lot to do, and I'm going to start on it now." Harvey cradles the phone and looks up at the television. Notre Dame had just scored a touchdown, but Harvey is thinking dollars, not points.

CHAPTER 27

HARVEY CALLS STILTON. They meet at the office and Stilton, showing more enthusiasm than Harvey had ever witnessed before, fills him in on how easy it was to slip into the Anchor's banquet kitchen and dump the SRSV solution in the salad.

While Harvey is explaining to Stilton the procedures they will employ in "harvesting these cases," the phone rings. It's Irving.

"I called Joe Murphy at the hospital. He said he wants you to represent him, and he would like you to come to the hospital as soon as possible. Murphy served in Vietnam and he says the place looks like a Vietnam field hospital with bodies everywhere."

"Irving, would it be possible for you to meet me at the hospital? I don't know your colleagues, and your introducing me to them will be a big help."

"Sure. When do you want me there?"

"In a half-hour. I'll wait for you outside the ER entrance."

SMALKIN INTRODUCES HARVEY to Joe Murphy. Harvey has with him a packet of contingency retainer contracts. The retainer contract provides that Harvey is entitled to a one-third fee of any recovery made against the Anchor Hotel and reimbursement for expenses advanced in furtherance of the case. Murphy listens carefully as

Harvey explains the conditions of the contract. Murphy reads the retainer agreement, looks up and says, "Let me see if I have this right. You are going to represent me, and if I don't recovery any money, I don't owe you anything."

"That's correct except that you remain responsible for money I advance in preparing your case for trial."

"Give me a ballpark estimate of the cost?"

"It shouldn't be a lot because I don't have to go out and buy medical experts. The emergency room doctors will be our experts. I would guess expenses of about one thousand dollars."

"If we recover, how much is a case like this worth?"

"Between $25,000 and $50,000."

"Fifty thousand dollars for an upset stomach! Hell, I'm in the wrong business." He takes a handkerchief from his pocket and wipes perspiration from his forehead. "Why so much money?"

"A couple of reasons. First it's going to be a tremendous black eye to Anchor's reputation, and Anchor is going to want this whole thing behind them as soon as possible. They are not going to want to litigate these cases. Whenever a defendant is anxious to settle and I sense it, my settlement price goes up." Harvey winks. "There is another reason why the hotel's lawyers won't want to try these cases." Harvey's eyes shift between Murphy and Smalkin as he speaks.

"What's that?" Murphy asks.

"Because the tort or the wrong occurred in Atlanta. Therefore, the cases will be tried in Atlanta. Atlanta is predominately black . . ."

"So what?" Smalkin says.

"Black folks are more generous than white people. They award more money. Atlanta's white silk stocking law firms know this and pay a premium to settle cases pending in Atlanta."

Harvey hands Dr. Murphy a pen. While Murphy signs the retainer, Harvey says, "Irving is going to introduce me to some of the other folks who were poisoned. Do you mind if he tells them you've retained me in this matter?"

Murphy looks up, his eyes red, his face tired, "Hell no. I hope everybody sues these bastards."

IRVING SMALKIN ESCORTS Harvey around the emergency room lounge and introduces him to his colleagues with the same soothing message, "This is my friend Harvey Slinger. Harvey is a terrific trial lawyer, and I recommend him. Harvey is representing Joe Murphy and several others, and he would be pleased to represent you."

Harvey shakes the prospective client's hand, mumbles his sympathy and how it was all the fault of the Anchor Hotel. When the response is positive, and it overwhelmingly is, Harvey jots down the client's name, address and phone number, has them sign the retainer, and promises to be in touch in a day or two. Each new client is given Harvey's business card with the advice, "If you know of anyone else who needs my services, please have them contact me."

CHAPTER 28

ALEX'S PLANE SETS down at Atlanta's Hartsfield International Airport at 8:10 p.m. Carrying only two bags he clears customs, hails a taxi and is in his apartment before ten. There is a message on his answering machine from Kia asking him to call her as soon as he gets her message. She gives no details. Alex lays his briefcase on the kitchen table and removes the video tape. He has heard the audio portion and is anxious to view the video. He dials Kia. "Hi. I just got in. Is everything all right with you?"

"Yes. How did it go in Paris?"

"I won't know for sure until I watch the video, but if it recorded without a glitch, it should be dynamite. Especially for . . ." The thought that his phone might be tapped crosses his mind. "I'd rather not discuss it over the phone. When can we get together?"

"Tomorrow night, if that's good with you."

"Great. I'll come by at seven. We have a lot to talk about."

"Why don't we have dinner here? It will be more private."

"Do you have a VCR?"

"Sure."

"Okay, dinner at your place, and I'll bring the wine and the steaks."

AT SEVEN ALEX arrives at Kia's place with two porterhouse steaks, cheese, crackers, a bottle of California cabernet sauvignon and the video cassette. As soon as he enters the apartment, Kia says, "Tell me what happened in Paris. I'm dying to know."

Alex tosses the video cassette on the kitchen table and points to it. "I won't have to tell you. You'll see it in living color. I'm worried that the lighting was too dim but . . ."

He shrugs. "We'll see. Let's have some wine and cheese while we watch it," he says, as he pulls the wine cork.

The video picture is grainy and shadowy, but the dialogue and performances of William Brannon and Madame Secour are very clear. They watch in silence the sexual machinations of the man recently designated by the governor of Georgia, "Family Man of the Year." When the video ends Kia turns to Alex and says, "What a skunk."

Contrary to her usual up-beat cheerfulness, Kia is quiet throughout dinner and Alex can't figure out why. He tries to keep the conversation going by talking about what happened in Paris but Kia doesn't seem interested. She's elsewhere with her thoughts.

Finally, Alex says, "Kia, is something wrong?"

"No. Why do you ask?"

"Because you haven't said more than ten words since we watched the video. If it's something I've said or done, tell me."

"No, no . . . it's . . . I guess it's just that I've developed a tremendous migraine. I get them from time to time."

What Alex had thought would be an exciting evening has turned sour. It is time to leave. "Kia, your migraine needs rest, and I'm still fighting jet lag. Let's call it a night. I'll call you tomorrow and see how you're doing. In the meantime, if you need anything, give me a call."

At the door, Kia says, "Now that you've got what you want on Brannon, what are you going to do with it?"

"I'll prepare a transcript of the tape, make a copy of the video, and get them to Brannon."

"How?"

"I'm not sure, but I'll think of a way. I told you I wouldn't use blackmail, and I won't. Brannon may think he's being black-mailed . . . He may even go to the police." He falls silent for a moment. "Brannon's the key to whether we succeed. That doesn't mean that Talbot and Foster aren't important, but he's the key."

"Are you still confident?"

He smiles. "Yes. Brannon's video is powerful stuff, especially how he paid for the prostitute's favors. Brannon may be all we need, but if we nail one of the remaining two that will be what you Americans call the icing on the cake."

IN THE MORNING Alex prepares a transcript of the Brannon vid-eo. He visits Rich's department store and purchases chocolate brown shorts and a brown short sleeve shirt that match the UPS summer uniform. At Staples he buys a machine similar to the machines used by UPS deliverymen to record deliveries and pro-vide receipts. He stops at an outdoor UPS station and picks up a delivery envelope.

Back at his apartment he wipes the video cassette and tran-script clean of fingerprints and, wearing latex gloves, places them inside the envelope and seals it. He changes into his new UPS look-alike clothes, glues on a mustache, dons a Braves baseball cap and wrap-around sunglasses, and heads to Coca-Cola head-quarters.

SURROUNDED BY AN iron fence, the Coca-Cola headquarters complex requires visitors to enter at a guarded check point. Alex parks three blocks away and walks to the Luckie Street entrance. When he starts through the entrance gate a guard stops him.

"I'm sorry sir, but UPS deliveries are made at our receiving department on Blair Street," the guard says.

"That's where I usually make deliveries, but this package is for William Brannon, the chief executive officer of Coca-Cola.

Mr. Jason Arminger, chief executive of UPS, and a personal friend of Mr. Brannon's, personally instructed me to deliver it here and see that a member of Mr. Brannon's staff accepts it. Mr. Arminger said that Mr. Brannon is waiting for it." Alex waves the package in front of the guard.

The guard hesitates and mumbles, "No one informed me." He enters the guard station and makes a phone call. A minute later he returns and points ahead to the headquarters building. "I've alerted the receptionist that you have a special delivery for the chief executive officer. She will accept delivery."

"Thank you." Alex gives the guard a salute and walks across the plaza to the executive headquarters building.

The lobby is empty. He walks directly to the receptionist and presents the package to the woman behind the desk. "This is for William Brannon, chief executive officer."

"I'll contact Mr. Brannon's office . . ."

"I don't have time to wait, lady. Please sign here." Alex shoves the machine in front of her. She signs. Alex turns and leaves.

CHAPTER 29

THE NEXT MORNING Brannon strides into his office and doesn't greet his staff with the usual pleasantries. Sheila Winslow, his secretary of eighteen years, knows his every mood and immediately senses a problem. "Is there anything that I can get you, Mr. Brannon?"

"I'm fine, Ms. Winslow, but I must confess I didn't sleep well last night."

She shakes her head sympathetically. "You're under such pressure. I don't know how you take it day in and day out. I was planning on putting together your itinerary for South America unless, of course, there is something more pressing you want done."

"No. The South American trip has top priority."

Sheila Winslow closes the door quietly on her way out. William Brannon leans back in his large leather desk chair with his chin resting in the palm of his left hand. Slowly he spins the chair around. In front of him is the Atlanta skyline, a skyline his work and efforts helped create. *Who's behind it? What's their game?* He needs help like he has never needed help before. Using his cellular phone he dials Lester Hammond's private number.

AT THAT MOMENT Lester Hammond is at a meeting in Rochester, New York with the chief financial officer and general counsel of the Eastman Kodak Company. They are discussing security for Kodak's top executives throughout the world. When Hammond's cellular phone vibrates silently against his left thigh, he knows the call is very important. Only seven people have his private number, and no one other than his wife and his chief deputy have ever called it before. Hammond's eyes sweep the room. "Ladies and gentleman, please excuse me. I must take a short break." Without further explanation he rises and walks out of the conference room.

In the hallway he answers the call. "This is Lester Hammond."

"Lester, this is Bill." There is a pause. "I need to talk to you."

"Sure, Bill. Go ahead."

"Can you come to Atlanta?"

"When?"

"Today."

Hammond's stomach tightens. He glances at his watch. It is nine-twenty. He has flown to Rochester in the company jet so transportation is available. "I'm in Rochester, New York now, but I'll come down. Where and what time shall we meet?"

"I have a full day of business engagements that I have to keep but . . . let's meet at my office at seven. Call Sheila and tell her that you'll be in Atlanta tonight and that you would like to stop by to see me. Sheila will convey that message to me, and I'll okay it for seven."

Hammond is relieved. He has enough time to finish his business here at Eastman Kodak and be in Atlanta in time for their meeting. "I will call Sheila as soon as I break free from here. Bill, is there anything you would like me to do before we meet?"

"No. And Lester, our meeting is confidential."

"I understand completely."

ON THE FLIGHT to Atlanta, Lester Hammond's thoughts turn to his twenty-five year association with William Brannon. As a young, rising star within Coca-Cola's executive ranks, the thirty-two year old Brannon was given the job of developing the company's security plans. After extensive study, Brannon recommended to the executive committee that routine matters such as interviews, employee assistance programs, and loss and prevention investigations be handled in-house with more complex matters such as surveillance, industrial espionage, and executive protection services handled by an outside company.

At the time, Hammond Investigative Services consisted of thirty employees housed in a six room office complex in a warehouse section of South Atlanta. Impressed by Lester Hammond's investigative knowledge and administrative skills, and a promise to prioritize all things relating to Coca-Cola, Brannon did not take the safe course and recommend a large and experienced company such as Pinkerton. Rather, he recommended Hammond Investigative Services. It was a risky decision but it worked out.

As Coca-Cola grew, Hammond's business prospered. His company now has forty offices strung around the world. He is a multimillionaire with homes in four countries. He enjoys the prestige and privileges that come with being rich and powerful, and he's never forgotten that it was Bill Brannon who gave him the opportunity to achieve his success.

As he steps off the company private jet and climbs into a waiting limousine, he resolves that there is nothing he won't do for Bill Brannon. *All he has to do is ask!*

CHAPTER 30

A SECURITY GUARD escorts Lester Hammond to Brannon's four-teenth floor suite of offices. He has been there many times and has no trouble finding his way through the support staff offices that lead to Brannon's working office. When he enters, Brannon is seated behind his desk, gaunt and tired looking. Behind Brannon a bank of windows look out across the Atlanta skyline.

"Still working?"

Brannon's head snaps up. He stands, waves Hammond in and comes around the desk to greet him. They shake hands. "Thanks for coming down," Brannon says, walking past Hammond and looking into his executive secretary's office and the reception area to be sure that they are alone. He returns, shuts his office door and gestures with his head for Lester to follow him into an ad-joining office that he uses for social purposes.

Hammond takes three steps into the room and stops. "Wow!"

Brannon spins around and grins. "Well, what do you think?"

Hammond stands for a moment taking in the scene. "Bold, elegant, wonderful, and I suspect, very expensive."

"Every piece of furniture in this room is eighteenth century American. All of the paintings are by Americans. That's a Sargent, that's a Homer, and on the far wall, a George Bellows."

"When I was last here, about a year ago," Hammond says, "this room was stuffed with modern kitsch."

Brannon walks over to a tall Chippendale secretary, opens the top doors and says, "What will you have?"

"Macallan's if you have it."

"Is the eighteen year old stuff good enough?"

"Absolutely."

"If I remember correctly, you like your scotch straight up."

"Bill, you remember everything correctly."

"Perhaps," Brannon says, as he places two glasses on a William and Mary oval tavern table and pours the Macallan's, "but I don't always do things correctly. That's why I asked you to come down." He turns and hands one of the glasses to Hammond and motions him to a large sofa. Hammond lowers his ample frame into the sofa and Brannon sits facing him. Brannon raises his glass, tips it in the air, and says, "Here's hoping we can solve my problem."

Hammond repeats the gesture, smiles and says, "We'll work it out."

They sip their drinks in silence. Waiting for Brannon to speak, Hammond remembers Brannon telling him years ago that if he didn't have sex at least twice a day he gets a terrible headache. Hammond recalls that they were playing golf at the Cherokee Country Club when Brannon made the remark. He wonders if that is still the situation.

Brannon sets his glass on an end table and leans forward, his forearms resting on his knees, his blue eyes staring at Hammond. In his left hand he holds a folder. Hammond has noticed that except for when Brannon mixed the drinks, the folder hasn't left his hands. "I'm going to be blackmailed."

Hammond's body tightens. "What makes you think that?"

"This was delivered to the lobby receptionist yesterday afternoon by someone dressed as a UPS driver." Brannon hands the folder to Hammond. "He told security that Bill Arminger, the

CEO of UPS had personally sent him to deliver the package to a member of my staff. He said I was waiting for the package. He had the woman at the desk sign for it."

Hammond studies the envelope. "What makes you think it wasn't a UPS driver who delivered it?"

"I checked with Bill Arminger who is a personal friend and golfing partner. He told me that he didn't send me a package. He also had the UPS records checked. There is no record of UPS making a delivery to me yesterday, nor do they have a record of anyone signing for a delivery to me." Brannon's eyes flash his anger.

Hammond puts his glass down. "May I have a look?"

Brannon nods. "Sure", and hands Hammond the folder.

Hammond opens the folder and removes what appears to be a transcript. "Is this what I think it is?"

"Read it." He glances at Hammond's drink. "It will help if I refresh your drink." He picks up Hammond's glass and moves toward the bar.

"Before I read this, is there a tape that goes with it?"

"Yes, a video. It's in the envelope."

He looks inside the folder. "Have you viewed it?"

"Yes."

"Does this transcript conform to the video word for word?"

Brannon nods, "Word for word."

"What's the quality of the video?"

"The lighting is terrible, but the sound is good. The bad news is that it's me, buck ass naked in bed with this . . ." He shakes his head and waves his hands in a dismissive manner. "That TV," he says, pointing to a television, "has a built in video, in case you want to view it."

Hammond opens the transcript and begins reading. Brannon refreshes Hammond's drink and places it on the table beside him. He returns to the bar, pours himself more scotch, walks into his working office, flops into his desk chair and stares out at the dark sky and Atlanta's pulsing lights.

Hammond reads the transcript and views the video. He walks into the working office and lowers himself into a chair facing Brannon, the transcript in his right hand. For a man trained to conceal his thoughts, Hammond's face shows his concern. "Do you have any idea who is behind this? The French woman?"

"I might. I'm not sure. But it's not the French woman. That was my first reaction. When I called her, she vehemently denied any knowledge of the situation but promised to find out what she could. She called back and told me they found the camera and the microphone hidden behind an exit sign in the stateroom. She said that only two people have unrestricted access to her boat, the captain and a first mate and both have been with her since she purchased the boat six years ago. After questioning them, she's convinced that they're not involved. Frankly, I wasn't convinced until . . ." His lips compress and cut off his words.

Hammond studies his friend. He has never seen Brannon when he was not in total control, except for now. Brannon's thin, drawn face and anguished eyes reveal his inner turmoil. "Until what? And what did you mean when you said you might know who's behind this but you're not sure?"

Brannon shifts in his chair. "This isn't easy for me to talk about." He rubs his cheek with his hand and glances away for a second. "There's a part of me that no one knows about, and it's caused by something I can't control. I've always had a very strong sex drive." He pauses and takes a deep breath. "Business takes me all over the world. My wife usually isn't with me. I . . . well . . . I get this urge. I've got to have a woman."

"I remember your telling me years ago that if you didn't have sex twice a day you got a terrible headache."

Brannon smiles, "It's probably diminished a bit since then, but it's still strong."

"That explains why you were with this woman in Paris," Hammond says, waving the transcript.

Brannon shakes his head. "That's not the point in my telling you this. There's a young woman that I recently had a small affair with."

"What do you mean, 'small affair?'"

"I mean, we probably didn't have sex more than ten . . . fifteen times. I had to call it quits with her. She was getting too demanding. She even suggested that I leave Virginia. That did it." Brannon stands and begins pacing behind his desk. "I told her I wasn't going to see her again. But two days ago I was sitting here and . . . and I got this tremendous sexual urge." He fingers his drink. "I called her."

"Where was she?"

"She works here . . . in the travel department."

Hammonds eyes widen. "And where did you plan on having sex with her?"

"In my private elevator."

"Your private elevator!" Hammond exclaims, coming half out of his chair.

"Yes. We did it there twice before. See, I would call her and she would meet me at my private parking area in the basement. I would take the elevator to the basement, and she would get on. I would take it up between floors and lock it out." His eyes shift from Hammond to the floor as he speaks. "It's not an ideal arrangement but better than nothing."

Hammond shakes his head as if to clear it. "What happened when you called her?"

"I suggested that she meet me and . . . she spat out, 'Why don't you go to Paris and get it from your French whore,' and hung up."

Hammond stares at his friend. The surprise of what he's hearing shows on his face. "What's this woman's name?"

"Kia Williams."

Hammond removes a Palm Pilot from his jacket and makes an entry. "I gather that because of her position in the travel department she knew that you were in Paris." Brannon nods. "But that doesn't account for how she knew about the prostitute," Hammond says, his head tilted back, eyes fixed on the ceiling. "Unless, unless . . ."

"I thought the same thing . . . that she followed me to Paris. I had Sheila discreetly check where everyone in our travel department was when I was in Paris." Brannon sips the last of his drink. "Kia Williams was here, in this building working when I was in Paris. Then I got busy and didn't think about it until yesterday afternoon when I opened that damned package," he says, pointing to the transcript resting in Hammond's lap.

"Someone told her about you and the woman in Paris, and she knows who that person is."

The two men, their scotch glasses empty, stare at one another in thoughtful silence, both thinking, *Who? Why?*

Hammond speaks first. "One thing is for sure. There's more behind this than the revenge of a woman scorned. Here's what I suggest. Don't do anything until you are contacted by the blackmailers. When you're contacted, call me immediately, and we'll decide what should be done next. In the meantime, I will put a twenty-four hour tail on Kia Williams and find out who she socializes with, who she sleeps with, and everything else about her from the day she was born." Brannon flinches. "Bill, don't worry, your name will not be connected in anyway with the investigation. If we come up with a suspect, and I believe we will, we'll also find out everything there is to know about that person. Then we'll get together and make some decisions as to what should be done."

DESCENDING IN BRANNON'S private elevator, Brannon turns to his friend. "If I get out of this mess, I'm going to keep it in my pants."

Hammond smiles and rolls his eyes. "Yeah, sure you are."

CHAPTER 31

BILL BRANNON IS pissed-off. It is Sunday afternoon and he planned on playing golf, but it's raining. He is restless. Never one for reading as a diversion, he clicks on the television and presses the remote until he gets the Falcons' football game. He immediately has second thoughts. *Screw the Falcons*, and presses ahead on the remote until he gets a tennis game. One of the players is Agassi. He likes Agassi. Agassi reminds him of a young version of himself, confident, smart, and aggressive. He pushes back in the sofa ready to enjoy the match when his cell phone rings. It's Hammond.

"Bill, this is Lester. Good afternoon."

"Good afternoon, Lester. Have you learned anything?"

"Yes, quite a bit. I take it that no one has contacted you?"

It has been almost two weeks since he and Lester meet at his office, and he has heard nothing. "No, Lester, I've heard nothing."

"I can't get away today, Bill, but if you're available tomorrow, I can be in Atlanta anytime you like. I think we should act on this information promptly."

"It won't be necessary for you to come to Atlanta. I'm flying to New York tomorrow. I have some business that will keep me busy most of the day, but I'm available in the early evening. Can we get together then?"

"Are you staying at the company condo?"

"Yes. Can you stop by at six-thirty?"

"I think it would be better if we discussed this matter in the privacy of my limousine."

"Okay, but can we finish in an hour?"

Hammond thinks, *nothing takes precedence over Brannon getting laid.* "Yes. I'll be by promptly at six-thirty."

"I'll be waiting."

THE NEXT EVENING at six-thirty, William Brannon strides from the entrance of a fashionable Park Avenue building to Hammond's waiting limousine. The chauffeur holds the door and he slides in across the soft, smooth, glove leather seats. They shake hands. Hammond waits until they are in the flow of traffic before speaking. "This car is sound proof. No one, including my driver, can hear a word we say, and what I have to tell you is very confidential." Brannon feels anxious. "Twice last week Kia Williams met a man by the name of Alexandre Ivanovich. Is that name familiar to you?"

Brannon shakes his head. "No. It sounds Russian."

"Alexandre Ivanovich is a Russian immigrant who lives and works in Atlanta. He has a small apartment in Midtown and operates a one-man limousine service. He came to Atlanta from Russia eight years ago sponsored by an uncle who owned the limousine service and guaranteed his cousin's employment. Ivanovich went to work for his uncle, and within a year the uncle died. Ivanovich inherited the business."

"Was the uncle's death natural?"

"So far as we know it was. There are no suspicions relating to the uncle's death. I'm just giving you background. Here's the interesting thing about Ivanovich. From September, 1973 until November, 1991 he was a member of the KGB reaching the rank of colonel at the age of thirty-one. I can tell you from personal knowledge of the KGB that is a damn fast climb. Through a highly confidential source I was able to secure a verbal synopsis of Ivanovich's CIA file."

Hammond reaches into his briefcase and removes a manila folder. He glances through it. "He was born in Vladavostock thirty-nine years ago. He is the oldest of three children, born of peasant parents. His father was a fisherman who died when he was seven. His mother raised the family working as a janitor. From an early age Ivanovich was something of a child prodigy excelling in math, sciences, and languages. He has a chemical engineering degree and is fluent in six languages, Russian, English, French, Italian, German, and Spanish. Following graduation from university at the age of nineteen, he was accepted into the KGB where he received a variety of special training including the equivalent of what we call special-forces training." Hammond looks up from his notes. "In other words, Bill, he knows how to kill with his bare hands."

Hammond returns to his notes. "Although he was a member of the Communist party, he was non-political, and his quick rise within the KGB seems to have been on merit alone. He spent his entire career in the Foreign Intelligence Directorate, the elite Directorate of the KGB, usually as a spy posing as a diplomat. He is six foot two, weighs about a hundred-ninety, and is known to be extremely strong. He works out four or five times a week at the Atlanta Centennial YMCA." Hammond closes the file and looks at Brannon.

"If he's so smart, why's he driving a limousine?" Brannon says, a smirk on his face.

"I can't answer that. There are a number of possible reasons, but I don't think that need concern us now. What's important is the fact that Ivanovich was in Paris the same two days that you were there." Hammond pauses, letting his words sink in.

Brannon's face flushes with anger, "The cocksucker."

"And there's something else. Do you remember a month or so ago when your head chemist got drunk and left his computer containing the Coca-Cola formula in a limousine?"

"Yes."

"You personally instructed me to get it back, and my men did. Well, the man who owned that limousine, and who had the computer in his apartment, is . . ."

Brannon's head snaps round, "Ivanovich?"

"That's right. I don't know if there's a connection, but it sure as hell is an unusual coincidence, isn't it?"

"Yes. It certainly is."

"Not only was he in Paris when you were there, but . . . Bill, two and two still make four. Kia Williams is the woman you spurned. She hates you. She's Ivanovich's friend. She knows you are going to Paris, she knows your exact itinerary, and she gives it to this son-of-a-bitch. He's a trained spy. He follows you, plants the listening and video devices, and records your evening on the boat." Hammond takes a deep breath and clenches his teeth. "Bill, there are some people on this earth that shouldn't be here. The world would be a better place without them. Ivanovich is one of those sons-of-bitches." His eyes glisten. Leaning toward Brannon, he whispers, "Would it disappoint you if Ivanovich disappeared from the face of the earth?"

The silence is so heavy they can hear their own breathing. They sit staring at each other with the shimmering lights of traffic casting shadows about them.

"Could you make that happen without anyone tracing it back to you or me?"

"I think so. I'll know after making just one phone call."

Brannon glances at his watch, locks his fingers together, and stares straight ahead. He doesn't answer for a long moment and then, as if tasting his words, he says, "If I could be sure that his death could never be traced back to us, then . . ." he pauses, "that would make me very happy."

Lester Hammond opens the hand rubbed mahogany bar and lifts out a bottle of 1990 Dom Pérignon. He pops the cork, pours two glasses, and says, "Somebody once said that life is more about dealing with shadows than absolutes. Getting rid of Ivanovich is an absolute." He touches his glass against Brannon's, "To a better world."

Brannon winks, "To a better world."

CHAPTER 32

WHILE WILLIAM BRANNON and Lester Hammond drive through Central Park plotting Alex's death, Alex works out at the YMCA and then heads to Manuel's for a beer. As he turns on to Virginia Avenue, his cell phone rings. "Where are you?" Kia asks.

"I'm on my way to Manuel's. Want to join me?"

"I'd love to but I promised to take my mother shopping to-night. Alex, this may not interest you but just before I left the office today we were notified that Nelson Foster, senior vice president and the chief financial officer, will be spending the next five days fishing in the Florida Keys."

"Did the notification give any particulars?"

"Yes. All executives must leave notice with the company at all times where they can be contacted in the event of an emergency."

"And where can Foster be contacted?"

"At a place called the Mooring's in Islamorada.

"Where in the Florida Keys is Islamorada?"

"I'm not sure."

Alex makes a U-turn and heads back to his apartment while they continue talking. "I don't know if following him would be worthwhile. I'll think about it. Thanks, Kia."

At the next traffic stop, he dials the Delta Air Lines reservations office and learns that there is an eight-fifteen flight leaving Atlanta for Miami that evening. He books an aisle seat. He packs an overnight bag and surveillance gear, checks the computer for directions from the Miami airport to Islamorada and makes a reservation for a rental car. He calls the Mooring's and reserves a room under the name of Randolph Geerman.

At the Miami airport he picks up his rental car, follows Route 836 to the Florida Turnpike and eventually eases into U S 1. An hour and a half later he crosses the Islamorada city line. He stops at a diner, orders a coffee and a sandwich, and gets directions to the Mooring's.

CHAPTER 33

THE FOOD POISONING of over two hundred people at the Anchor Hotel has turned the Law Office of Harvey Slinger into a swirl of activity. Every day from early morning until late evening Harvey and Stilton are consumed with phone calls, interviews, advising clients and prospective clients, obtaining and reviewing medical records, writing letters of representation, preparing contingent fee contracts, and a host of other related activities.

It is nine in the evening and Harvey has not taken a break since arriving at the office early that morning. He tells Stilton he's going out for a bite to eat. As soon as he walks out the door, the phone rings. Stilton answers.

"Is this the Law Office of Harvey Slinger?" a woman asks.

"Yes," says Stilton.

"My name is Helen Frederick. Is this Mr. Slinger?"

"No. Mr. Slinger stepped out for a moment. This is his associate, Stilton Geronsky. Can I help you?"

"I want to talk with Mr. Slinger about representing me about . . ." The voice trails off in sobs. "My husband died yesterday. He attended the dinner at the Anchor Hotel in Atlanta Friday night. When he got home Saturday evening, he wasn't feeling well so . . ."

Stilton interrupts, his palms sweating. "Where do you live?"

"In Memphis. My husband went straight to bed but spent the entire night in the bathroom with diarrhea, terrible stomach pains and uncontrollable vomiting. I called our son, Arthur, and he took his father to St. Francis Hospital. He was admitted and remained there for two days. After he got home he was better for a day or so, but he was still very weak and couldn't eat anything except tea and a little chicken noodle soup. Then last night, in the middle of the night, he had an attack of dry heaves. Actually, it was more like a seizure, and it went on and on. I called 911, my son, Arthur, and our family physician, but . . . but . . . by the time the paramedics arrived, Thomas was dead."

Stilton, hunched at his desk, his body and thoughts paralyzed with fear, hears the woman ask, "Are you still there?"

"Yes. How old was your husband?"

"He would have been seventy-nine tomorrow."

Stilton is sweating and his skin feels prickly. "Were you told why your husband died?"

"Yes." The woman sighs, "The physician at the hospital told me that the convulsive dry heaves were caused by dehydration and his heart gave out."

"What caused the dehydration?"

"Food poisoning."

Stilton's heart leaps. "Ma'am, give me your name and telephone number. I'll have Mr. Slinger call you when he returns."

Harvey returns to his office and ducks into Stilton's office to find out if he has any telephone messages. He finds Stilton slumped over his desk, his head between his arms, crying. Harvey doesn't know what to make of this hulk of a man crying like a baby. After standing in the doorway for a few moments, he walks over and shakes Stilton's shoulders. Stilton turns his head and looks up, his eyes swollen and red, his face pale. "You said we wouldn't hurt anybody, you said we wouldn't hurt anybody," he says through loud sobs. Stilton puts his head between his arms and continues crying.

Harvey grabs Stilton's hair and yanks his head up. "What the hell's the matter with you?"

Stilton's hands flop across the desk until he finds the scrap of paper on which he wrote the woman's name and telephone number. "Here," he says, holding the piece of paper out to Harvey, "this woman said her husband died last night because of being poisoned by food at the Anchor Hotel."

"Why did she call us?"

"She wants you to represent her," he says, pointing his finger at Harvey, "but you can't because we killed him!" His eyes are alive with fear.

Stilton bolts from his chair and grasps the telephone on his desk with both hands. His eyes dart wildly around the room. He lifts the telephone, and shakes it. "We've got to call the police and tell them what we did!"

Harvey slaps Stilton across the face and pushes him back into the chair. "You dumb bastard, get hold of yourself." Stilton slouches in the chair, his tear blotched face resting on his chest. "Now listen to me," Harvey says. "I'm going to call this woman and find out all the details, things that I'm sure you didn't ask her. While I'm doing that, I want you to sit here and do nothing. Nothing! Do you understand?" Stilton nods. "Remember, you are to just sit here until I return. You are not to make or receive phone calls. Do you understand what I'm saying?" Stilton nods. Harvey goes to his office.

Twenty minutes later Harvey returns to Stilton's office, quietly closes the door and observes his associate still crying, head down and folded in his arms. Harvey's conversation with Mrs. Frederick has convinced him that Dr. Frederick did indeed die from food poisoning. It is also clear to Harvey that Stilton will tell the police everything. If he allows that to happen, he will be indicted for murder and sent to prison. In a flash the solution becomes clear.

He turns on his heel and races back to his office. He goes to his desk, unlocks the top right drawer and removes a .38 Smith &

Wesson Body Guard five shot revolver. He checks the chamber; it's loaded. He removes the safety lock, slides it into his right jacket pocket and walks back to Stilton's office.

He enters the office, closes the door, and stands for a moment observing Stilton, still at his desk, facedown, softly sobbing. Harvey quietly crosses the room and stands behind Stilton. With Stilton giving no indication that he is aware of his presence, Harvey removes the gun from his jacket, places the tip of the barrel within an inch of Stilton's right temple, and pulls the trigger. Stilton's head jerks and the sobbing stops.

Harvey removes a handkerchief from his trousers and carefully wipes the revolver clean of all traces of his fingerprints. With the gun still held in the cloth, he wraps Stilton's right hand around the gun with his index finger inside the trigger housing and places his hand and the gun beside Stilton's head. He studies the scene and decides that it is not quite right. He maneuvers Stilton's arm, hand, and the gun ever so slightly until he has them positioned exactly as if Stilton shot himself. He checks his clothing to be sure blood has not splattered on him. He finds none. The only blood he sees is a trickle that runs from the entrance wound down along Stilton's cheek.

Harvey reaches down and feels Stilton's left wrist. There is no pulse. He's dead. He takes a deep breath, picks up the phone and dials 911. In an excited voice he says, "This is Harvey Slinger calling. I heard a noise, like a shot, ran into my associate's office and found him slumped at his desk with a gun beside his head. He shot himself! Please, send an ambulance and the police." After the operator secures a few other particulars, such as his office address, Harvey lays the phone in the receiver and says to himself, *I'd better gild this lily a little better.* He runs downstairs screaming, "Stilton shot himself! Stilton shot himself!"

Stilton's apparent suicide makes the front page of the *Atlanta Journal-Constitution.* The article reads in part: "In what police believe to have been a self-inflicted wound, Stilton Geronsky, age

31, died last night from a .38 caliber bullet that entered his right temple just above the ear. Mr. Geronsky, a member of the Georgia and Atlanta Bar Associations, was an associate in the Atlanta law office of Harvey Slinger. A reliable source reports that nothing was found at the scene that would enable the police to establish a motive for the suicide. Mr. Geronsky's employer, Harvey Slinger, who discovered the body, is reported to be under sedation and unavailable for comment at this time. Major Marcus Andrews, the Atlanta Police Department spokesperson, reports that the investigation is continuing."

Lieutenant Harold Johnson of homicide, a veteran of twenty-five years on the Atlanta Police Department, is in charge of the investigation into the death of Stilton Geronsky. After visiting the scene Lieutenant Johnson's first impression is that the deceased killed himself. There is, however, no suicide note and, after interviewing Stilton's elderly and bereaved mother, no apparent motive for committing suicide.

According to Margaret Geronsky, her son was not depressed and never owned a gun. In fact, so far as Mrs. Geronsky knows, Stilton never fired a gun. These revelations have put the lieutenant on notice that Stilton's death might be something other than a routine suicide.

Photographs of the Stilton's body are thoroughly analyzed and reveal nothing suspicious. The lab reports that all blood samples match those of the deceased, as do the fingerprints recovered from the revolver. The firearms identification expert confirms that the bullet removed from Stilton's brain came from the gun found at the scene.

Lieutenant Johnson personally interviews Dr. Armando Romerez, the pathologist who conducted the autopsy. Dr. Romerez reports that the gunshot pattern is to the right side of the deceased's head and a half inch above the right ear. It is identified by a small oval entrance wound. Considerable gunpowder residue was found around the entrance wound, which indicates

146 · JAMES GABLER

that the tip of the gun was within an inch or two of the side of the deceased's head when it was fired.

Doctor Romerez was able to trace the bullet's course and trajectory because of the hemorrhage and damage it left to the brain. Dr. Romerez's opinion is that the cause of death was a single gunshot wound to the right side of the head, and the trajectory of the bullet consistent with a self-inflicted wound.

Lieutenant Johnson's investigation turns up no evidence of foul play and under manner of death, he writes, "self-inflicted." Accordingly the investigation into the death of Stilton Geronsky is officially closed.

Stilton's humble birth, struggle to become a lawyer, and support and loyalty to his ailing, elderly mother captured the attention of local and national media and he achieved in death what had eluded him in life—recognition.

CHAPTER 34

THE NEXT MORNING Alex arises before dawn. At the registration desk he sees an elderly man drinking coffee and reading a fishing magazine.

"I see that the dining room's not open yet. Any chance I might be able to get a cup of coffee?"

The man looks up, "I've got a pot of coffee in the back. I'll get you a cup."

As soon as the old man disappears from view, Alex slips behind the counter, scans the registration book and sees that Nelson Foster is registered in Cottage 13. He has barely returned to the guest side of the counter when the old man reappears carrying a Styrofoam cup. "Here," he says, "I brewed it not more than ten minutes ago."

With coffee in hand and instructions from the old man on how the cottages are numbered, Alex has no difficulty locating Cottage 13, a pink stucco, two-room bungalow facing the ocean and surrounded by hibiscus and bougainvillea. He waits in a grove of mangrove trees and watches the morning sun burst across the sky. After a wait of about ten minutes a man of medium height, carrying a rod and reel, wearing a fishing jacket, rubber hip boots, a Braves baseball cap and sunglasses emerges from Cottage 13.

Alex follows him along a gravel path that leads to the main

lodge. As the man passes the reception desk, the old clerk says, "Mr. Foster, your fishing guide called and said that he'll meet you here at seven."

Foster glances at his watch, "Thank you," and continues into a small dining room where breakfast is being served.

Alex saunters over to the desk. "That was very good coffee. Thanks."

The old clerk smiles, "I got another pot brewing. Want some more?"

"No, thanks, one cup is about all my nerves can handle. This is my first time in the Keys. What kind of fishing do you do around here?"

"Oh, just about any kind, but in the flats is some of the best bone fishing in the world."

"Is that what that fellow you just spoke to is going for?"

"Yeah, he told me last night that this is his first time bone fishing. But he's an experienced fisherman, and he's got the best guide in these parts, so he'll do fine."

"Are bonefish fighters?"

"You better believe it. Pound for pound they're as strong as any fish there is and lightning fast. Once they take the fly, you've got your hands full. Battles of seven or eight runs are common. Believe me you gotta be in shape to be a good bone fisherman."

"Maybe on my way back from Key West, I'll give it a try. Any particular guide I should ask for?"

"Yep, same guide that fellow's using, Sammy Plitt," the old man says, pointing to Nelson Foster who is walking toward them from the dining room.

"Excuse me, but you look familiar. I've been trying to figure out where I know you from. I'm Nelson Foster from Atlanta."

Foster is not wearing the baseball cap or the sunglasses, and though the lighting is dim, it gives Alex his first good look at his face. Foster is seven or eight inches shorter than Alex, with thinning brown hair, and delicate, almost effeminate facial features.

"I'm Randolph Geerman," Alex says, extending his hand. "I don't think we've met before. I've never been to Atlanta."

"You don't happen to do business with The Coca-Cola Company in any way, do you?"

"No, I'm a professor of economic history," he says in his most cultured English accent. "We don't drink much Coca-Cola at the university."

"I'm sorry to hear that. Coca-Cola's good for you. Are you going bone fishing?"

"Not today. I'm heading to Key West for a few days, but maybe on my way back, I'll give it a try. It was nice meeting you, Mr. Foster, and I hope you have a lot of good fishing."

ALEX RETURNS TO his room and spreads the surveillance equipment on the bed. He glances at a standard brown clock radio on the night table. In color and size it looks almost identical to the Semco clock radio that he has with him. The Semco includes a functional AM/FM radio, clock and alarm, but it is also equipped with a microminature .25W transmitter, color camera, microphone and antenna, and capable of transmitting for two hours. It is designed for indoor surveillance, and it is easy to operate, plug it in and set the clock. Alex packs the Semco clock radio in with the other equipment and thinks how easy the task will be if Foster's bungalow has a clock radio like the one on his night stand.

Check out time is not until noon. Alex decides to wait an hour or so to be sure that all the fishermen are gone. To pass the time, he rummages in his carry bag and pulls out a dog-eared paperback of *Crime and Punishment*.

At eight o'clock, Alex stops by the reception desk and learns that all registered male guests have gone fishing. The old clerk volunteers, "Just a few wives and children left. When are you heading to Key West?"

"I'm not sure. I thought I would sit by the pool for a couple of hours and read."

"Be sure you wear plenty of sunscreen. It's going to be a scorcher."

Alex returns to his room, puts on bathing trunks and wraps a towel around the bag containing the audio-video surveillance equipment. The pool and deck are empty of people. Alex selects a lounge chair that is out of sight from the reception desk and lays the towel, novel, and sunscreen on it. With the bag strung over his shoulder, he moves down a narrow path to the water's edge. Keeping close to the verdant foliage, he edges his way toward Cottage 13.

The bungalow is not equipped with an alarm system. Wearing latex gloves and using his master keys, he quickly opens the front door. Inside he looks through the dresser drawers and finds bras, black lace lingerie, silk panties and silk stockings. Hanging in a garment bag in the closet is an elaborate Victorian-style woman's dress, a fifties mini-skirt, and a low-cut cotton blouse. *Wow! a cross-dresser.*

The cottage consists of a small combination living room-kitchen, two bedrooms and a screened porch. The clock radio is identical to the one in his room. He substitutes the Semco surveillance clock-radio for it, and sets it to start recording at 8 p.m. He positions it so that the camera is focused on the bed, the area in front of the bed, and the doorway entrance. He closes and locks the front door and returns to the pool area.

He has almost twelve hours before the video turns on. He has heard many nice things about Key West from his neighbors, David and Richard, and it is only two hours away. Where did they say to have lunch? Blue Heaven, yes, I'll drive to Key West, have lunch, and spend the afternoon sight-seeing.

CHAPTER 35

IT IS NOON when Alex drives across the causeway onto the island of Key West. After stopping for directions, he finds the Blue Heaven restaurant and has lunch. After lunch Alex goes sightseeing. Following a typical tourist path, he visits the Ernest Hemingway Home and Museum where the famous writer lived in the 1930s. He is surprised to find over thirty cats roaming the premises as cats did when Hemingway lived there. After walking through the coach house where the famous author did his writing, he does what Hemingway did every afternoon at about one o'clock when he quit writing, he goes to Sloppy Joe's and has one of Hemingway's favorite drinks, a Daiquiri.

Wanting to see how an American president lived while on vacation, he visits the Harry Truman Summer White House and is amused to learn that President Truman often jump-started his vacation days with a morning shot of whiskey.

The last couple of hours on the island Alex spends exploring the marinas, docks, streets, restaurants and pubs of the Historic Seaport District. He wants to stay for the famous Key West sunset, but he knows that staying means not getting back to Islamorada until after eight.

Alex leaves Key West at five-thirty and times his return to

Islamorada so that he is parked on Industrial Drive outside the Mooring's at ten minutes to eight. A cloth briefcase fitted with a frequency audio-video receiver, a 6.5 MHz audio sub-carrier and a 3db dipole omni-directional antenna lay on the front seat beside him. He places the 12VDC adapter in the cigarette lighter and plugs the power supply line into the cigarette lighter.

At eight o'clock he hears footsteps, a cough, and other sounds that tell him the audio portion of the transmitter is operating. After waiting about five minutes he hears Foster say, "Miss Bernhardt, my name is Albert Lonigan, and I am a staff reporter with *The New York Times*."

Foster's voice, Alex says to himself. *Does he also play Sarah Bernhardt?*

A squeaky, high pitched voice says. *Parlez vous Français?*

"I'm sorry Miss Bernhardt, but I don't speak French. My editor told me that this interview would be conducted entirely in English."

"*Non! non*! I am Sarah Bernhardt, the greatest actress of the 19th century. Even when I toured the United States, I did not perform in English, always in French!" There is a pause. "It annoys me that Americans never make the effort to learn any language but their own."

"Does this mean that I've traveled all the way from New York for nothing? My editor told me that you requested this interview in order to reveal something historically significant about your life. It would seem unfair to deprive history of a worthy footnote simply because of my language limitations."

"You are, of course, quite right. I assume young man that you have properly prepared for this interview by reading about my career and life."

"Yes, Miss Bernhardt. I've read everything I could find that's been written about you, and that's quite a lot."

"Millions of words have been written and recorded about my life, but no one has told the world about the consuming passion of my mature years. Why? Because I never revealed it. It is an omission that needs correcting. I want the world to know about it."

"Forgive me for interrupting Miss Bernhardt, but isn't the dress you are wearing similar to the dress that the painter Alphonse Mucha painted in his famous graphic to promote your role in the play *Gismonda*."

"Yes! Yes! Your astute observation brings me to the secret that I wish to reveal. When I saw Alfons's finished design, I loved it, and I asked to see the artist. When that beautiful Czech walked into my salon, it was love at first sight. No poet has or ever will be able to express in words the emotional force that swept through me when I first saw Alfons. And you must spell his name Alfons and not Alphonse for that was his preference."

"How old were you at the time?"

"As I recall it was near Christmas, 1894. I was fifty, and my dear Alfons was thirty-six. History has recorded that the *Gismonda* graphic launched Alfons's career, and it did, but it also led to a bond of love between us that allowed Alfons to transcend his earthly talents and create the beautiful, sensuous Mucha women that still captivate the art world. Alfons often told me that every woman he ever painted after he met me was infused with his love for me."

"That is a very touching story, Miss Bernhardt, and a part of your life that I certainly have never read."

"It is, I suppose, but a footnote, as you put it, but a significant footnote that I wish to share with history." There is a pause. "If you are going to be here tomorrow, you will have an opportunity to hear Marilyn Monroe in spiritual levitation reveal that her death was not suicide but murder. She will tell you who the murderer is. It will shock the world."

"Can you tell me in advance?"

"No! No! You must be here tomorrow to find out."

I would like to stay for that myself, Alex thinks.

CHAPTER 36

ALEX DRIVES BACK to the Miami airport, but it is too late for a flight to Atlanta. He books a morning flight and stays at a nearby airport hotel. Early the next morning while reading the *Miami Herald,* his eye catches the byline: "Atlanta Lawyer Commits Suicide." His body tightens when he reads, "Harvey Slinger, the deceased's employer, said that he could think of no reason why Mr. Geronsky would take his own life. . . ."

KIA HAS JUST finished showering when the phone rings. It is Alex.

"Kia, have you heard about Harvey Slinger's associate?"

"I didn't know he had an associate."

"He killed himself."

"What? Who killed himself? What are you talking about?" she says with a trace of annoyance.

"I read in this morning's *Miami Herald* that a man by the name of Stilton Geronsky, who worked in Slinger's law office, killed himself last night at Slinger's office."

There is puzzled silence at Kia's end. "I went to bed early. I didn't listen to the late news. This is the first I've heard about it."

"I'll be back in Atlanta before noon, and I'll give you a call. Find out as much as you can about this Geronsky suicide."

"You went to Florida?"

"Yes."

"How did you make out?"

"Beyond belief. Can we get together tonight?"

Kia thinks for a moment. "Let's meet here at six-thirty."

KIA AND ALEX view the video of Nelson Foster prancing around his cottage bedroom dressed as Sarah Bernhardt. Later at dinner Kia mentions something of interest to Alex.

"Natalie Johnson, Miss Talbot's girlfriend, stopped by today and said that she and Miss Talbot are traveling to Berlin tomorrow for two days."

"Why Berlin? Did she say?"

"Yes. Miss Talbot has business there. From Berlin they're going to Prague where Miss Talbot is going to buy turtles for her Japanese garden."

"Why did Natalie stop by to talk with you?"

"She didn't come by specifically to see me. She stopped in for information on sights to visit in Berlin while Miss Talbot is working. She just happened to ask me. She's very nice, very friendly."

"Did she say what kind of turtles?"

"No, just that their shells have beautiful yellow and black colors that resemble a starburst. She said that Prague is the only place where they can be purchased."

Why would Talbot go to Prague to buy turtles for her Japanese garden? Alex wonders. It is 5 a.m. in Prague. It is too early to call his ex-KGB friend, Mikhail, in Prague, but he will email him when he gets home.

CHAPTER 37

ALEX ARISES THE next morning and goes for a run through Piedmont Park. While Alex jogs through the early mist, Lester Hammond is in his New York penthouse pouring a cup of freshly-brewed coffee. He checks his Palm Pilot for the private number of Boris Forsenko, a Russian underworld acquaintance he met a few years earlier. He jots the number on a post-it, puts it in the pocket of his tailor-made silk slacks, and takes the elevator to street level. He walks east two blocks, turns into the lobby of a well-known hotel, finds a bank of public telephones, and makes a call.

BORIS FORSENKO STEPS out of the shower and is toweling down when the telephone rings. He answers, "Forsenko here."

"Boris Forsenko, this is Moscow. I want to cash-in that chit you gave me."

For a split second the message doesn't register, and then Forsenko remembers. "You name it, Moscow, and you got it," he says, with a heavy accent.

"I suspect that your phone may be tapped. Write this number down and call me back from a pay telephone." There is a pause. "Can you do that in the next fifteen minutes?"

"Yes," Forsenko says.

Hammond gives him the number of the pay telephone he is calling from.

Sixteen minutes later the phone rings. Hammond picks up, and Forsenko asks, "What's your name?"

"Moscow," Hammond says. "Are you calling from a pay phone?"

"Yes, but what makes you think my home phone is bugged?"

"Common sense. What I have to say is confidential so we must meet alone."

"I always travel with bodyguards, but I trust you, Moscow. You tell me where, and I'll leave the boys outside."

Lester Hammond thinks quickly. Some place public where he will not be recognized, and where Forsenko will not feel threatened. The Brooklyn Botanical Garden pops into his head. He attended a Christmas party there at the Palm House sponsored by the Edison Corporation. The party included a visit next door to the Steinhardt Conservatory. He remembers it well, and the tropical plant section would be perfect.

"Let's meet at ten o'clock at the Brooklyn Botanical Garden."

"Where's that?" Forsenko says. "I've never been there."

"The parking lot for both the Brooklyn Museum and the Botanical Garden are located on Washington Street. Traveling from Brighton Beach, the parking lot is on the left, a half block before you reach Eastern Parkway. The entrance gate to the Botanical Garden is opposite the rear of the museum. I want you to meet me in the Tropical Pavilion located in the Steinhardt Conservatory. Just follow the signs along the walkway that lead to the Steinhardt Conservatory. The Tropical Pavilion is located on the lower level. There are three pavilions on the lower level, but you can't confuse it with the other pavilions because the word 'Tropical' is written on the glass door." *He's never going to remember all this.* "Maybe," Hammond suggests, "you should write the directions down."

"I have."

"Good. When you enter the Tropical Pavilion there is a circular path, walk to your left until you meet me. And Boris, come alone. What I have to say to you is very confidential."

"I understand."

STANDING IN THE Tropical Pavilion between coffee and tea shrubs, Lester Hammond thinks back to when he first met Boris Forsenko in the bar at the International Hotel on Red Square in January 1992. It was a bitter cold night with a snowstorm swirling outside. Hammond had come to Moscow a week earlier for the purpose of finding out if it was politically possible to establish a business beachhead in the emerging new Russia. After a series of talks with high level Gorbachev bureaucrats, he concluded that with the dissemination of the proper bribes his investigative business would receive the cooperation of the Russian authorities.

Feeling good about the prospects of opening a new office in Moscow, and in anticipation of his departure from Russia in the morning, Hammond was about to order a brandy when the man next to him said in halting English, "You look happy. I'll buy you a drink. I'm not happy, but I'll buy me a drink too. What will you have?"

Hammond gave the man a quick once-over. He was well dressed, had a pleasant smile, and Hammond felt like talking to someone. All of his business associates had left for the United States. *Why not*, he thought. "Thank you. I'll have a Courvoisier."

The man gave the drink order in Russian. While the bartender prepared their drinks, they introduced themselves. The Russian's name was Boris Forsenko, and he blamed his sadness on not being allowed to immigrate to the United States to join members of his family in Brooklyn, New York. He explained that the American immigration authorities had rejected his application for a green card because of a sullied background that included a number of minor criminal run-ins with the Communist justice system. As their conversation continued into the night, accompanied by many drinks, Hammond grew to like Forsenko and decided to help him immigrate to the United States.

Hammond's direct intercession through well-connected immigration officials resulted in the department reversing itself and allowing Forsenko to immigrate in October 1992. At each step along the way, Forsenko was made aware of Hammond's efforts on his behalf. Three days after his arrival in Brooklyn, Forsenko called Hammond.

"Mr. Hammond, I know the only reason I'm here is because of you. I hope someday I'll be able to return the favor. If you ever need something done that you can't get done through your own resources, call me, and I'll do it for you. Introduce yourself as Moscow. Moscow will be the code name for me to remember this promise. Here's my number."

THE STEINHARDT CONSERVATORY is a complex of all-glass greenhouses. From where Hammond is inside, he can see the pathway leading to the entrance. He watches as Forsenko approaches accompanied by four men. His companions stop at the entrance, and Forsenko enters alone.

Within a minute Forsenko swaggers around the Tropical Pavilion gravel path. He is a bit heavier and grayer than when Hammond last saw him in Moscow but better dressed. He is wearing a brown English tweed suit that fits his fireplug-like physique. He is about five feet six inches, has large arms, a thick chest and a large head. He stops three feet from Hammond and places his hands on his hips. His face breaks into a grin. "You ain't changed a bit. In fact, you look better than when I last seen you."

"How can you remember?" Hammond says, with a chuckle, "You were drunk."

"So were you!"

They shake hands. Stepping back, Hammond says, "I can't say that what I've heard has been nice, but I've heard that you've been very successful since reaching our shores."

"Yeah, yeah," Forsenko says, pleased with himself. Suddenly his face stiffens. "Where'd you hear that?"

"You forget, Boris, I operate the largest investigative company in the world. It's my business to know what everyone is doing, especially those whom I sponsor into this country."

"Yeah, Mr. Hammond, if it wasn't for you I wouldn't be here, and I'll never forget that."

They are standing not more than two feet apart and an awkward silence sets in. Finally Forsenko says, "Who is he, and where does he live?"

"His name is Alex Ivanovich. He's an ex-KGB scumbag who lives in Atlanta, Georgia. He's what you call in Russian, a *necheta*." Hammond reaches inside his suit jacket and withdraws an envelope. "Everything you need to know about this man is in here." Hammond hands the envelope to Forsenko.

Forsenko notices that Hammond is wearing gloves. Hammond continues, "Where he lives, where he works, his KGB background, everything including photographs of him."

"You want him killed?" Hammond nods. "Ex-KGB, it'll be a pleasure."

"Boris, there is to be no connection in this matter to me. Recopy the information in the envelope and then destroy everything that you now hold in your hand. Do you understand?"

"I understand."

"This is the last time we will speak. I'll read about Ivanovich in the Atlanta newspapers."

They shake hands. Hammond watches through the glass wall as Forsenko joins his entourage and trudges back toward the parking area.

WHEN FORSENKO ARRIVES at his office, he calls his principal operative in Moscow and explains that he needs an experienced hit man, a professional assassin, who can fly to New York immediately for the assignment details, do the job, and return to Russia before discovery of the body.

The Moscow contact says, "I know the man for the job. He

speaks and reads enough English to make his way. It is a question of his availability. He is much in demand, but Boris, he is very expensive."

"Under the circumstances, a price within reason will be no problem."

"I will contact him and let you know something as soon as possible."

At 3 p.m. New York time, 11 p.m. Moscow time, Forsenko hears back from Moscow. The assassin, Igor Kalogin, "is the best in the business, available and prepared to leave Moscow whenever you wish. His price: $35,000 plus expenses."

"Tell him to get on a plane, and we'll meet him when he arrives at Kennedy Airport," Forsenko says.

IGOR KALOGIN IS met in the reception lounge at the John F. Kennedy International Airport by Forsenko and his first-in-command, Vladimior Roskovsky, and whisked off to a nearby hotel. He is thoroughly briefed on the assignment and given a ticket for travel to Atlanta in the morning aboard Delta Air Lines flight 695. It is agreed that upon the successful completion of the assignment Forsenko will wire $35,000 and expenses to the Russian's numbered account in the Cayman Islands.

In a humorous exchange between the assassin and Forsenko, Forsenko says, "How will I know you've completed the job so that I can wire the money?"

"I'll call you. But if you want real proof, I'll ship his body to you."

"No, no, don't do that," Forsenko says, laughing, "just call. I'll take your word."

CHAPTER 38

FOUR DAYS AFTER Forsenko meets the Russian assassin at Kennedy International Airport a crate arrives at the Brighton Beach Moscow Social Club. A pounding on the front door catches the attention of a Forsenko underling who, on seeing the size of the crate, orders it taken to the backyard. It is standard procedure at the Russian social club to x-ray every in-coming package. The underling and an assistant plug the portable x-ray machine into an extension cord and x-ray the contents of the crate.

The x-rays reveal a human body inside the crate. They run into the house screaming.

Roskovsky and Sadkov are in their offices on the second floor and hear the commotion. They race to the yard, turn on the x-ray machine, and verifier that inside the crate, in a fetal position, is the body of a large man. Sadkov wonders whether it is the body of Ivanovich or the assassin. The x-ray views are blurry and a positive identification cannot be made. Forsenko is in East Rutherford, New Jersey at the time, and Roskovsky alerts him to this startling development.

"That crazy bastard really sent the body to me? I thought he was kidding." Forsenko says. "No wonder I never heard from him."

"We can't tell whose body's in the crate. Too many shadows," Roskovsky replies.

"Take the box to the basement," Forsenko orders, "and find out who it is. I'll be back in an hour."

The four men carry the crate to the basement and take it apart.

Forty minutes later, Forsenko bursts through the front door, hurries down the basement steps and finds his associates in a huddle. He shoves his way between them and halts abruptly. On the floor surrounded by wooden shards, half in and half out of a large plastic bag, are the remains of one of Russia's most feared assassins.

Forsenko lets out a gasp and turns away. "The dirty son-of-a-bitch sent the rotten corpse back to me. He'll pay for this. He'll pay for this if it's the last thing I do."

FORSENKO IMMEDIATELY CONTACTS a concrete contractor in the Red Hook section of Brooklyn. He orders a six inch thick concrete shell measuring seven feet by four feet by three feet. Forsenko has used the services of this particular contractor on other occasions, and he knows their transaction will remain secret.

"When can you have the form ready for the deposit?" Forsenko asks.

"When do you want it?" The contractor replies.

"It's almost four now. I think we should bring the deposit over after dark. To be on the safe side, let's make it at ten."

"It will be ready. Come to warehouse number three. I'll leave the outside lights on."

"After we make the deposit and you pour the concrete over the deposit, how long will it take for it to set and dry?"

"Ten or fifteen minutes."

"That's all?"

"Yeah."

"How's that possible?"

"It depends on how much calcium chloride I add to the water to be mixed with the cement. If you're in a hurry I'll add twenty percent, and it will set and dry in a few minutes."

"Add the twenty percent. I want to give the deposit a quick bath." Forsenko pauses, "The last time we did this, you provided a truck with a hitch and a trailer to move the form to the boat. Do you still have them?"

"Yeah, where's your boat docked?"

"Sheepshead Bay."

"Okay. I'll tow it there myself but have the boat waiting. You'll also need strong men to carry it on board. And, Mr. Forsenko, bring ten thousand dollars cash."

CHAPTER 39

WITHIN THIRTY-TWO hours of learning that the president of Co-ca-Cola is heading to Prague to buy turtles, Alex is aboard an airliner for Paris with a connection on to Prague. Alex has puzzled over why Sharon Talbot is traveling to Prague to buy turtles. Why Prague? He can't figure it out, but he plans on spending a day there before Talbot arrives to try and find the answer.

AN HOUR AFTER Alex's Delta 747 leaves Atlanta for Paris Kia is in the kitchen cleaning up from dinner with her back to the television. A local news reporter is giving an up-date on the Geronsky suicide. She turns and glances at the television. She physically flinches when she sees the portrait photograph of Stilton Geronsky. She looks more closely at the photograph. It is the face of the strange looking man she passed in front of the Hyatt Hotel. There is no doubt in her mind. It is Stilton Geronsky she saw at the Hyatt.

Before going to bed, Kia turns on the ten o'clock news and watches an interview between Harvey Slinger and a local news reporter.

Reporter: Were you aware that your associate kept a gun in his office?

Slinger: No. I had no idea. In fact, I still haven't been able to find out when or where he purchased the gun. If I had known he had a gun, I would not have allowed him to bring it to the office, certainly not without a permit. And it's my understanding that no permit had ever been issued for this weapon.

Reporter: I take it that you don't approve of keeping firearms in your law office.

Slinger: No, of course not. I've never owned a gun and never felt the need to have one.

Kia is stunned by Harvey's last remark. *That's not what you told me, you liar.*

THE FIRST TIME Kia met Harvey was at the Atlanta Athletic Club. After working out, she stopped by the club restaurant for a quick snack. A few minutes later Harvey sat at her table. He introduced himself and they fell into conversation.

Kia remembers Harvey telling her at their first meeting that because "my law office is in a tough neighborhood, I keep a .38 Smith & Wesson revolver in my desk drawer." He even told her that he bought the gun in Trenton, New Jersey.

She turns off the television when the phone rings. "Kia, it's Harvey."

"Funny you'd call. I was just watching you on television."

"It was really terrible."

"I'm sure."

"Kia, there's something I need to talk with you about. It's important."

Kia glances at the bedside clock. It is almost ten-thirty. "Okay, go ahead."

"Not over the telephone. I know you don't have time to come to my office, so I thought we might meet for a drink after work tomorrow."

Tomorrow she is supposed to meet her friend Patty for dinner, she remembers. "What's it about?"

"It's confidential, but it will interest you."

"If what you have to tell me won't take more than a half hour, I can meet you at Veni Vidi Vici's at six. I'm meeting a friend there for dinner at six-thirty."

"Perfect. I'll be waiting in the bar area."

CHAPTER 40

ALEX'S PLANE SETS down in Prague in mid-morning. He clears customs and walks into the international reception lounge carrying a suitcase. He sees Mikhail standing near a far wall smoking a cigarette. Mikhail is wearing jeans, cowboy boots, and a black leather jacket. The past eight years have been good to Mikhail. He has put on a tad of weight, and his sandy hair had thinned and grayed a bit, but otherwise he looks fit and prosperous.

Seeing Alex, Mikhail throws his cigarette on the ground, steps on it, and moves toward him. They meet, hug, laugh, and in a brief moment renew their long friendship.

"How are Zhanna and your little one, Jana?"

"Zhanna is fine. She is pleased with my teaching position at the university, loves living in Prague, stays in shape by playing a lot of tennis, and is excited to see you. The little one, Jana, is no longer little. She is a beautiful young woman in her second year at university and, of course, has a boyfriend."

"What about you, Mikhail? You look terrific. Are you happy teaching chemistry and metallurgy?"

"Yes. I enjoy the prestige of being a professor and the daily contact with young people. It keeps me young. I'm not getting rich, but we live comfortably on my salary and have a nice house provided by the university. What about you, Alex? How do you like America?"

"I like America, but I haven't seen much of it because my vacation time each year is spent in Russia visiting Grigory. But I like the American people. They are friendly and generous. As for my job . . ." He shrugs equivocally. "It's not challenging, but it has its advantages."

"What do you do? I've heard that you own a limousine service."

Alex smiles, "If you consider owning one car a limousine service, then yes, that is what I do. I drive business executives around Atlanta."

They have reached Mikhail's car in the parking area outside the terminal.

They climb in and Alex asks, "What kind of car is this?"

"It's a Skoda, and it's made here in the Czech Republic."

"It's very attractive," Alex says, pushing back in the seat seeking more legroom.

"To move the seat back further, push down on the lever on the right side of the seat." Alex pushes on the lever and the seat slides back.

"My job is boring but it got me out of Russia at a time when my life was coming unraveled—my job, my marriage . . ." Alex falls silent as he gazes out the window and watches the countryside change from rural to urban as they approach the city. "After nineteen years in the KGB, I find that being my own boss and having time to myself is a nice change of pace." Alex's head is tilted upward against the headrest, his face expressionless. "Yes," he says, "I've become bored with what I've been doing but lately that has changed."

His last remark and tone of voice cause Mikhail to turn and look at him. Their eyes lock. "As much as I would like to stay with you and Zhanna, I can't."

"What? Zhanna will . . ."

Alex hushes him with a motion of his hand. "Mikhail listen to me. I've become involved in something that has already resulted in one attempt on my life. I survived that attempt only because I was warned in advance by a member of HAC."

"Who initiated the hit on you?"

"Although I have a strong suspicion, I don't know for sure who initiated it, but the assassin was a member of Boris Forsenko's crime syndicate that operates out of Brooklyn, New York. Whoever it is who wants me dead probably won't stop with one attempt, and I don't want you or Zhanna caught in the crossfire. That's why I can't stay with you."

They are crossing the Altava River at the Cechuv Bridge when Mikhail says, "I received your e-mail raising the question of why people come to Prague to buy turtles. I made some inquires and a friend tells me that he knows the answer." Mikhail lights a cigarette. "He is willing to talk with you provided that you agree to keep confidential what he tells you, and never reveal him as the source of the information."

"I have no problem with that. What's his name?"

"He wants to remain anonymous."

"Okay. If I don't know his name, I can't possibly tell anyone who it is that gave me the information."

Mikhail glances over at Alex. "I thought we would go directly to see my friend. He's going to talk with you in my office at the university." Mikhail snaps his fingers, "That's it. That's where you can stay. No one will find you there."

"Where?"

"In my office at the university. It has a sofa and a bathroom with a shower. Alex, it will be perfect!"

WHEN ALEX ENTERS Mikhail's office, he finds an old man is seated at a bare wooden table. The old man stands and acknowledges Alex with a nod and sits back down. Alex takes a seat across from the old man. The old man removes a slip of paper from his jacket pocket. He speaks in Russian with only a slight accent. "I am going to talk with you because our mutual friend, Mikhail Slavonovich, has assured me that whatever I tell you will be kept secret, and that you will never reveal that I'm the source of the information. With Mikhail here as a witness, do you agree to those terms as a condition of my talking to you on the subject of the procurement and sale of reptiles and other endangered species?"

"Yes," Alex says, without hesitation.

The old man's eyes show his ambivalence. "If it ever becomes known that I am the source of information that results adversely in any way with what goes on here, it will mean my death." The old man folds and unfolds the piece of paper as he speaks. "And though I am old, I am not yet ready to die."

"I understand your concerns, and I will never reveal what you tell me."

The old man reflects for a moment, and nods. "I believe you." The old man extends his hand. They shake hands. Mikhail excuses himself and leaves the room.

The old man folds the piece of paper, places it in his jacket, all the while studying Alex with small gray piercing eyes. "Why are you in Prague?" he asks.

"I'm here to find out why a certain person is coming to Prague to buy turtles and to use whatever information I obtain as an advantage in business negotiations."

"Blackmail?"

"No."

The old man continues staring at Alex. "Very well, we have our agreement. What is it you wish to know?"

Alex feels his body relax for the first time since entering the room. "The other night I learned that . . . I will refer to the person in question as 'this person.'" The old man nods, but he does not take his eyes off Alex. "I learned that this person comes to Prague to buy turtles for her Japanese garden. When I asked what kind of turtles, I was told that it is a turtle with a bright yellow

and black starburst on its shell. When I asked why she comes to
Prague to buy the turtles, I was told because Prague is where you
buy them. I've been to Prague many times, and I have never heard
that it is a clearing house for turtles."

The old man takes out a pack of cigarettes, lights one, and
sucks in deeply. When he exhales, the smoke curls in tight ringlets
and the muscles in his wrinkled face seem to relax. He holds the
pack of cigarettes out to Alex. Alex shakes his head. "You are wise
not to smoke. I've been trying to quit for many years. I've not
been able to quit, but I've cut back to five cigarettes a day." He
smiles, and then as if putting on a mask, his face becomes expressionless. He places the pack of cigarettes back in his jacket and
leans forward, his elbows and forearms resting on the table. "This
person has come to Prague to buy what are known as radiated
tortoises." He takes another pull on the cigarette. "It has a yellow
head and a domed shell that radiates yellow and black and gives
the impression of a starburst."

"Is it indigenous to Czechoslovakia?"

The old man shakes his head. "It is indigenous to only one
place on earth—Southwestern Madagascar."

"Then why doesn't this person go to Madagascar to buy these
tortoises? Why Prague?"

"It is illegal to sell them in Madagascar. They are an endangered species and protected by the Convention on International
Trade in Endangered Species."

"If it is illegal to buy them in Madagascar, why is it legal to
buy them here? It seems to . . ."

The old man interrupts with a wave of his hand. "Let me explain how the system works. The illegal traffic in rare and endangered animals and plants is conservatively estimated to be between
ten and twenty billion dollars a year. Mikhail told me that you now
live in the United States. That country alone spends more than
three billion dollars a year on such illegal sales. So you see, the
world has an insatiable appetite for rare animals. The value of a

radiated tortoise is determined by three factors. The condition of the tortoise as reflected in the brilliance of its shell's starburst colors. The sex of the tortoise is important. A mature female is worth the most because it can bear offspring, and, of course, availability, or what our new capitalistic system calls supply and demand."

"How much does a radiated tortoise in excellent condition sell for?"

"Twenty thousand dollars. I mentioned that the radiated tortoise lives only in Madagascar, a biological paradise. But Madagascar is also one of the poorest countries in the world. Its impoverished people know that in other countries these tortoises are valued as pets, and they can sell as many of them as they can capture, or steal. The radiated tortoise population is an endangered species, rapidly dwindling, which makes it one of the most desired species of tortoise on earth. And soon they will all be gone."

"How do the turtles get from Madagascar to Prague?"

"Through smuggling which of course is limited only by one's imagination. Ironically, tortoises are ideal contraband because they can survive long trips without food and water."

"What is the most common method of smuggling?"

"Madagascar lies in the Indian Ocean off the southeast coast of Africa. It is separated from Africa by a narrow channel only two hundred and fifty miles wide. The looters confine the captured tortoises to holding pens until moving them to smugglers' boats waiting offshore. The tortoises are then transported to South Africa or the Island of Reunion where they are mixed with tortoises that were bred in captivity. The smugglers fit the illegal tortoises with forged permits that certify that they never lived in the wild, that is, that they are captive-bred. For this system to work the authorities must look the other way, and they do, for which they are handsomely paid. With the new legal certificates of captive-bred, the smuggled tortoises are freely transported in commerce."

"If the false papers can be obtained in South Africa, why come to Prague?"

"Because an old law still on the books here permits dealers to possess animals that fall into the endangered species classification but does not allow those dealers to export them. Of course, with falsified documentation a common practice, exportation became easy and, over time, Prague became an emporium in the illegal trade of endangered species." The old man shrugs. "I guess you might call it tradition to come to Prague. Besides, Prague is such a beautiful city."

"How many dealers are there in Prague who specialize in Madagascar starburst tortoises?"

The old man stares at him, and a palpable silence hangs in the air. The old man pushes back in his chair. "There are several," he says, standing and walking to the window. He looks out for a moment at the well-kept lawn, then turns and faces Alex. "But there is only one with whom the rich deal—the House of Havlacke."

"Why is that?"

"The House of Havlacke sells only the highest quality reptiles, whether lizards, snakes or tortoises. As you probably know, wealthy people want the best. The Havlackes have been in business for almost a hundred years and have survived two world wars and communism. The business is operated today by a fourth generation Havlacke, Milos Havlacke."

"If I wanted to discuss the purchase of starburst tortoises with Milos Havlacke, where would I find him?"

"At 20 Parizska."

"Is that off Old Town Square?"

"Yes. Parizska is one of Prague's most fashionable business areas, and the Havlacke business is on the fifth or top floor of one of the most beautiful nineteenth century mansions in Prague."

"I take it that the Havlacke family is wealthy."

The old man nods slowly. "Yes, quite wealthy."

It is obvious to Alex that the old man has at some time worked for the Havlackes. His knowledge of their business and manner of speaking is far too detailed and confident to be based on hearsay.

"Is there any particular room or place in the building where Milos Havlacke conducts the sale of tortoises?

"One place only, his office." Anticipating Alex's next question he adds, "It is the large, elegantly appointed office to the right of the reception area. From his balcony, clients have a magnificent view of Prague and the Altava."

Both men fall silent, holding one another's stares. The old man speaks first. "If you are planning on visiting Mr. Havlacke's office alone, you will need to know the security code. The office is protected by an alarm system that was manufactured in France. If the correct code is not entered into the system within thirty seconds after the front door is opened, an audible alarm sounds in the office and at the police station three blocks away." The old man pauses and closes his eyes.

"I'm planning on visiting Havlacke's office, but I don't know the code."

The old man's heavy-lidded eyes open partially, but he says nothing. Alex feels his heart quicken as he frames the next question. ""I would appreciate if I could learn the code, and under no circumstances will I ever reveal how I came about it."

The old man turns and looks out the window, his small frame silhouetting the picturesque campus beyond. After a moment he turns and faces Alex. "The code numbers are 0726. Can you remember that without writing it down?"

Alex repeats the number to himself and nods.

"This is important," the old man says shaking his index finger for emphasis. "When you leave, reset the alarm by reversing the numbers 6270."

Alex repeats the numbers out loud, and nods. He walks over and extends his hand. The old man takes it. "Thank you for sharing this information."

The old man nods and leaves the room.

CHAPTER 41

WAITING FOR MIKHAIL to return, Alex looks around the office. In addition to the table where Alex and the old man talked, there is a desk, a computer, and a leather sofa along the far wall and a window. Along the back wall is a bookcase and a closed door. Alex opens the door and steps into a small bathroom containing a sink, toilet, and shower stall. Nothing fancy, but adequate for his stay in Prague.

A few minutes later Mikhail arrives. "Well," he says, "did you learn why people come to Prague to buy turtles?"

"Yes. Thanks."

"Have you had a chance to inspect my office?" Mikhail says, waving his hand around.

"Yes. It will do very nicely, but won't your colleagues question my presence here?"

"No. This is not the Soviet Union. While you were talking with my old friend, I contacted most of them and explained that you are a friend and will be staying here for a couple of days." Mikhail hands Alex two keys. "The large key is to the building and the small key to my office." Alex pockets the keys and gives his friend a hug. "Now, we must get you a car."

"I won't need a car today. My business here doesn't begin until tomorrow, and I would rather use public transportation and walk.

It will give me more flexibility. From what I hear, parking in Prague is terrible."

"You have heard right. It's awful."

"I want to take you and Zhanna to dinner tonight. Where would you like to go? I hope it can be someplace casual where we can sit outside, drink beer and enjoy this beautiful weather."

"I know the restaurant. It's in Old Town Square. It's called U Prince. You can't miss it. It's just across the square from the Astronomical Clock. Although they don't take reservations, I know the owner, and I'll get reservations for eight. Will that give you enough time?"

Alex glances at his watch, "More than enough. I'll see you and Zhanna there at eight. Tell Zhanna I'm excited to see her."

Alex decides against sight-seeing Prague. Instead, he takes a nap.

He has just finished showering and dressing when the phone rings twice and stops. A few seconds later it resumes ringing, the signal he and Mikhail arranged. He answers.

"Alex, it's Mikhail. I just received a phone call from Vladimir Kushner in Odessa. He . . ."

"I remember Kushner. Didn't he spend most of his career in the Fifteenth Directorate, Security of Government Installations?"

"Yes. He lives in Odessa now. I saw him a month ago there when I went to visit my mother. We had lunch and reminisced about some of our KGB experiences. Your name came up, and he remembers you. He works for the Ukrainian Government in counter-intelligence. As you know, he's a member of HAC. He called to tell me that he learned from a reliable source in the Russian underworld that a Russian gangster living in New York by the name of Boris Forsenko has offered a $100,000 reward to anyone who kills you." Alex's heart drops. "Alex, you must be extremely careful. A small Russian criminal element lives in Prague, and it is possible that one of them will spot you. Many of these men will kill their mothers for $100,000."

Mikhail lowers his voice, "I have a gun in the office. I think you should take it with you. It's in the bottom desk drawer on the right. The desk key is taped to the inside cover of *War and Peace*. The book is located on the bottom shelf of the bookcase."

Alex walks over to the bookcase, bends over and pulls out *War and Peace*. He opens it and the key is taped to the inside front cover. He unlocks the desk, pulls open the bottom right drawer, and there, wrapped in a white towel, is the standard issue of the Russian military and the KGB, a double action Makarov automatic. The clip is fully loaded. He slips it between his belt and waist, and picks up the phone. "I have it, Mikhail, and I feel better already. I'll see you at U Prince in an hour."

CHAPTER 42

ALEX ARRIVES AT U Prince wearing a light-weight black leather jacket, khakis, and carrying a small black case containing the transmission components of an audio/video surveillance system that he plans installing in Milos Havlacke's office.

Zhanna and Mikhail are seated at an outside table located across the square from the old astronomical clock. The waiter is putting a pitcher of Staropramen beer on their table when Zhanna sees Alex. She jumps up, runs to him, throws her arms around his neck, and kisses him on both cheeks. "It is so good to see you, Alex." She looks up at him. "You haven't changed a bit."

"It's great to see you, Zhanna. You really haven't changed, still vibrant and beautiful." She is in her early forties, long blonde hair, sparkling blue eyes and not an ounce of fat on her body.

Zhanna takes Alex's hand. As they walk to their table, she points to the black case. "Is this going to be a business meeting, or dinner with old friends?"

"It's something I have to take care of after dinner."

Mikhail pours three glasses of beer. They tip their glasses together and Zhanna says, "Just before you arrived, I had closed my eyes and thought back to that wonderful week that you, Tatyana,

Mikhail and I spent in Lucerne. Remember that lovely cottage on the lake we shared and the motor boat trips around the lake . . ."

"And taking the cable car and tram to the top of Mount Pilatus," Mikhail adds.

"How long ago was that?" Zhanna asks.

"Thirteen years," Alex says.

"Before we order dinner," Zhanna says, "I want to hear all about America."

AS THEY TALK, Alex senses someone watching him. He casually looks around and catches the stare of a chain smoking, seedy looking man at a nearby table. The man quickly looks away.

He's trying to figure out if I'm Alex Ivanovich. Damn it. I should have worn a disguise.

The man pulls out money, slaps it on the table, and hurriedly leaves after casting a glance at Alex.

During dinner Alex notices a man walking slowly in front of the outdoor tables, attempting to appear nonchalant as he looks into the crowd, his eyes hesitating a second too long on Alex. Moments later, the man, his eyes on Alex as he passes their table, enters the restaurant. *He's been sent to confirm my identity. They'll be waiting for me when I leave.*

It is almost midnight when Zhanna, Mikhail and Alex call it a night. Alex pays the bill, but when offered a ride to the university by Mikhail, he declines. Zhanna looks at Alex, her eyes clearly troubled. "Will I see you before you leave."

"I'm not sure you'll see me before I leave, but this I guarantee, lovely Zhanna; you'll see me again." They hug. The old astronomical clock strikes midnight.

CHAPTER 43

THERE ARE NO astronomical clocks in Atlanta to announce the time, but Harvey Slinger is punctual, and at six o'clock he's at Veni Vidi Vici's, nursing a martini in the bar area when Kia arrives. He stands and holds the chair for her.

He must want something, Kia thinks.

"What would you like to drink?" Harvey asks.

"Nothing, thank you," Kia says. "What's this about, Harvey?"

Looking down at his drink, Harvey runs his index finger around the rim of his glass. He looks up, glances around the room, and then focuses on Kia. "I suppose you're meeting your Russian co-conspirator here?"

"Now what's that supposed to mean?"

Harvey leans forward, pushing his face so close she can smell his bad breath. She pulls back. "You and that Russian are cooking up something that involves the Coca-Cola formula, and I want to know what it is."

Kia sits staring at him, the turned down corners of her mouth expressing her revulsion.

"I meant to get in touch with you earlier, but I've been consumed with these Anchor Hotel food poisoning cases."

"Oh? You're involved in that?"

"Yeah, I already have over seventy of those cases."

"You were at the dinner Friday night?" Kia says, curious to know more.

"Yeah, I even got sick myself after eating the salad. Fortunately, I didn't need hospital treatment."

"Your associate, Mr. Geronsky, did he also get sick?"

"No, no, he didn't attend." Kia doesn't believe him. "You know, Kia, a funny thing happened last week. A new client came in. He had an accident, injured his back, as so many of my clients do. A friend referred him to me."

Kia inches forward in her chair, wondering where he is going with the conversation. "I don't remember how it came about, but he mentioned that his grandfather invented the recipe that is used today to make Coca-Cola."

He glances at his glass; it's empty. He signals for the waiter's attention and waves him over. He looks at Kia. "Are you sure you won't reconsider and have a drink?" She shakes her head. He looks at the waiter. "I'll have another."

Harvey's grinning. "Now, where was I? Oh, yes, I was talking about my new client. Guess what he told me? He told me that your sleazy Russian boyfriend cheated him out of the Coca-Cola formula. A family heirloom handed down to him from his grandfather." He belches. The smell is repulsive. "And guess what else? Mr. Calderman has retained me to get his formula back."

Kia forces herself to smile. "Why are you telling me? Why don't you tell Alex?"

"I wanted to tell the son-of-a-bitch, but he won't return my phone calls. In the past two days I've left three messages on his answering machine, but he hasn't had the decency to call me back. And you know what else I'm going to do?" he says, shaking his finger in her face. "I'm going to have that Communist bastard shipped back to where he came from—Russia!"

A flash of anger races through her. She bites her lower lip to keep from saying anything, but as she stares at his arrogant,

THE SECRET FORMULA · 183

smirking face, the pieces began to fall in place. What started as a vague suspicion is now a clear indictment. She brushes a strand of hair from her forehead, leans forward, and says, "And do you know what I'm going to do for you? I'm going to see that you go to prison."

Harvey flinches, and the smirk fades. "What . . . what . . . are you crazy? You, you . . . you bitch."

"You and your associate arranged to poison those psychologists at the Anchor Hotel, and then you killed him. Dead men can't talk, can they, Harvey? I saw Geronsky at the Anchor Hotel Friday evening, and I have a witness." She pauses to let her words sink in. Slinger's face grows pale and beads of perspiration dot his forehead. "You shot Geronsky with a gun that you purchased in Trenton, New Jersey." Harvey's eyes widen. Kia senses he's scared. Savoring her words, she says, "It was your gun Harvey, not Geronsky's. Don't you think the police would like to know that? Guess what I'm going to do tomorrow morning? I'm going to tell the police what I know. They will trace the gun to you, Harvey. I also heard at work today that the health authorities are suspicious that the food poisoning was a deliberate act. I saw your associate coming from the Anchor Hotel, and I'm sure others saw him there too. And if that's the case . . ."

Kia's dinner companion Patty enters the restaurant. She sees Kia and approaches their table. "Hi Kia, I hope I'm not . . ."

Harvey gulps down his drink and jumps up. "You're full of shit Williams, and I'm not going sit here and put up with any more of your bullshit. I'll see you and your Commie friend in court." He brushes abruptly past Patty as he hurries out.

Kia sits back in her chair feeling enormous satisfaction. Her accusations were shots in the dark, but from his reactions, she hit the bull's-eye. *Yes, definitely, I'll go to the police tomorrow.*

Patty follows Harvey's departure in shocked surprise. Turning to Kia she asks, "What in hell was that all about?"

WAITING FOR THE valet attendant to bring his car, Harvey is furious and his mind a jumble of thoughts. *Killing Geronsky was easy and exciting. This bitch knows too much. If she tells the police that I bought the gun in Trenton, they'll trace it to me. How'd she find that out? If the police reconstruct Stilton's death with me in mind, they might conclude that I killed him. Did any of the kitchen-help see Stilton?* By the time the attendant pulls up with his car, Harvey has decided what he must do.

Harvey returns to his office, turns on the computer, brings up the contract he prepared for Kia and Alex, and jots her address on a piece of paper. He then goes online to www.mapquest.com, types in his office address and Kia's address, and prints a map with detailed directions to Kia's apartment.

Harvey's thoughts now turn to where and how to kill her. *In her apartment, of course, but how? Bludgeon her with a tire iron or strangle her?* He looks at his hands. His hands are small, but they are strong from daily exercise of squeezing a rubber ball. *But what if she screams? Put a pillow over her mouth. I'm ahead of myself. What if I can't get into her apartment? I'll have to kill her in the parking lot when she gets out of her car.* Harvey studies the directions to Kia's apartment and slips them into his pocket.

CHAPTER 44

ALEX WATCHES ZHANNA and Mikhail walk across the square in the direction of their car, and he thinks about the task ahead. The Coca-Cola president, Sharon Talbot, is flying to Prague in the morning so he must install the surveillance system in Milos Havlacke's office before she arrives. Parizska Street and the Havlacke building are just off the square, three blocks away. He is sure, however, that he will be followed. He decides to walk in the opposite direction, toward the river.

As he leaves the square and turns into a dark, narrow, twisting street, he senses that he is being followed. He glances over his shoulder. In the illumination from a street light, he sees a figure down the street moving in the building shadows toward him.

Alex continues walking at a normal pace until he comes to another dark, narrow street. He turns into it, sprints ahead, crosses the street and jumps into a storefront doorway.

Within seconds a man comes charging around the corner. He stops abruptly, his head jerking from side to side in an attempt to determine where Alex has gone. After a moment of hesitation, he races forward but stops at the end of the street. Seeing nothing, he turns and looks back down the street. There are many dark doorways fronting the buildings that line its long, narrow passage.

Alex smiles to himself. The game is now even. The hunted is about to become a hunter.

The man starts down the street looking for Alex hiding in one of the doorways. He moves from one side of the street to the other side, peering into each doorway. He carries something in his right hand. Alex, crouched against a near wall, thinks it's a gun. Alex removes the Makarov from under his belt. He checks it to be sure the safety is off. He will use it only as a last resort. A shot will attract attention. He moves the gun to his left hand.

The dark figure steps into the doorway. Alex springs forward sinking his fist into the assailant's stomach. The man doubles over. Alex clubs him behind the head with the butt of his gun. As the man falls to the ground his arms wrap around Alex's legs and pull Alex down. The man rolls on top of Alex, his hands flailing and reaching for Alex's throat. Swinging the Makarov with his left hand, Alex strikes him along side of the head. The man lurches backward. Alex jams the palm of his right hand under his assailant's chin and pushes up. The man falls on his side and rolls onto his stomach. Alex jumps on top of him. The man attempts to rise on his knees. Alex drops his gun, puts both hands under the man's chin and yanks his head up and twists it sideways. There is a loud crack. The man's body slumps to the ground. Alex again yanks the head. It wobbles in his hands. He feels the man's pulse. There is none. He's dead. Alex pulls the body completely into the doorway.

Alex rests on one knee, breathing in quick, short bursts. When he regains his breath, he picks up his gun and looks around for the dead man's weapon. He sees it in a corner of the doorway. Using his handkerchief, he picks it up and stuffs it in the man's jacket. He looks up and down the street. It is empty. Leaving the corpse in the doorway, he retrieves his black case and starts out. He takes only a few steps when he sees a large manhole cover. He reaches down and pulls up on the iron handle. The cover is heavy, but he manages to slide it to the side.

He returns to the doorway, takes hold of a leg, drags the body to the opening, dumps it in, and hears it splash in the sewer below. *That's your coffin, you bastard,* he says to himself as he slides the manhole cover back in place.

He looks around. There is no one in sight. He walks back to the doorway, picks up his black case, brushes himself off, runs his fingers through his hair, adjusts his clothing, and walks out into the night.

Walking back toward Old Town Square, Alex feels nauseous. The events of the past ten minutes have unnerved him. He begins thinking about his own mortality, a thought that rarely occupies his thoughts.

THE HAVLACKE BUILDING is easily identified. It is a five story nineteenth century gothic mansion made from local quarried stone, and the most imposing building on fashionable Parizska Street. Alex walks around to the street at the rear of the building and discovers that a seven foot iron gate blocks entrance to the back doors. He pulls on latex gloves and climbs over the gate. He faces two large oak doors with glass paneling. He shins his flashlight along the edges of the paneling and along the inside walls looking for a security system. There is none. Using a KGB skill learned years ago, he picks the lock and enters.

He bounds up the steps two at a time until he reaches the top floor. A small brass plaque on a large mahogany door reads, "Havlacke Enterprises." Using a flashlight he examines the lock. It is the standard bolt type, and he quickly picks it.

On entering he moves the flashlight beam along the left reception wall and spots the security pad. He punches in the numbers the old man gave him: 0726. He waits. The alarm does not sound. The old man's information is correct. The system is disarmed.

On the opposite side of the reception area he sees Milos Havlacke's office. It is furnished as the old man described, an elegant combination of classical French antiques, Oriental rugs, and

French impressionist paintings. Alex moves the flashlight beam around the room and across the high vaulted ceiling looking for a hiding place for the surveillance equipment. Bookshelves lined with books, paintings and decorative objects form the entire back wall of the office.

An opaque glass sphere with a removable top catches his attention. It sits at eye level on a shelf and faces into the room. The sphere is about the size of a basketball, hand blown, and patterned with alternating black and white geometric squares. It is perfect. He drills two small holes into the sphere with a special glass bit. He drills two larger holes opposite the pinholes to allow for the antennas. He loads the transmitter, battery pack, and antenna connector into the sphere. Next, he positions the camera lens and microphone behind the pinholes, extends the antennas through the larger holes, and replaces the top. He finishes the installation in less than a half-hour.

Before leaving, he resets the alarm system by following the old man's instructions. He punches in the numbers 6270, steps into the hall and closes the door. He pushes on the door to be sure it's locked. He leaves the building the way he entered.

CHAPTER 45

WHEN ALEX LEAVES the Havlacke building and heads back to Mikhail's office, Harvey Slinger is executing his plan to murder Kia. On the drive to Kia's apartment, Harvey is surprised at how calm he feels. Killing Stilton was easy. He is proud to have proved to himself that he could kill another human. It makes the task in front of him much easier. *I've got to do it,* he tells himself.

Using the Mapquest directions, he has no difficulty finding Kia's apartment. He parks out front, walks into the apartment-unit foyer and checks the directory. He is relieved to find that her apartment is on the ground level. He returns to his car, drives to a street outside the apartment complex and parks. He removes the tire iron and a flashlight from the trunk, slips the tire iron inside his belt, and the flashlight in his pants pocket.

Keeping in the shadows, he walks to the rear of her apartment. The area behind the apartment is dark. He picks his way through the darkness by staying close to the building. The only sounds in the night air are the chirping of crickets and the crunch of his feet on the gravel walkway. Stopping beneath a window to Kia's apartment, he places the flashlight against the window frame and turns it on. He studies the window and the frame carefully and decides that the apartment is not equipped with an alarm system. Aiming the light beam on the window lock, he removes the tire iron from his belt and breaks the glass above the lock. He slips his hand inside, and releases the lock. He remains still and listens. He can vaguely hear a television playing in one of the apartments. Satisfied that he has not been seen or heard, he lifts the window and climbs in.

Inside he lowers the window but having decided to leave the way he came he does not lock it. Flashing the light beam around the room he discovers he's in Kia's bedroom. He moves out of the bedroom. Using only the flashlight, he explores the apartment. In addition to the master bedroom and bathroom, there is a kitchen, a small adjoining dining room and a living room. He studies each room carefully, noting the position of the furniture, the location of the light switches, and the areas that allow movement from one room to another.

He now turns his attention to how to kill her, but a troubling thought keeps interrupting his thinking. What if she doesn't return alone? She mentioned that Alex is out of town, and he saw Kia's dinner companion as he was leaving the restaurant. Still, she might return with someone, and he has to plan for that contingency. Her bedroom is, he decides, the most strategic place to wait for her. If she brings someone home, he will use the tire iron. If she is alone, he will strangle her when she enters the bedroom and smother her screams with a pillow.

The bedroom light switch is located to the right of the bedroom entrance. He removes a pillow from the bed, positions a chair inside the bedroom doorway near the light switch and settles down to await her return. The pillow and the tire iron rest in his lap.

WHILE HARVEY SITS anxiously checking his watch in anticipation of Kia's return, Kia and her friend, Patty, enjoy dinner, a bottle of wine, dessert and café latte.

At dinner Patty says, "I know it's none of my business, but I'm still going to ask. Who was that creepy-looking guy you were talking to when I came in?"

Kia explains that she arrived early and while waiting for Patty, "That creep came up with a martini in his hand, sat down and started talking about how much money he's making in the stock market." Kia shrugs and rolls her eyes, "I told him to get lost."

Patty shakes her head. "How does a creep like that think he's got a chance with a woman that looks like you. Besides, he's probably married with kids."

Kia and Patty haven't seen one another in three months and their conversation turns to work and the lack of a significant other in their lives. Kia is tempted to mention Alex but decides against it.

Kia and Patty leave the restaurant at nine o'clock and walk to the garage next door. The attendant brings Kia's car first. She and Patty say goodnight, promising to get together soon.

During the fifteen minute drive home, two men occupy Kia's thoughts—Alex and Harvey. She wonders how Alex made out in Prague, whether he is safe and well. His flight from Paris is scheduled to arrive Monday evening at eight-thirty. She will meet him. As she drives into her apartment complex, she thinks about how little evidence she has to support her suspicions of Harvey. She questions whether she should go to the police in the morning.

As Kia inserts the key into her apartment lock, she is still trying to decide whether to go to the police with her suspicions. The question has been at the back of her mind all evening. But the gun isn't a suspicion. Harvey told her that he owned a Smith & Wesson revolver, and that he purchased it at a gun shop in Trenton, New Jersey. Yes, she will go to the police, but for now, straight to bed.

Harvey hears her put the key into the lock. He stands up. There are no voices. He hears the door close. No voices are heard. *She's alone.* He lays the tire iron on the chair and presses his left shoulder against the light switch with the pillow in his left hand. He will wait until she touches him.

Without turning on a light, Kia moves through the darkness. Stepping into the bedroom she reaches for the light switch. Her hand brushes Harvey's left arm. He swings his right arm forward and around her throat and yanks her toward him. His chokehold is so tight and strong she can feel her breath rushing from her body. Instinctively her karate training comes into play. In a series of fluid, rhythmic motions not lasting more than a few seconds, her hands reach up to the choke hand and pull it away, relieving the pressure on her throat. At the same time she assumes the classic Tae Kwon Do horse stance, bending and spreading her feet parallel and two shoulder-widths apart and lowering her center of gravity. With a quick bowing motion, and using her right hip as the fulcrum, the one hundred and forty-five pound Slinger flips completely over her. His head and back slam onto the floor and his legs strike the doorframe. Kia jams her right knee into Slinger's right shoulder, pinning him to the floor. At the same time, she forces his left wrist back and by twisting it to the right rolls him onto his stomach. She then bends his left arm up behind his back in a hammerlock, and places her left knee in the small of his back. She leans backward, reaches up and switches on the light.

Her assailant is lying face down. She turns his head to see who tried to strangle her. She's shocked to see that it's Harvey. Looking down at him, she says, "I forgot to tell you that on Tuesday's I skip lunch and take karate lessons at the Coca-Cola fitness center. Harvey, if you move, I'll break your arm." She spots her purse on the floor near Harvey's head, pulls it to her, takes out her cell phone and dials 911.

CHAPTER 46

IT IS 6 A.M. and Alex has had little sleep with a recurring dream of falling into an abyss and tumbling through black space. He has been awake since five a.m. and his eyes are puffy and bloodshot. He is exhausted physically and emotionally. He hesitates to call Mikhail so early but he must talk to him about what happened after he left the U Prince.

He calls. "Good morning Mikhail." He hesitates. "There's something I must talk to you about. Is it too early?"

"Are you okay?"

"Yes."

There is an edge of distress in Alex's voice and Mikhail hears it. "I'll be right over with a thermos of coffee and a loaf of bread. Stay put."

Mikhail arrives in less than a half-hour and notices Alex's puffy, dark-circled eyes and haggard look. "You look terrible. What's wrong?"

"I didn't sleep well."

"It's more than that, Alex. Out with it."

They sit on the sofa. Mikhail pours coffee into their mugs. "Mikhail, what am I going to do?"

Mikhail lights a cigarette and waits for Alex to continue. "I was followed after I left the restaurant. The man had a gun and he tried to kill me."

"Was he a Forsenko bounty hunter?"

"I'm sure he was."

"Did you shoot him?"

Alex walks to the desk, opens the lower right drawer and shows Mikhail the Makarov wrapped in the towel. "No."

"But you did kill him?" Alex nods. "Will his body be discovered before you leave?"

Alex shakes his head. "He is resting in a cool, deep place. He may never be found." Alex sighs. "Mikhail, I've given you only bits and pieces of my problems with Forsenko. I need your advice and help, so let me start from the beginning so you'll see the complete picture with all its complications." Alex tells Mikhail the chronology of the events that began with Vanderbork's computer being left in his town car.

When he finishes, Mikhail asks, "When are you leaving?"

"Tonight on a seven-fifty flight to Paris. Do you remember Yuri Natskov?"

"Yes, of course."

"He's going to meet me at the airport, and I'll spend the night at his place in Paris. My flight to Atlanta isn't until four to-morrow afternoon."

"Why delay?"

"I haven't seen Yuri in over three years, and I want to spend some time with him. By the way, your old friend explained why the person I'm investigating is coming to Prague to buy turtles. To complete my investigation I'll need your car."

"Here are the keys, but you can't go outside without a disguise. It's too dangerous. The fact that you were recognized last night means that Forsenko circulated a photograph or composite drawing of you throughout the Russian underworld."

Mikhail reaches behind his desk and brings out a wooden box. It looks like an artist's paint box. He opens it. The box contains foundation creams, tubes of make-up of various colors, acetone, spirit gum, and a tray of brushes. "I may not be a master of disguise, but I'm pretty good at it. When I'm through, you won't recognize yourself."

Mikhail positions his chair beside the desk and motions Alex to bring a chair forward and sit facing him. He opens and peers into a bag that he lifted from a shelf behind the desk. He empties its contents of human hair on the desk. He fingers through the assortment and selects three gray pieces of hair. "I'll make you a beard from these." He douses a cloth with an astringent and cleans Alex's face.

"Mikhail, tell me all you know about Forsenko."

Without looking up as he cuts and trims the beard, Mikhail says, "Forsenko was a well-known crook when he lived in Russia. He spent time in prison twice that I know about."

"For what?"

"The first time for pimping and the second time drug running. He honed his criminal skills in Russia and brought them with him to America."

"And his operation is in Brooklyn?"

"Yes. Kushner tells me that his operation includes everything he practiced in Russia, drugs, prostitution, the sale of illegal passports, birth certificates, drivers' licenses, any type of paper. You name it and Forsenko's gang will provide it. Kushner said that he's now into money transactions, laundering it and making it."

"What do you mean, making it?"

"Counterfeit money so good it's almost impossible for even an expert to tell the difference. Kushner thinks the counterfeit money is made in Budapest. He said Forsenko's money and drug businesses reach around the world. Now hold still," he tells Alex, as he places double-sided toupee tape along Alex's chin and jaw and sets the beard in place. He selects a matching mustache, sets it in place and trims it. He holds up a mirror. "What do you think?"

Alex studies himself in the mirror. "It looks real."

Mikhail lifts a gray wig from the pile. Looking at Alex's full head of hair he says, "This is a stretch wig and is supposed to fit any size head, but with so much hair, I'm not sure it will fit your head."

"Then let me help," Alex says, yanking the black wig from his head.

Mikhail's eyes widen. "What the hell is that about?"

"Remember, I told you that someone broke into my apartment and split my head open. Well, the hospital people shaved my head before the doctor sewed me up, and I bought a wig."

"I can't believe I didn't notice."

Using foundation creams, a flat brush and his fingers, and following the natural creases and wrinkles, Mikhail deepens Alex's forehead creases, the crow's feet, and adds dark circles under the eyes. He places the net wig cap on Alex's nearly-bald head, fits the wig, and secures it with stick tape.

Mikhail leans back and admires his work. "Ah, your hair, beard and mustache are gray but your eyebrows are black. That will never do." He takes a white stick liner and runs it against the direction of the hair growth several times. "Voila! You are now at least twenty-five years older." He holds the mirror for Alex to see.

Alex studies himself. He does indeed look twenty-five to thirty years older. "A terrific job. I'm just glad I don't feel as old as I look."

"An important point. You must not only look old, but you must act old. Can you simulate a slight limp and not stand so damned ramrod erect?"

Alex stands. He bends his body forward, and walks with a limp.

"Too much!" Mikhail shouts. "Much too much! You are too bent forward, and the limp too pronounced. You look like a cripple. That will draw attention. The purpose of the disguise is that people will not notice you. Try it again. Less bend, less limp. Make it more of a slight shuffle."

Alex shuffles across the room holding his left shoulder slightly forward of his body and his right leg partially stiff. "Perfect!

You look and walk like a tired old man. Believe me Alex I would not know you myself."

"There's one problem."

"What's that?"

"How do I convince the passport officer that I'm me, and not my father?"

"Good question," Mikhail says stroking his chin with his left hand. "Just before you go through passport control, go to the men's room and substitute your wig for the gray wig." He selects from the box a small bottle containing a clear liquid. "Take this with you when you leave this evening. It's acetone. If you have trouble removing the beard and mustache, rub the acetone underneath. It's a remover and will free them from the tape. It will also clean the tape from your face. You can wash the foundation creams off with soap and water."

Mikhail is worried. He sees in Alex's eyes lonely despair.

"Alex, you have asked for my advice. Here it is. You must kill Forsenko!"

Alex's head snaps up. "With Forsenko alive you will be hunted like a wild beast and, eventually, they will kill you. Forsenko feels that he must kill you to save face.

"But do you think for a second that the man who replaces Forsenko will give a rat's ass about paying $100,000 for your murder. He will have no interest in you. He will have his hands full with a hundred other details, not the least of which will be consolidating his power. You will be a forgotten item. In fact, secretly he will feel indebted to you. For you to live, Alex, you must kill Forsenko!"

Alex gazes at the coffee mug in his hand. His eyes lift. "I've been thinking the same thoughts all night, and I've thought of several ways I might do it. Do you remember those time-bombs we used during combat training?"

"Yes, very well. I helped build many of them," Mikhail says.

"I have a general recollection of how they are made, but I don't remember the specifics about them. And if I use one, it must work perfect. There will be no second chance."

198 · JAMES GABLER

"Tell me how you plan to employ the bomb so I have an idea of the type of bomb you want."

"The easiest and safest method will be to blow up Forsenko's car with him in it, but I'll need to know more about his daily travel habits. By that I mean, does he drive his own car, is he chauffeured, what type of car he uses, what is his daily routine? Then I can decide on the best method."

Mikhail walks behind his desk and turns on the computer. "I'll create a couple of different kinds of bombs. In preparing the formulas, I'll allow for contingencies. It will take me several hours, but I'll have them for you before you leave tonight.

CHAPTER 47

THE GULFSTREAM V carrying Sharon Talbot, president and chief operating officer of Coca-Cola, and her girlfriend, Natalie Johnston, arrives in Prague at 8 a.m. on a sun drenched October morning. They are met by a company limousine and driven to Prague's most elegant hotel, The Intercontinental, located in Prague's Old Town and just one block from the Havlacke building. Standing at the far side of the plaza that separates the hotel from Parizska Street, Alex watches the two women enter the hotel, their faces alive with excitement.

Sharon Talbot is fifty-six years old, five feet four inches tall, and though not obese, she is slightly overweight. Her gaunt, wrinkle-free face, the product of a recent face and neck lift, is in sharp contrast to the soft, roundness of her body. She wears her color enhanced chestnut hair in a short bob, and although she usually dresses in conservative women's business suits, today she sports a two-piece lavender Escada pantsuit.

Talbot, a graduate of Emory University and the University of Pennsylvania's Wharton School of Finance, has succeeded in the male-macho dominated environment of Coca-Cola for two reasons—she is smarter and harder working than her male counterparts.

At ten-thirty Talbot and her friend come out the hotel entrance and get into a waiting limousine. The limousine edges forward, turns left on to Parizska, and stops halfway down the street in front of the Havlacke building. A frock-coated attendant opens the passenger door and assists the women out. They walk up three marble steps that lead to the building's entrance and disappear behind two massive oak doors. The limousine moves off down the street.

Alex walks down the street to where he has parked Mikhail's car and climbs in. He lays the black case he's carrying on the front seat. It contains the necessary equipment to video the events about to take place in Milos Havlacke's office.

He waits a minute or so before plugging the 12 VDC power supply into the cigarette lighter. His equipment does not include a viewing screen so he cannot see what the camera records, but if the transmitter works properly, he will hear what takes place. He presses the remote control button activating the transmitter. Silence. *Damn it!* Then voices resonate inside his car.

"Madame Talbot, it is a thrill to see you again," Milos Havlacke says with a English-Oxford accent. "It has been how long? Two years? And how are our precious pets?"

"It has been two years to the day that I was last here. My pets are divine and will surely outlive all of us."

"No doubt, no doubt. The Madagascar starburst tortoise has a life expectancy in excess of a hundred years. The tortoises that I have for you today are not only beautiful, but in superb condition."

"Surely, Monsieur Havlacke, you remember my friend, Miss Johnston, who accompanied me on my last visit."

"I do, indeed. Miss Johnston, it is a pleasure to see you again, and to have you as our guest in beautiful Prague."

"It is a pleasure to be here, Mr. Havlacke," Natalie Johnston says.

"Before we talk business, may I offer either of you a glass of wine or tea?"

"I think not, Monsieur Havlacke," Talbot says. "You received my e-mail regarding my needs?"

"Yes, yes, and I have taken every precaution, and made every effort to fulfill your wishes. I believe when you see what I have for you, you will agree that I have succeeded. Peter, please bring in the tortoises."

After a brief silence, Havlacke says, "Are they not magnificent? Eight of the most beautiful starburst tortoises I have ever seen and I have been in the business over forty years."

"They are exquisite," says Talbot.

"And the great tragedy, Madame, is that because the Madagascar starburst tortoise is being poached indiscriminately, they will soon be extinct. Can you believe that at this moment these beautiful creatures are being smuggled into parts of Africa where barbaric tribal chiefs eat them as aphrodisiacs."

"And I presume, Monsieur Havlacke, that your concern centers on your fear that the barbaric habits of these tribal chiefs will put you out of business," Talbot says.

"Madame, Madame," Havlacke sniffs, "please do not believe that the antiques you see in this room, the Louis XIV chair on which you sit, the impressionistic paintings that adorn the walls, the exquisite Oriental rugs that cover the floors, made by the same hand techniques used to weave the ancient treasures that covered the floors of the royal palaces of Rajasthan, resulted solely from the sale of Madagascar tortoises."

Annoyed by Havlacke's pretentious arrogance, Talbot has a sudden impulse to leave but restrains herself. "How much?"

"Twenty thousand dollars each."

"Twenty thousand dollars! Two years ago they were ten thousand dollars."

"Madame Talbot, the diminishing supply of the Madagascar starburst tortoise is not something I've made up. Unfortunately, it is real. In another two years, you will probably not be able to buy this quality of tortoise at any price. In addition, the men who smuggle these unique creatures from Madagascar run great risks, and they demand more money with each delivery of their precious wares, to say nothing of the increasing risks that confront me in forging the documentation, and shipping them around the world. I am sorry the price has increased so much, but it is simply a question of supply and demand and increasing risks." Havlacke's tone and mannerisms clearly show his distaste for price bickering. He takes a sip of water before continuing. "Madame Talbot, I have at least twenty Japanese clients who will gladly pay $25,000 or more." He stands, indicating that he is ending the conversation. "Remember, Madame, it is the things we don't buy that we later regret, not the things we buy."

"Yes, I must have them. Do you have the paper work from our last transaction?"

"I have it in front of me."

"Fax your invoice to my Swiss banker, Monsieur Graudet, in Geneva. I will call him today and approve the payment. As soon as you receive payment, I want my pets delivered to my estate in Atlanta by personal courier."

"You realize, of course, that personal delivery will add eight thousand dollars to the bill."

"Considering what you've charged me that is a small price to insure their safe arrival."

Milos Havlacke bows but makes a mental note that this will be his last business transaction with Sharon Talbot.

The two women leave the Havlacke building and walk hand-in-hand down Parizska Street toward Old Town Square.

CHAPTER 48

IT IS A warm, sunny day, and Alex has five hours before he is scheduled to meet Mikhail back at the university. When he was in Prague fifteen years ago, it was shrouded in industrial smog and the depressive gloom of Communism. He wants to see the new, liberated Prague, and feels confident that with his disguise he can move about without detection. He locks the car. Slinging the black case over his left shoulder, he crosses the street and roams the area that was once the Jewish ghetto, located just to the west of Parizska. He looks in through an iron fence to the oldest cemetery in Europe, passes the Maisel and Klaus Synagogues, and spends time in the Jewish Museum viewing an exhibit of silver and textile objects.

He moves through the congested narrow streets of the Old Town section and walks until he comes to the U Fleku Brewery. Here he drinks a couple half-liters of tmave, a dark lager. He hops aboard an electric streetcar and takes it back to Old Town Square. He visits the Prague Castle, a complex of the ancient royal palace: a cathedral, a monastery, galleries and gardens. While climbing the Petrin Outlook Tower, he hears the Astronomical Clock in the tower of the Old Town Hall strike four. He returns to Old Town, retrieves Mikhail's car, and drives to the university.

WHEN ALEX ENTERS Mikhail's office, it is nearly five o'clock. Mikhail is working at the computer. Without looking up, he says, "I'm almost finished." Alex walks into the bathroom and checks his disguise. It still looks neat and fresh. When he returns to the office, Mikhail removes six sheets of paper from the printer and hands them to Alex. "Here, two different methods for exploding the bomb. Method A employs the standard timing device. Method B is my own invention and requires some explanation."

With the papers in hand, Alex walks to the window and begins reading. After a few minutes, he turns. "I've not heard of igniting a bomb in the manner set out in Method B. Will it work?"

"I have no personal experience with a bomb of this type, but, yes, I believe it will work very well."

Alex rereads the papers that detail the Method B bomb. "I have a degree in chemical engineering but it's been a long time since I've lifted a test tube. I would appreciate your explaining in simple language how I build this bomb and how it works."

Michael nods, "Okay, I'll start from the beginning. But first let me explain why the bomb works as it does. For more than a year now, two colleagues and I have been working on pyrophoric metals, metals that when exposed to oxygen in the air self-ignite and create tremendous amounts of heat."

Michael opens the right top desk drawer and removes a small box. "In this box," he says, handing it to Alex, "is a spiral pyrophoric wire. Take it with you because the wire is essential to exploding the bomb. To build the bomb you will need the chemical materials listed under item A and the equipment listed under item B."

Mikhail runs his fingers through his hair, and joins Alex by the window. Lowering his voice, he continues, "When you decide to build the bomb remove the wire from the box and follow the procedures that are detailed in the formula. Once the bomb is built, to explode it all you need do is break the plastic case that holds the bomb and allow in air. The oxygen in the air reacts with the pyrophoric wire creating great heat that ignites the explosives."

"I don't want to sound vain," Alex says with a wry smile, "but there is one little point you've not covered."

"What's that?"

"After I've crushed the plastic case to let in air, how do I avoid being blown up?"

"Indeed, Alex, an important point. My formula, however, calls for you to coat the wire with these two chemicals here," Mikhail says, pointing. "If you apply them in the exact percentages by weight as I've detailed, it will prevent oxygen reaching the wire for ten seconds, the time it takes for the chemical coatings to evaporate." Alex is about to say something but Mikhail continues, "But I urge you to conduct your own experiments to be sure of the ten second delay. You can't make a mistake, Alex, or you won't be around to take Zhanna and me on that vacation to Switzerland."

Alex nods reflectively. "The pyrophoric wire acts as both the explosive catalyst and timing device."

"That's right," Mikhail says. "It's essential for both."

ON THE DRIVE to the airport, Alex says, "You know, Mikhail, I'm alive only because Demitri Sadkov left a message on my answering machine advising that Forsenko was sending someone to kill me."

"Yes. You mentioned that earlier. I knew Demitri was in New York, but I didn't know he was working for someone like Forsenko."

"I'm glad he is. How well do you know Demitri?"

"We were very close during the two years we served together in Japan,"

"It would help if I knew Forsenko's habits, especially his daily travel itinerary. I assume that he has bodyguards. It would also help if I knew something about his security. It's me against them, and the more I know, the better my chances. Unfortunately, I don't know Demitri well. In fact, he is one of only five in our group whose e-mail address or telephone number I don't have."

Alex looks over at his friend, "Mikhail, I hate to ask this of you, but would you contact Demitri, find out if he will provide me with this information, and if he will, how I can contact him."

Mikhail lights a cigarette, expels the smoke in a steady stream, and lapses into pensive silence. After a few moments, he says, "I'll do better than that. I'll contact Demitri, obtain the information, and e-mail it to you."

"If you think it necessary, tell Demitri why I want the information."

Mikhail gives his friend a quick smile. "I can assure you that won't be necessary. Demitri is very bright, and in view of what he already knows about your situation, he'll know why you want the information. Also, I think he'll consider it a favor if Forsenko dies." Mikhail takes a final drag on his cigarette and flips it out the window. "Think about it. With no connection to Forsenko's death, who better to replace Forsenko than Demitri?" After a contemplative pause, Mikhail continues, "Yes, the more I think about it, the more convinced I am that Demitri will welcome Forsenko's death."

DISGUISED AS AN old man, Alex enters the terminal and sinks into the crowds. Before entering the passport checkpoint, he enters the men's room, removes paper towels from the towel holder, opens a toilet stall, closes the door, sits down, removes the wig, and with the help of the acetone, removes the beard and the mustache. He places them in a plastic bag. He rubs away most of the makeup and foundation grease with water, and flushes the towels down the toilet. On the way out, he washes away the remaining make up and drops the plastic bag in the trash receptacle. He passes through passport and security controls without incident, and boards his flight for Paris.

ALEX'S FLIGHT FROM Prague lands at Charles De Gaulle Airport on time. He clears customs and meets his friend Yuri in the international reception lounge. They drive into Paris and spend the evening at a bistro on Place Pigalle eating, drinking, and talking primarily about Alex's Forsenko problem. Alex tells Yuri about the bomb Mikhail has invented with the ten second explosion delay. Yuri's advice is the same as Mikhail's—"Kill Forsenko!"

Alex spends the night at Yuri's apartment on the sofa bed, and he sleeps better than he has since learning of Forsenko's plan to murder him. He awakes at nine. Yuri has gone to work. He has breakfast at a local bistro. After breakfast he visits the Georges Pompidou Centre.

He meets Yuri back at the apartment at one o'clock. Yuri insists on driving him to the airport. On the way to the airport they again discuss the Forsenko situation. Without taking his eyes off the road, Yuri says, "Last night when I had too much to drink, I told you to kill Forsenko. Now, in the sober light of this beautiful day, I repeat—kill him!" Yuri lapses into silence for a long moment. "I did a lot of thinking this morning about a Forsenko solution and I have an idea." Alex turns in his seat and faces Yuri. "Run the experiments to determine whether the chemical coating of the wire does insulate it for ten seconds from a heat reaction with oxygen. If it does . . . Remember the motorcycles we rode when we were in England?" Alex nods. "I would build Mikhail's bomb, find out how he travels, go to this Brooklyn place where Forsenko lives, steal a motorcycle, ride up behind his car, smash the plastic bomb case against the rear window, and get the hell out of there."

A smile breaks across Alex's face. "I like it! It's a great idea. I'll have to coat the plastic case with an adhesive that makes it to stick when I slam it against the car window, and make sure the plastic breaks, but if Forsenko's car is stopped, that should be easy to do. And ten seconds, that should give me enough time to get away before the explosion."

Yuri looks over and smiles. "At a speed of thirty miles an hour you're moving about forty-five feet a second. In ten seconds you're 450 feet away when the bomb explodes. Unless you're planning

on blowing up the whole neighborhood, you'll be safe." He pauses. "Steal a big Harley, and when you gear up and pop the clutch,
it will move a lot faster than thirty miles an hour."

Alex leans back in the seat, stretches his arms over his head
and closes his eyes. They drive in silence. Yuri pulls in front of the
departure terminal. They shake hands.

"Thanks, Yuri. It's been fun. The next time I come to Paris,
I'll give you more notice."

CHAPTER 49

ALEX'S PLANE TOUCHES down at Atlanta's Hartsfield International Airport shortly before 8 p.m. Passport and customs procedures are routine, and when he steps into the international reception area, Kia is waiting.

"I'm glad to see you're still in one piece," she says.

"Thanks for picking me up, Kia. I'm in one piece, but barely."

"What does that mean?"

Alex takes Kia by the arm and heads to the exit, "We must have a serious talk."

"About what?"

"Things are happening that you must know about."

"What is it?"

"It can wait until we get in the car."

Kia asks Alex to drive. As they start out of the garage, she bursts into tears. "Harvey . . . Harvey broke into my apartment Friday night and tried to kill me."

Alex slams on the brakes and stops. Between sobs, Kia tells Alex about Harvey calling her, their meeting at the restaurant, his breaking into her apartment and attempting to strangle her. "I've spent a lot of time at police headquarters giving them the details."

"Why did he do it? Do you know?"

Kia tells Alex the details about accusing Harvey and his associate of being responsible for poisoning the psychologists, and her threats to tell the police about Harvey's ownership of the gun that killed Stilton. "He tried to kill me to keep me from going to the police."

Alex eases the car out of the garage. When they are on Route 85 heading to Atlanta, Kia says, "We can't go to my place. This thing with Harvey has newspaper reporters from all over the country swarming over Atlanta. Their trucks, cameras, microphones, all kinds of equipment completely surround my apartment building. A police spokesman and a lawyer from the District Attorney's office both suggested that I not talk with them, and I haven't."

Alex looks over and smiles, "That sounds like good advice." He checks the rear view mirror to see if they are being followed. Satisfied that they're not, he says, "Let's go to my place. Kia, this thing with Harvey highlights what I want to talk to you about. For your own safety, you have to get out of my life."

Shocked, Kia tries to keep control of her emotions, "Why? Harvey's in jail."

"This isn't about Harvey. It goes beyond Harvey. It's about what happened in Prague, why it happened, and why it will happen again."

"What happened in Prague?"

"In one respect, we did well in Prague. I was able to record and video Talbot making an illegal purchase of eight internationally protected turtles. I have it here." He pats the black case. "I haven't had a chance to view the video, but the voice recording is clear."

"What are you talking about? Protected turtles?"

"Let me back up. In 1975, a hundred and thirty countries signed the Convention on International Trade in Endangered Species, laws that protect endangered animals, reptiles and plants. The United States is a signatory to that treaty. Talbot's purchase of those turtles might not seem like a serious crime, but under our federal laws, if caught, she could go to prison for five to fifteen years."

"What's that have to do with me getting out of your life?"

"It has nothing to do with Talbot."

"Then . . ."

"It's very complicated and . . . I'll tell you about it when we get to my place." They drive in silence.

AT ALEX'S APARTMENT he opens a bottle of red wine, pours two glasses, and hands a glass to Kia.

She looks at him, her eyes narrow and cold. "Alex, I've put my complete trust in you, but now I'm not sure. Are you trying to dump me so that you can keep all the money?"

"No, Kia."

"Then why are you telling me to get out of your life?"

"Sit down, Kia."

She sits in a chair at the kitchen table and Alex takes a seat directly across from her. "I'm not sure what caused this to happen, but someone has set in motion murderous actions that are spinning out of control. Here's what's happened that you don't know about. I should have told you about it sooner, but, at the time, I wasn't entirely sure it involved what we're attempting to do with the Calderman formula. Besides, I didn't want you to know that I killed a man."

"What! You killed a man?"

"About two weeks after I delivered a copy of Brannon's video and the transcript to the receptionist at Coca-Cola's headquarters, I received a call warning me that a man was coming to Atlanta to kill me. I was told when he was coming, how he would arrive, and who sent him. Although I've been trained to kill, I'd never killed anyone before. But I was left with only two choices—kill or be killed."

"You killed him?" Alex nods. "Who sent him to kill you?"

"A Russian gangster in New York by the name of Forsenko."

"Why?"

"That's what I don't know. Unless . . ."

"Unless what?"

"Forsenko was hired by Brannon."

Her remark to Brannon, *Why don't you go to Paris and get it from your French whore*, comes to mind. She gasps.

"What is it?"

"Nothing," she says, lowering her eyes to avoid his stare. "Are you sure you didn't know this gangster from when you were in Russia? Something you did to him or his gang when you worked for the KGB?"

"I've thought about it ever since he came here to kill me, and I can't make a connection. What I can't figure out is how Brannon knew that I followed him to Paris. But I have a gut feeling there's a connection between Forsenko and Brannon."

"What did you do with this man's body?"

"I shipped it back to Forsenko in New York."

"You did what?" she says, coming out of her chair.

For the first time a smile forms around the corners of Alex's mouth. "I shipped the body back to Forsenko. It was a way to get rid of the body, and I figured it would send him a message." Alex rubs his tongue across his lips. His mouth is bone dry. He pours a glass of water and empties half in one gulp. "It sent him a message, but it was the wrong message." He gives Kia an odd smile. "I'm told it infuriated him, and he put the word out through the Russian underworld that he would pay a hundred thousand dollars to anyone who kills me."

"No!"

"There's more. In Prague I went to dinner with friends. When I left the restaurant, a man followed me." Alex shakes his head, as though trying to clear his thoughts. "He tried to kill me. We had a fight, and I killed him."

Kia throws her hands across her face. "Why? Why is this happening?"

"It's quite simple. Every thug in the Russian underworld wants to collect Forsenko's $100,000 reward."

"Oh Alex, what are we going to do?"

"Kia, listen to me. If you don't get out of my life, what they're trying to do to me, they'll do to you. I'm sorry I got you into this, but I had no idea it was going to turn out like this."

"I don't want out!"

"For your safety, you must." She shakes her head. "Your parents need you, and as they get older, they're going need you more."

"If I drop out, will you continue?"

"I don't know. It will depend on something I have to do. If I'm successful, I'll go on. If I'm not . . . then . . ." He throws his hands out in a gesture of resignation. "If I continue and sell the formula, I promise that you'll get your share."

Kia's hands, shaking moments ago, now rest steady on the table. "And what's this 'something' you have to do? Alex, look at me, what is it you're going to do?"

Alex lifts his head and their eyes meet. "I'm going kill Forsenko before his goons kill me. But there are no guarantees I'll succeed."

They stare at each other for a long moment. "Then I want to help you kill him."

"That's a very generous offer . . . probably the most generous offer anyone has ever made to me, but I can't accept it."

Kia's hand grasps Alex's. "Alex, I'm serious. I want to help you?"

Alex shakes his head. "I can't let you get involved in this. It's too dangerous. If we fail, the consequences will ruin your life. I think too much of you to allow you to . . ."

"You have a strange way of showing it. Surely you know how I feel about you. I've made that very clear. Yet, you've never even kissed me . . ." Her lips quiver.

Alex goes to her, puts his arms around her, lifts her to her feet and kisses her hard. He feels his body come alive with desire. She throws her arms around his neck and kisses him back, hard, open-mouthed. He lifts her in his arms and moves to the bedroom. Kia, her arms around his neck, whispers, "Alex, I want you so much."

EXHAUSTED FROM HIS flight from Paris, Alex sleeps curled on his side, his face buried in the pillow. Kia is wide-awake, still savoring the sensual emotions of their lovemaking. Suddenly, her remark to Brannon about the French whore strikes her with the pain of a stabbing knife. *That's how Brannon found out about Alex and ar-ranged his murder. It's my fault.*

Alex awakes at six-thirty. A crack of sunlight slivers in be-tween the bedroom curtains and spreads across the room. His mouth is dry and sour. He slips out of bed and brushes his teeth. Returning to bed he cups his naked body to Kia's and runs his right hand along her thigh. Kia whispers, "Don't move. I'll be right back." Kia jumps out of bed, races to the bathroom, brushes her teeth, climbs back in bed, laces her arms around Alex, and says, "I'm ready."

AT BREAKFAST KIA says, "What's this Russian gangster's name."

"Forsenko."

"How are we going to kill him?"

"Kia, we decided last night that you can't become involved."

"No, Alex, you decided." She looks at him, her eyes pleading. "Alex, there's something I must tell you. It's been on my mind since last night. I feel so guilty."

Kia tells Alex about her three month affair with Brannon, why she broke off their relationship and how her anger caused her to blurt out the French whore comment when Brannon called attempting to rekindle their relationship.

Alex leans back in his chair, a relieved smile on his face. "Thanks for sharing that with me, Kia. It puts a lot of things in perspective." His voice is soft and even.

"But I still don't understand how my remark to Brannon connects me with you?"

"That's easy. Brannon had you followed. When they saw us together, they checked me out and learned of my KGB background. That discovery, I'm sure, set off all kinds of alarms. When they dug deeper, they found out that I was in Paris the same two days as Brannon." He takes a sip of coffee. "They then hired Forsenko to kill me."

"Are you angry with me?"

"No," he says, and kisses her.

She looks up at him, her eyes reflecting her determination, "I want to help you, and there's a way I can help now."

"How?"

"Do you know how you're going to get a copy of the Talbot video to her?"

"I haven't figured that out yet, but I will."

Kia holds her hand out. "Give it to me. I'll deliver it to her."

"Do you see her at work from time to time?"

"No, but I'll make it a point to see her," Kia says with quiet determination.

Alex reaches in his briefcase, removes the video and hands it to her. "Can we get together Friday?"

"Sure. Provided the reporters are gone, what about my place at seven?"

"It will be safer if we meet at Manuel's."

"Okay, Manuel's at seven."

CHAPTER 50

AFTER KIA LEAVES Alex checks his e-mail. There are dozens of postings but the one from Mikhail gets his immediate attention. It reads, "Demitri advises that Forsenko has a Friday night routine that rarely varies. The Brighton Beach Moscow Social Club at 6 Brighton Street in Brooklyn, New York, is Forsenko's headquarters. Promptly at eight he leaves from there for Lundy's Seafood Restaurant on Emmons Avenue. He always travels in the middle car of a three-car caravan. The first and third cars contain a driver and two armed bodyguards, one in the front seat and one in the rear. Forsenko rides in an armor-plated limousine with a driver, front and rear seat bodyguards and one or two guests who are usually members of his organization. Demitri is sometimes one of Forsenko's guests and, of course, he doesn't want to be there when your party begins. So, let me know when it begins so I can notify Demitri.

"Forsenko's route to the restaurant is as follows: South on Brighton 6 a half block to Brighton Beach Avenue. Left or east on Brighton Beach three blocks to Coney Island Avenue. Left or north on Coney Island two blocks to Neptune Avenue. Right or east on Neptune and within a block or two Neptune becomes Emmons Avenue. Lundy's is located on the north side of Emmons at its intersection with Ocean Avenue. On the south side of

Emmons is the Sheepshead Bay channel inlet that opens into the Atlantic Ocean. Lundy's has a parking lot located in the rear and facing Voorhies Avenue. The exit and entrance to the parking lot fronts Ocean Avenue.

"Everyone goes to dinner except the drivers. They remain with the cars. Forsenko's group dines at a table that looks out across Emmons to Sheepshead Bay. You can set your watch by when Forsenko leaves the restaurant, always at eleven. Throughout dinner everyone drinks vodka and lots of wine.

"The route from the restaurant is as follows: Right or south from the parking lot for a half block to Emmons. The intersection is controlled by a traffic signal. Right or west on Emmons to Coney Island Avenue. Left or south on Coney Island one block to Ocean View. Right or west on Ocean View three blocks to Brighton 6. Left or south on Brighton 6 to the Brighton Beach Moscow Social Club.

"Forsenko is creature of habit, and these routes never vary except for occasions when a street is blocked for repairs. If you need additional information, let me know. And please don't forget to e-mail me the date your party is to take place. Zhanna and I send our love. Mikhail"

Alex prints the message and rereads it. The fact that the drivers stay with their cars eliminates any possibility of attaching a bomb to the undercarriage of Forsenko's limousine and detonating it by means of a timing device.

The phrase "these routes never vary except for occasions when a street is closed for repairs" gives Alex an idea. He remembers seeing a repair sign on a side street in the Virginia-Highlands area before he left for Prague. The sign consisted of an orange square cloth attached to a metal stand with the words, ROAD CLOSED. Two orange cones on each side of the sign blocked entrance into the street. With so much work taking place on Atlanta's aging streets, similar signs are a daily part of the landscape. Alex decides to put the next such sign he sees in the trunk of his car. The cones he'll buy at Lowes or Home Depot.

A plan of using a road sign to block a street and stop Forsenko's limousine in route from the restaurant to the social club excites Alex. It is a perfect fit for Mikhail's bomb, and Yuri's method of delivery. But how does he block the roadway? He thinks of Kia's offer of help. He tries to push it from his mind.

The next morning, Alex stops at a chemical supply store and buys all the chemical ingredients listed under A and all the materials listed under B in Mikhail's formula. He pays cash for them. In the afternoon, while returning from a trip to the airport, he passes a side street blocked to traffic by orange cones and a sign mounted on a metal stand that reads, "Closed Road Work." Alex backs up to the sign, pops the trunk lid, bounds out and throws the sign into the trunk. That evening he drops by a Lowes and buys the remaining necessary materials for making the bomb and four orange traffic cones. He pays cash for all his purchases.

He remembers Yuri's statement, "I wonder if bikes are as easy to steal now as they used to be." He decides to examine the current crop of motorcycles, with special attention to the ignition locks. He checks the yellow pages and tears out seven pages of listings for motorcycle dealers. That night, and over the next two days, whenever he has a break in his work schedule, and in the evenings, he visits bike dealers in Greater Atlanta and inspects new and used models. He discovers that he can get several motorcycles running in a few minutes with just a screwdriver, and others with a screwdriver, a pair of pliers and a hammer.

ON FRIDAY NIGHT Kia and Alex meet at Manuel's. They sit at a table in the room to the left of the bar.

"Are the reporters still camped out around your apartment?" Alex asks.

Kia shakes her head. "It's wonderful. They're gone and I'm so glad."

"Why'd they leave? I'd think that a lawyer breaking into a

young woman's apartment and attempting to kill her would be hot news."

"I'm told they took off for a hotter story in California where a physician was arrested for killing his pregnant wife. I don't know whether there's any truth to it, but somebody said that anything short of murder or a celebrity sex crime doesn't hold the media's attention."

After the waitress leaves with their orders, Kia says, "Is Forsenko still on your agenda?" Alex nods. "When?"

"Next Friday."

"Are you prepared?"

Alex tells her about the bomb formula, how the bomb works, his understanding of Forsenko's Friday night travel route, the need to select a road to block, stealing a motorcycle in order to deliver the bomb, and planning an escape route back to Atlanta.

When he finishes explaining the setup, Kia says, "You need help, and I'm going to help you."

"I can't let you do it, Kia. You have elderly parents to care for and . . ."

Kia's eyes flare with an intensity that he's never seen before. "Alex, if my son Tony were alive, it would be different. The only people in this world I love are my parents and you. If I told my parents about the situation you're in, why you're in it, and how I feel about you . . . and what I want to do to help you, do you know what they'd say to me?" Her mouth tightens and tears well in her eyes. "They'd say, 'Kia, we've lived our lives, now go live yours.'" Kia edges back in her chair. "Think about it, Alex. How are you going to steal a motorcycle and not leave your car at the scene of the theft? And driving a Lincoln Town Car around Brooklyn will be a lot more conspicuous than my Toyota Corolla." She pauses. "And who's going to set up the road block for you?"

The waitress places a pitcher of beer on the table between them. Alex pours their glasses.

"I'll tell you who is going to drive you around Brooklyn until you find a motorcycle, and who's going to place the road block," she says, jabbing her index finger at her chest, "I am."

"You really want to do this, don't you?"

She nods. "It's my fault that you're in this situation and I want . . ."

Alex's hand shoots out. "We don't know for sure that Brannon's behind this."

"Alex, don't talk foolishness. Before I told you about blurting out about the Paris whore, you said yourself that your gut feeling was that Brannon was behind the assassin coming here to kill you." She glances around the room to see if anyone is listening to them. Leaning forward, she says, "I've given this decision a lot of thought, and I know the risks. I want to do it."

Alex reads in her eyes that she means every word she's said. He nods, "We'll leave here Thursday night at about ten. We'll use your car, if that's okay?" Kia nods. "We'll get to Brooklyn about one or two in the afternoon, allowing us time to check out Forsenko's travel route to the restaurant, and what street we're going to block off. Forsenko leaves the restaurant at eleven, so we should start looking for a motorcycle at about nine."

"That only gives us two hours. Suppose you can't find one in that time?"

"We'll find one. I've checked the Brooklyn Yellow Pages and the place is loaded with motorcycle dealers, which means a lot of folks in Brooklyn ride motorcycles." Alex drinks the last of his beer, calls the waitress, pays the bill, and stands.

Kia looks up. "Where are we going?"

"If the coast is really clear, I was thinking your place."

A smile breaks across Kia's face, her first smile of the evening. "Now that, Alex, is a very good idea."

CHAPTER 51

THE NEXT SIX days are a busy time in Alex's life. He carries on his regular limousine service but takes on nothing extra, concentrating his efforts on preparations for the trip to Brooklyn. He e-mails Mikhail, and advises, "My party will take place this coming Friday." He suggests that Kia have her car inspected, and it's a good thing she does because a damaged water hose is found and replaced. From the computer he obtains maps and directions to Brooklyn, and lays out his precise route, a distance of 855 miles.

He buys a Hagstrom map containing the street details of "Little Odessa-by-the-Sea," the informal name given to Brighton Beach because of the influx of Russian immigrants to the area since the early 1980s. He arranges for Avon Jones to handle his business assignments. He conducts five coating experiments of the nickel wire and confirms that it takes ten seconds for the decane, dodecane mixture to evaporate, the time he'll need to avoid being blown up. He is ready.

On Thursday evening, Alex assembles all the chemical ingredients and materials listed in Mikhail's formula and sets about making the bomb. When he finishes, he uses a soldering iron to heat-seal the plastic box. To guard against accidentally crushing the bomb, he places it inside a Styrofoam picnic cooler and surrounds it with plastic pellets.

He showers, dresses in jeans, a pullover cotton sweater and soft crepe-soled shoes. He wraps a screwdriver, a hammer and a pair of pliers in a towel and slips it into his backpack along with a roll of double-sided permanent mounting tape.

At ten o'clock Kia arrives. She is also dressed in jeans and a sweater. She appears at ease. Stepping inside, she says, "Are we ready?"

"I think so. Do you have the food?"

"Yes. I've packed sandwiches, cheese, peanuts, and crackers. We won't get hungry." She studies the objects Alex has placed by the door for transfer to her car. "Where's the, uh . . . bomb?" Alex points to the Styrofoam cooler. "Will it be safe there?"

"Yes, so long as we don't have an accident, especially a rear end collision." Alex picks up the stacked orange cones and the metal stand, "Let's start putting this stuff in the car." Kia carries his overnight bag. Alex returns for a box containing six one liter bottles of water and throws it on the back seat. Lastly, he lifts the cooler and puts it on the floor behind the driver's seat. Alex gets behind the wheel. He looks over at Kia, "Did you bring your cell phone." She reaches into her purse, and pulls it out. "Good, I have mine. How do you feel?"

"I feel good, no second thoughts. But I didn't sleep at all last night, so I'm really tired."

"You look tired. It's going to take between fifteen and sixteen hours to get to Brooklyn, so why don't you try to get some sleep?"

Kia lays her head back against the head rest, closes her eyes, and murmurs, "Okay."

By the time they have cleared Atlanta and are heading north on I 85, Kia is asleep. He drives through the night never exceeding the speed limit. At 8 a.m. he stops at a service area outside of Baltimore, Maryland. He has traveled 500 miles, at an average speed of about 55 miles per hour. While refueling, Kia wakes up.

"Let's take a break," Alex says.

They stretch their legs, go to the restrooms, purchase large coffees, eat sandwiches, and resume their journey north with Kia behind the wheel. By the time they cross the Susquehanna River, Alex is asleep.

It is a clear, crisp morning, and with nothing in front of her but the road ahead, Kia is alone with her thoughts. They center on her parents and Alex's admonition not to exceed the speed limits.

Alex asked to be awakened when they arrive at the Verrazano Narrows Bridge exit. Kia shakes him as they approach the exit. "Alex, we're approaching the Verrazano bridge exit."

"When you stop for the toll, I'll take over."

Kia stops at the toll. Alex flings open the passenger door and runs around to the driver's side. Kia slides across the seat. He has studied a map of Brooklyn and knows that the Russian immigrant community, Brighton Beach, is concentrated in an area adjacent to Coney Island.

After crossing the bridge, he follows the Belt Parkway and the signs leading to Coney Island. He turns off the parkway and ends up on Surf Avenue in Coney Island. He drives east on Surf until he reaches Brighton Beach Avenue, the main street through Brighton Beach. The streets intersecting Brighton Beach Avenue are labeled Brighton 1 through 15.

He stops the car and reads Mikhail's e-mail that details Forsenko's travel route to and from Lundy's Seafood Restaurant. Starting at Brighton 6 he follows Forsenko's route to the restaurant and arrives at the intersection of Emmons and Ocean Avenues five minutes later. Lundy's is located on the northwest corner of the intersection. When the traffic signal turns green, Alex makes a left turn onto Ocean Avenue and an immediate left into the restaurant parking lot. A skinny attendant instructs him to park next to a white Lexus. It is two o'clock.

"Are we going in?" Kia asks.

"Don't you want to see what the place looks like and have lunch?"

The entrance door opens into a small foyer. They are met by an attractive young woman with a pleasant smile. "Can I help you?" she asks.

Alex peers in at the empty tables. "Are we too late for lunch?"

The hostess picks up two menus from the counter, "No. Would you like a table looking out to the bay?"

"Yes, that would be nice," Kia says.

The hostess seats them at a table that looks across Emmons Avenue to Sheepshead Bay. Kia orders a salad. Alex orders penne pasta and two glasses of water. As they wait for their food, two men set up a circular table around which they place nine chairs. Alex leans forward and whispers, "I suspect that's Forsenko's table."

It is almost three when they leave Lundy's. With Alex driving, they follow the route that Forsenko will take when he leaves the restaurant that evening. When they turn onto Ocean View Avenue, his head moves from side to side, sizing up the traffic patterns.

Approaching Brighton 6, Alex points to his left, "Kia, note that Brighton 6 is one-way south. That's terrific."

"Why?"

"I'll explain after I get a few more things worked out." Alex continues west on Ocean View until he reaches Ocean Parkway, a wide boulevard running north and south through Brooklyn. He turns right onto Ocean Parkway and sees a service street on the right that extends three blocks north, ending at the eastbound entrance ramp to the Belt Parkway. Alex stops the car and looks around. There are cars parked on both sides of the service street with houses on the right and the parkway on the left. "This is absolutely perfect. If I had written the script, I couldn't have done better."

"I don't get it," Kia says.

"Okay, let me explain. I haven't worked out all of details but this much is clear.

"When Forsenko and his goons leave the restaurant, I'll call you on your cell. You'll be parked at the intersection we just left, Ocean View and Brighton 6. The distance from the restaurant to

Brighton 6 is about twelve blocks, and it will take Forsenko about five minutes to cover the distance. When you get my call immediately set up the sign and the cones along the south side of Brighton 6. Because Brighton is one-way southbound, we don't have to block traffic coming in the other direction. As soon as the sign and cones are in place, drive down Ocean View, turn at Ocean Parkway, as we just did, and drive into this service street and park wherever there's a space. But, Kia, be sure to leave your parking lights on so that I'll know where you are."

"What if there are no parking spaces available?"

"Then drive to the end of the third block and double-park. And remember, I'll be right behind you. If everything goes right, you'll hear the explosion, and after that I should be here in a few minutes. When I see your car, I'll ditch the bike and join you."

Pointing ahead, he says, "Do you see the ramp that goes off to the right where the service road ends?" Kia nods. "Do you know where that leads?"

Looking at a map of Brooklyn she says, "According to this map, it enters onto the Belt Parkway."

"Yes, and six miles farther on is the Verrazano Narrows Bridge, and three miles after that the New Jersey Turnpike."

Kia smiles, "Sounds too good to be true."

Alex nods. "We'll do a dry run, but first I want to go back to Lundy's because I'm not sure how I'm going to follow Forsenko's car after it leaves the restaurant."

Alex drives back to Lundy's. At Ocean Avenue he turns on to Voorhies and drives west hoping he can use it as a parallel street to reach Ocean View and Coney Island Avenue before Forsenko's car arrives there. After driving two blocks, however, it is clear that the Belt Parkway blocks southbound access from Voorhies. Alex makes a U-turn and returns to Lundy's. He sits in the car for a few minutes studying the intersecting streets and their traffic patterns. He puts the car in gear and follows the Forsenko travel route back to Ocean View and Brighton 6. Before entering the

226 · JAMES GABLER

intersection, he pulls to the curb and stops. Pointing to Brighton 6 on his left, he says, "That's the street he'll turn down to return to the social club."

Alex looks in all directions before continuing. "Here's the plan. I don't know whether you've noticed, but on the opposite side of Voorhies Avenue where Ocean Avenue goes under the Belt Parkway there are concrete abutments. Tonight, when Forsenko and his gang leave the restaurant, I'll be waiting under the parkway next to an abutment. From that position I'll have a clear view of the restaurant and the parking lot. You should park where we're parked now, or on the other side of the intersection. When Forsenko leaves the restaurant, I'll call you. You'll immediately set out the sign and cones and drive to the service road and wait for me."

"What will you do when they leave the restaurant parking lot?"

"As soon as they turn onto Emmons, I'll follow. When they reach here, I'll be crossing Brighton 7. The lead car will start to turn into Brighton 6, see the 'Closed Road Work' sign and cones and stop in the intersection on an angle. Forsenko's car will stop either just before entering the intersection, or perhaps slightly into the intersection. Either way, when Forsenko's car stops, it will be essentially facing straight ahead, leaving enough space between the rear of the lead car and the front of Forsenko's car to allow me through. The third car will have stopped behind Forsenko's car."

"How will you get the bomb to Forsenko's limousine?"

"Don't forget, I'll be behind them and closing the gap. When Forsenko's car stops, I plan on being right about there," Alex says, turning slightly and pointing to a spot in the street just to the rear of their parked car. "I'll brake to about ten miles an hour and slam the bomb on the rear window of Forsenko's car. If the bomb works the way it should, I'll have plenty of time to get out of there."

"When is the last time you rode a motorcycle, Alex?"

"About twelve years ago."

"Are you sure you are going to be able to handle this?"

Alex smiles, "Don't worry, Kia, it's like riding a bicycle. Once you know how to do it, you never forget." He puts the car in gear and starts forward, "Let's do a dry run."

CHAPTER 52

AFTER THE DRY run, there is time to spare before looking for a motorcycle. They walk through Prospect Park and drive around Brooklyn familiarizing themselves with the streets.

At nine they begin the hunt for a motorcycle. They cruise Brooklyn's main and side streets. It is just after ten when Alex sees the bike he wants. It is a blue and diamond ice Harley-Davidson Electra Glide Ultra Classic. It is in front of a restaurant on Smith Avenue. An attractive, well-dressed young woman is being assisted off the bike by an attendant who, at the same time, is gesturing to the operator. The young woman, helmet under her arm, walks into the restaurant. Her companion drives forward and turns at the corner. Alex follows him. He watches the biker park his motorcycle in the lot behind the restaurant and dismount. Carrying his helmet the biker enters the back door to the restaurant. Alex wants this bike for two reasons, it is easy to steal, and it is extremely powerful. There is, perhaps, a third reason; it's a beautiful bike and he'll enjoy riding it.

Alex turns to Kia. "By the time he discovers his bike missing, we'll be driving south on the New Jersey Turnpike." Alex reaches into the back seat and brings forward a backpack. He opens one of the pockets and removes the towel containing pliers, screwdriver and hammer. He again rummages in the back seat, lifts out a helmet and puts it on.

Kia looks surprised. "You brought along your own helmet?"

"Didn't you notice, the biker and his companion both took their helmets with them. A biker rarely leaves his helmet with the bike." Alex gets out of the car, opens the right rear door and removes the cover of the Styrofoam cooler holding the bomb. Using both hands, he feels around inside and lifts the bomb out. Kia watches his every move. He holds the plastic box in his right hand. "As you can see, it's not large. The tape covering this side of the bomb is a double-sided adhesive that sticks to glass. It will hold the bomb on the car window."

Kia grimaces, "Are you sure?"

With an equivocal shrug, he says, "It worked every time I tested it."

Alex places the bomb in the large pocket of the back pack, and slips the backpack onto his back. "When I ride out of the lot, follow me, but stay at least three car lengths back. I won't lose you. If I notice at some point you're not behind me, I'll stop and wait for you. Okay?"

Kia nods. "My hands are sweating."

"If we get lost from one another, you have the map and you know what to do. Kia, you must promise me that after you park in the service road that you'll wait for me no longer than ten minutes. If I'm not there in ten minutes, you are to leave, drive to Atlanta, and forget you ever met me. Is that a promise?" She nods. "Let me hear you say it. Is that a promise?"

"Yes, except for the part about forgetting I ever met you."

"Everything is going to be okay," he says, leaning back into the car and kissing her.

Alex walks across the street and into the parking lot. He glances around. There is no one in sight. Approaching the Harley, he takes out the screwdriver, places it under the ignition lock hood and pushes up. The hood flies off. He places the head of the screwdriver inside the ignition and turns it clockwise. The indicator light flashes green showing that the bike is in neutral. He hits the starter button and the engine fires into action. He mounts the bike, flips the kickstand up with his foot and drives off the lot waving to Kia to follow.

Alex has developed a feel for the streets of Brooklyn and he has no trouble finding Ocean Avenue. He drives south on Ocean Avenue. When he reaches Kings Highway he pulls over and stops. Kia stops behind him. Alex walks back to her car. "We still have nearly forty minutes to kill. It might be a good idea if you take up your position at the intersection of Brighton 6 and Ocean View. If you follow this street and turn right when it ends, you'll be on Emmons. Don't forget to wear latex gloves, the baseball cap and sunglasses when you set the sign and cones out.

"And what are you going to do?"

"I love riding this bike, so I might ride around for a while. There's a full tank of gas."

"Alex, please don't do anything so foolish. That motorcycle attracts attention."

He leans in, kisses her, and says, "Wish me luck."

Holding back tears, she squeezes his hand, "Good luck, Alex."

KIA'S COMMENT ABOUT the big Harley attracting attention makes sense. He noticed riding down Ocean Avenue how the bike turned heads. He remembers that the map showed a park located at Manhattan Beach, an area east of Brighton Beach, and not more than a five minute ride to Lundy's. The park, he figures, should be a quiet place to wait out the remaining time. He rides to the eastern end of the park and stops on a deserted street that runs between the park and a community college.

At ten-forty-five, Alex shoves-off and rides east on Oriental Avenue, turning right at Western Shore Boulevard and right again at Emmons. He has to stop for a red light at its intersection with

Ocean Avenue. As he waits for the light to change, he wonders if Forsenko is looking out the window. The light changes and he turns on Ocean. He sees no on-coming traffic and makes a U-turn under the Belt Parkway, stopping next to an abutment. He glances at his watch, the luminous dial shows ten-fifty-two. He reaches back, releases the Velcro flap that holds closed the pocket containing the bomb, and lifts it out. He examines the cord tied around the bomb. It is securely attached. He slips the cord over his head. The plastic box now rests against his chest. He removes the strips covering the double-sided adhesive tape and turns the box so that the adhesive faces away from his body. He has carried out several experiments, and he's satisfied that the adhesive adheres well to glass and that it will hold the one pound bomb on the limousine's rear window.

The next few minutes are like no other time in his life. As he sits on the motorcycle waiting for Forsenko and his men to leave the restaurant, waves of excitement sweep through him. He is eager to deliver the bomb and surprised that he has no fear of dying.

Precisely at eleven, Forsenko and his gang leave the restaurant laughing, arms around one another, walking with the lurch of too much to drink. He lifts his cell phone from a side pocket and calls Kia, "They've just left the restaurant."

"Then I'd better get moving," she says.

ALEX FOCUSES ON Forsenko's limousine and watches five men enter it. Two men each get into the other two cars. The motorcade drives off the parking lot with Forsenko's limousine in the middle.

Alex waits until the three vehicles turn onto Emmons before he roars off in pursuit. When he sees the Forsenko motorcade turn left onto Coney Island Avenue, he accelerates. He is a block behind when the three vehicles turn down Ocean View. Alex crosses Brighton 7 at thirty miles an hour and sees the lead car begin its turn into Brighton 6. Its brake lights flash, and it stops abruptly. Forsenko's limousine brake lights flash and it stops suddenly.

Alex engages the clutch and brakes and his bike fishtails slightly on the macadam surface. With his right foot still on the rear brake, he releases the front brake, rips the bomb from his neck, heels the bike to the right, and slams the bomb container into the rear window. He can feel the plastic case break. As soon as the bomb strikes the car, he rolls the throttle and pops the clutch. The big Harley shoots forward leaving behind a trail of ear-splitting noise.

A split second before Alex delivers the bomb Forsenko hears the roar of the approaching motorcycle, turns and sees something smack onto the rear window. Immediately sensing danger, he screams, "A bomb! Get it! Get it!" The bodyguard on his left lunges sideways, grasps the door handle and yanks down on it. The door won't open. Frantically Forsenko charges to his right and pulls down on the door handle. It's locked. Terror stricken, Forsenko turns, pounds on the glass partition that separates the passenger compartment from the driver, and screams, "The lock button! Release the lock button!" To his horror, the driver's seat is empty!

The driver, hearing Forsenko scream "It's a bomb! Get it!" throws open his door and jumps out, but in his haste he fails to release the lock button controlling the other doors.

Forsenko's deputy, Roskovsky, seated in the jump seat, keeps his wits and lowers the left passenger window and starts toward it. Forsenko sees what he's up to and pulls him back with such force that his head strikes and shatters the glass partition. Forsenko lunges for the open window. But it's too late. Ten seconds has elapsed. The bomb explodes!

Alex hears the explosion, down shifts, slows the motorcycle to a normal speed, and watches as people scurry from restaurants and houses and run excitedly in the direction of the blast. Turning onto Ocean Parkway he sees cars stopping and traffic snarls developing.

He wheels into the service drive and looks for Kia. Every parking space on both sides of the service drive are occupied. Midway in the second block he sees a car's red taillights. He pulls next to a parked car, leans the motorcycle against it, removes his helmet and puts on a baseball cap and sunglasses. Carrying the helmet under his left arm, he crosses to the sidewalk, and with shouts of excitement and car horns blowing behind him, he walks to the car with the lighted taillights. He opens the door and slides in.

Kia throws herself across the seat, her arms encircling him, "Alex! You're safe!"

Alex gently removes her arms, "Kia, let's get out of here!"

Kia puts the car in drive and moves slowly along the service drive stopping where it merges with Ocean Parkway. Keeping to the right, she spins up the ramp, stops at the top, clears traffic, and roars out onto the Belt Parkway. Eight minutes later they cross the Verrazano Narrows Bridge and head south on the New Jersey Turnpike.

They ride in silence, immersed in their own thoughts. Alex breaks the silence, "How do you feel?"

"Tired, anxious, happy, sad, I feel a lot of different emotions, but mainly I'm tired. I'll feel better after I've had some sleep."

Alex points ahead, "I see a service area. Pull in and I'll drive." She turns into the service area and stops. He climbs behind the wheel, "We should be in Atlanta at about three. You try to sleep. If I get tired, I'll pull into a rest stop. "

Kia hands him a bottle of water. "Do you want a sandwich?" Alex shakes his head. "Do you know if anyone besides Forsenko and his men were injured?"

"Only Forsenko and the men in his car."

"How do you know that?"

"When I entered the intersection, there was no other traffic, either behind me, on-coming, or approaching from the right. Also, I deliberately made the bomb charge small so that the blast would not be destructive beyond a ten foot radius."

234 · James Gabler

"Then how . . ."

Alex interrupts her with a wave of his hand, "An explosion creates heat and gas under very high pressure that travels outward as a blast wave. The pressure dissipates the farther the wave moves outward. By limiting the explosive charge, I limited its explosive effects. But if the bomb was on the car's rear window when it exploded, and I'm sure it was, an implosion was created as well as an explosion. The blast effect from the implosion was confined to the space inside the car, and its destructive force is far greater than the explosion." He looks over at her, "Does that make sense?"

Kia sighs. "That makes me feel much better. All week I've worried that some innocent person might be killed or injured." She leans back and closes her eyes.

CHAPTER 53

W<small>HILE</small> A<small>LEX</small> D<small>RIVES</small> south on I 95, tired and smelly, and still not half way to Atlanta, Lester Hammond arises, leaving his thirty-four year old trophy wife sleeping soundly in their luxurious bedroom. It is six-thirty. Even on Saturday mornings, Hammond's restlessness leaves him unable to sleep late. After showering, he puts on a silk robe and velvet slippers, walks to the kitchen, pours a cup of coffee, and enters the den.

Hammond is proud of his turn-of-the-century four story Upper East Side townhouse, and he feels especially at ease in the den, a room that combines the elegance of Oriental rugs, rich fabrics, and English antiques with the comfort of mahogany paneled walls, a fireplace and recessed bookshelves.

Hammond picks up the remote, flicks on the television, and strolls to a bank of windows that look east. He glances down at boats moving on the East River, and sipping his coffee watches a brilliant orange sun climb above the horizon. It is quiet moments like this, no matter how transient or brief that cause him to pause and appreciate his life. He has a beautiful wife, wealth, position, power, and prestige. He is feeling very good about himself when his thoughts are distracted by a television announcement: "Police report that a car bombing in the Brighton Beach section of Brooklyn late last night resulted in the death of six men who were occupants of a limousine owned and occupied by Boris Forsenko . . ."

The coffee cup falls from his hand, crashes on the floor, and spills on his slippers and the rug. Hammond rushes to the telephone and dials the private number of Harry Bricker, his chief of operations in New York. Bricker answers on the second ring.

"Harry, this is Lester. Have you heard about the car bombing in Brooklyn?"

"There was a message on my answering service from a confidential Brooklyn police source when I checked about ten minutes ago. The message advises that it occurred . . ."

"Harry, I want you to personally find out everything you can about the bombing and get back to me as soon as possible. I particularly want to know if the police have any ideas as to who committed it." Hammond looks down and notices the coffee stain on his slippers. Mess repulses him, and he kicks the slippers off. "Ariana and I are leaving for Paris on the Concorde at noon. We will leave here by helicopter for Kennedy at ten-thirty. Get me a preliminary report before I leave."

"I'll get right on it and call you as soon as I've something more than what's being reported on television."

CHAPTER 54

KIA AND ALEX are about four hours from Atlanta when Lester Hammond's cellular phone rings. He is leaving his limousine and about to board the helicopter. It is Harry Bricker. Bricker fills him in on all details known to the police, but the bottom line is that the police don't have a clue as to who the bomb-throwing motorcyclist is. Lester Hammond does.

Hammond calls Tommy Miers, his Atlanta chief of operations. Miers engineered the break-in of Alex's apartment when they recovered the Vanderbork computer. He led the investigation that turned up Alex's presence in Paris. Tommy is about to tee off on the third hole at the Cherokee Country Club when his private cell phone vibrates. He motions his golfing partners that he will have to take the call, and he listens patiently while Hammond explains the bombing and his suspicion that Alex Ivanovich is the mysterious motorcyclist.

"You know how much I enjoy golf, and I truly hate interrupting your game, but it might be important to know where Ivanovich has been for the past several days, whether he is in Atlanta now, whether he worked yesterday, and whether he purchased a train, bus or airline ticket to New York City. Tommy, I want you to get one of our best men on this immediately."

Because it is Saturday morning, it isn't easy locating his best operatives, but at eleven-thirty Miers catches up with Alan Brunson who was involved in the recent investigation of Ivanovich. Miers fills Brunson in on what he knows about the bombing, Hammond's suspicions, and the need for immediate action.

While speaking with Miers, Brunson switches on his computer and brings up their file on Ivanovich. Brunson hangs up from Miers, and dials Alex's telephone number. The answering machine comes on. He drives to Midtown and parks on Myrtle Street, a block north of Alex's apartment.

It is a lazy Saturday afternoon, and at twelve-thirty the sun is already hot. Brunson is dressed casually, khaki pants, a blue short sleeved silk shirt, and loafers. He walks south on Myrtle, left on 3rd Street, and stops at the alley. He looks around. There is no one in sight. He walks up the alley and sees only one car in the parking space next to Alex's apartment. It is Alex's town car. He knows from the past investigation that the other parking space belongs to the second floor tenant in the main house. Brunson continues up the alley another fifty yards and turns. As he walks back he studies Alex's cottage. There are no lights on inside or accumulated newspapers out front. He decides to knock and pretend that he has the wrong address if anyone answers. The door leading onto the porch is locked. He knocks loudly. There is no answer and no sign of activity inside. He thinks it curious that the Alex's car is here but no one at home. *Where did Ivanovich go without his car?*

He cuts through the yard and climbs the steps leading to the main house. He pushes the buzzer for the second floor apartment. The nameplate shows the occupant is Roland Walters. Then Brunson remembers, Walters works for a dot com company in Atlanta but his family lives in Charleston, South Carolina, and he visits his family on weekends.

The first floor apartment lists the occupants as David Steen and Richard Warlick. He presses the buzzer. A few moments later a voice answers, "Who is it?"

"A friend of Alex Ivanovich."

"Mister Ivanovich doesn't live here."

"I know. I'm trying to locate him. May I talk with you for just a moment?"

"You are talking with me."

"I mean personally, face to face, just for a moment."

David releases the speaker button and turns to his roommate Richard. "Should I?" Richards shrugs and points to a chair where copies of Alex's Friday and Saturday *New York Times* and *Atlanta Journal-Constitution* lay unopened, "Don't let him come in here."

David waltzes out through the foyer and cracks open the front door. The man standing on the other side is in his late thirties, well groomed with close-cropped hair. The thought, *a plainclothes cop*, immediately strikes David.

"I'm a friend of Alex's. I just got into town and came by to see him. I knocked on the porch door but there was no answer. I thought you might be able to tell me where I can find him."

"Are you a police officer?"

"No, just a friend who wants to say hello."

"What is your name so that I can tell Alex that you stopped by?" Brunson stares at David. "I'm afraid I can't help you, sir," David says with a giggle and slams the door.

Alex and Kia are about 185 miles north of Atlanta when Brunson mutters, "Fucking queer," and turns and leaves.

Walking back to his car an idea occurs to Brunson. What about the Russian's friend, Kia Williams. Is she at home? Has she been absent from work this week? He checks the file for her address and phone number, and notes that she owns a 1996 Carolla Toyota. He calls the office and leaves instructions with an associate to start checking on whether Alex Ivanovich or Kia Williams rented a car, or purchased airline, train or bus tickets to New York in the past week. He calls Williams and gets her answering service. He drives to her apartment.

Her car is not in the parking area. Brunson walks into the apartment unit hallway and presses the buzzer to Kia's apartment. No answer. He presses the buzzer of the neighbor in apartment 1B. No answer. He decides to return to the office and contact Harry Bricker in New York for more details about the bombing before reporting to Tommy Miers.

CHAPTER 55

WITH KIA AT the wheel they enter the city limits of Atlanta sixteen hours and twelve minutes after leaving the entrance ramp to the Belt Parkway. Alex, emotionally and physically drained, is thinking of nothing more exciting than taking a shower and going to bed when Kia says, "Alex, would you mind terribly if I dropped you at your apartment. I promised my parents that I would visit them tonight. I'm dead tired."

"I think it's a good idea that we not be seen together. Drop me off at Jupiter and 5th. I'll get my car and meet you at the turn around in Piedmont Park. We'll transfer everything from your car to my car."

IT IS NOT quite five and still daylight when Alex returns from the park and parks outside his apartment. He decides to wait until dark before removing the gear from the car trunk. David and Richard are his friends, but they are also busybodies. The less they know, the better. Alex enters his apartment and looks around. Everything appears as he left it. He is about to check his messages when the phone rings. It's David.

"Alex, you had a visitor this afternoon."

Alex waits, but David does not continue. "Okay David, I'll bite. Who was it?"

242 · James Gabler

"I don't know. He said he was an old friend of yours that he had just gotten into town and stopped by to see you. He wanted to know if I knew where you were. I told him the truth that I didn't know where you were."

"What did he look like?"

"He looked like a cop, Alex."

Alex feels his pulse quicken. "Aside from looking like a cop, what were his physical features?"

David thinks. "You might even say he was handsome, if you like that kind. I don't. Do I Richard?" he calls out.

Alex smiles to himself. David is teasing him. "Help me David. What does 'that kind' look like?"

"Well, he was about your size, dressed casually but neatly, and I would guess in his late thirties. He had brown hair, high cheekbones, and a thin, straight nose. When I asked his name so that I could tell you that he had stopped by, he just stared at me. That's when I slammed the door."

Alex thanks David. He hits the rewind button on the answering machine. His attention is attracted to three calls that are unidentifiable because the caller hung up. Suddenly, he is overwhelmed with fatigue. He undresses, showers, gets in bed and falls asleep.

ALEX AWAKES AT six the next morning. He has slept twelve hours. He brushes his teeth, starts a pot of coffee, and opens his laptop computer. He goes to the Internet connection, types in "nytimes.com." The web page, "The New York Times on the Web" appears. He clicks on "National/NY" and then on "New York Region." The top of the screen reads, "Six Men Dead in Brooklyn Car Bombing." The article continues, "Late Friday night six men died in the bombing of a limousine in the Brighton Beach section of Brooklyn. The bombing took place at the intersection of Ocean View and Brighton 6. Police officials said that the limousine, occupied by six men returning from a restaurant in

Sheepshead Bay, and attempting to turn south on Brighton 6, was required to stop at the intersection because of a street blockade. Witnesses in a car stopped behind the limousine reported that a motorcycle entered the intersection traveling west on Ocean View. As it passed the stopped limousine, the motorcyclist placed an object on the rear window of the limousine and sped away. Seconds later a bomb exploded. The Commissioner of the Department of Public Works, Ronald Dickson, reports that there was no road work in progress or any record of traffic restrictions at the intersection in question.

"The dead were identified as Boris Forsenko 52, Viktor Tabakov 41, Vladimir Roslovsky 44, Sergei Komeskov 27, Andrei Chubatis 29, and Anatoly Chermonya 31, all Russian immigrants and Brighton Beach residents. The limousine was owned by Boris Forsenko.

"A spokesperson for the Brooklyn District Attorney's Office disclosed that Boris Forsenko was under investigation but refused to reveal the nature of the investigation. An official admitted that the police are unsure of the motive for the bombing but are investigating whether it was mob related. An anonymous source reported . . ." Alex turns the computer off and pours a cup of coffee. He has not worked out in three days.

Alex decides to go for a jog.

CHAPTER 56

AFTER DINING WITH her parents, Kia goes home, showers and crashes in bed. In the morning she checks her phone messages and learns that Sharon Komat, the lawyer assigned by the State's Attorney's Office to prosecute Harvey Slinger, has left a message that she wants to meet with Kia as soon as possible.

At work on Monday Kia contacts Komat's office and makes an appointment to meet attorney Komat at her office at 4 P.M. Other than what she has read in the newspapers and heard on television and radio, she's had no further contact with the authorities since she gave them a detailed account of Harvey's attempt to strangle her, and her suspicions that he murdered his associate. She is curious to know if the police have reexamined the circumstances surrounding Stilton's death. and what, if anything, they have uncovered.

WALKING DOWN THE gloomy corridor leading to attorney Komat's office, Kia wonders what Komat wants to talk to her about. She sees the meeting as a chance to find out the status of the case, and she is thankful for it.

The receptionist leads Kia into Sheila Komat's small, tidy office. Komat rises when Kia enters, and extends her hand. Komat is a tall, large framed black woman whose haggard appearance and puffy eyes suggest that she spent a restless night. Komat has a law degree from Yale, has been a prosecutor for fifteen years, and has acquired a reputation as a tough but fair prosecutor.

"Please have a seat," Komat says, directing Kia with a motion of her hand. Kia sits on a wooden chair that faces Komat's desk. "I'm Sheila Komat. I've been assigned to prosecute Harvey Slinger." Kia nods. "I asked you to come here for several reasons: to meet you, to bring you up to date on where we are with the case, and to tell you about what I would like to see as the eventual disposition of the case."

"Disposition?"

"Yes. Slinger's lawyers have approached me with a suggested disposition, and although their proposal has some rough edges that will have to be worked out, overall I find it reasonable, subject, of course, to court approval."

"You mean you're not going to prosecute him?" Kia says, rising from the chair. "He broke into my house and tried to kill me."

"Please," Komat says, "hear me out. We are prosecuting him. It's just . . ."

"You call it plea bargaining, don't you?"

The prosecutor stares back at her with tired, blood-shot eyes, and nods.

"Why?"

"Why? See those filing cabinets," Komat says, pointing to a corner of her office.

"They're filled. Over four hundred cases assigned to me alone. And every lawyer in this office handles at least as many cases. Do you think for one second that the criminal law system in this city could survive without plea bargaining?" She is on her feet, her face red. She stops. "I'm sorry. I don't mean to shout at you, but I get so frustrated with people saying that we're always taking the easy way out." She slumps into her chair.

"Well, isn't that what it is?"

"In a sense, yes, but it's necessary, and nobody understands that better than the lawyers and judges who are responsible for administering the criminal justice system in Atlanta. Let me explain what I've been talking to Slinger's lawyers about," Komat says, her lips compressed in frustration. "Slinger will be sentenced to a total of fifty years, to be served concurrently, which under present guidelines means that if he doesn't get into trouble in prison, he'll be eligible for parole after fifteen years. It doesn't mean he'll be released after fifteen years. It means only that he'll be eligible for release. In addition, he'll voluntarily accept disbarment, which will prevent him from ever practicing law again."

"What about Slinger's involvement in the death of his associate?"

Komat shakes her head. "Slinger steadfastly maintains that he had nothing to do with Geronsky's death, and although the police have reinvestigated the matter, they have found nothing pointing conclusively to Slinger. The evidence trail is cold."

"And if he did do it, and I believe he did, he gets away with murder.

"Yes," Komat says with sad resolution, "and he won't be the first person to get away with murder."

Komat's words strike Kia forcefully. Komat has made up her mind, and there is nothing she can say or do to change it. She stands. "Thank you, Ms. Komat, for taking the time to explain. Whatever you decide, I'm sure will be best for everyone."

They shake hands, and Kia leaves.

CHAPTER 57

THE CHAUFFEUR HOLDS the door open as Nelson Foster, senior vice president and chief financial officer of The Coca-Cola Company, climbs into the waiting limousine in front of company headquarters. Foster is on his way to the Fulton County Airport to board the company Gulfstream for a flight to Beijing and a series of important meetings with Chinese officials. While settling comfortably in the posh leather seat, he sees a Lincoln Town Car pull up and stop a few feet away. The driver jumps out and snaps opened the passenger door. As his limousine starts forward, Foster shouts, "Stop!" The chauffeur jams on the brakes.

Foster spins around and stares through the rear window at the town car driver. *Holy shit!* He removes a Palm Pilot from an inside jacket pocket and enters the license number of the town car. There is no doubt about it. The driver is the man he spoke with early one morning at the Mooring's in Islamorada. Foster remembers approaching him and asking if they had met before. *The man spoke with an upper-class English accent. The son-of-a-bitch told me he was a professor of economic history.* Foster rarely forgets a name, but a face—never!

Foster opens his cell phone and calls Cola-Cola security. A male voice answers, "Security, how may I direct your call?"

"Stanley Masland," Foster says. Masland is director of Coca-Cola's in-house security.

"I'm sorry, sir, but Mr. Masland is presently out of the office."

"Then let me speak with his chief deputy. Tell him that Nelson Foster is calling."

"Yes sir."

Within seconds Adrian Smoose is on the line, identifies himself as an assistant to the director of security, and asks how he might assist Mr. Foster.

"Adrian, I want you to check this license number." He gives the number to Adrian. "It's a black Lincoln Town Car. Find out who the owner is, but more importantly, the name of the driver of the car who just moments ago arrived at our headquarters with Mildred Pittson, a Coca-Cola executive."

Adrian Smoose checks the time; it is 2:27 p.m. He jots it down and continues making notes as the chief financial officer speaks.

"I want you to find out everything you can about the driver, his age, where he lives, whether he's married, children, education, everything. Do you understand?"

"I understand completely, Mr. Foster. When do you want the report?"

"I'll be out of the country for the next seven days. I want it on my desk when I return."

"Yes sir. It will be on your desk when you return."

Adrian Smoose is short and pudgy with a sallow complexion, a receding hairline, and enormous fat lips that overwhelm the rest of his face. What makes Smoose's appearance even more distracting is his habit of smacking his lips together when he speaks. Because of how he looks, fellow employees refer to him behind his back as the "geek," "dork," "sweet lips." He is, however, a hard worker, and during the thirty-five years he has been with Coke, he has worked his way up from a stock boy to one of five assistants to the director of in-house security. Smoose is extremely pleased that a senior officer has requested his help. It makes no difference that Foster's call was intended for his superior. The job is now his.

Checking ownership of the vehicle is an easy task. The Coca-Cola Company has influential contacts throughout the world, and the Georgia Department of Driver Services is no exception. Smoose e-mails his request for information on the ownership of the vehicle to Coca-Cola's contact at the appropriate department and prioritizes the request as "URGENT." Within a half hour he receives an e-mail reply advising that the owner and operator is Alexandre Ivanovich, and the additional details of his address, age, etc. One entry particularly catches his attention, Ivanovich is a Russian immigrant.

With the information in hand, Smoose places a call to Thomas Miers, vice-president and chief of operations for Hammond Investigative Services for the southern United States. He thinks that an investigation on behalf of Mr. Foster warrants going straight to the top. Besides, he wants the right people to know that he is handling such an important assignment.

Miers' private secretary answers the call. Smoose identifies himself but is advised that Mr. Miers is in a meeting. He stresses the importance and urgency of his call. The secretary promises to inform Mr. Miers as soon as he is free.

Adrian Smoose sits at his desk wondering why the senior vice-president of The Coca-Cola Company wants information about some Russian immigrant. He rereads the information the Department of Driver Services has sent him. He shakes his head. It doesn't help. He busies himself with routine matters and at 4:50 p.m., while tidying his desk, the telephone rings.

"Hello, Adrian? Tommy Miers. I haven't seen you since that computer espionage seminar we attended. How are you?

Smoose is pleased that Miers remembers him. "I'm fine Mr. Miers, how . . ."

"Adrian, please call me Tommy."

Smoose feels uncomfortable addressing an important man like Thomas Miers by his first name but, if that's what he wants, he'll do it. Miers continues, "I understand you called and said it's urgent."

"Yes. Our senior vice-president and chief financial officer, Mr. Foster, has given me an assignment to find out everything possible about a man by the name of Alexandre Ivanovich." Miers stiffens. "And I'm going to need your office's help. Mr. Foster instructed me to have the report ready for him in seven days."

Questions flash through Miers' mind as he listens. *What the hell is going on? Hammond, now Foster. Why does Foster want information on Ivanovich?* "Of course, we will help. It might assist our investigation if we knew why Mr. Foster wants the information."

"I can't help you on that score, sir. Mr. Foster didn't say why he wants the information."

"Did Mr. Foster say why he needs the information in seven days?"

"Yes. He's away on a business trip and wants the report when he returns."

Pulling up the Ivanovich file on his computer, Miers says, "Adrian, I'll personally be back in touch with you tomorrow."

"Thanks, Mr. Miers."

Miers immediately calls Lester Hammond and is put right through. "Lester, Tommy. There's been a development that I think you should know about." He tells his boss about the telephone conversation with Adrian Smoose. When Miers finishes, Hammond suspects he knows the answer to why Foster wants to know about the former Russian spy. *Foster's been compromised.* "Tommy, what I'm about to ask of you is probably the most delicate assignment of your career."

He pauses. "It must be accomplished with great discretion and known only to you and the operatives you select." He pauses again, letting the silence emphasize what he is about to say.

"When Nelson Foster returns to Atlanta, I want to know his every action, where he goes, who he sees, and especially if he sees Ivanovich."

Miers knows better than to ask his boss why. Hammond will tell him when he wants him to know. "What about that funny looking guy, Smoose? How do I handle his request?"

"Give him just enough information so that Foster knows who he's dealing with, KGB background, how he came to live and work in Atlanta, that sort of thing," Hammond says, as he walks to the window and stares down at the evening traffic creeping along Madison Avenue.

CHAPTER 58

THE GULFSTREAM V pilot has clearance from air traffic control and is on the final approach to the Fulton County Airport. Nelson Foster sits back in his seat gazing out as the Atlanta skyline fades behind the deepening evening shadows. He is thinking, not about the enormous success of his business trip (the prospect of all China being opened for the sale of Coca-Cola—over a billion people!) but about the town car driver. He has thought about him a hundred times over the past seven days, always reaching the same conclusion, *He's the son-of-a-bitch behind it.*

It has been three weeks since he received in the mail, addressed "private and confidential," the video cassette showing his Sarah Bernhardt performance. Still, he has not been contacted. His thoughts on how to deal with the driver are interrupted by the flight attendant's announcement that they have landed. The strain of the trip and his worry about the videotape has left him exhausted. He will deal with the situation in the morning.

THE NEXT MORNING before sunrise, Foster is on his way to the office totally unaware that a GPS navigation device is attached to the undercarriage of his car. In his office he shuffles through his mail until he finds what he is looking for—Adrian Smoose's report on the town car driver. It is labeled, "Personal and Confidential." His right hand tears away the envelope flap. His eyes pour down the page. His head jerks back when he reads, "Ivanovich is an ex-KGB colonel who served nineteen years in the Foreign Service Directorate."

If there was any doubt in Foster's mind as to who was behind the taping of his evening in drag, it is gone. He reads the rest of the report with one thought in mind, how to handle the situation. He runs through his options: he can notify the police or he can notify Lester Hammond but either way the reason for the blackmail will become known, and he can kiss good-bye his chances of succeeding William Brannon as Coca-Cola's next chief executive. He knows that a lot of executives' mistakes and bad habits, both business and personal, are tolerated, but cross-dressing is not one of them.

He turns in his chair and looks out across the Atlanta skyline and thinks about his future. Nothing has been said officially, but unofficially members of the board of directors have made known to him that he, not Sharon Talbot, is their choice to succeed Brannon. He has two other options: he can do nothing and wait for Ivanovich to make the next move, or make the next move himself. "Don't put off for tomorrow what you can do today" has been a guiding principle throughout his life, and it has served him well. He glances at his watch, it is 7:20 a.m. He decides to call Ivanovich. The Russian's cellular business telephone number is listed in Smoose's report. Foster dials it.

Alex is on his way to pick up a client when his phone rings. "Is this Star Limousine Service?"

"Yes sir," Alex replies.

"My name is Donald Pickens. Your name was given to me by a friend who said you're a reliable service. I need a ride to the airport at four this afternoon. Are you available?"

"Yes sir. Where shall I come for you?"

"The Capital City Club. It's located at Harris and Peachtree but the entrance is on Harris. When you come in give the girl behind the desk my name, and she will notify me."

"I know the location. I'll be there at four."

ALEX PARKS IN the Capital City Club lot, enters and advises the woman at the desk that he is there for Donald Pickens. The woman disappears momentarily. Alex, standing facing the entrance door with his back to the club's interior, hears a voice from behind say, "Mr. Ivanovich?" He turns and on seeing Nelson Foster, he tries to hide his surprise.

Dressed in a blue worsted suit, white cotton button-down shirt, regimented blue and gold tie, and black wing-tipped shoes, Foster does not resemble the transvestite who pranced about the Islamorada motel room dressed as Sarah Bernhardt. Foster senses that the Russian recognizes him.

"Mr. Pickens?"

"Yes. For now," Foster says, "Pickens will do."

Aware that Foster has staged the meeting, Alex wonders what lies ahead. He opens the passenger door of the town car and Foster slides in. Turning toward Foster as he gets behind the wheel, Alex says, "What airline, sir?"

"I don't want the airport, Mr. Ivanovich. I want to talk to you, so just drive."

As Alex turns left on Peachtree and heads north, he glances in the rear view mirror and sees a black Buick emerge from Harris Street and follow behind. "I see that your colleagues are following us."

"If anyone is following us, it's not at my direction."

"Then I take it that you want me to lose them?"

"Absolutely!" Foster turns and peers through the rear window.

Approaching the next intersection, Alex faces a red traffic light. He slows for it. When almost to a stop, he presses down on the accelerator and the car shoots forward reaching sixty within seconds. Through the rear view mirror he watches the Buick hesitate at the intersection, and then speed through the light. But Alex has gained the momentum. After a series of quick turns through the downtown streets, he doesn't see the Buick and feels confident he has lost it.

Traveling now in the normal flow of traffic and feeling relaxed, he says, "I'm afraid I won't be able to talk with you, sir."

"Why not?"

"Because you're recording our conversation."

Foster removes a small recorder from his jacket, flicks it to the off position, and throws it onto the front seat. "I'm not now."

Alex glances in the rearview mirror. "I'll talk with you but not in this car."

Foster thinks for a moment. *Where can we go and I won't be recognized?* "I'm a member of the health club at the Four Seasons. Drive there." Foster relaxes.

Alex makes a U-turn and heads north on Peachtree. Turning onto 14th Street he swings into the Four Seasons' circular driveway and valet parks. He follows Foster through the hotel lobby into the health club. Foster signs in, and they are given locker keys.

In the locker room, Foster removes his shirt, holds his arms out to the side and says, "See, I'm not wired. But I assume, Ivanovich, that you are aware that electronic eavesdropping equipment is now so sophisticated that a recording device can be implanted under one's skin and you can't see it."

They strip naked and Foster motions with his head for Alex to follow him. They walk down a hall, enter the sauna and sit facing each other on redwood benches.

"What do you want to talk about?" Alex asks.

"When are you going to officially blackmail me?"

Alex fixes Foster with a searching stare. "I have no idea what you're talking about."

"Oh, come now, don't try to bullshit me. I know your KGB background. It's no coincidence that you showed up at the Islamorada fishing resort where I was staying, and that same evening a hidden camera recorded me in my room doing you . . . " He waves his hand in a gesture of disgust, "you know what."

256 · JAMES GABLER

"Why don't you say what's on your mind?"

"All right, I will," Foster says, his fists clenched, jaw jutting. "That scurrilous video showing me in a woman's dress . . ."

"What about it?"

"What about it?" He stands and moves to within a foot of Alex's face, the veins bulging in his neck. "Do you know that blackmail is a serious crime?"

Alex, seated on the bench, his eyes level with the smaller man's eyes, says, "Do you know that murder is a serious crime."

"Murder? What are you talking about?"

"I am talking about someone at Coca-Cola who contracted for my murder, and as far as I can determine, the contract is still out."

They hold each other's gaze. Alex doesn't know why, but he feels he can trust Foster. He also sees Foster as the opening he's been looking for and decides to confide in him. Alex tells Foster about the break-in of his apartment, why he thinks it occurred, and the two recent attempts on his life.

When he finishes, Foster says, "Who do you think is behind it?"

"Brannon."

Foster stares at Alex, a quizzical look on his face. "Bill Brannon? Why?"

"He also received a video, and he's afraid the world might find out about it. I suppose he's decided to eliminate the source."

"It's that bad?"

"Brannon must think so."

Sweat is coursing down both of their bodies. "So you admit it."

A vague smile tightens around Alex's lips. He nods almost imperceptibly.

"What do you want?" Foster says.

"I want The Coca-Cola Company to do what it agreed to do, pay for the cola formula that it's been using illegally since 1921. That's what I want."

"What the hell are you talking about?"

"In case you don't know, Mr. Foster, seventy-eight years ago the United States government sued Coca-Cola in the Federal District Court here in Atlanta. The government won the case. As a result, Coca-Cola was required to change its soft drink formula. The president of Coca-Cola at that time, Roscoe Hatfield, asked a local chemist by the name of Thomas R. P. Calderman, to submit a new Coca-Cola formula. Calderman submitted a recipe for a new Coca-Cola, and Hatfield and Calderman entered into a written agreement that provided that if The Coca-Cola Company used Calderman's recipe, Coca-Cola would pay Calderman one percent of future gross revenues derived from the use of the recipe."

"I know there was a lawsuit, but I've never heard of Calderman or a Calderman formula. But let's assume that what you say is true, what makes you think that Calderman's formula is the same as today's Coca-Cola formula?"

Alex explains the airport incident with Vanderbork and how his curiosity about the formula led him to open Vanderbork's computer and read the formula. "Having read what Vanderbork records as the secret formula, I can tell you with one hundred percent certainty that the Calderman formula and today's Coca-Cola Classic formula are identical."

Alex also tells Foster about how his negotiations with Simon Calderman led to his purchase of the Calderman formula.

The smirk on Foster's face confirms his skepticism. "Do you have the original documents that support what you've told me?"

"Yes. I have the original contract entered into between Roscoe Hatfield and Thomas Calderman, and the original Calderman recipe that's been used by Coke since then." Alex stands and throws water from his cup on the hot coals. Turning to Foster he adds, "Do you know how much The Coca-Cola Company owes me as the owner of the Calderman formula?"

"I have no idea."

"As the company's chief financial officer, I thought you might have a ballpark figure in mind. I can't give you an exact figure,

because even though it's public information, I don't know how to
accurately access all the information. As you know, there's an electronic billboard display here in Atlanta that shows daily the total
number of drinks Coca-Cola has sold since it was founded. The
last time I looked the figure stood at more than six trillion two
hundred and sixty-five billion drinks."

"So what?"

"Extrapolating from those figures, I calculate that in the
past seventy-eight years Coca-Cola has earned gross revenues of
over one trillion dollars from sales relating solely to the
Calderman formula. You don't have to be a mathematical genius
to figure that one percent of one trillion is ten billion. If you
allow six percent compound interest, which is the legal rate of
interest in Georgia, Coca-Cola owes me about one hundred and
fifty billion dollars."

They stare at each other in silence. The smirk returns to Foster face. "That makes you richer than Bill Gates and Warren Buf-
fett combined."

"Yes, in theory it does, but I don't have the money yet."

The suggestion of a smile creases his lips. "I'm glad to see that
you've retained your sense of humor." Foster takes a sip of water.
"As a finance person I'm curious as to how you arrived at the ten
billion dollar figure."

Alex shrugs. "Easy. I figured seventy-five percent or four trillion seven hundred billion of the drinks sold resulted from
Calderman's formula. During that seventy-eight year period, the
price of a bottle or glass of Coca-Cola went from five cents to a
dollar. I arbitrarily, but conservatively, calculated the average cost
per drink at twenty-five cents. Four trillion seven hundred billion
multiplied by twenty-five cents . . ."

Foster interrupts. "One trillion one hundred seventy-five billion dollars."

Alex wets his lips. "You would agree, would you not, Mr. Foster, that if my ten billion dollar figure is correct, compound interest

on sales over seventy-eight years would increase the amount owed to over one hundred and fifty billion dollars."

"Everything you've said is ridiculous, and I don't know why I'm sitting here listening to it." Foster says, wiping his face with a towel.

"Do I take it that our meeting is over?"

"Have you ever heard of the statute of limitations? Georgia has a two year statute of limitations!"

"I've talked to a lawyer about that, and limitations don't attach where there's fraud. Here there's fraud from the beginning of the contract. Hatfield deliberately and willfully failed to pay Calderman's estate in accordance with the agreement, and succeeding Coca-Cola executives have willfully and fraudulently denied the existence of the contract to both Thomas R. P. Calderman's son and grandson." Alex reaches back, picks up his towel and wipes his face. "That's fraud, Mr. Foster, and Georgia courts allow punitive damages for fraud."

"I don't want you to read anything into what I'm about to say, but I want to find out where you're coming from. Okay?" Alex nods. "If Coca-Cola offered to buy the formula that you claim to own, are you prepared to sign the necessary documents conveying clear and unencumbered title to Coca-Cola?"

"If the price is right, yes."

"You haven't answered my question about blackmail," Foster says.

"I don't recall hearing you ask about blackmail. I've never said anything about blackmail to you, Brannon or Talbot."

"Sharon Talbot has received a video?"

Alex nods. A grin breaks across Foster's face. "Now, isn't that interesting." He pauses. "Do Brannon or Talbot know about my video?"

"No. I haven't spoken with either of them, so they don't know."

"Ivanovich, if Coca-Cola decides to buy its formula from

you, what would become of those videos? And by that I mean, all traces of them, copies, transcripts, photographs, everything."

"Whatever Mr. Brannon, Ms. Talbot and you decide."

"How much do you plan on charging us . . . I mean . . . Coca-Cola for its formula?"

"You keep saying 'its formula.' It's my formula."

"I understand, but you must forgive me because all my life I've thought of it as the property of The Coca-Cola Company." They lapse into silence, staring at each other.

Foster repeats, "How much?"

"As of two o'clock today Coke's stock market capitalization exceeded one hundred and thirty-six billion dollars. The formula is the ingredient most responsible for creating that wealth, so I don't think asking for one-tenth of one percent of that amount or $136,000,000 is asking too much."

"I don't mean to disillusion you, or denigrate the Coca-Cola formula, but let me explain something. The formula is not the most important factor in Coca-Cola's success, although it certainly has played an important part. The formula does contain, as you know, secret ingredients that set Coca-Cola Classic apart from other colas and makes it, in my opinion, the best tasting soft drink in the world. As such, it is a priceless asset. The factor most responsible for creating the company's wealth, however, has been its unceasing advertising over the years. There is almost no place on this earth that you can go and not see or hear the name Coca-Cola. Coca-Cola has become more American than apple pie, and through advertising we have spread the company name and goodwill to every corner of the globe."

"If you didn't have a product, what would you advertise?"

"You have to have more than a product. You have to have a product that people want to buy. The formula is responsible for that part of Coca-Cola's success, but what I'm saying is that if people don't know about the product, they won't buy it."

"I know nothing about marketing, but it seems that what

you're saying is that the two go together, and one without the other will not succeed. If Coca-Cola doesn't own the formula, there is nothing to advertise, and the largest part of its asset base will evaporate."

"Perhaps, Ivanovich, you should have been in marketing, rather than spying."

Alex smiles, "Perhaps I would have been had I been born in the United States."

"Before I make a proposal, I must know the answer to this question. Do you have other compromising information of any kind relating to anyone at Coca-Cola other than Brannon, Talbot and me?"

"No."

"Your asking price of $136,000,000 not only won't fly, it won't even get off the ground. Listen to me, Ivanovich. Listen very carefully. I will agree to help you sell the formula to Coca-Cola in exchange for two promises from you. First, you agree to accept $15,000,000 in full settlement in exchange for the Hatfield letter and the 1921 Calderman formula. Second, upon payment of $15,000,000, you'll turn over to whomever, wherever, whenever, and however I designate the original and all copies of the videotapes, photographs, transcripts, and anything else you have relating to Brannon, Talbot and me."

Foster stands and empties his cup on the hot coals. "If the figure I've suggested is acceptable, you should write a letter to our General Counsel, Felix Ungerschmidt, outlining what you've told me about owning the formula, why it's your property and not the property of Coca-Cola, the amount of money you claim Coca-Cola owes you, and enclose copies of all your documents. Your assertion that Coca-Cola owes you in excess of ten billion dollars will get Felix's attention. He'll seek a conference with Bill Brannon. That should get things moving."

"Let's get out of here," Alex says.

They leave the sauna and walk to the water fountain. After

refilling their cups, Alex says, "You want me to give up $136,000,000 in exchange for $15,000,000. Is that right?"

"Look, Ivanovich, let me explain the facts of life. The Coca-Cola Company has made more Georgians millionaires than all other businesses in this state combined. The people of Georgia are our friends. There's no judge or jury in this state that's going to award an ex-KGB Russian spy ten cents against The Coca-Cola Company. In fact, Ivanovich, and you can trust me on this, as soon as you file suit, it will be dismissed by the judge, and your ass will be on a plane heading back to Russia."

Alex feels a flush anger. "And do you know what I'll do before I get on that plane? I'll open a Website on the Internet and publish your secret formula for all the world to see and copy. And if you and your fellow ivory tower executives don't think people in third world countries won't start producing and selling it without a license, you're nuts!"

This guy is a live wire, Foster thinks. "Let's simmer down. We aren't going to get anywhere hollering at each other. If money is to be paid to you, it will have to be approved by the Coca-Cola Board of Directors. They will only consider approving it if it comes with Brannon's endorsement. And only if they feel that it is an amount that is justified in order to simply eliminate the risks of a law suit, the bad publicity attached to such litigation, and the possible damage to the franchise that might occur by your publishing the contents of the formula on the Internet. So, it has to be a realistic figure, a figure that Brannon can bring to the board and have taken serious. Common sense tells me that the figure can't be more than $15,000,000. Now, do we have an agreement or not? No guarantees, but I'll put forth my best efforts to get a settlement of $15,000,000."

"I have a partner who has an interest in any settlement. I'll have to talk with . . ."

"I want a commitment from you now. Because when I leave here, we're probably never going to talk or see one another again."

Alex reads in Foster's eyes that he is not bargaining. This is a first and final offer.

"Okay. I'll commit for my partner. Fifteen million dollars and we'll have a deal."

As they walk back to the locker room, Alex says, "I'm curious. Why are you doing this?"

The executive stops and looks up at the larger man. "Because you're a loose cannon that's about to explode, and when you do, I don't want to be a part of the damage. I'll tell you something else, Ivanovich. You had better keep your word, or you'll never get to spend the money." Foster turns and strides off.

Alex comes out of the shower at the same time as Foster. As they towel down, Alex says, "I want to remind you that someone was following us when we left the Capital City Club. That means that whoever it was knows that we were together today. If that tail was meant for you, rather than me, as I suspect it was, they'll be following you again, perhaps when you leave here."

"I'll keep that in mind."

CHAPTER 59

WHILE ALEX JOGS through an early morning fog in Piedmont Park, Coca-Cola's General Counsel, Flex Ungerschmidt, sits at his desk at Coca-Cola headquarters struggling with the most momentous decision of his well-structured life. Should he ask his wife of twenty-nine years for a divorce? She has been a caring and faithful partner and a good mother to their four children. But last night in San Francisco his twenty-eight year old girl friend rolled over in bed, braced her beautiful blonde head between the palms of her hands, and issued an ultimatum. "Felix, it's either your wife or me. You have two weeks to decide."

He flew back on the red-eye, and though tired and confused, he came straight to the office. Reading through the mail on his desk, Ungerschmidt's thoughts are three thousand miles away when his eyes read the words, "I am the legal owner of the cola formula that The Coca-Cola Company has been illegally using since 1921." He stops reading, refocuses, and reads: "Dear Mr. Ungerschmidt: My name is Alexandre Ivanovich and I reside in Atlanta. I am the legal owner of the cola formula that The Coca-Cola Company has been illegally using since 1921. I am enclosing a copy of the recipe that Thomas R. P. Calderman invented and submitted to Coca-Cola at the request of Coca-Cola's President, Roscoe Hatfield, and the contract that Coca-Cola entered into with Thomas R. P. Calderman based on the company's acceptance and use of Calderman's recipe. I own the originals of these documents.

"The contract between The Coca-Cola Company and Thomas R. P. Calderman, sets out in clear language The Coca-Cola Company's promise to pay Calderman, his heirs or assigns, one percent of future gross revenues from the sale of Coca-Cola produced from Calderman's 1921 recipe. A month after the execution of the contract Calderman died from a heart attack. Seventy-two days after Calderman's death, The Coca-Cola Company sold its first shipment of cola produced from the Calderman recipe.

"Over the past seventy-eight years the son and grandson of Thomas R. P. Calderman have asserted claims against The Coca-Cola Company based on that contract. In response to those claims, Coca-Cola has falsely denied the existence of the contract, and has knowingly falsely denied that it ever used the Calderman recipe in the production of Coca-Cola. Although a veil of secrecy is used by the company to avoid disclosure of its formula, I've seen the Coca-Cola formula, and it's identical to Calderman's 1921 recipe.

"As the owner of the 1921 Calderman recipe, The Coca-Cola Company owes me ten billion dollars exclusive of interest. These figures are calculated on the basis of Coca-Cola's sales resulting in the illegal use of the Calderman recipe from November 3, 1921 to present. Applying the legal rate of six percent interest, compounded annually, the amount owed to me exceeds one hundred and fifty billion dollars. I am advised by my attorneys that punitive damages for Coca-Cola's fraudulent use of the Calderman recipe are also a viable issue to be decided by a jury.

"I request a meeting with authorized representatives of The Coca-Cola Company to determine whether a settlement can be reached without the need for litigation. I can be contacted at the above telephone number." The letter is signed, "Alexandre Ivanovich."

Felix Ungerschmidt leans back in his chair, smiles and shakes his head. *What kind of kook is this?* He is about to drop the letter and enclosures into the wastebasket when a thought occurs to him. He reaches into a desk drawer and pulls out the company organizational chart that lists the corporate officers since the inception of the company.

From 1911 to 1928, Roscoe Hatfield is listed as president. He reads the letter that purports to represent the contract between Thomas R. P. Calderman and Coca-Cola. It is signed by Roscoe Hatfield. He looks at the other enclosure. It consists of one page, and is titled, "Recipe for new Coca-Cola, submitted by Thomas R. P. Calderman, 7/7/1921," and at the bottom of the page a different handwriting appears, "This recipe is accepted on behalf of The Coca-Cola Company in accordance with the terms of the contract between Thomas P. R. Calderman and The Coca-Cola Company, dated July 7, 1921 and is made a part of the contract." It is signed, "Roscoe Hatfield, President." It is dated, "July 23, 1921."

Ungerschmidt compares the signatures on the two documents. They appear identical. He does not know the contents of the Coca-Cola formula and cannot verify whether it is identical to the formula on his desk. He rereads Alex's letter and the contract.

He stands, walks to the window and stares out at traffic below. He glances at his watch. It is 7:50 a.m. Brannon will not be in for another hour or so. Even though the letter and enclosures are undoubtedly the work of a kook or prankster, Ungerschmidt feels that because the allegations are so serious, the company's chief executive officer must be advised of them.

At nine-fifteen Ungerschmidt walks down the hall to the corner suite of offices occupied by Brannon and his staff. He sticks his head in the office of Sheila Winslow, Brannon's executive secretary, "Good morning, Shelia."

Winslow's head snaps up. She smiles. "Well, good morning to you Mr. Ungerschmidt. I thought you were in San Francisco."

Felix smiles. *She knows everything that goes on in the company.*
He steps into the office. "I got back a few hours ago. Is Mr. Brannon in?"

"He came in about five minutes ago." Her smile broadens, "Is there anything I can help you with?"

"No thanks, Sheila. When Mr. Brannon has a free moment, would you tell him I would like to speak with him."

Winslow's smile fades. "Is it important?"

Ungerschmidt shrugs. "I don't think so, but it is something I think he should know about."

Winslow scribbles on a pad and then says, "Mr. Brannon is leaving this afternoon for the conference in Dravo, Switzerland, after which he's going to stay in Switzerland for a few days of skiing. Can it wait for a week?"

Ivanovich didn't set a deadline for a meeting and Ungerschmidt says, "I suppose so."

UNGERSCHMIDT IS BUSY reading a legal brief when he hears a noise, looks up, and sees Brannon standing in the doorway. "I'm sorry," Ungerschmidt says, standing.

With a hand gesture Brannon motions him back into the chair. "I would have said something, but I didn't want to break your concentration. I didn't know legal briefs were so interesting." He flashes a grin. "Sheila said you wanted to see me." He sits in a chair facing Felix.

"Bill, I know you have a lot of things to do before you get out of here and this can wait."

"Well, I'm here now, so what is it."

Felix fingers Alex's letter and the enclosures. "I hate to waste your time with this because it's undoubtedly from a kook, but the allegations are so serious I thought you should know about it."

Brannon's face is expressionless. "What is it?"

"While reading my mail this morning, I came across a letter from an Alexandre Ivanovich . . ." He notices Brannon flinch. "He claims he owns a formula that Coca-Cola has been illegally using since 1921. He's enclosed copies of a contract and a recipe . . ."

Brannon, his stomach churning, reaches out with his right hand, "Let me see the letter."

Ungerschmidt hands him the letter and watches as Brannon's eyes scour the page, his lips moving in unison with the words he reads. *So this is the son-of-a-bitch's game.* Without looking up, Brannon holds out his left hand, "The enclosures."

Felix hands them to him and thinks, *Brannon knows something I don't know.*

After reading the contract and the recipe Brannon hands the papers back and leans back in the chair. "Sounds like a kook to me too." Brannon stands and starts toward the door.

"Don't you think," Felix says, feeling uncomfortable challenging his boss's dismissive attitude, "we should find out if this formula is the same as our formula. If they're not the same, then we trash this stuff. That's the end of it."

"Suppose they're the same."

Ungerschmidt stares open mouthed at his boss, thinking, *Well, are they the same? You know the formula.* Instead, he says, "Then the company might want to look into the situation further."

"For Christ sake, Ungerschmidt, you're the lawyer. Don't be naïve. What about the statute of limitations? And what about latches? Every time a lawyer's client gets caught with his pants down, the lawyer starts babbling about latches." Moving toward Ungerschmidt, and jabbing his finger in the direction of the puzzled lawyer, Brannon says, "How can anyone sit on their rights for seventy-eight years and do nothing? Isn't that what latches are about?"

Ungerschmidt stands. He has never seen Brannon in a situation when he exhibits less than complete control. And yet, in the past few minutes, he has witnessed Brannon's mood swing from composure, to excitement, to nonchalance, to anger. For some reason, Ivanovich's letter has tapped an emotional reservoir in Brannon that he has never seen before. "Bill, this is all moot if the two formulas are not the same." He pauses, "You know the Coca-Cola formula, Bill. Are they the same?"

"I have access to the formula, and, of course, I've seen it. But I've not memorized it, so I don't know."

"We both know someone who does know, and I saw him this morning when I came in."

"Vanderbork?"

Ungerschmidt nods. "Why don't we ask him?"

Brannon ponders the question. *I may as well pacify him,* he thinks. "Okay. Have copies of that letter, the recipe, and the so called contract sent to my office. I'll summon Vanderbork, and when he arrives, I'll let you know."

BRANNON RETURNS TO his office and instructs Shelia that he doesn't want to be disturbed. He immediately calls Lester Hammond's private phone number. Hammond, strolling down La Croisette Boulevard in Cannes with his wife, feels the vibration and senses that the call is from Brannon. He removes the phone from the holster, indicates with a hand gesture to his wife that he will have to take the call, and continues walking along the elegant promenade as he presses the talk button. "This is Lester Hammond."

"Lester, something is developing here with that Russian. I think I know what he's up to, and I don't like it," Brannon whispers.

"Bill, you are going to have to speak up for me to hear you. There's a lot of street noise."

Brannon repeats the statement and adds, "Where are you?"

"In Cannes with Ariana."

"I hate to interfere with your vacation, but I have to see you. This situation needs your immediate attention. I'm leaving for London this afternoon and I'm staying at Claridge's. Can you meet me there tomorrow? I have a couple of matters I must take care of, but we can get together for dinner at the hotel."

Giving his wife an apologetic look, Hammond says, "Bill, you are the only person in the world I would do this for, but, yes, I'll meet you in London tomorrow. Let's meet for dinner at Mirabelle's. It's an old timer but still my favorite. I'll make the reservations for eight, if that works for you."

"I'll make it work, and thanks, Lester. Please tell Ariana I send my love and apologize for this intrusion."

Brannon swings around in his chair and gazes out the window, letting his eyes move along the horizon framed by Atlanta's soaring skyline. The scene always pleases him because he is proud of the part he has played in helping build modern Atlanta. His computer beeps and he spins back around. The computer screen reads: "Mr. Vanderbork is waiting." He has Sheila notify Ungerschmidt. When he arrives both men are ushered into Brannon's office.

Ungerschmidt hands the chief executive a folder containing Alex's letter, and copies of the contract and Calderman's 1921 cola formula. Brannon glances at the enclosures and then lets his eyes rest on Vanderbork. Vanderbork looks tired, he thinks.

"Harold, are you looking forward to retirement?" As soon as the words come out, he realizes he has said the wrong thing.

"I'll find out in twenty days."

"I'm sure you'll enjoy sleeping late, playing golf . . ."

"I've never played golf."

Feeling the conversation is heading in the wrong direction, Brannon says, "I'm sorry."

"You needn't be, sir. It was my deliberate choice. I never felt that I had time to chase a silly little golf ball."

"Harold, I really didn't ask you here to talk about golf." He pauses. "You know every detail of the Coca-Cola Classic formula from memory, don't you?"

Vanderbork's eyes, reflecting his puzzlement by the question, sweep from Brannon to Ungerschmidt and back to Brannon. He nods and waits.

"Is this," Brannon asks, as he hands Vanderbork a copy of Calderman's 1921 recipe, "in any way similar to our Classic Coca-Cola formula?"

Vanderbork studies the document. His face gives no clue to his thoughts. He looks up, glances at Ungerschmidt, but fixes his eyes on Brannon. "They are identical."

"You're sure?"

"I'm absolutely sure." He is tempted to ask where Brannon obtained the formula, and explain how dangerous it is to have the formula in the hands of unauthorized personnel such as Ungerschmidt and Xerox operators, but thinks, *to hell with him*. He has no respect for Brannon. A year ago he sent a written re-quest to Brannon for a waiver of his mandatory retirement, *and the prick didn't have the courtesy to answer me*.

"Thank you, Harold," Brannon says, his head aching and feeling the need for a drink.

CHAPTER 60

AT 8 P.M. Brannon's limousine pulls in front of Mirabelle's. Before the chauffeur opens the passenger door, the Coca-Cola executive bounds out and strides down the steps into the restaurant. He looks around the art deco foyer; it is empty. He walks into the bar area. Hammond is standing at the bar.

They shake hands. Hammond hands his friend a glass of scotch. "I knew you would be on time. Our reservation is for eight, but we have the table for the rest of evening, and we can go in whenever we like. Would you like to talk here for a while?"

Brannon nods. They walk from the bar and stand at a high round table along a far wall.

Brannon briefs Hammond about the events of yesterday morning including the contents of the Ivanovich letter, the contract, the recipe, and Vanderbork's verification that the Coca-Cola Classic formula is identical to the Calderman 1921 recipe.

"Do you have copies of those documents?"

Brannon reaches into his inside jacket pocket, removes an envelope and hands it to Hammond. "I thought you might want to see them."

Hammond reads Alex's letter, the recipe and the contract. He whistles 'whew' when her reads the amount of money claimed by

Alex. Hammond hands the papers back and takes a sip of his drink. "Assuming everything Ivanovich says is true, what did Ungerschmidt say the law is?"

"He wasn't sure, said he would have it researched by our outside counsel and get back to me."

"Bill, there's something that I've found out that I haven't told you about because I've been trying to bring it into clearer focus. But in view of these developments I think you should know about it," Hammond says, coughing and waving away a cloud of cigarette smoke blown in their direction.

"These damn smokers are not only killing themselves but trying to kill the rest of us. Let's go to our table," Brannon says. They walk quickly out of the bar and into the dining area.

The dining room is a rectangular space separated by an arched wooden divider decorated with over-sized vases containing unusual floral arrangements. Their table is in the rear of the room. Hammond orders a 1990 Leoville-Las-Cases, a red Bordeaux from St. Julien. "This is the same wine that Steve Case and Gerald Levin drank at a dinner celebrating their agreement to merge AOL and Time-Warner."

"Well, considering how that flopped," Brannon says, "I'm not sure we should drink it." They laugh.

"You said you've learned something I should know about. What is it?"

"Did you read or see on television about a week ago where a Russian Mafia boss and his colleagues were blown up in a car bombing in Brooklyn?"

Brannon feels an anxious twitch. "I read the *Wall Street Journal* every day, and I recall reading something about it. I think it was also in the *Journal-Constitution*."

"It also made the front page of *The Times* and all the major television networks," Hammond says, leaning forward and lowering his voice so as to make it impossible for other diner's to hear. "Well, that Mafia boss, whose name was Forsenko, is the man I hired to kill Ivanovich."

Hammond stops talking as the sommelier approaches, presents the bottle for inspection, uncorks it and pours a splash into his glass. Hammond swirls the wine, smells it, takes a sip, and lets it run over his palate. With a nod of the head he indicates to the sommelier to pour the wine.

The waiter arrives and they place their orders. Hammond remains silent until the waiter leaves. "I told you the operation failed and, in my judgment, no further attempts should be made. You agreed. I told Forsenko to call it off. What I didn't tell you is that the man Forsenko sent to Atlanta to do the job was shipped back to Forsenko in a wooden crate, dead, his neck broken." Brannon feels a shiver. "With thugs like Forsenko, saving face is important. When Forsenko reported to me what happened, he was outraged, screaming that he would personally kill Ivanovich. I extracted a promise from him not to harm Ivanovich within the United States. A week or so later I learned that Forsenko spread the word through the Russian underworld that he would pay a reward of a $100,000 to anyone who killed Ivanovich anywhere outside of the United States. Forsenko knows Ivanovich visits his son in Russia the first two weeks in June and . . ."

"Well, where do we go from here?"

Hammond raises his hand. "I'm not finished. From the beginning, the police viewed the bombing as gang related. But as soon as I heard about the bombing, my suspicions turned to Ivanovich."

"Why?"

"At the time it was a gut reaction, but now that I've learned something about Ivanovich's activities that weekend, and have had time to think about it. I'm convinced that he's the motorcyclist who bombed Forsenko's limousine."

Brannon leans into the table, his mouth drawn tight. "What have you learned about that bastard?"

Hammond explains how he initiated an immediate investigation of the whereabouts and activities of Ivanovich and Kia Williams and learned that they were not in Atlanta on the day Forsenko was murdered.

"Look, Lester, the fact that this guy and Williams weren't in Atlanta doesn't mean they were in Brooklyn. They were probably shacked up for the weekend. Besides, whoever killed Forsenko did us a favor.

"You mean, like dead men tell no tales?"

Brannon nods.

Hammond starts to reply but notices the waiter approaching with their meals: Dover sole meunier with dauphine potatoes and spinach for himself, and roast rack of lamb with mint pesto, rice and a vegetable galette for Brannon. When the waiter leaves Hammond says, "Are you aware that Foster made a request to Coca-Cola's in-house security to find out about Ivanovich?"

Brannon's head snaps up. "Nelson Foster?"

"Yes."

"When?"

"Just before he left for Beijing. When he returned, the Russian's file was on his desk." Hammond pauses and a grin forms around the corners of his mouth.

"How do you know this?"

"Because your security requested that my Atlanta office obtain the data, and I was alerted by Tommy Miers. I gave approval to supply the info, but instructed Tommy to put a very discreet tail on Foster to find out why he wanted the information." Hammond takes a sip of wine. "What do you think Foster did the afternoon of his first day back from China?"

"I'd like to know."

"At three-thirty, he left his office and had his driver drop him off at the Capital City Club. A little early to start drinking, don't you think?" He takes a bite of the sole. "This is the best damn fish in the world. Whoever said red wine doesn't go with fish. The problem with these so called wine experts is . . ."

"Cut the shit, Hammond. What did Foster do when he got to the club?"

"He waited for Ivanovich. At four o'clock a Lincoln Town Car pulled up, Ivanovich got out and went into the club. A few minutes later Foster and Ivanovich came out, got in the town car and drove north on Peachtree. Ivanovich's spy training apparently alerted him that he was being followed because he ran a red light, accelerated to a high speed, and lost my guys."

"Do you know where they went?"

"No."

"Do you have any idea why Foster wanted information about Ivanovich, and why he met with him?"

Hammond rolls the stem of his glass between the thumb and index finger of his right hand. "My first reaction was that he also received a compromising video. Another thought, however, occurs to me. It may sound preposterous, but I'm not so sure that it is."

The sommelier steps forward and pours the last of the wine. Brannon looks around the room. No one appears to be paying attention to them. Still, he leans in and whispers, "Let me hear it."

"Foster is in cahoots with Ivanovich in an attempt to shake down the company."

Brannon's facial muscles tighten and his eyes narrow. "Now days nothing surprises me." He waves the cheese cart away. "What do you think . . ." He stops in mid-sentence, eyes bulging as he watches a beautiful young woman with long shapely legs strut through the dining room.

Hammond smiles, ""You were saying?"

"Where was I? Yeah, what do you think we should do?"

"I think we should pay a surprise visit to Foster and find out why he wanted the information, and why he met with Ivanovich. Only then will we know how to evaluate the situation."

"I agree. When can you do it?"

"Sunday, does that work for you?"

"I'll make it work," Brannon says, standing. "Let's go to the Harvard Club for a real drink."

AS THE TWO executives climb into Brannon's waiting limousine, three thousand miles away Nelson Foster sits on a metal folding chair in his garden, a slouch hat pulled down over his ears, binoculars held loosely in his right hand. His Coca-Cola colleagues are all ardent golfers, but his sport is more solitary and better suited to his gentle nature—bird watching. His enthusiasm for birding has taken him to Thailand's Khao National Park, Sri Lanka, and Australia's Outer Banks. He is the current president of the Atlanta Audubon Society and a past president of the Georgia Ornithological Society. It is a sport that he shares with his wife of thirty years, but not today. She is off in Buckhead with her personal shopper looking for a dress to wear at their daughter's approaching wedding.

Foster's immediate thoughts are not concentrated on the beautiful red robed Cardinal perched on the branch of a tree a hundred feet distant. Unaware that an opportunity will present itself on Sunday, he is trying to figure out how to initiate his promise to settle Ivanovich's claim against the company.

THE NEXT MORNING Lester Hammond is aboard his private jet heading to Cannes to resume his vacation. He is troubled by what he has learned about Brannon's recent behavior: a sexual addiction so strong that he was screwing an employee in his private elevator, breaching fiduciary duties by paying off a French whore with confidential company information knowing she intended to use it for financial gain, consenting to a contract murder of a man he'd never met, and a noticeable increase in his alcohol consumption. *Is Brannon coming unhinged?* Regardless, common sense tells him that Brannon's behavior is aberrant, and it will eventually reflect adversely on the operations of the company. He has a lot of Coca-Cola stock. He decides that on Monday he will take a long, hard look at whether he should start unloading some of it.

CHAPTER 61

AFTER SUNDAY CHURCH Nelson and Maria Foster return to their home in Buckhead, one of Atlanta's most exclusive residential areas. The Foster residence, a five thousand square foot Georgian house, is set back from the road and surrounded by towering oak trees. By Buckhead standards, it is modest in size. The house, pool, patio and gardens occupy only an acre and a half of the twelve-acre estate. The Fosters, interested in bird watching and concerned about the environment, have left the remaining ten and a half acres in its natural state.

Foster changes into casual clothes and leaves the house carrying binoculars, a metal folding chair, and a bottle of spring water. He crosses the patio and follows a trail into the woods that winds through a ground cover of English ivy, honeysuckle, holly fern, purple winter creeper and mondo grass. A hundred yards further on he stops in a small clearing surrounded by a grove of Georgia oak trees. He opens and sits on the chair.

BRANNON WATCHES AS Hammond's jet turns onto its final approach to the Fulton County Airport. He wonders what suggestions Lester will have about bringing up the subject of Foster's secret meeting with Ivanovich. He has thought about it long and

THE SECRET FORMULA · 279

hard since London, and he has decided to simply confront Foster about the meeting and ask why it occurred.

The jet taxies to a private terminal. Hammond emerges casually dressed in silk beige slacks and a white polo shirt. On the drive to Buckhead, Brannon explains how he plans to question Foster. Hammond agrees.

SURROUNDED BY RED maples, Georgia oaks, dogwoods and white pines, Foster's thoughts have turned to William Brannon. Although not social friends, they have worked well together for many years. Several years ago Brannon confided to Foster that he would recommend to the board of directors that Nelson succeed him when he reaches mandatory retirement age. Over the past couple of years, however, Nelson feels that something has changed, not just between them, but within Brannon himself. The change in Brannon's behavior is subtle, but it's there. Brannon has become more irritable, less tolerant of the opinions and conduct of his colleagues, and he rarely seeks advice before making business decisions.

Foster's job often brings him into contact with the company's bottlers, and on several occasions he has heard oblique remarks that question Brannon's leadership. Foster also senses an erosion of morale within the company, and within the ranks of a number of bottling partners. But his concerns are not reflected in the company's stock price or in conversations with other company executives or the board of directors. Could the problem be with himself and not Brannon? His thoughts are interrupted by his wife, "Nelson, Bill Brannon and Lester Hammond are here to see you."

He spins around, surprised to see Brannon and Hammond clomping through the underbrush toward him. "What have I done to merit an unannounced Sunday visit from two such distinguished gentlemen?"

They shake hands, exchange small talk about the weather, the pleasures of bird watching, and when golf comes up, Foster says,

"To get you two off a golf course on a beautiful sunny afternoon like today means that what you want to talk about must be very important. Would you like to return to the house?"

"No," Brannon says. "I can't think of a more private spot than here. I'll get right to the point Nelson. It has come to my attention that you recently met secretly with an ex-Russian spy by the name of Ivanovich." Brannon's shirt is wet with perspiration and his tone accusatorial. "I have reason to believe that at this meeting you discussed matters concerning The Coca-Cola Company."

Foster removes a bottle of water from his pants pocket, unscrews the cap and takes a swig. He recaps the bottle and places it back in his pocket. "We did discuss the company. In fact, assuming that what he claims is true, we discussed the survival of the company and worked out an agreement, subject, of course, to your approval and the approval of the board of directors."

Brannon's mouth flies open. "What are you talking about? Have you lost it? What right do you have to discuss The Coca-Cola Company business with some kook? Do you know what I'm going to do?" Brannon says, jabbing his right index finger in the direction of Foster's chest. "Tomorrow at the board of directors meeting, I'm going to recommend that they authorize me to fire you."

Hammond places a restraining hand on his friend's shoulder. "Bill, please, slow down. Let's hear what Nelson has to say."

Standing in the shade of two-hundred year old oaks, Foster starts by telling about receiving a registered package labeled, "Personal and Confidential." Without disclosing what was in the package, he admits that the contents were embarrassing.

He explains his subsequent actions including the details of the conversation he had with Ivanovich at the Four Season's Health & Fitness Club.

When Foster mentions that Ivanovich claims The Coca-Cola Company owes him more than one hundred and fifty billion dollars, Brannon flies into a rage. "You're as crazy as that Communist spy. We won't pay him a cent. I will personally see that he's shipped back to Russia with nothing more than the shirt on his back." Breathing hard, his face crimson, voice shrill, arms flailing, he shouts, "As for you, Foster, you're finished! Conspiring with that Russian to shake down the company for millions of dollars is going to earn you an eight by eight concrete cell at the state penitentiary."

Sensing that Brannon is on the edge of a hysterical collapse, Hammond reaches out, places his arm around his waist, and sits him gently on the folding chair.

After waiting a few moments for Brannon to regain his composure, Foster places his hand on the trunk of a towering oak. "This oak is over two hundred years old and still in perfect health. The Coca-Cola Company is over a hundred years old, and with love and care it will grow older and remain as healthy as this oak. But our company isn't quite as lucky as this oak, which has nature as its caretaker. In order for Coca-Cola to sustain healthy growth, it must be nurtured by the decisions of wise men. For the most part, it has received good guidance and healthy nurturing."

Brannon sits motionless, head down, face drained white. Foster walks over to him and places his right hand on his shoulder. "Your first ten years as CEO were probably the most brilliant and productive of any ten years in the history of the company. But that has not been the case in the past couple of years."

Foster looks over to Hammond who is standing behind Brannon. Their eyes meet, and in that brief moment before Hammond turns away, Foster reads in his eyes the pain and sadness he is feeling.

"Every important decision you've made in the past two years you've made without consulting me, or Talbot, or any of your senior executives. You need only read the newspapers to know that our bottling operations are in disarray around the world, and our job cuts are the largest in the history of the company. Your decisions have cost the company billions of dollars in failed projects in Europe and

Asia, to say nothing of billions of profits in lost opportunities that will never see the bottom line."

Trance-like, Brannon stares at the ground as Foster continues. "Friday afternoon, Felix stopped by my office unannounced. From the moment he stepped through the door it was obvious that something was weighing heavily on his mind, and it didn't take him long to tell me what it was. He told me about receiving a letter from Ivanovich with a copy of the 1921 formula and contract."

Foster opens the water bottle and takes a drink. He looks as cool as if he had just stepped out of the shower. "He also told me of the meeting that you had with Vanderbork, and Vanderbork's confirmation that the Calderman recipe is identical to the formula Coca-Cola has been using since 1921. Felix mentioned that he is having the legal consequences of the Russian's claim researched by outside counsel. He said that nothing in the law is ever certain, and that the final results are never known until litigation fully plays out."

"Nelson," Hammond says, stepping forward, "I think I should get Bill home so that he can rest. I understand there's a board of directors meeting at two tomorrow. Bill still has a lot to do to get ready for it."

"Nothing he has to do is more important than what we're now discussing. Let me tell Bill a few other things I think he should know before he summarily refuses to settle Ivanovich's claim.

"Ivanovich has a video tape of you, and he tells me you've seen it. He believes, and says he can prove, that you put a contract out through the Russian mafia to kill him. When I threatened to have him sent back to Russia, he said that if that happened he would give the Coca-Cola formula to the world by publishing it on the Internet. He said nothing about what he might do with the videos that he has of you and me. Might they too end up on the Internet?"

Brannon, a glazed look on his face, stands. As Hammond reaches for his friend's arm, Foster says, "Lester, Bill Brannon trusts you more than any man alive. Bill still controls the board of directors. Try to talk some sense into him. Why bet the company and risk the reputations of its three top executives. This whole thing, the risks and all of the sordid parts will go away for fifteen million dollars."

Hammond catches Foster's reference to "three top executives," *Was Foster's comment a slip or deliberate?* Either way, Hammond thinks the remark suggests that Ivanovich has an incriminating tape on Sharon Talbot.

Foster watches as Brannon, his body stooped, his gait shaky, follows the trail back to the house. It is a side of Brannon that he has never seen before. Brannon's aura of invincibility is gone.

HAMMOND OPENS THE front passenger door and motions Brannon in. "I'll drive you home," he says. As they approach the entrance gate to Brannon's estate, Brannon says, "The code is 1020, then hit pound." Hammond punches in the numbers and two large gates swing open. After navigating the half mile driveway, Hammond stops at the mansion's front entrance. Looking at his colleague for the first time since leaving Foster's house, Brannon says, "I hope you can stay over. I need to talk with you before the board meeting tomorrow. You are welcome to stay here."

"Thanks, but I think it better that you get some rest. We can talk early tomorrow." Brannon nods. "I have a number of matters that I need to take care of. I'll spend the night at the company apartment. Bill, I'll need to borrow one of your cars." Brannon nods.

"What time would you like to get together in the morning?"

"Can you be at my office by eight?"

"Sure."

WHEN BRANNON'S CAR leaves his estate, Nelson Foster calls Sharon Talbot. Nelson explains that serious and important developments have come up that she should know about before the board of directors meeting tomorrow. Sharon, scheduled to host a dinner party that evening, asks, "If we meet early tomorrow morning, will that allow sufficient time to completely cover the problems and still give me time to make an intelligent decision on what should be done?"

"Yes. I'll need about an hour of your time."

"All right, let's meet in your office at seven."

CHAPTER 62

FOSTER IS WATCHING a ribbon of clouds lift across the horizon and settle just below the Atlanta skyline when his door opens. Sharon Talbot, Coca-Cola's president and chief operating officer, stands in the doorway neatly attired in a dark blue Armani suit. Aware that Foster is her main competition to succeed Brannon as chief executive officer, she is suspect of his reasons for wanting to meet confidentially before a board meeting.

As Foster pours coffee, Talbot says, "I hope there's good reason for my being here at this early hour."

"There is. Please hear me out before asking a lot of questions. In that way you'll hear the whole story." Foster relates the events that started with his receipt of a confidential package containing personally compromising data and ending with yesterday's confrontation with Brannon.

Talbot is astonished by what she is hearing. *Can he be so stupid,* she thinks. *What makes him think that I would agree to pay this horrid ex-spy $15,000,000?* When he finishes speaking, she asks to see a copy of Thomas R. P. Calderman's 1921 formula and the contract between Calderman and Roscoe Hatfield.

She reads the documents and returns them to Foster. "Your problem and Brannon's problem," she says, "though similar, are not identical. This horrible man has totally compromised you, and by advocating that we settle his specious claim, you are being dishonest and prostituting your fiduciary responsibilities to the company. When you recommend to the board that it pay this despicable man $15,000,000, you must also tell them about the compromising video that he has of you." Her eyes narrow and bore in. "If you don't, I will."

Her response catches him totally by surprise. At first he thinks, *The hypocritical bitch.* Then another thought strikes him. *She doesn't know there's a video of her. Or is there?*

"How is Brannon's situation different from mine?" he asks.

She stands. "Although this horrible man has compromised Bill, by refusing to pay the son-of-a-bitch, Bill is, at least, intellectually and ethically honest. That's the difference." Moving toward the door she calls back, "Remember, Nelson, confession is good for the soul."

CHAPTER 63

LESS THAN THREE miles away, Alex sits in the Caribou Coffee House drinking coffee and reading the morning paper. He doesn't have a client pick up until nine o'clock. His cell phone vibrates. He walks outside before answering. "Good morning. This is Star Limousine Service."

"This is Nelson Foster. Lying to me is not only going to cost you a chance for $15,000,000, but it's going to cost me my job."

"What the hell are you talking about?"

Foster briefs him on his conversation with Talbot and adds, "You told me that you have a video of her, but her arrogant, 'I'm better than you' reaction, clearly indicates that you don't."

A sickening feeling sweeps through Alex. *Did Kia fail to deliver the video to Talbot?* "I have a video of Talbot in Prague illegally buying tortoises smuggled from Madagascar. I can't believe she doesn't have it."

"Well, she doesn't, and unless you get that video into that sanctimonious bitch's hands before the board meeting today, I'm finished here and your settlement is kaput."

It is 7:50 a.m. Alex calls Kia. She is driving to work. "Our settlement with Coke is going down the toilet. I told Foster that we have an incriminating video of Talbot, and he met with her earlier this morning to enlist her help. Instead of agreeing to support the settlement, she turned on him and demanded that he confess to the board of directors at their meeting today his involvement with me, and resign. Kia, Talbot obviously doesn't know that she's been compromised."

"Oh, Alex, I'm sorry! I'm sorry! I forgot to deliver it to her."

The silence is deafening. Then in a tone of voice she has never heard Alex use, he says, "How could you forget, Kia! Damn it! You've ruined everything!"

"It's no excuse, and I never told you, but the day you gave me the video my mother had a stroke. It was a mini-stroke, but she was in the hospital four days, and between visiting her and taking care of my father, I forgot about everything. I'm sorry, Alex! I'm sorry!"

"I'm sorry to hear about your Mom. How's she doing?" he asks perfunctorily.

"Good, Alex. She's doing good."

Alex says nothing for a long moment. "Kia, our only hope of salvaging this thing is to get the video to Talbot and make her aware that what she did in Prague is a crime subject to imprisonment for up to fifteen years. If we're able to do that, she will realize that she stands in the same shoes as Brannon and Foster. Do you still have the video?"

"Yes, it's in the trunk of my car along with the transcript. Alex, I promise I'll deliver the video to her this morning."

LEAVING FOSTER'S OFFICE, Sharon Talbot returns to her office and reflects on what Foster told her. *Foster's finished. He'll resign before the board convenes. I'll tell the board why he resigned and what he told me about his involvement with that despicable Russian and their plan to shake the company down for $15,000,000. As dumb as Foster is, he's right about Brannon. Brannon's leadership the past couple of years has been wretched, and from what Helen Van Sante said last night, some board members know it. Foster said the*

Russian has a video of Brannon. I wish I knew what it's about, but knowing Brannon, it's something horrid. Should I confront him about it now or at the board meeting? If I question him now and he fails to deny it, that will mean it's true. Yes, I'll do it now.

Talbot opens a closet door and looks at herself in a full-length mirror. She was never the prettiest girl in the class, but she was always the brightest. She turns slowly so she can see herself from all angles. She likes what she sees. She is confident that before the day is over she will be the new CEO of Coca-Cola.

CHAPTER 64

WHILE SHARON TALBOT is contemplating how to administer the coup de grace to William Brannon, Lester Hammond is in Brannon's office urging him to recommend to the board the $15,000,000 settlement.

"Look, Bill, not to settle the claim means that the company runs the risk of losing to Ivanovich. I don't think that will happen, but like Ungerschmidt said, when you present a complicated set of facts to a jury, anything can happen. Juries do some crazy things. I can tell you from personal experience, litigation is a lose-lose situation.

"It's time consuming and distracting. In the next two or three years you should be devoting all of your time and energy to getting Coke back on track, not sitting in some lawyer's office preparing for your deposition testimony. Litigating Ivanovich's claims puts the company at risk, because should he win, he owns the company. Why risk that for a measly $15,000,000?"

Seated behind the desk is the old Bill Brannon, the Bill Brannon that Hammond has known for more than thirty years: calm, charismatic, and in total control. "Are you finished, Lester?"

"No. There are considerations that go beyond what I've said. Those considerations should be obvious to you, but since I'm on my soapbox, let me go over them. Litigating this case, and this is so whether you win or lose, runs the risk of the video of you and the French woman finding its way into the public domain. If that happens, it will not help your leadership position here at Coca-Cola, your reputation in the community, and most importantly, your marriage and family." Hammond pauses, his eyes fixed firmly on Brannon. "With regard to your marriage, I'm not thinking of you. I'm thinking of Virginia. I think a public airing of your philandering will almost kill her. Fighting Ivanovich is not worth inflicting that kind of pain on people you love." He pauses and nods. "Okay, I'm finished." He can read in Brannon's eyes that he has not gotten through to him.

After a long a moment of silence, Brannon says, "I appreciate your thoughts and your friendship, but I can't give into extortion . . ."

"But it's not . . ."

"It may not appear that way to you, but that's how it strikes me, and I intend to deal with it accordingly. I'll have that ex-spy's ass out of this country before he has a chance to contact a lawyer. Thanks, Lester," Brannon says, standing and extending his hand. "I know how I'm going to deal with that son-of-a-bitch."

What Brannon does not know is how he will deal with Sharon Talbot who five minutes earlier entered his outer-office and asked to speak with him.

When told by Miss Winslow that "Mr. Brannon is in conference and has left instructions not to be disturbed," Talbot replied, "Well, tell him to see me when he's free," and stalked out.

ON HIS WAY to the elevator, Hammond passes by Foster's office. *Christ*, he thinks, *he deserves to know.* He sticks his head in the outer-office. Foster's secretary looks up and sees him, "Mr. Hammond, it's nice to see you. What brings you to Atlanta?"

"It's great to see you, Beverly. I'm here briefly on a little business matter. Is Mr. Foster in?"

"Oh, yes, and I know he'll want to see you. I'll tell him you're here."

She disappears into the inner-office. Within moments she re-appears and holds the door open. "Mr. Foster is delighted that you stopped by to see him."

Foster stands when Hammond enters the office. Hammond immediately notices that he isn't the same calm, confident Foster that castigated Brannon yesterday afternoon.

He appears troubled.

They shake hands. "I spent an hour trying to talk sense to Bill." Hammond says, shaking his head. "He refuses to settle the Russian's claim. I gave it my best shot, because I truly believe settling this matter would be best for everyone. He won't do it."

"Did he say why?"

"No, he just said he has a plan for dealing with the situation. Anyhow, I thought you should know." He turns to leave and adds, "Life does get screwed up, doesn't it?"

CHAPTER 65

SHEILA WINSLOW IS fuming over what Sharon Talbot said and how she said it. *She ordered Mr. Brannon to see her. Has she forgotten that Mr. Brannon is the chief executive officer?*

When Hammond leaves Brannon's office, Sheila enters and tells her boss about Talbot's visit and the arrogance in her voice in demanding to see him.

That's not like Sharon. She's always deferential toward me. Couldn't be her period. She went through menopause several years ago. He shrugs and dials her private number. "Sharon, I understand that you would like to see me . . . I can see you now, if you like."

Minutes later Talbot enters. She sits facing him. "How did your dinner party go last night?" Brannon asks.

"Fine. I'm sorry you and Virginia had to cancel at the last moment. Is Virginia feeling better?"

"She's a bit better today, but those damn migraines leave her washed out for a couple of days. She had such a bad attack I didn't feel comfortable leaving her alone."

"I understand." Her eyes bore into him. "Bill, is there something that I should know about before today's board meeting that I've not been made aware of?"

"Yes, and I was going to come see you about it even before Mrs.

Winslow said you wanted to see me." Bill Brannon spends the next thirty minutes briefing the president on the events surrounding Alex Ivanovich and his determination to vigorously reject the Russian's claim and take all necessary action to have him deported.

When he finishes, she says, "Bill, I think you've conveniently left out a couple of important matters."

"What's that?"

"The fact that this Russian has videos that compromise the integrity and character of you and Nelson."

Brannon's jaw sags and he bites his lower lip. *So it's true*, she thinks. "Bill, I admire your determination not to give in to blackmail, but this video of your activities is going to fall into the public domain via the Internet whether you arrange to ship that bastard back to Russia on the Concorde or a banana boat." She pauses to allow her words to take effect.

Where did she hear this? Has she seen the video? How much does she know?

Little beads of sweat form on his forehead and tell her he's frightened. *I have the bastard.* Feeling an inner exhilaration, she continues, "The Company means more than any one person, regardless of how much we love and respect them." She runs her tongue over her lips. She can taste the nectar of the words she is about to speak. "Bill, do the honorable thing, and do it today at the board meeting."

Stunned, Brannon sits motionless. He knows what she is asking, but he is determined to hear her say it. "Do what at the board meeting?"

She pushes back in her chair and studies him. "Resign, Bill. Resign and take that golden parachute of benefits that awaits you, your pension, stock options, consulting fees, private office and use of the company jet. You've earned them. Don't let a stupid indiscretion do you out of them." She leans forward, "It will be too late when the board finds out about the video."

He stands and walks wearily to the window. Usually he loves

looking out at the burgeoning Atlanta skyline, but not now. He turns and sees her sitting ramrod straight, a smirk flickering around her pursed lips. "I'll give serious consideration to your suggestion. I'll let you know before the board meeting."

She stands. "Thank you, Bill. I know you'll do the honorable thing." She extends her hand. He refuses it.

CHAPTER 66

IMMEDIATELY ON RETURNING to her office, Talbot calls her girl-friend, Natalie Johnston. Sharon's call catches Natalie sitting by the pool under a beach umbrella having just opened the first volume of Marcel Proust's, *Remembrance of Things Past*. Natalie and Sharon recently joined a women's book club, and Natalie agreed to read Proust's monumental work and provide the members with a monthly ten minute synopsis of her progress.

"This is Natalie."

"What are you doing, sweetheart?"

"I've just started Proust's *Remembrance of Things Past*. I don't think I'm going to like it."

"Why not?"

"His sentence structure is terrible. His sentences ramble on and on. I'm trying to read one now that's been running on for a page and a half. What's up?"

"I've got some good news. It's not definite yet, but before the day is out I think I'll be the new CEO here."

Natalie jumps up from the chaise lounge, "That's wonderful! How did it happen?"

Talbot hears a loud commotion outside of her office door. "I'll call you back."

The door bursts open and Kia charges in followed by Talbot's secretary.

"I tried to stop her but she pushed past me. I'll call security."

Kia walks across the office and tosses the video cassette on the desk. "And here's the transcript in case you don't have a VCR," she says, throwing it on the desk.

Talbot says to her secretary, who stands transfixed in the doorway, "Alert security, but have them wait outside. And, please, close the door."

Talbot stares at Kia who is standing in front of her with her hands placed defiantly on her hips. "I notice you're wearing an employee's badge. Who are you?"

"My name is Kia Williams." Pointing to the cassette, Kia says, "Don't you want to know what's on that video, and who it's from?"

Talbot's eyes run over Kia and shift to the cassette. "What is it?"

"The original of that video is owned by a friend of mine— Alex Ivanovich."

Repeating what Alex told her to say, she continues, "It shows a scene that took place in Prague at the House of Havlacke starring you, your friend, Natalie Johnston, eight starburst turtles, and Mr. Havlacke. It runs twenty-four minutes. It involves the international crime of the illegal purchase of endangered tortoises from Madagascar, a crime punishable by five to fifteen years in prison."

Talbot's face turns ashen and she slumps into her chair. "That's right, Madam President, five to fifteen years in prison. I see that you have a VCR on the credenza. I suggest that you watch the video." Kia turns and leaves.

CHAPTER 67

IN THE HALLWAY Kia calls Alex. "Mission accomplished. I just left Talbot's office. I gave her the video and the transcript and repeated exactly what you told me to say about her crime being subject to as much as fifteen years in prison."

"That's great. Thanks," Alex says in a flat, dull voice.

"What's bothering you? I thought you'd be elated."

"I received a call from Foster. Hammond was not able to convince Brannon to go along with the settlement. Brannon said he has a plan to deal with me that includes shipping me back to Russia."

Kia feels a rush of anger. She looks up and down the corridor. She remembers Brannon telling her that he has a corner office. "I'll talk to you later."

She strides down the corridor in search of the chief executive's office. At the southeast corner she sees a small brass plaque on a door. It reads, "William W. Brannon, Chairman and Chief Executive Officer." With her heart pounding and the adrenaline flowing, she pushes open the door, steps inside and looks left and right.

The receptionist's head snaps around, but before she can react, Kia charges past her and down a hallway on the right. The hallway leads to the spacious, well-appointed office of Sheila Winslow. Winslow, at her desk working at a computer, looks up, startled. "Who are you?"

"I'm Kia Williams and . . ." Turning, she sees the receptionist and a young man dashing toward her. Her hands fly out, "Don't touch me." They stop. Edging toward Winslow and the door leading to Brannon's office, Kia keeps up a constant chatter, "See my badge. I'm an employee of Coca-Cola. I work in the travel department. I've been an employee for over ten years. What I have to tell Mr. Brannon is very important." She is standing in front of the door to Brannon's office. She turns, grips the door handle and twists it. It's locked.

Kia studies her three adversaries. The receptionist and the young man look scared and confused, but Winslow, a smirk on her face, says simply, "Why don't you sit down. I've called security."

Kia spins around and strikes the door with both fists. "Brannon, you coward, this is Kia Williams. If you don't come out, I'll kick the door in."

The door opens. Brannon stands in the doorway, tie askew, hair disheveled, eyes red and swollen. "What's going on?" he asks.

"Please, Mr. Brannon, get back inside. This woman is out of control. I've called security," Shelia Winslow says. "They should be here any moment."

"No," Brannon says. "Cancel security. I know this woman."

"You know this . . .?"

"Yes. And Sheila, I don't want any interruptions." With that Brannon steps aside as Kia enters his office. He closes and locks the door. He motions her to a chair facing his desk.

Kia refuses the offer and stands glaring at him. "You look like shit."

"You and your Russian boyfriend have done me in."

"No, we didn't do you in. Your own stupidity has done you in."

Brannon rubs his eyes and runs his right hand through his hair. "The video of me in Paris . . . Sharon Talbot knows about it and has demanded that I resign before the contents of that video become public knowledge. The board might forgive me for having an affair with a prostitute. I suspect that half the male members have done the same thing. But they will never forgive my disclosing highly confidential company information in payment for her services. That's a breach of trust, and among business executives an unforgivable sin."

Kia walks over and sits on the edge of Brannon's massive desk, her long, shapely legs almost touching the floor. "How in hell does she know what's on that video?"

"Foster told her."

She shakes her head. "No, he didn't."

"How do you know that?"

"Because Alex told me, and unlike you, Alex doesn't lie. Alex told Foster that he had a compromising video of you, but he didn't reveal the nature of it." Kia eases off the desk and sits in a chair. "If I told you something that could save your ass, will you recommend settling Alex's claim?"

"Yes if it saves my position as CEO."

"You have lied to me before. Why should I trust you now?"

He leans forward, so close he can smell her perfume. "Are you and the Russian in this thing together?" She nods. "Trust me."

I have to; I don't have a choice, she thinks. "You should ask Talbot to tell you what she did in Prague that if reported to the feds will send her to prison for five to fifteen years."

Brannon bounds from his chair. "Did I hear you right?"

Kia nods. "Before coming here, I personally delivered a video to her that she is probably watching now. It shows her in Prague illegally buying endangered species turtles. In case you don't know it, those turtles are protected under international laws to which the United States is a signatory. Violators are subject to imprisonment for five to fifteen years."

Brannon's eyes flash, reflecting his excitement. "Fabulous!" He darts into his private bathroom. A few minutes later he emerges wearing a clean white shirt, a neatly knotted tie, and his hair freshly combed.

Kia eyes him suspiciously. "You're going to recommend the settlement?"

"Yes, but what I can't figure out is how your boyfriend is going to be able to enjoy all that money from prison."

"What do mean by that?"

It's a long shot, but the look on her face tells him that Hammond is right – Ivanovich blew up Forsenko's limousine. He holds her stare. "I know something that only you and your Russian boyfriend know, and I'm willing to keep it a secret, but there's a price."

"What do you think you know?"

"That Ivanovich is the motorcyclist who blew up those six men in Brooklyn."

"That's the dumbest thing you've ever said." She turns away.

"Kia, look at me." She turns back and their eyes lock. "I'm not bluffing.

"Ivanovich laid the bomb on the car and you helped him. You and your boyfriend are about to become millionaires because I'm going to recommend the settlement to the board of directors, and the board will approve my recommendation. But if I tell the police what I know, you'll both go to prison, and Coca-Cola will get its money back." He pauses.

"If you really love this guy, you'll make his dream come true, not destroy it and yourself."

"What's the price?"

"You!" Brannon lets the silence do its work before adding, "As soon as you get your share of the money, you'll leave Ivanovich."

Her eyes flash and hold his. She feels sick to her stomach. "Why? So you can keep me in the closet like you did before." She turns and heads for the door.

"Remember, Kia, money in a Swiss bank account can disappear as quickly as it got there. Like cotton candy, now you taste it, now you don't. Or in the case of money, now you have it, now you don't." He pauses. "I want your answer soon, so don't take too long to decide."

Kia storms down the corridor toward the elevator. A few minutes later Brannon walks out of his office and stops at Shelia Winslow's desk. "If you need me, I'll be in Sharon Talbot's office."

CHAPTER 68

MARTHA MARKS HAS been Sharon Talbot's secretary for fifteen years. Her severe almost Victorian-styled clothing and thick dark-rimmed glasses make her look less attractive than she is. What no one knows is the secret crush she has on William Brannon. Almost every day she fantasizes about having sex with him in exotic places around the world. She doesn't realize how easy it would be to turn her fantasies into realities.

Martha Marks is surprised to look up and see Mr. Brannon standing in front of her desk. "Mr. Brannon, how are you?"

"I'm fine, Martha. How's the world been treating you?"

"Oh just fine Mr. Brannon. Last Friday I went to a perfectly wonderful restaurant with some girlfriends and . . ."

"Martha, I do want to hear about it, but right now I'm in a time crunch. Is your boss available?"

Hiding her disappointment, she smiles. "She asked not to be disturbed, but I'm sure that doesn't mean you, Mr. Brannon. Let me go in and check." A few seconds later Martha reappears. "Ms. Talbot said for you to come in, but Mr. Brannon, she doesn't look well."

"I won't take much of her time."

Talbot remains seated when Brannon enters. In the several

hours since he last saw her, her appearance has changed. Her rosy complexion had turned ashen, her normally piercing blue eyes are red and watery, and her sharp facial features appear sunken. One look at her tells him that she has seen the video.

As he pulls up a chair he thinks back to when she triumphantly left his office. She played her hand with skill, thinking that she held all the best cards. It turned out, however, that the Russian had the trump card, and through his partner Kia, he played it brilliantly.

Her eyes are glazed. Brannon, concerned she might not hear him, says, "Do you hear me, Sharon?" She nods. "Here is what I've decided to do. I've changed my mind about the Ivanovich settlement. I'm going to support it. I'm going to introduce the subject to the board, and recommend that in exchange for ownership of the 1921 Calderman formula, the board authorizes payment of $15,000,000.

"You will second my recommendation. Nelson and Felix will then fill in the details, explain why we're unanimous in our support of the settlement and answer any questions members might have. A secret part of the settlement, however, will be the return of all copies of the videos and anything else relating to the videos such as transcripts and photographs. The Russian must comply with this part of the deal before the transfer of money takes place. When we receive all of his clandestine crap, I'll personally deliver yours to you. Can I count on you to second my recommendation?"

Again, she nods.

"I want to hear you say yes or no."

"Yes."

"Sharon, you understand that your disloyalty cannot be forgiven."

She stares blankly at him for a long moment. "I understand."

"When the board of directors' meeting winds down, I'll expect you to submit your written resignation." She winces. "I know exactly how you feel." His voice hardens. "You will recall that you put me through this same ordeal earlier this morning."

"I'm so distraught that I don't think I'm emotionally able to write a resignation."

Tears streak down her face.

"If you don't feel that you can handle a written resignation, then resign orally, but keep it simple. Tell the board you've talked it over with me, and you're resigning for personal reasons that you don't wish to discuss at this time. Tell them a written resignation will follow. Remember, Sharon, a wonderful package of financial and other goodies await you if you resign voluntarily. Those goodies will not be available if the board has to ask for your resignation. And keep in mind, your resignation will eliminate your criminal conduct becoming known.

Brannon reaches over and hands her his handkerchief. "The Russian's videos of Nelson and me are mere peccadilloes. You've committed a serious crime punishable by imprisonment. Do I make myself clear?"

"I will resign," she says through a torrent of tears. "And now, I would like to be alone."

As he starts for the door he wonders if she is contemplating suicide. *That would be the perfect solution.*

CHAPTER 69

ON LEAVING BRANNON'S office Kia passes the office of Nelson Foster.

He's been on our side from the beginning. He deserves to know that Brannon has agreed to recommend the settlement. She opens the door and looks around. Compared to the reception offices of the chief executive and the president, Foster's reception area is small.

There are just two desks. The room is empty. A hallway about ten feet in length runs off to the left, at the end of which is a door. Kia opens that door and looks in. She sees a man seated at a desk looking out at the Atlanta skyline. She can't see his face, only the back of his head.

"Hello."

He turns. "Well, hello yourself," he says with a smile.

"Are you Mr. Foster?"

"Yes, I'm Nelson Foster. Can I help you?"

Kia walks in and extends her hand. "I'm Kia Williams, Alex Ivanovich's partner."

He stands and shakes her hand. "To what do I owe the pleasure of your visit?"

She immediately likes him, a firm handshake, an easy smile, and she senses that he is genuinely pleased to meet her. "I just finished visiting Ms. Talbot and Mr. Brannon and was heading for the elevator when I saw your name on the door. I thought you might like to know about my visits with them, and I decided to come in."

"Well, thank you for coming to see me. And, please, have a seat and tell me about your visits." He motions her to a chair.

Kia tells Foster about the Prague video and delivering it to Talbot, the details of her visit to Brannon and his commitment to support the settlement.

Foster hangs on her every word, and when she finishes, he flashes a big smile.

"Maybe I won't have to resign after all."

"Resign? You're going to be promoted."

A HALF HOUR after Kia's visit, Foster receives another visitor, an ebullient William Brannon, the antithesis of the confused and uncertain man that visited him yesterday.

Much of what Brannon tells Foster is repetitious of what Kia told him, but he pretends it's new information and shows appropriate enthusiasm. Brannon lays out the procedures for obtaining the board's approval of the settlement. First, he will brief the board on the situation and recommend that Coca-Cola settle for $15,000,000. "Talbot will then advise the board that after conferring with me, Ungerschmidt and you, she also recommends the settlement. Then it's up to you, Nelson, with Ungerschmidt's assistance, to take over, fill in the details, and set out the reasons why the board should authorize the settlement.

"My commitment to recommend the settlement includes a secret agreement that all videos, transcripts, photographs, and everything else Ivanovich has relating to Talbot, you, and me will be turned over to us. Ivanovich must comply with this part of the agreement before any money is transferred. I leave it in your capable hands to work out the details and make this nightmare disappear."

"I'll take care of it," Foster says confidently.

Brannon places both hands on Foster's shoulders. "I wasn't myself yesterday. I don't know what got into me—questioning your integrity. That's over. Oh, and some other good news. Toward the end of today's meeting, Sharon is going to resign."

CHAPTER 70

THE BOARD OF Directors meeting convenes at 2 p.m. The board consists of twenty members, only two of whom work directly for the company—Talbot and Brannon. The other eighteen members are an elite country club mix of bankers, lawyers, chief executives, a socially concerned activist, and a prominent philanthropist.

When the issue of new business comes up, Brannon briefs the board on the Ivanovich claim. Most board members are astonished to learn that the Calderman cola formula is identical to the formula The Coca-Cola Company has been using since 1921.

A few members voice skepticism about the authenticity of the Calderman formula but no one offers a reasonable explanation for why the formulas are identical. All of the board members complain about the amount of the recommended settlement and are generally offended that a Russian immigrant will get so much money.

Any thoughts of rebellion are quickly quashed by Nelson Foster's presentation.

"Like so many of our shareholders, my family's financial security is tied to Coca-Cola stock. If you reject this settlement and we lose the case, Coca-Cola stock will shrink by more than half. That's a mathematical certainty. But consider what the psychological impact of losing this case will have on the stock price. It will be devastating. On the other hand, if the Ivanovich claim is settled, it will cost less than a penny a share."

Foster's eyes move around the room making contact with every member. He knows the answer to his next question before he asks it. "Is there anyone in this room willing to risk the future of this great company and the financial security of its employees and shareholders and their families for a penny?" A palpable silence provides the answer.

ALEX HAS JUST dropped off his last customer for the day. He is leaving the Atlanta airport and his cell phone rings. It is Nelson Foster. He has been thinking about this call all day, and his heart jumps.

"The board of directors has approved the settlement provided that it is kept completely confidential. Is that agreeable?" Foster says.

"Yes."

"Good. I want to get together with you and Kia and work out the details. Can we meet at my office tomorrow at ten?"

"Yes, of course," Alex says, his heart pounding.

Alex Ivanovich, the man with nerves of steel, is excited. He pulls his town car onto the shoulder of the road, stops, and calls Kia. When she answers, he says, "Are you sitting down?"

"No," she says, with a chuckle, "I'm cooking dinner for my parents."

"You're a millionaire."

There is a long moment of silence. Then in a weak, almost pleading voice, she says, "Please, Alex, don't kid me."

Alex takes a deep breath to calm his own excitement. "Kia, I'm not kidding. I just heard from Mr. Foster. He wants to see us at ten tomorrow to work out the details. Do you want to get together tonight and celebrate?"

There is a pause. Then in almost a whisper, Kia says, "Yes," followed by a booming, "Yes! Yes!"

Alex smiles, his first smile of the day. He looks at his watch. "Can you be ready by seven-thirty?

"Absolutely."

"I'll be by at seven-thirty."

CHAPTER 71

THE NEXT DAY Alex and Kia meet with Foster in a small conference room that forms a part of Felix Ungerschmidt's office. Alex advises Foster and Ungerschmidt that Kia is entitled to $5,000,000 of the settlement. To insure confidentiality Foster recommends that the money be deposited in numbered Swiss bank accounts. Foster explains, however, that The Coca-Cola Company cannot open the accounts in their names.

"Why?" Alex asks.

"Because under Swiss law no one but the person who will own the account can open it. What I can do through my Swiss banking friends is set it up so that when you and Kia do apply to open the accounts, you will be guided through the procedure by a bank representative. At the time you open the accounts, the bank will require that you make a full disclosure of personal information and the source of the money."

"What will we need in the way of personal information?" Kia asks.

"Your passport, driver's license, a letter of reference from your bank here in Atlanta, and a certified copy of your birth certificate. I'll check further on this, and if additional information is required, I'll let you know."

"And what do we say about the source of the money," Alex says.

"I will have advised the bank that the transfer will be made from a company account at J. P. Morgan Chase in New York, and it is payment for the purchase of corporate software. When that question is asked of you, simply say you sold software to The Coca-Cola Company."

"At what bank in Zurich should we open the accounts?" Alex asks.

"I would prefer you open the accounts at UBS in Geneva."

"UBS?" Kia says.

"It stands for Union de Banques Suisse. UBS and Credit Suisse are the two largest banks in Switzerland. Coca-Cola does billions of dollars of business with both banks, but because I have a personal friendship with the president of UBS in Geneva, I'm confident that the entire transaction will move seamlessly, and remain completely confidential. And as you know, the confidentiality factor is important to Coca-Cola."

Ungerschmidt enters the room. "Felix," Foster says, "this is Kia Williams and Alex Ivanovich. Kia, Alex, this is Felix Ungerschmidt. Felix is General Counsel of Coca-Cola. He has personally prepared the settlement documents."

Seated at a small table, Ungerschmidt hands Kia and Alex a one page document.

"The document that I've given you is the release. A release must be signed before any money is transferred to your Swiss bank accounts. Please read it carefully and, if you have questions, I'll answer them. Nelson and I will leave you alone. After you have read the release and discussed it among yourselves, knock on the door and we will rejoin you. Please take your time." Foster and Ungerschmidt leave the room.

Kia studies the release for a minute or so and says, "Maybe we should hire a lawyer to help us with this."

"Let me read it." Alex reads the release.

314 · JAMES GABLER

GENERAL RELEASE

IN CONSIDERATION of the sum of FIVE MILLION DOLLARS ($5,000,000) paid to Kia Williams and the sum of TEN MILLION DOLLARS ($10,000,000) paid to Alexandre Ivanovich, receipt of which is hereby acknowledged, we, Kia Williams and Alexandre Ivanovich, being of lawful age and sound mind, for ourselves and our heirs, personal representatives, successors and assigns (hereinafter the "RELEASORS"), do remise, release and discharge forever THE COCA-COLA COMPANY, and all other persons, firms, partnerships and corporations, known and unknown, who are or might be liable to us, and their respective present and former heirs, beneficiaries, employees, agents, directors, officers, subsidiaries, affiliates, partners, divisions, corporations, successors and assigns (hereinafter the "RELEASEES"), from each and every claim, right, debt, and cause of action whatsoever, known and unknown, foreseen and unforeseen, against the RELEASEES which the RELEASORS have or may have upon or by reason of any matter, cause or thing whatsoever from the beginning of the world until the date of this General Release, including but not limited to any matter or thing or cause arising from or in any way related to The Coca-Cola Company formula or recipe for making, producing and manufacturing the syrup that is the basis for the carbonated cola drink known today as Coca-Cola Classic. This General Release specifically covers but is not limited to the 1921 Coca-Cola recipe and/or formula created and provided to The Coca-Cola Company by Thomas R. P. Calderman.

Although this General Release may be executed in Switzerland, it is the intention of the parties that it be subject to and construed in accordance with the laws of the State of Georgia and, therefore, it shall be deemed to have been executed in the State of Georgia and be binding on the RELEASORS, their heirs, personal representatives, successors and assigns.

IN WITNESS WHEREOF, the undersigned RELEASORS set their hands and seals this _____ day of _____, 1999.

_____   _____

Witness Kia Williams

_____   _____

Witness Alexandre Ivanovich

Accepted on behalf of The Coca-Cola Company this ___ day of ___, 1999.

_____

Alex finishes reading the release and looks up. Kia says, "Well?"

"The way I read the release Coca-Cola gives us $15,000,000 and we give up all rights and interests that we have in the formula. That's the deal we made, and it looks okay to me."

"If you're satisfied Alex then so am I."

Alex walks to the door and knocks. Foster and Ungerschmidt enter the conference room.

Looking at Kia and Alex, Ungerschmidt says, "Is there anything in the release that you don't understand?"

"Tell me if I'm wrong, Mr. Ungerschmidt, but we understand the release to mean that once the money is paid to Kia and me and we sign the release, then it's over, it's done. Coca-Cola owns the 1921 Calderman formula, and any claims for money relating to my ownership of the formula are extinguished."

"That's exactly what it means," Ungerschmidt says.

Alex and Kia exchanged glances. "That's what we agreed to. We have no problem signing the release," Alex says.

"Keep these copies" Ungerschmidt says. "You'll want to compare them with the releases you sign in Geneva to be sure they are identical."

"Give me a date when you can go to Geneva," Foster says.

Alex looks at Kia, then back to Foster, "Tell us when you want us there and that's when we'll be there. We'll wait to hear from you, Mr. Foster, but keep in mind we'll need a couple of days to make flight and hotel reservations."

"My favorite hotel in Geneva is the Beau-Rivage," Foster says, as they shake hands.

As Alex and Kia start to leave, Foster says, "Oh, Alex, don't forget to bring with you the other items of our agreement."

"I'll have them with me, Mr. Foster. All of them."

CHAPTER 72

IT IS 8:45 A.M. when the Delta Air Lines Boeing 747 lands in Zurich.

Fifty-five minutes later Kia and Alex's connecting flight to Geneva is airborne. By 11 A.M. they have cleared passport and customs and are met by André, the Beau-Rivage chauffeur. A half-hour later while registering they are told by the clerk that their room is "not quite ready."

Speaking French, Alex asks the concierge, "What is the best restaurant in Geneva for lunch?"

"La Perle du Lac."

"How far is it from here?"

"Oh, it's an easy ten minute walk along the lake." Pointing, he says, "Go out the front door, cross the street, turn left and follow the walkway that borders the lake. In about ten minutes you will see an attractive chalet in the park. That is La Perle du Lac. I should think it a little too chilly for lunch on the outside terrace, so I will call and make a reservation with a window view." He glances at the wall clock, "For twelve o'clock in La Salle L'Orangerie."

KIA AND ALEX walk hand-in-hand beside Lake Geneva taking in the beauty of the lake, the mountains, the architecture, the gardens, the flowers, and the people. At the restaurant they are shown to a table beside a picture window that looks out across the park to the lake and the distant Alps. They order fresh mountain trout, and Alex selects a white wine from the Valais region of Switzerland. After the sommelier has poured the wine, Kia raises her glass. "You are a genius, Alex, and an incredibly exciting man. I never knew that places like this, or views like this, existed," she says with a sweep of her hand taking in the park, the lake and the mountains beyond. "I have you to thank."

Alex reaches over and takes Kia's hand. "We're going to visit a lot more places like this before our money runs out."

Later, when Alex is signing the bill, Kia says, "Alex, do you really believe that this time tomorrow we're going to own Swiss bank accounts worth millions of dollars."

Alex lays the pen on the table and looks up. "Why else are we here?"

"To trick us into leaving the United States with the videos and then steal them. Maybe even kill us. I'd put nothing past Brannon."

THEY CHECK INTO their room at the Beau-Rivage. It has salmon colored walls, a fireplace, gold gilt mirrors, a king-size bed, replica Louis XVI furniture, and floor to ceiling windows that open onto a balcony with a panoramic view of Lake Geneva, Old Town and Mont-Blanc.

Alex makes a telephone call and speaks Russian.

When he finishes talking, Kia says, "Who was that?"

"An old friend."

Kia and Alex walk along fashionable Rue du Rhone window-shopping Geneva's clothing and jewelry stores. As they leave a women's shoe shop, a tall, swarthy looking man approaches Alex. He speaks Russian and hands Alex something. Alex pays the man with Swiss francs. The man glances at Kia and leaves.

"What did that strange man give you?" Kia asks.

Alex removes from his pants pocket a clenched fist. He opens his fist, and cupped in his palm is a miniature revolver. He closes his fist and puts it in his pocket. "It's for our safety."

Later Kia's attention is attracted to a $4,000 floral chiffon dress with a lace camisole top and matching lace wrap in a shop window. She enters the store and tries it on. Outside she says, "I love that dress, Alex. It fits me perfect. But $4000 for a dress, that's crazy."

Further up the street she pulls Alex into a shop that sells only women's hair pieces. She tries on a blonde wig. Alex almost doesn't recognize her when she comes out of the dressing room wearing the wig.

"How do I look?"

The wig doesn't match her African-American complexion, and he tells her so. To his surprise, she buys the wig, muttering something about "blondes have more fun."

After nearly three hours of shopping, Kia says, "It's been fun but I'm tired. Let's call it a day. But if we get the money tomorrow, I'm going to buy that fancy dress."

"Why do you doubt we'll get the money?"

"Because I don't trust Brannon."

"I think we're going to be just fine," Alex says, with less than total conviction.

"Our dinner reservations aren't until eight-thirty. Let's go back to the hotel and relax."

Hand-in-hand they cross the street and head over the Pont des Bergues to the Beau-Rivage.

AFTER DINNER THEY stop at The Atrium, the hotel cocktail lounge, for a champagne nightcap. They sit in the front room at a table beside French windows that open onto the balcony with a view across the lake. Kia steps out on the balcony and Alex follows her. There is a soft breeze and Geneva's pulsing lights gild the darkness and reflect off the lake. Kia rests her head on Alex's shoulder. "Alex, it's so romantic."

CHAPTER 73

THE NEXT MORNING Kia and Alex are dressed and ready to go by seven o'clock. They have breakfast on their balcony overlooking the lake. They can see the UBS bank on the other side of the lake, not more than ten minutes away. But in deference to Kia's safety concerns, Alex orders a taxi to take them to the bank.

The taxi crosses the lake at Pont des Bergues, skirts the shoreline for a couple of blocks, and stops at the entrance to the UBS headquarters building at Rue des Commerce.

Following Foster's instructions, they walk to a desk located in the lobby just beyond the entrance and identify themselves to the man at the desk. The man asks them to follow him. They ride an elevator to the third floor and follow the man down a long carpeted hallway. The man opens a door and they enter a small windowless mahogany paneled room.

They are greeted by a well-dressed young man who speaks fluent English. "I am advised," he says, "that you wish to open numbered Swiss bank accounts."

"That's correct," Alex says.

The young man, seated behind a computer, asks for their passports. He enters their names, addresses, dates of birth, and nationalities. He inspects and makes copies of their drivers' licenses and bank references, and asks, "What is the source of the money to be deposited?"

"The money is in payment for corporate software that we sold to The Coca-Cola Company," Alex says.

After typing for a few minutes, the young man strikes the keyboard with a flourish and within seconds papers emerge from the printer. He glances over the papers and hands them to Kia and Alex. "Please read these carefully and let me know if the information is correct?"

They read the documents and verify the accuracy of the information.

The young man leaves the room.

Alex whispers, "Did you notice that he didn't ask the amounts to be deposited?"

Kia nods.

Minutes later a tall man carrying a black leather briefcase enters the room. He is about forty-five, has black curly hair flecked with gray, blue-gray eyes and sharp facial features. He is wearing a dark blue pinstriped double-breasted suit, a white monogrammed shirt with gold cufflinks, a gold Hermès tie, and black wing-tipped shoes.

His handshake is firm. He introduces himself as François Berelly, the bank president.

Kia's spirits soar. "It's for real," she says aloud.

"What is for real?" the bank president asks.

"Nothing, nothing, it's just an expression I sometimes use."

Berelly examines the documents the young man prepared. "I need strike but three keys to convert this information into your numbered UBS accounts." He removes from his briefcase two papers. "Here are the releases that you must sign before the settlement money is electronically transferred from J. P. Morgan Chase to this bank. I will serve as the witness to each of your signatures." He lays the releases on the table.

"Before we do that, I understand, Mr. Ivanovich, that you have brought with you certain items."

Alex lifts a backpack from between his feet and places it on the table. "They're in here."

The bank president stares at the backpack, "A representative of Coca-Cola will verify and take possession of those items, after which the releases will be executed and the money transferred to your respective accounts."

Berelly leaves the room and a moment later Nelson Foster enters.

"Well, what a pleasant surprise," Kia says.

Foster smiles as he shakes their hands.

"It's all in here," Alex says, pointing to the backpack.

Without taking his eyes from Alex, Foster says, "All three videos, the copies, and the transcripts?"

"Everything."

"You know, Alex, this part of the agreement is a matter of trust."

"You can trust me, Mr. Foster. I've retained nothing."

Foster picks up the backpack. "I trust you."

The door opens and Monsieur Berelly enters. He sits at the computer and punches three keys. "Your UBS numbered accounts are open. What the accounts need now is money." He slides the two releases toward Kia and Alex. "Please read the releases carefully to be sure they are identical to the releases you previously agreed to."

Alex removes the copy of the release that he was given by Ungerschmidt in Atlanta and reads the releases side by side. Satisfied that the releases are identical, he nods his approval to Kia and says, "We're ready to sign."

Kia and Alex sign the releases, Berelly witnesses their signatures, and Foster signs on behalf of Coca-Cola.

Berelly types a code into the computer. Within seconds the printer fires up.

Berelly removes a document from the printer tray, folds it, and hands it to Kia.

"This is your numbered UBS account that now contains five million dollars."

Kia stares at the document, her eyes blurring as she reads "$5,000,000." She looks up at Monsieur Berelly, "There's a dress down the street in Valentino's that costs $4000. If I decide to buy it, how do I get money out of this account to pay for it."

Berelly smiles, "Like you do with any other bank account, with checks. Let me finish with Mr. Ivanovich and I'll have that explained to you." He hands Alex his account document. "Please check the amount. It should read ten million dollars."

Alex examines it. "It does."

"Good, my associate will be here in a moment with several packets of checks for each of you, and a manual explaining all the intricacies of how your accounts work."

They shake hands all around, and Foster and Berelly leave the room. Alone, Kia and Alex stare at one another. Kia's mouth opens as if to say something, but Alex places his index finger against his lips and shakes his head back and forth.

The session with Berelly's associate takes about a half hour. When they leave the bank it is noon. It is a beautiful day. The sun is shining and there is not a cloud in the sky.

"Let's go to Valentino's. I want to buy you that dress," Alex says.

"That's sweet of you, Alex, but I've been thinking about that dress and, right now, I don't have any place to wear it but maybe someday."

"You're sure?"

"I'm sure, but thanks."

"Then let's go back to the Beau-Rivage and celebrate with a bottle of champagne."

CHAPTER 74

THE TWO HAPPY millionaires run across the Tour de L'Île Bridge and back along the quays to the Beau-Rivage. They bolt up the hotel steps, cross the lobby and enter The Atrium lounge. There is no one there except a bartender polishing glasses.

Kia throws her arms around Alex's neck, pulls him to her, and kisses him. As they kiss, Kia's right hand lowers to Alex's jacket pocket. Her hand goes inside his pocket and removes the miniature revolver.

When they break free, Kia says, "I'll be in the next room."

Alex steps up to the bar, "Do you have a well-chilled bottle of Dom Perignon?"

"Yes sir."

"We'll have it."

Alex enters the front room and is surprised to find Kia sitting at a table in a corner against the wall between the two rooms. The table by the French windows overlooking the lake is empty. Pointing to that table, Alex says, "Let's sit where we did last night."

Kia shakes her head. "I feel reclusive. I don't want to share my feelings with anyone but you, not even with nature."

Alex shrugs, and sits down. Seconds later the bartender places an ice bucket containing the champagne next to their table, pops the cork and pours their glasses. They clink their glasses together and sit facing each other, sipping the wine in thoughtful silence. Alex breaks the mood. "How is all this money going to change your life?"

"Do you know something, Alex, until a few moments ago I was afraid to think about it. I've always doubted that it would happen. Being sent to Switzerland to collect the money struck me as some scheme to get us out of the United States."

"When did your paranoia end?"

"When that handsome man entered the room and introduced himself as the president of the bank."

"Okay, now that you know it's for real, how's $5,000,000 going to change your life?"

"Probably no differently than what I told you that night at Lafayette's. Take care of my parents, go to college, buy a house and some new clothes." She takes a sip of wine.

"What about you, Alex? What are your plans?"

Alex replenishes their glasses. "My main object has always been to get custody of my son. So, the first thing I'll do is return to Russia, find out how much it will take to get his mother to sign the necessary papers awarding me custody, and pay her off. Of course, there will be others in the custody chain that I'll have to be pay off, but that's the way it works in Russia." He twirls the stem of his wine glass and his tone changes. "I like the United States and I like the American people, but I'm not going to live there."

Kia looks at him in stunned silence. "So, that's it. Now that you have your money, I'm thrown out like dirty dish water."

"No!" Alex says, reaching across the table and taking her hand." I want us to live here in Switzerland and . . ."

"No, " Kia snaps. "I could never leave my parents. Four years ago my dad had a stroke and they both depend on me." She bristles. "Why aren't you coming back to Atlanta?"

"Because most of my life has been spent in Europe, and I'll feel more comfortable living in Switzerland. Kia, I want you to live here with me. You'll love Switzerland. The Swiss don't have the prejudices toward African-Americans that you face in America. As for your parents, we'll buy them a condominium near us, and you can see them every day. They'll love Switzerland too."

"Where will we live in Switzerland?"

"Near Lugano. It's up near the Italian border. It has a mild climate, clean, crisp air, beautiful scenery, and an excellent school system. Now that we're here, let's spend some time traveling through Switzerland. We'll go to Lucerne, take boat trips on the lake, swim, have leisurely lunches, take the cable car to the top of Mount Pilates for one of the greatest views you'll ever see. We'll go to Lugano and take side trips into Italy, Lake Como, Milan, Venice."

"I would love to but . . . but . . ." She jumps up. "I've got to go to the room." She runs out.

Kia's absence stretches from a few minutes to ten minutes. Restless, Alex refills his glass and strolls through the open French windows onto the balcony. It is a clear, cloudless day and visibility is unobstructed. He can see the snowcapped peak of Mont-Blanc in the distance. As if imprinting the scene on his memory, he takes in the contours of Lake Geneva and its shore lined parks, the stately mansions, the Old Town, the centuries old Cathedral of St-Pierre, and the bridges spanning the lake. Glancing down he sees the Beau-Rivage limousine parked to the left of the hotel entrance. A taxi pulls in front of the limousine and stops. A blonde woman wearing dark wrap-around sunglasses dashes down the steps to the sidewalk and jumps in the taxi. The taxi starts forward. Suddenly, Alex's entire body stiffens. The champagne glass falls from his hand and crashes on the balcony. He gasps, *My God! It's Kia!* Before he can call out the taxi moves around the island street divider and stops for a red traffic light controlling entrance onto Quai du Mont-Blanc.

Alex bolts out of the lounge, crosses the lobby, and runs down the steps. As he hits the sidewalk the taxi is turning left onto Quai du Mont-Blanc. He yanks open the front passenger door of the hotel limousine. André, dozing behind the wheel, is startled by Alex's appearance. Shoving a one hundred Swiss franc note in André's hand, and pointing with his other hand at the taxi, he says, "André, follow that taxi!" André does not hesitate. He swings the limousine around the island and out into Quai du Mont-Blanc. They skirt the park, pass La Perle du Lac, and head away from the lake.

"Where's that taxi going?" Alex asks.

"I thought perhaps, monsieur, it was heading to the International District in Arianna Park you see on the right. But that is no longer possible because the taxi has passed the entrance." André falls silent for a moment. "It is going to the airport."

"Are you sure?"

André glances at him. "I'm sure, monsieur. There is no other destination out this far."

For the first time since he entered the limousine Alex leans back in the seat. *That's why she wanted to sit in the corner and not at the table facing the balcony. She didn't want me to see her leave the hotel. But where's she going?*

As the taxi approaches the passenger departure terminal, it turns right onto a side road and follows the perimeter of the airfield away from the terminal. The taxi stops in front of a glass building located behind a chain-link fence.

"What's that building?" Alex asks.

"That, monsieur, is the private aircraft terminal. A great many private planes fly in and out of Geneva."

Kia jumps out of the taxi. Still wearing the blonde wig and sunglasses, she runs to the fence and opens the gate.

"André, pull up to the gate," Alex orders.

André's limousine screeches to a halt at the gate. "André, don't wait for me."

Alex bounds out, runs to the gate and watches helplessly as Kia runs across the tarmac to a Gulfstream V, its engines roaring.

Clutching the miniature revolver in her left hand, Kia climbs the steps. She is still undecided what she'll do. The cabin door opens and out steps William Brannon. He leans forward, cups her buttock's in his hands, and kisses her.

He's not worth it, she thinks, and lets the revolver drop into her jacket pocket.

Pushing away from Brannon with both hands, she slaps him across the face.

Shocked and confused, Brannon stares at her, his mouth wide open. Kia removes an envelope from her right jacket pocket and thrusts it at him.

"What's this?"

"It's my insurance policy, my guarantee that you'll never say anything about Forsenko's death. You don't remember, but one night when we were in Antigua you got very drunk and said things that no one in the world was supposed to ever hear or know about. If there is ever an attempt to connect Alex and me to the bombing of Forsenko's limousine, I'll know where it came from. If that happens, I'll mail the original of what's in that envelope to the United States Attorney in Atlanta with copies to the Attorney General of Georgia, and to every member of the Coca-Cola Board of Directors. And believe me, Brannon, you won't survive it. Do I make myself clear?"

Brannon nods, his face a mask of disbelief.

Kia turns, walks down the steps, and runs back across the tarmac.

Alex vaults over the fence and runs toward her. At the edge of the tarmac they meet. Kia pulls off the wig and throws her arms around Alex.

"Oh, Alex, I'm so glad you're here."

Alex rolls her into his arms and kisses her. Pointing to the Gulfstream, he says, "What was that about?"

She smiles up at him, "Let's go to lunch and I'll tell you all about it. As for our future together, there's no one on earth I'd rather be with than you."

THE END

Dear Reader,

I hope you have enjoyed *The Secret Formula*. If you have I hope you'll tell your friends about it. Nothing sells a book better than word-of-mouth from satisfied readers. Likewise, I hope you'll take the time to contact me and leave your impressions of *The Secret Formula*. Nothing helps an author improve better than constructive criticism from readers. My email address is bacchuspr@aol.com. Below is a list of other books that I have written that are currently available for sale. Again, thank you for reading *The Secret Formula*.

OTHER BOOKS

God's Devil: A Papal Quest, a novel about a Catholic priest who is obsessed with becoming the pope and he let's nothing stand in his way. EBook $9.99. www.amazon.com/dp/ B0064QEG2C

Be Your Own Wine Expert, a beginner's guide to learning about wine quickly and easily, an expanded e-book version of Gabler's popular *How To Be A Wine Expert*. $9.99. www.amazon.com/dp/ B0064D6LI2

An Evening with Benjamin Franklin and Thomas Jefferson: Dinner, Wine, and Conversation. You, the reader, sit down with Jefferson and Franklin in the comfort of Jefferson's residence in Paris and they tell you in *their own words* the most interesting stories of their lives. Available in both paperback and eBook editions.

Passions: The Wines and Travels of Thomas Jefferson. Winner of the 1995 Veuve Clicquot Wine Book of the Year award. An intimate portrait of Thomas Jefferson at leisure, enjoying two of his passions—wine and travel. $29.95, available in hardcover from amazon.com.

Wine into Words: A History and Bibliography of Wine Books in the English Language. "No one in the world of wine has achieved anything approaching the perfection, the comprehensiveness, of James Gabler's masterful harvest of English-language wine-related items." Dr. Kevin Starr, State Librarian of California. $67.50, available from amazon.com.

ACKNOWLEDGMENTS

I acknowledge and thank Carrie Cort, Eileen Houston, Dona Gibbs, and George Williamson for reading the manuscript and offering valuable suggestions that improved the story.

Also special thanks to Michael Alcorn for his computer acumen and the password recovery or "cracking" information, to Jay Block for the motorcycle information, to the late Alfonso Baldi for technical assistance, and to my wife Anita for her patience and computer skills.

Made in the USA
Middletown, DE
26 July 2024

57886941R00189